PENGUIN BOOKS

You Need to Know

Nicola Moriarty is a novelist, copywriter and mum to two small (but remarkably strong-willed) daughters. In between various career changes, becoming a mum and studying at university, she began to write. Now, she can't seem to stop. *The Fifth Letter* was her UK debut novel, followed by *Those Other Women* and *The Ex-Girlfriend*.

You Need To Know

NICOLA MORIARTY

PENGUIN BOOKS

PENGUIN BOOKS

UK | USA | Canada | Ireland | Australia
India | New Zealand | South Africa

Penguin Books is part of the Penguin Random House group of companies
whose addresses can be found at global.penguinrandomhouse.com

First published in Australia by HarperCollins Publishers 2021
First published in Great Britain in Penguin Books published 2021
001

Set in 12.5/14.75 pt Garamond MT Std
Typeset by Integra Software Services Pvt. Ltd, Pondicherry
Printed in Great Britain by Clays Ltd, Elcograf S.p.A.

The authorized representative in the EEA is Penguin Random House Ireland,
Morrison Chambers, 32 Nassau Street, Dublin D02 YH68

A CIP catalogue record for this book is available from the British Library

ISBN: 978-1-405-93745-0

www.greenpenguin.co.uk

For Dad
I miss you so bloody much

'Do you know who sank the boat?
Was it the little mouse,
the last to get in,
who was lightest of all?
Could it be him?'

— Pamela Allen

If Mimi had been asked if she was capable of taking a life, she would have said, no. Never.

Prologue

Christmas Eve

Mimi

She had learned from a young age that it's never like it is in the movies. For one thing, there's no soundtrack. In a film, if something dramatic happens, or something horrific or frightening or desperately sad, the music will tell you how to feel. It will swell or thrum or thump. Violins might pierce your soul. A bass drum might crash around inside your ribcage. But the thing is, it changes the whole feel of it. You start to imagine that a terrible accident could be an exciting event. A chance to step in and save the day.

Whereas the truth of this type of situation is vastly different. When she was small, maybe seven years old, Mimi was at a restaurant with her family when a teenage girl at another table started choking. Most people will have seen somebody choking on television or in a movie, but they might never have seen it in real life. On the screen, it's often comical. The person might be gesturing wildly, eyes bulging. Someone else doesn't get what's going on. A hero swoops in and expertly performs the Heimlich manoeuvre. A piece of chicken flies across the room. People applaud.

1

In real life, it doesn't work that way.

The first thing Mimi noticed was the silence. She remembered she was blowing bubbles in her lemonade. The restaurant was noisy, chaotic. There might have been a shriek, or the clatter of a fork being dropped onto a plate, but she dismissed these as a normal part of the chaos. Then the hush fell. And from the silence, two or three panicked voices.

All around her, people seemed to have frozen in place. Her eyes were drawn to the table in the centre. A mother and father standing either side of their daughter. The daughter's gaping mouth. Someone else, an older brother perhaps, leaping to his feet and his chair crashing to the floor. The noise of it landing made Mimi jump in her seat.

And then the wailing started. Everyone responds to crisis situations in different ways. There are the capable types who calmly assess the situation, step in and help. The people who throw their hands up and back away, and the people who fall apart. The mother was falling apart. She didn't know how to help her daughter, her daughter who couldn't breathe and was turning redder by the second. And maybe without even realising it, she'd begun to scream. That scream was the most sickening noise Mimi had ever heard in her entire – albeit short – life. She couldn't say what it was about it. Was it the anguish she could hear within it? The fear? The rawness? It was strangled and it was animalistic and it was frightening and she wanted it to stop.

In the meantime, other diners had converged on the table. Mimi couldn't see the teenager's face anymore. Someone had hoisted her out of her chair and now they were attempting to do the Heimlich manoeuvre. But from the frustrated shouts, it didn't seem to be working. That's when Mimi's mum took her by the hand and led her out of the restaurant. Maybe she saw the look on her face, or maybe she was afraid they weren't going to be able to save the girl, that she might die right here in the middle of the restaurant and she didn't want Mimi to witness that. They wandered up and down the footpath outside and her mother chatted to her about different things. She couldn't remember now what they spoke about, but she could recall that sense of knowing. *She's trying to distract me.*

Soon there was the wail of a siren.

Mimi never found out whether that girl was okay, but she did think about it a lot. She replayed the scene in her mind as she fell asleep at night. She heard the sound of the mother's cries and her skin would crawl and her stomach would churn, and sometimes tears would sting her eyes and she didn't really understand why.

Thirty years had gone by since that night at the restaurant and, tonight, Mimi had found herself thinking of that mother again. It was Christmas Eve, so she shouldn't be thinking about her. She should be thinking about happy things. Warm, feel-good things. *Must remember to hang the stockings tonight when we arrive at the holiday house. Was the turkey I bought too big for that oven up there? I should have double-checked with Jill. Did Pete's brother, Darren, remember to pick up the prawns this morning? And was he smart enough to pack them in an esky with ice for the drive up?*

Did we buy enough gifts for the twins? They're only babies, I know they won't remember their first Christmas morning. And there's very

3

little that they need – what with all the hand-me-downs from Callie and Tara. But still, I don't want them to miss out.

This is what I should be thinking of.

Mimi loved the lead-up to Christmas. She always had. The way the world felt different. Not just festive, that was a given. But magical. She still got a funny little jump in the pit of her stomach when a shopping centre Santa waved at her.

So why was she thinking about that woman right now, instead of about eggnog and candy canes?

It was because of the accident on the freeway.

It was just like when that girl was choking in the restaurant. There was an eerie silence. Then, the sound of someone grunting in pain.

And finally, something else. A woman's tortured screams. She sounded just like the mother in the restaurant and Mimi was thinking: *No. Not this again. No, no, no.*

But then she realised. *The person who's screaming is me.*

I

Tuesday 1 December

Mimi

Mimi lay on her stomach on the rug, her sketchbook and pencils in front of her. A bead of sweat slipped down from her forehead and curved around her cheek. She should hop up and turn on the aircon. Summer had well and truly arrived.

The twins were side by side on their backs, both gazing up at the colourful mobiles hanging from their play gym. She should have been giving them some 'tummy time', but they hated being on their stomachs at the moment and she rather preferred happy, gurgling twins over anguished, screaming ones. Not to mention the fact that Elliot had recently mastered the art of rolling front to back. Now, as soon as Mimi put her on her stomach, she immediately flipped back over anyway. So what was the point? If anything, it would only mean Elliot showing off in front of James. What if that created some sort of rift between the sisters? What if years in the future, James was sitting in a therapist's office, explaining how her inferiority complex first stemmed from the days when her mother placed her next to her capable, rolling twin while she stayed stuck on her stomach and screamed.

Actually, they were probably both going to end up in therapists' offices, complaining that their parents had wanted boys, not girls, as evidenced by their two very boyish names. Which wouldn't be fair, really. Mimi was perfectly happy with having girls. It was Pete who'd been hoping for boys. He might have tried to hide it but it was bloody obvious. Whereas Mimi, well, Mimi hadn't wanted *any* more children at all.

She put down the pencil she'd been drawing with and gave her hand a small smack. *You're not supposed to have thoughts like that, not consciously.* Yes, it was true that Pete had been the one pushing for another child, but it wasn't his fault they'd ended up with two for the price of one.

That was life. It liked to play funny tricks on you. Sometimes they were small pranks. Like when she stayed up until one in the morning finishing her daughter's school project – she knew she wasn't supposed to do the work for her, but she also knew that every other parent was probably up late creating the papier-mâché sculptures of the earth too. She knew because she and the other mums joked about it at school pick-up. 'How did you go with your homework this week?' *Ha ha, wink, wink.* But anyway, the next day when she woke up bleary-eyed, her daughter woke with a bad cough and couldn't go to school, and Mimi realised she could have watched Netflix and drunk wine and gone to bed at eleven.

But other times, it was an extra funny trick. A real zinger. Twins! When your husband convinced you to have just one more baby. That with three children your family will be complete. That it'll be so much easier this time, because Callie is sixteen and Tara is eight and they're self-sufficient and they're great kids and they'll help out with the baby.

The problem was, Mimi had felt their family was complete. She'd had such an unexpected path to motherhood. As young newlyweds, they'd been completely blindsided by the discovery that Mimi had fallen pregnant with Callie at twenty-two. The pregnancy was smooth, the delivery unexceptional. And then Callie had been a dream baby. She fed well, she slept well. So before long, they figured they may as well have another. It hadn't been their plan to have children in their early twenties, but why not?

Apparently, the reason why not was Mimi's uterus, which decided it wasn't going to be so compliant the second time around. And so, they'd gone through years of heartache trying to fall pregnant. That's why there was such a huge age gap between their two eldest girls. When Tara had come along, Mimi had felt such a sense of relief. Of contentment. As though for years she'd been trying and failing and trying and failing to do this one simple task: bring Tara into the world. And now that she'd done it she could relax. She could breathe again.

She'd thought she and Pete were on the same page about that. But then she'd understood. He was aching for a son. A bit of an annoying cliché really. What could a son do for him that their daughters couldn't? It didn't help that he'd grown up with two brothers and was missing being surrounded by all that bloody testosterone. So, despite knowing she was done, Mimi had given in and they'd started to try again. And for whatever reason, her uterus had decided it was back to being amenable and she'd fallen

7

pregnant with the same speed and ease as she had back in her early twenties. *Thanks a lot, uterus.*

She licked her upper lip and tasted salt. Sweat. Their house was meant to be ecologically designed for environmentally friendly heating and cooling, but she'd never found it to be as effective as flicking the switch on the aircon. She wished they'd put in a swimming pool last summer when they'd suffered through the heat and begun to discuss the idea. But then everything had changed. The twin pregnancy. And of course, entangled with the news of new life was the news of loss. In the end, a swimming pool was the last thing on their minds. Besides, Pete had pointed out they'd forever be scooping leaves from the water because of the bush behind their house. So, in a minute she'd give in and resort to technology to cool herself down.

If she was honest, today had been a pretty good day. Although she did have a new bar for what was considered a good day now that she had twins. But Callie and Tara had both got ready for school and out the door on time for once this morning – without any arguments. And Callie had even changed one nappy for her. That was a particularly big deal, because soon after the twins were born, Callie had made a family declaration that she was never changing any nappies. In stark contrast, Tara's response had been to morph into a very capable – if a little short – live-in nanny.

The funny thing was, when Mimi was pregnant she'd assumed Callie was going to be the one helping out and that maybe Tara might act out a bit because she'd been replaced as the baby of the family. But instead Callie had been more and more withdrawn lately, spending increasing amounts of time locked away in her bedroom, while Tara seemed to have matured five years in the space of a month. Of course it was to be expected that Callie would go through a teenage stage like this, but it was still a shock because right up until this year, Mimi had thought Callie had somehow skipped the scary teen stage. They'd remained close, right through the start of high school and through Callie getting her first period and pimples and awkward growth spurts. Callie had kept confiding in her and joking with her. But now, along with retreating to her room all the time, she'd become snappy and irritable. It was as if she was a different person.

Meanwhile, Tara was so helpful that Mimi needed to be careful she didn't start to lean on her too much. She was eight, for goodness sake! She still needed to be a kid and have fun and not take on the burden of motherhood. She needed to enjoy being the big sister. Her responsibilities shouldn't extend beyond keeping her room tidy, doing her homework, helping out with some family chores.

On more than one occasion Mimi had been slow to rouse herself and climb out of bed in the night when the twins had woken for a feed, only to find Tara already in their room, scooping one out of the cot to comfort her, an expert arm reaching in to give the other a tender pat while she waited for her mother.

And the temptation was there for Mimi to accept her help, to allow Tara to hold James while she picked up Elliot and started warming the bottles. But she stopped herself and sent Tara back to bed. The only one helping her should be Pete. Tara was a child; she needed her sleep.

Thankfully, on her way back to bed, Tara always snuck into her parents' bedroom and nudged her dad awake so he'd know Mimi needed the help.

Mimi picked her pencil back up and had another go at the sketch she'd been working on, but she wasn't feeling inspired. She was meant to be creating a cute little monkey for a jungle scene and the little bugger wouldn't sit right in the trees for her. She checked the time. Was it too early for a glass of wine? Often just one glass helped her to relax and get her creativity flowing. It wasn't even midday. Maybe she could have one later with lunch. That was the upside of bottle-feeding – she was allowed alcohol again.

She'd struggled to breastfeed the twins from the beginning. Both Callie and Tara had been good feeders. They'd latched on in the exact way all the breastfeeding literature described. She could remember looking at other mothers in the hospital having trouble feeding and couldn't understand why it was so hard for them. She was ashamed to admit that a small part of her thought she was somehow superior because her babies could feed.

Now she wanted to go back in time and hit herself over the head with a breast pump. She wanted to reach back and comfort those mothers, shield their eyes from her smug face as she sat and nursed her daughters. Because now she got it. She bloody well got it. Breastfeeding was not the easiest, most natural thing in the world. It was fucking hard. And her success the first two times had nothing to do with some innate ability she possessed as a mother. It was dumb luck.

And so, the twins had been supplemented with more and more formula from the day she came home from hospital until, eventually, her abysmal supply of milk dried up. But she hadn't cried about it. And she hadn't felt like a failure. She'd celebrated. Because fuck she'd missed wine.

She felt her phone buzzing in the back pocket of her jeans and slipped it out. It was Jill, her mother-in-law. As Mimi slid her thumb across the screen to answer, Elliot opened her mouth and let out a huge wail, as though she'd been waiting for the right moment.

Jill

Dear Frank,

Three Hail Marys this morning. Sitting up here in bed. That's all I could manage for my sins. I suspect if I went to a priest he wouldn't think that was enough. And I'm supposed to get down on my knees to do it. But I was tired. And cranky. So three was the magic number today. Besides, I know what you would say: 'Why are you bothering with that, woman? God isn't sitting around waiting to count your prayers. He's got better things to do.'

But I don't know how else I'm supposed to atone.

Love,

Jill

Jill folded up the piece of paper and placed it on her bed-side table. Later she'd put it in an envelope, seal it up, address, stamp and post it. A waste of time, but she'd still do it. When she first started, the letters were longer. In them, she would beg for forgiveness. She would tell detailed stories about her days, about the boys. Sometimes as she wrote, spots of ink would be smudged with her tears. But that hadn't happened for some time now.

She smoothed her hands across the floral bedspread on her lap and briefly considered pulling it right back up. Easing herself down flat again. Closing her eyes and praying for sleep. But she knew it wouldn't come. Sleep never seemed to come when she wanted it anymore.

She always used to start the day with a cup of tea in bed. Frank would bring it to her. Place it on the bedside table right where the letter was sitting. Now if she wanted to start the day with a cup of tea she had to get out of bed and make it herself.

Most days she hated him for leaving her. She hated that with Frank gone, it sometimes felt as though she'd lost all of her best parts along with him. Her sense of humour. Her patience. Her compassion. Actually, that wasn't entirely true. They weren't gone, not completely. They were muted.

She glanced sideways at the folded paper. Considered picking it back up and rewriting it. She'd been far too brusque. Far too dismissive. But then, what else would she say? She had no news to share. No cute little stories.

Besides, she knew full well why she was so cranky today. It was because of the date. The first of December. Christmas was coming and there was no way she could stop it. Her friend Marjory had suggested she do something different this year for the holidays. But Marjory didn't know why it was so important that Jill stuck with tradition.

She twitched back the covers and placed her feet on the floor. Her whole body seemed to creak and groan. She hated this part of the day, when her bones hadn't woken yet and they protested against every move. She collected her thick blue dressing gown from the armchair in the corner and pulled it on. It might have been the beginning of summer but she still needed to wear it first thing. This house was always cold in the mornings, and her bones wouldn't loosen until she warmed up. She slid her feet into her slippers and headed out to the kitchen to put the kettle on.

While the kettle boiled, she leaned against the bench and wondered what she might do today. It was already 11 am, so she'd used up a good portion of the day just lazing in bed, writing to Frank and feeling sorry for herself because there was no one to bring her a cup of tea.

Marjory kept trying to convince her to come and volunteer at the Salvation Army charity store with her. She said it would be a good way for her to get out of the house. But Jill had no interest at all in joining Marjory at the Salvos. Marjory had told her stories of what the other women were like – the ones who'd been there the longest and had unofficially appointed themselves as management, who sniped at Marjory if she discounted a second-hand pair of shoes or tutted if she rearranged the racks in a different way to what they thought was best. Marjory laughed with Jill about their self-importance, but Jill knew she wouldn't be able to stand being bossed around by a bunch of officious women when she used to run an entire staff of teachers and had control over eight hundred students at Wattle Crest High before she'd retired.

Sometimes she thought she'd retired too early. Sometimes she felt she could walk into Wattle Crest and step right back into the principal's shoes today. Other days she knew everything had changed in the schooling system since she'd left and that her ways wouldn't cut it anymore.

She could call her daughter-in-law, check if she needed any help with the babies. But she didn't want to seem overbearing. Pete's wife had been the first to marry into their family. Mimi – an absolute goddess with her long black curls. Tall and striking, way out of her son's league. Weak and strong all at once. Despite the physical imbalance, they were the perfect match. Better suited even than she and Frank had been all those years. There was just something about them. They were equals. Best friends. You could tell there were no secrets in that marriage.

And Mimi always made sure Pete took on his fair share of the housework and the parenting. Not like when she was raising three boys with Frank. Yes, it was the new way but it was also Mimi. Strong and firm. Yet somehow, Mimi had let Pete railroad her into another pregnancy. A weakness.

It was clear she didn't want to have anymore children, especially after all the trouble they'd had falling pregnant with Tara. And Jill knew the age difference made it difficult at times for the sisters to bond. The gap particularly widened when Callie hit her teen years and had been stretching ever since. After all, what did a sixteen-year-old have in common with an eight-year-old? But at the same time, they were still sisters and they did love one another. Jill could see it in the way Callie was protective of her younger sister and in the way Tara looked up to her, even as she pretended she didn't.

The big shock had been finding out that the third pregnancy was twins. *Now you've gone and done it*, Jill had thought when she heard the news. *This might be the end of you both. The end of your marriage.*

But it wasn't, at least not yet. So far, Mimi was coping. Just. But she didn't even have her parents here to help her out. Another example of Mimi's bravery – emigrating from England to Australia all alone when she was only eighteen.

Maybe Jill should call her. At least to check in. She was closer to Mimi than she was to her other daughter-in-law, but that made sense. Mimi had been a part of their family for so long, whereas Tony met Andrea much later. Married less than two years ago. And Andrea was harder to read, which was surprising, considering she was a high school teacher – Jill ought to have more in common with her. But they simply hadn't bonded yet. In terms of looks, Andrea was Mimi's polar opposite in every way. Where Andrea was short and slim with petite features, Mimi was all hips and breasts and she towered over pretty much everyone in their family. While Mimi had those long dark curls, Andrea kept her light-brown hair closely cropped in a pixie cut.

The other thing that brought Jill closer to Mimi was the grandchildren. Apparently Tony and Andrea didn't want to have children. Ever. But who was the driving force behind that decision?

There had almost been a third daughter-in-law. They'd all thought Darren was going to marry his long-term girl-friend Charlotte but last year they'd discovered they were all quite wrong, and Darren had been alone ever since. Sometimes Jill worried that he was running out of time if he wanted to have a family. But then she'd remember – men had all the time in the world, didn't they? It was women who had a ticking time bomb in their uterus. Unfair.

The kettle boiled and she poured her cup of tea, then picked up her phone to call Mimi. For a moment, her thumb hovered over the mail icon. The email had arrived three days ago. It had taken her a few minutes, but eventually, she had recognised the sender's name. It was a name that gave her a nasty feeling in the pit of her stomach. And it was highly unusual that she would be writing to her.

Then she'd read the subject line: 'You need to know'. Her skin had prickled with irritation. What on earth could this woman have to say that Jill apparently *needed* to know? The presumptuous tone annoyed her so she'd closed the app and ignored it.

Her thumb moved away from her inbox now and instead, she phoned Mimi.

Andrea

'Miss, what if I was anaphylactic? Would I still have to make a cake?'

'If you were anaphylactic, it would depend on what you were allergic to. But you're not, so it's irrelevant.'

'Okay, but what if I had a religious reason? Like, it's against my faith to use flour or something.'

'I can't say I've heard of any religions that are against flour. But as I'm confident that's not the case for you, it's once again irrelevant. Get baking, Menasse.'

There weren't many enthusiastic faces in the class in front of her and Andrea wasn't overly thrilled with being roped in to cover for the food tech teacher herself. She wasn't supposed to have any classes on this afternoon and her plan had been to mark her Year Eleven history assignments.

They had the ceiling fans turned up to the highest setting but it was still sweltering in the classroom. Although Andrea shouldn't complain; one of her university friends had ended up picking up a teaching job out in the far west of Sydney. At least here on the North Shore it didn't get as hot as it would out there.

Now that Grant Menasse had stopped trying to argue his case against baking, the class settled down and started on their recipes. Andrea did a lap through the tables, checking in on them all, and then headed up to the front of the classroom and sat down at the teacher's laptop, which was sitting open on his desk. Apparently he'd left in a hurry after lunch. Food poisoning. She wondered if it was from tasting his students' food. Either way, she wasn't planning on doing any taste-testing herself during today's lesson.

She found his password on a Post-it in his top drawer – very secure – and logged in. She opened up the web browser and found herself idly googling 'religious beliefs against flour'. She clicked through to an article on religion and dietary choices and was skimming through it when she heard snickering coming from the class. She looked up and the snickering erupted into full-blown laughter.

'What? What's the joke I'm missing?'

Several students pointed behind her and she turned around to see that the smart board was mirroring the laptop screen. They could all see her search.

Grant was looking positively delighted. 'She took me seriously,' he shouted. 'She actually believed me.'

Andrea pursed her lips and minimised the browser

17

window before snapping the laptop shut. 'I did not,' she said. 'You made me curious, that's all.'

Thank God she hadn't been looking at something worse. Imagine if she'd been googling something like 'weird rash from underwear' or if she'd logged into her Facebook account, which included photos of the big night out she'd had last weekend with six other teachers from Redmond High. She was always careful to keep her Facebook account locked down tight so that students and parents could never find her on social media, but that wouldn't help much if she splashed it across the screen at the front of the class for everyone to see.

Right, from now on, always make sure the mirroring feature is turned off before using any computers in class. Lesson learned.

'Excuse me, Miss, did you find anything?' Chariot Stevenson asked politely.

Andrea smiled despite herself. She'd been caught out, she might as well run with it. 'I don't think so,' she said. 'Although I suppose there could be a fringe religion with an aversion to flour. Didn't someone create their own Jedi religion once? Maybe Jedis are anti-flour.'

'Nah, I reckon Jedi's thing would be veganism,' Ahn called out from the back of the class.

'Are you kidding me? No way Jedis would be vegans. What about Scientologists? They're into some weird shit, right?' This from a student Andrea didn't know.

'Oy! My mum's a Scientologist,' said Grant.

'Yeah, and?'

'Yeah, fair enough, she is into some pretty weird shit.'

Andrea knew she should be reprimanding them for swearing, but she couldn't really be bothered. She was kind of enjoying the religious debate that had sprung up. Only a few students were still keeping up the pretence of following the recipes. The rest of the class had abandoned their mixing bowls.

'What about food that needs to be halal, or what's the other one . . . kosher? Is flour kosher?' put in a student from the back row.

'I think it is, isn't it? Kosher is about meat, right?' said Ahn.

'All animal products,' clarified Kiara.

'I eat halal,' Tanisha said. 'And I do Ramadan.'

'Oh my God. Do you lose, like, heaps of weight?' asked Chariot.

'It's not a *diet*!'

Was this discussion healthy or disrespectful? Maybe Andrea ought to steer them back to their recipes.

She was dead tired by the time she arrived home. After the food tech class, she'd been pulled into a meeting with the head of the English department who wanted to plan the Year Nine excursion for early next year, which Andrea thought really could have waited until January. And then she'd begun marking the history assignments, which started off so promising with a well-thought-out piece from Rashida Hamdi but immediately took a turn for the worse when she moved on to Jessica Kingston, and had been progressively more disappointing from there on. It was funny how often kids thought she was out to get them when she gave them a poor mark, when in reality she wanted nothing more than for them to succeed. She wanted every one of these assignments to be well thought out, well-researched, well-written, kick-ass commentaries on 'The role of Nicholas II in the collapse of the Romanov Dynasty'. Because then it would mean she was reaching them, that they were listening in class, that they cared. Instead she was dishing out marks that barely scraped by as a pass.

She was so tired that she almost didn't go to check on apartment 5A. The last few days everything had been fine, so maybe it was better to leave them be, and besides, Tony hadn't been too keen on her interfering. But at the last minute she felt a wave of guilt. What if everything wasn't fine? What if she didn't check and something happened? So, she headed down the hall past her own apartment door to 5A.

The funny thing was, in this type of apartment block, in this part of Sydney, you never would have imagined anything close to what was taking place behind the door of 5A. And yes, it might have been classist of Andrea to assume these problems only happened in lower socio-economic areas, but it had still shocked her when she'd seen what was going on.

The apartments here cost at least five times the amount she would have been able to afford had it not been for Tony. The real estate brochure had described their home as 'an executive haven of total opulence with show-stopping 180-degree harbour views and grand scale proportions'.

Andrea still remembered poring over the photos and feeling a heady combination of disbelief, desire and nausea. The sprawling balcony with porcelain tiles. The double-height ceilings and the gourmet stone kitchen. The herringbone timber floors and the plush bedroom carpet. And downstairs, a huge, sparkling swimming pool with an infinity edge, overlooking the harbour. She desperately wanted to live there, of course she did; it was stunning and luxurious. Never in her wildest dreams would she have envisioned one day living in a place like this. But wasn't it too much for one couple? Too indulgent? Too extravagant?

In truth, when Andrea first met Tony, he wouldn't have been able to afford it himself. He'd been working as an accountant, doing well enough for himself but certainly not wealthy. But then earlier this year he'd sold his book. It had been a huge shock. He hadn't even told anyone he'd been working on something.

His two younger brothers were already published authors. There was Pete, the middle brother, who earned a decent living writing an adventure series for middle-grade readers. And Darren, the youngest, had won the Esther Arlo Prize for an unpublished manuscript.

Andrea had been astonished to discover that both his brothers were published authors. Tony had shrugged it off though. *Is it any different to families of actors or singers?* he'd said, perhaps a little defensively. Later, she'd understood why he was defensive about it. He'd been secretly working on something himself and was nervous to admit he was following in his younger brothers' footsteps. He was afraid he might not live up to their success.

But everything changed when Tony's crime novel, *Don't Breathe*, was put out to auction and there was a frenzied bidding war for the rights. It hadn't even been released yet but he'd already made more money than his two brothers combined with the exorbitant advances he'd received from all over the world. They'd started looking at new apartments almost the second the first payments hit their bank account. The book was due out in February and the publicity campaign was ramping up. Meanwhile, Tony was already hard at work on the sequel.

It had been a big adjustment for Andrea to get used to an author husband as opposed to an accountant husband. Especially when they'd only been married such a short time before everything had changed. It was almost as though a personality shift had accompanied the professional switch. Not necessarily in a bad way . . . just different. She still wasn't sure if she was entirely used to the new him. One of the things she'd always loved about Tony was his gentlemanly nature; he had an almost old-world charm, the way he would hold doors open or insist on walking on the road-side of the footpath. Some women might have found it sexist for this day and age, but Andrea had always thought it was sweet, if a little formal at times. And it was such a divergence from her previous relationships. Before Tony, she'd made some bad choices. She'd mistakenly believed she wasn't worth better treatment. Tony had shown her that she was.

But lately, it wasn't that he'd lost those tendencies, it was perhaps that they'd become a little stiff, a little more perfunctory this past year. Or maybe it had nothing to do with the change in career and it was simply a case of him becoming more complacent as their second year of marriage progressed. That was normal, wasn't it? The honeymoon period couldn't last forever.

Although was it normal for the sex to slow down as much as it had? When they'd first started sleeping together, Andrea had discovered that in contrast to his old-fashioned ways, he was quite adventurous in the bedroom – keen to experiment with role-play or games. Andrea felt like it added an extra dimension to their relationship. It was exciting knowing that the conservative man everyone else saw was unexpectedly wild in the bedroom – and that she was the only one who got to see that side of his personality. Although as much as she enjoyed his exploratory side, she did have to suggest that once in a while they might just relax and have some ordinary vanilla sex.

Was that why things had slowed down? Was he disappointed that she didn't always want all the extra bells and whistles, metaphorically speaking, of course. Although now that she thought about it, there might have been a game involving a bell once. Perhaps she needed to try harder, put more effort in.

As Andrea approached 5A now, she stepped lightly and slowly, creeping up on the door so she could listen and decide whether or not it was necessary to knock. When she reached the door, she held still, leaned up close and pressed her ear against it. At first there was nothing, but eventually, as her senses tuned in and she blocked out everything else, she heard it. The sound of quiet crying.

Her heart broke as she closed her eyes and took a deep breath. Then she knocked.

Darren

Seeing Charlotte's name flash up on his phone still gave him that jolt, deep in his gut. And this frustrated him. He knew it wasn't going to be the phone call he dreamed about – the one where she would tell him she'd made a terrible mistake and she wanted him back. The truth was, even if her new relationship broke down, she'd still never come back to him. She was playing for the other team now. And as much as he'd held out hope that her switch of allegiances would be temporary, he understood now that it was permanent. This was her life. Her truth. And he could see how happy it made her.

So he'd accepted the consolation prize she'd offered him. Friendship. Even though it killed him every time he saw them hold hands. Every time they kissed. Every time she looked at her new girlfriend the way she used to look at him. Actually, it wasn't the way she used to look at him. It was better. Deeper. An extra twist of the knife. A few of his mates joked that he ought to enjoy the show any time they kissed in front of him. He only just managed to stop himself from punching them. Dickheads. They didn't get it. He was still in love with Charlotte.

Besides, if he was completely honest, he was proud of her for working it out. As much as he desperately wished it hadn't meant losing her, he was impressed with the strength of character she'd shown in recognising who she was, midway through her thirties. Especially as she came from a staunchly religious family who were refusing to accept her revelation. Recently she'd called him crying because she'd invited her parents out to dinner to meet Steph, her partner. Her dad had been a no-show and her mother had only turned up to let her know that they would never approve. Darren had always got along well enough with Charlotte's parents, but he was furious with them for the way they were treating her. To let her believe they were going to join her for dinner only to show up and deliver that crushing message was the last straw as far as he was concerned. He couldn't see how any parent could do that to their own child whom they supposedly loved. He'd have had a go at them himself if Charlotte hadn't told him not to.

Darren raked his fingers through his hair now and picked up the call, crossing his fingers that she wasn't going to be in tears again. She deserved happiness.

'Char, what's up?' He stood up from his computer and wandered out onto his small balcony to chat to her in the late afternoon sunshine. His one-bedroom, one-bathroom flat on the Lower North Shore was compact and in need of some updates, but he was fond of it nonetheless. There were multiple bars and cafes within walking distance, and if he leaned out over the railing on his terrace he could just catch a glimpse of the city skyline through the purple flowers of a huge jacaranda tree.

By contrast to the last phone call, the voice that greeted him was bright and bubbly.

'Babe! How are you?'

He hadn't been able to bring himself to ask her to stop calling him babe. It would come across as petty, like he was doing it to get one back at her. She called most of her friends babe, she didn't mean anything by it. But it was what she'd called him back when they were together, so it was hard to hear.

'I'm good. Great. Yeah, doing really great. You?'

'Same! But hey, listen, there's something I need to talk to you about. Something important. Can we meet? Friday night, if you're free?'

That little jolt in his stomach struck again. She wanted to talk. About something important. What if he was wrong about there being no hope for him? What if she had changed her mind?

He had to keep his voice steady when he replied, had to clear his throat to stop his tone from rising to an unnatural level.

'Sure. I've got some things to shift around, but I can make that work.'

'Oh, are you certain? I don't want to put you out.'

The truth was he had nothing going on this weekend apart from Netflix and a couple of beers on the couch.

'It's cool, don't stress. Cross Street Bar okay with you? Seven?'

'Perfect. I'll see you then.'

He hung up the phone and took a few deep breaths. *Don't get ahead of yourself, Daz. She wants to talk. It could be anything. But still, she'd said 'I'll see you then' not 'We'll see you then'.*

The last few times he'd caught up with Charlotte, Steph had always been by her side. Maybe this time it would just be the two of them.

He checked the time on his phone. Five pm. Time to finish work. He snorted. That was an absolute joke; as if he'd achieved a single thing sitting in front of his computer all day today. He may as well have chucked his board in the back of his car and gone surfing at Freshwater Beach instead.

Maybe tomorrow would bring inspiration.

Andrea

'Andrea?' came a small voice from the other side of the door.

'Yes, it's me, sweetie.'

She heard the clunk of the lock turning and then the door swung open. Andrea looked down at Violet, her six-year-old neighbour. She was slight with bright blue eyes and wispy blonde hair pulled back in a ponytail. Violet wiped her nose on the sleeve of her school shirt and moved back to let Andrea in.

'Is she here?' Andrea asked.

Violet shook her head.

'Oh honey, how long have you been alone?'

She avoided eye contact. 'Little while.'

'Are you hungry?'

She looked shy for a moment, then she nodded.

'All right, let's see if we can find you a snack.'

Violet followed Andrea around the kitchen as she opened cupboard doors and the fridge, looking for something a child would like. Caviar, truffles, quail eggs. Four bottles of champagne. Blue cheese. Smoked salmon.

The woman had expensive taste. She also had expensive habits. In Andrea's opinion, Heather was a high-functioning drug addict. Although Heather probably wouldn't consider herself an addict at all. Mainly because she wasn't broke and she didn't have track marks, and she took her drugs with famous rich people at exclusive parties. The problem was, she didn't always wait for a babysitter to show up before she left Violet to head out to one of her parties. Andrea had tried alerting social services to Heather's neglect, but when they turned up to check on things, she'd presented herself as the perfect parent.

Eventually, Andrea found crackers, cheddar cheese and some fruit. She tried to chat animatedly with Violet while she sliced the cheese, cut up the fruit and placed the snack on a plate. She asked her about school and homework and friends. Andrea used to see a nanny coming and going from Heather's apartment, but it seemed she had quit abruptly and never been replaced. From the hints Violet gave her, Andrea gathered the nanny's sudden departure had something to do with Heather's wild lifestyle and the different men she frequently brought home.

Andrea kept hoping that maybe Violet's school would pick up on the home-life issues and register their concerns with social services, so that it wasn't just coming from the neighbour down the hall. But somehow, Heather always sent Violet to school in pristine condition. It helped that she had a driver who took Violet door to door, so she never missed a day or turned up late. Not to mention Violet herself took great care in completing her homework, often asking for Andrea's help to make sure she had it done in time.

Andrea had only spotted the driver once or twice, but she got the feeling he cared about Violet too. She'd noticed him fixing Violet's plait for her as he walked her down to the car. He wasn't what she would have imagined of a chauffeur either. He was casually dressed and he seemed to have this relaxed, cool air about him. He had a shaved head, neatly edged stubble and kind eyes.

Andrea put the plate down in front of Violet and sat next to her, trying not to watch her too intently while she ate. Violet had always been tiny and Andrea suspected that was just her build, but it was still nice to see her eat something. Her arms were quite thin.

Andrea certainly couldn't ever remember her own

mother making her a snack after school, or watching her eat, or caring about whether or not she was satisfied. She was lucky if her mum made her any meals at all.

Andrea had been slight as a child too. Arms and legs like sticks. The kids at school called her Skinny Minnie. Not in a kind way. In her late teenage years, she'd packed on the weight as she tried to get her body to fill out, but it appeared in all the wrong places and she constantly felt out of proportion. Thankfully though, by the time she'd reached her thirties, she'd finally settled into her body shape. Accepted her petite form for what it was. Now the only time she ever looked curvy was when she ate something that didn't agree with her and her stomach became bloated and poked out like a beach ball.

'Is it good?' Andrea asked as Violet ate slowly and neatly, making sure to chew with her mouth closed. She had better table manners than Andrea's sixteen-year-old niece.

Violet swallowed and gave her a big smile. 'Really yummy,' she said. 'Want some?'

'Nope, I'm good. That plate is all for you, my dear.' Andrea paused. 'Did Mum say what time she'd be back?'

Violet looked up at the clock on the wall, her face a picture of concentration. Eventually she said, 'Little hand on the six.'

'Six o'clock?' Andrea looked at her own watch. It was almost six. 'Okay, so she's supposed to be home any minute now. I'll stay with you until she gets here though, okay?'

Almost immediately she heard the sound of a key in the lock and she swung around to face the door.

'What are you doing here?'

'Checking on Violet,' Andrea said, standing.

'Well there's no need. I was only around the corner picking up some groceries.'

Andrea's eyes flicked to the bag her neighbour was holding. It looked as though the only 'groceries' she'd bought were bottles of alcohol.

Heather clocked her looking. 'The rest is in the car, Miss Detective. My driver is bringing them up.' She stepped back to the door and opened it wide. 'Thanks, but you can go now.'

Andrea glanced back at Violet, gave her a quick, warm smile and then headed for the door. When she reached Heather, she paused briefly and leaned in. 'I'm keeping an eye on you,' she whispered.

Heather reached out and grabbed her arm, fake nails digging into Andrea's skin. 'Stay away from my daughter.' Her voice was a harsh hiss.

Andrea wrenched her arm free and swung back around to call out to Violet in as cheerful a voice as possible. 'Lovely to see you, honey. I'll see you again soon.'

Then she stepped past Heather and out into the hall. The door slammed behind her. Andrea held still for a moment, her arm tingling from where Heather had grabbed it. Okay, so maybe tonight she'd only ducked out for a quick trip to the shop, rather than out partying with friends, but still, six was too young even for that. And Andrea didn't believe for an instant that her driver was bringing up other groceries. Heather had gone out for what she considered 'essentials', nothing more.

There was also no way Andrea was going to stay away from Violet. The little girl needed someone to look out for her.

Christmas Eve

The first driver went right by. She was a P-plater on her own.
And when she saw the pile-up loom out of the darkness on the
side of the freeway, she was too stunned to react. She sailed
on past, her heart pounding. It looked bad. It looked really
bad. And it looked as though it had only just happened. She
knew she should stop, call emergency services. But her hands
seemed locked into place on the steering wheel, her right foot
unflinching on the accelerator. She was already a full kilometre
beyond the accident before her body unfroze and it crossed
her mind that now she knew what type of person she was. The
type of person who doesn't stop to help. She would have called
the police except that her mum made her keep her phone
in the boot of the car ever since her brother had dobbed her
in for texting while driving. In the end, she convinced herself
it would be okay because the next car would stop and get help.

Later, when she heard on the news that there was a fatality
from the accident, and that another person was critical, she
wondered whether or not a life could have been saved if she'd
helped.

2

Friday 4 December

Mimi

The thing that irritated her about it the most was the tone. She knew Pete was trying to sound a bit jokey, trying to make it seem like a casual suggestion, but she could tell there was an underlying note of concern.

'Should we *really* be opening another bottle of wine tonight?'

Okay, yes, they'd already sped through a bottle of sav blanc that afternoon. It was meant to be a pre-dinner drink and then finish off the bottle with dinner. But it was Friday and it was sunny and Mimi was still making up for lost time. So the drinks had gone down easy as they'd sat out on the patio overlooking the backyard and listened to the tranquil sounds of the bush.

She supposed he was right. The twins would wake in the night and getting up to prepare bottles for them after several wines would probably be a nightmare. Not that she'd have to do it alone. Pete always helped out . . . well, when he was jabbed awake he did, anyway. The man could sleep through a semi-trailer driving through the lounge room. But he didn't do it on purpose. As soon as he was awake, he was out of bed and heating up bottles or rocking the girls while Mimi mixed up the formula.

That was the handy thing about having a husband who worked from home. It meant he was very hands-on with their kids. He'd turned one of the bedrooms at the back of the house into his study and it looked out over Lane Cove National Park. He said it was the perfect place to write because looking out at the bush gave him all the inspiration he needed to create his adventure stories.

When they met, he'd just finished writing his first book and was nervously preparing to submit it to a publisher. He let Mimi read his manuscript and, for fun, she'd started doodling drawings of the main characters. When he saw the drawings, he said they'd given him the courage to send the book out, because she'd brought his characters to life for him. He'd included Mimi's sketches with his submission and now, seventeen years later, he'd written and she'd illustrated twenty books in the *Timid Tongue-Tied Timmy* adventure series. She'd studied graphic design before they met and she continued to work at a small printing firm in the early days, but once the books took off, she left to work on the illustrations full time. Art had always been her passion above design.

People often asked them how they did it – lived and worked so closely together. *I'd go insane if I didn't get my eight hours at the office away from my husband,* several of the school mums said. But the truth was, it was easy for Mimi to spend so much time with Pete because he was her best friend. And it helped that she was still bloody attracted to the guy. Even after spending almost two decades with him, even after he'd started to lose his hair and had to shave it all off, even with those few extra kilos around the middle, he could still stir something inside her when he looked at her in just the right way. Her favourite thing about him was his arms – they were muscular and strong and she liked nothing better than snuggling into his chest and having him wrap those arms around her.

So, right now, as she stood in the kitchen with the second bottle of wine in hand, she really shouldn't be feeling irritated with him. Because he was only being sensible when he suggested they not open the second bottle of wine.

But at the same time, he hadn't had to give up drinking for nine months' worth of pregnancy. She was just playing catch-up. That first sip of wine had felt like coming home. Ha. She was kidding. She wasn't that bad. She just didn't realise how much she'd missed the taste, the comfort, the warmth. The way her whole body began to relax with each mouthful. Her jaw would unclench and the tension in her neck would release and her shoulders would drop, and it felt like everything else clicked into place from there. She'd imagine her spine slotting into place, one piece of Lego on top of the other. Click, click, click, click. Her hips would loosen. The warmth would spread down her thighs, circle around her calves, all the way to her feet until she felt her toes uncurl. *Who wouldn't want to sustain that experience?*

Plus, just a few weeks ago, Pete had come home after taking Callie out for one of her driving lessons and downed five Bacardis in a row. Callie was actually quite a good driver, but apparently she'd somehow missed a stop sign and had consequently taken ten years off Pete's life. And *that* had been a Wednesday night. Back before the twins, they used to try to restrict their drinking to weekends only. But throughout the past year, Pete had proclaimed that 'helping Tara with her homework' or 'taking Callie out for driving lessons' were exceptions to the no mid-week drinks rule.

Hence, Mimi's irritation at him now judging her for wanting to open another bottle on a Friday night. She forced herself to shrug it off and put the bottle of sav blanc back in the fridge. 'Fair call.'

'Sorry. Didn't mean to be a buzz kill.'

She must have sounded more disappointed than she'd meant to.

'Nah, you're right. I'm all good. Meant to tell you your mum dropped by this morning while you were out.'

Pete had been out most of the day for a meeting with their literary agent followed by lunch with their publishers. Usually Mimi would join him for those, but someone had to be home with the twins and it made more sense for the writer to be in the meetings than the illustrator.

'Oh yeah? How was she?' he asked.

'Seemed fine. Still determined about Christmas, so it looks like we're definitely going ahead with the usual plans. She was more concerned with how I was. I think sometimes she forgets that you work from home and you're usually here with the twins. I could tell she was probing, trying to see if I'm coping.'

Pete made a face. 'Sorry, was that annoying?'

Mimi folded her arms. 'You don't need to apologise for your mum, she's lovely. It's nice that she cares.'

Tara appeared from the hallway and leaned against the island bench. 'Twin report,' she announced. 'Elliot was stirring so I popped her dummy back in and she settled. James is fast asleep.'

Pete and Mimi exchanged a brief look. They both loved the way Tara had picked up all the little mothering terms like 'stirring' and 'settled'.

'Thanks, sweetie. I want them to make it through till two tonight, so that's perfect. You hungry?'

'Yep. What's for dinner?'

'Ask your father,' said Mimi.

He twisted his mouth, thinking. 'Takeaway too many times lately?' he asked.

Mimi raised her palms and deferred to Tara. 'What do you think?'

She considered the question for a minute. 'I think pizza is allowed. We haven't had pizza for a while.'

Mimi nodded. 'I agree with the wise one. Oh, wise one, advise us which pizza place to choose tonight. George's Gourmet or Christina Christina?'

'Christina Christina. Because blonde Christina always gives me lollies when I go with Dad to pick it up.'

'But what happens if it's redhead Christina who serves you? Will you be disappointed?'

'A little, but I'll live. Can you plait my hair before I go with Dad?'

'Sure, sweetheart.' Tara had inherited Mimi's tight curls and after a full day at school, they'd sprung out into a frizzy tangle around her head.

They all turned as the sound of a bedroom door slamming upstairs was followed by footsteps stomping across the landing.

'Tell me she hasn't woken the twins,' Mimi said.

They collectively held their breath as they waited for the cries, but there was silence. Callie appeared at the bottom of the stairs. 'What's for dinner?' she asked.

'Oh, hi Mum, hi Dad, hi Tara,' said Pete. 'How is everyone tonight? Good? Had a nice day? Yeah, not too bad. How about you, Callie, haven't seen you since you got home, disappeared into your room and stayed there ever since. You been well?'

'Shut up. I've been busy.'

'Don't say shut up, it's rude,' said Tara.

'Then why do Mum and Dad say it to each other all the time?'

'We do it in a jokesy way,' Mimi replied. 'Don't we?' she added, feeling slightly guilty.

'Yeah, course,' said Pete.

Mimi took a step towards Callie. She'd been missing her since she started retreating into her room whenever she was home. They used to have lovely long chats over chai lattes in the afternoons. Callie used to hug her with abandon. She used to confide in her. But it felt like a switch had been flipped several months ago.

She'd also started ironing her curls dead-straight every single morning. Mimi had always taken such pleasure in the way her daughters had embraced the curls they'd inherited from her. She knew it was naïve to presume Callie wouldn't change her look as she grew, but flattening those perfect ringlets was akin to blasphemy in Mimi's mind.

'Are you okay? How was your day?'

'Fine. What's for dinner?' she repeated.

'Pizza.'

'Ugh. Can't you guys cook for once?'

Mimi saw Pete's nostrils flare and she gave him an almost imperceptible shake of her head. Yes, Callie was being rude, but she was trying to pick her battles with their teenage daughter at the moment. If they reprimanded her, it would only lead to another fight.

Pete rolled his eyes but when he spoke, his tone was light. 'You're sixteen,' he said. 'You could cook. Besides, I made bolognese yesterday.'

'From a jar.'

'And?'

'Peyton's parents make their own sauce from their *own* tomatoes from their backyard.'

'Peyton's parents don't let Peyton have her own phone. Do you really want us to be more like them?'

'That's completely beside the point. Is it really that bad that I want to eat healthy?' She swung around and stomped back up the stairs.

Mimi's mind immediately started doing exactly what it had been doing on and off for the last few months: cycling through all the potential reasons for Callie's new attitude. The twins. Trouble at school. Bullies. Friends. Social media. A boy. She has a crush on someone. Someone has a crush on her. Was she suddenly worried about weight? Potential eating disorder. That was a new one to add to the list.

Her concerns must have been manifesting themselves on her face because Pete was pulling the bottle of wine straight back out of the fridge.

'I rule an exception on stopping at one bottle, due to having a teenager in the house,' he said. 'Let's have the pizza delivered.'

'Thank God.'

He realised his mistake the moment he stepped into the crowded bar, scanned the room and spotted Charlotte. There was an arm slung around her shoulder. The arm was attached to Steph. Steph, with her short sharp platinum-blonde hair, her sharp features and sharp angles. Her bright red lipstick. A complete juxtaposition to Charlotte's softness, her long dark waves, soft olive skin and natural makeup-free features. Her lipstick-less lips that he used to be allowed to kiss.

He was an idiot for starting to create a sliver of false hope for himself. He knew better. And it was insulting to Charlotte to keep thinking she'd go back on this decision, because it wasn't a decision, was it? It was a revelation of who she was. He needed to pull himself together and accept their relationship for what it was – friendship. Because if he wanted to keep Charlotte in his life that was all it could ever be.

He made a conscious effort to fix his body language, pulling his shoulders back and lifting his chin so he wouldn't look disappointed. Then he started weaving his way through the Friday night crowd of men in suits with loosened ties and women in cute blazers, short skirts and high heels. Sometimes he missed working a normal nine-to-five job. Being able to head out with his colleagues at the end of the week to cut loose, sharing a drunken pash on a hot summer's night with someone from the office as the night drew to a close. Before he'd quit to write full time he'd worked as a sales development manager for a finance company in the city. He hadn't been all that great at his job, just barely hitting his targets each month. He suspected his boss had accepted his resignation with some relief when he'd scored his publishing deal.

'Ladies,' he said as he reached Charlotte and Steph's booth but remained standing. 'Grab you something from the bar before I sit down?'

Charlotte jumped up and gave him a kiss on the cheek while Steph stayed sitting but smiled at him. 'All good,' said Charlotte. 'We've ordered and we've got a beer coming for you as well.'

'Asahi?'

'Asahi.'

He grinned and pulled out a chair while Charlotte dropped back into her seat. He thought Steph's smile might have become a little fixed throughout the exchange and wondered if it bothered her that Charlotte still knew him well enough to order him a beer before he'd even arrived to choose it.

Now that it had been confirmed her invite really did have nothing to do with wanting him back, he was curious to find out what the important thing was that she wanted to talk about. Unfortunately, she wasn't in any hurry to enlighten him.

'What's going on? How have you been?' she said before he could jump in and ask her what she wanted.

'Not much. The usual. You guys?'

Steph went to answer but Charlotte spoke over the top of her. 'Oh, us? We're boring. Tell us more about you. The usual? What does that mean? Come on, tell us about your "exciting author life".'

Darren cocked his head to the side. Charlotte's voice

seemed to have switched to high-speed mode and it was a tad shriller than usual. She was nervous about something.

'Err, my exciting author life? Charlotte, you know that's a myth. There is no exciting author life. It's just me and my laptop and a looming deadline.'

'Yeah, but no interesting writing events of late? Like that time you got mad drunk in front of Markus Zusak and then you came home crying because he's your idol?'

'Well, thanks for bringing that up. Nope, can't say anything like that's happened lately. Anyway, didn't you have something –'

Charlotte cut him off. 'Oh, I meant to say, thanks so much for those Netflix recommendations you sent me. Steph and I have been binging *Lucifer* nonstop . . .'

Charlotte paused briefly as their drinks arrived and then continued on, describing in surprising detail the plot of the episode she was up to, before jumping to a review of the movie she and Steph had seen the previous night and then a meandering anecdote about the best way to make guacamole. Neither Steph nor Darren could get a word in as she continued to swing wildly from one topic to the next, clearly intent on avoiding broaching the reason she'd asked him out.

Eventually, she had to pause for breath in the middle of a story about the new wireless headphones she wanted to buy and Darren took his chance. 'Char, sorry to interrupt, but you mentioned there was something important . . . something you needed to talk with me about. And I'm guessing it's not guacamole recipes or Bose versus Beats.'

'Umm, yeah. There is. Do you need another drink though? I think you're almost empty.'

Darren glanced down at his beer; it was more than half full. 'I'm right,' he said.

He watched as Steph placed a hand over the top of Charlotte's on the table. 'You're okay, hon,' she said. Charlotte visibly relaxed under Steph's touch.

Darren swallowed a pang of jealousy.

'Okay,' said Charlotte. 'I guess I need to come right out and say it. Steph and I . . . we have a favour to ask of you. I mean, it's not really a favour, it's bigger than that, it's huge, it's . . . I don't know how you describe the magnitude of what we want to ask you.'

'Char,' Darren said, 'all you do is ask.'

'We want your sperm.'

Darren held very still, trying hard to compose his face so he didn't look shocked. On the one hand, it was the most obvious answer. Of course this was why she wanted to talk to him. He'd always known how much she wanted kids, but when she'd come out, he hadn't ever stopped to think about how much harder it would be for her to fulfil that dream. But at the same time it completely blindsided him.

All those times he'd imagined one day marrying Charlotte, having a family with her, he'd envisioned what their kids might look like. And now she wanted him to hand that imaginary child right over and allow her to raise him or her with someone else.

Then there was the second bombshell.

Now that she'd spilled the truth, she was back on high-speed mode. 'So, I know it's a big ask, a huge decision. But if you did say yes and if it did work, if Steph fell pregnant, we want you to know there'd be zero responsibility on your shoulders. We'll have a contract drawn up, something to say that you'd never be financially liable –'

Wait a minute, if Steph fell pregnant?

Darren held a hand up to cut her off. 'Sorry, hang on. Steph's the one who'd be . . .' He motioned a rounded stomach out in front of himself. For some reason he seemed to have lost basic vocabulary skills.

'The one who'd carry the baby, yep,' said Charlotte.

So, it wouldn't be that same imaginary child at all. She didn't even want his sperm for herself, she wanted it for her girlfriend. The baby wouldn't be half-Darren half-Charlotte. It would be half-Darren half-Steph.

Charlotte took off again, rushing through all the reasons he'd make the perfect donor for them, explaining how happy it would make them, how hard it was to find the right man to ask, how desperate they were to start a family, how ready they were.

And Darren found himself staring straight at Steph. He could barely hear the words Charlotte was saying. Instead he was conjuring up a new image. A tiny girl, with his own ears that stuck out just a little too far, with his dirty blond hair, his dimples. But now he was adding in new features. Steph's high cheekbones, Steph's pale skin.

It was all wrong! It didn't work. The features were clashing. When he used to picture the child he and Charlotte would have together, everything blended together perfectly. Her button nose made up for his big ears. Her olive skin matched his brown eyes. For some reason, this new child was remarkably resemblant of Dobby the elf.

Darren realised that Steph was now staring straight back at him and he dropped his eyes, embarrassed at being caught out examining her face with such intensity. But Steph surprised him with an impressive level of insight.

'You were trying to figure out what a baby created from you and me would look like, weren't you?' she asked, interrupting Charlotte's flow.

Darren grabbed his glass and took a large gulp. 'Maybe,' he said. 'A little.'

Charlotte opened her mouth to speak but yet again Steph spoke over her. 'Darren, this is a huge thing we're asking you. You'll need to take some time, but it's also okay if you want to say no.'

Once again, Darren was surprised. His jealousy had meant that he'd never really put a lot of effort into getting to know Steph. Instead he'd kept her at arm's length, preferring to see her as the imposter within his world. But right now, she was displaying real compassion. And he appreciated it. He smiled and nodded. 'Thanks, Steph.'

But now he looked back at Charlotte and saw that her face had dropped. It was clear she was hoping for a yes. And quite possibly hoping he was going to give them that yes, here and now. Considering the excitement and animation in her voice as she'd chatted on and on about all the reasons he was the perfect choice, he wouldn't have been surprised if she'd whipped a jar out of her handbag and asked him to nip into the men's room and bang out a specimen for them right now.

He couldn't stand to see her looking so disappointed. The words were out of his mouth before he could stop himself.

'I'll do it.'

Charlotte was on her feet in an instant. She flung her arms out to gather him into a difficult hug, considering there was still a table between them. 'Thank you,' she gushed. 'Thank you, thank you. You don't know what this means to us.'

Steph, meanwhile, had remained sitting and when Charlotte finally released him, Darren saw that she was looking worried.

'Are you sure about this?' she asked. 'Honestly, you can take more time if you need it.'

Charlotte dropped back into her seat and whacked Steph with the back of her hand. 'Jesus, Steph, he said yes. Don't try and talk him out of it now.'

Steph smiled. 'I'm not. I only want to make sure he's certain.'

Darren looked away and briefly caught the eye of a petite redhead by the bar. He grinned at her and then turned back. 'When you think about it, I'd be stupid not to. It's a chance to give two people a family. And all I have to do is jerk off. Not a bad gig really.'

'Oh my God, Darren!' Charlotte laughed and then stood up again. 'I'm going to the bar. We need to celebrate.'

As soon as she was out of earshot, Steph leaned forward. 'Really,' she said, keeping her voice low. 'You don't have to say yes. I know you still have feelings for her. And I know you'd probably do just about anything for her. I don't want you to do this out of obligation or because . . .'

She trailed off and Darren felt one of his eyelids twitch. He knew what was coming.

'Because what?'

'Because you might think that if you do this for her, that she'll somehow . . . that she might come back to you.'

He could tell Steph was feeling bad about saying it but it still pissed him off. Sure, she might have been on to something, but did she have to call him out on it like that? This was his problem to deal with alone. And in truth, he was embarrassed that it was that obvious. He'd lost his appreciation for her compassion.

'Honestly, I'm fine,' he said. 'I'd do this for anyone.'

'You really think that?'

'Yep. Why the hell not? Blokes donate to sperm banks all the time, what's the difference?'

'The difference is that you're still in love with Charlotte.'

'You're mistaking friendship for love.' He hesitated before moving on to an outright lie. 'Anyway, I've moved on. I'm seeing someone else.'

The corner of Steph's mouth twitched. 'Are you?' she said. 'Charlotte never mentioned it.'

'It's only new.'

'Well, in that case, don't you think you need to consult your new girlfriend before you agree to do this?'

'Not really. Like I said, it's only early days. She has no claim over my junk.'

Steph leaned back and folded her arms. 'All right,' she said. 'Fair enough.' She paused. 'Thank you. We do really appreciate this. Both of us.'

Darren softened a little. He could see the relief in her eyes. She wanted this as much as Charlotte did. Now he just hoped she didn't start asking him a whole heap of questions about the imaginary girl he was supposed to be dating.

Jill

Dear Frank,

I've made it to Friday. Although Fridays don't really matter anymore when you're retired, do they? But still, it's another week and so it feels like an achievement. Another week of mediocrity. Another week of boredom and loneliness and insomnia. Another week without you.

I'm being dramatic. I'm sorry. Are you sick of me telling you I'm sorry? You probably are. But I don't know what else to do. I don't know how else to make up for it all. I suppose in truth I simply can't. Nothing can make up for any of it. No amount of Hail Marys. No amount of waffling letters. No number of apologies. But I may as well keep writing. Because what else can I do?

I skipped my Hail Marys this morning. I just couldn't be bothered. I was too angry. But I will do them tonight before I go to sleep. As many as I can. I'll chant them until I'm too tired. And then I'll lie awake with burning eyes and beg for sleep.

But do you think it'll make any difference in the long run? When my time comes to be judged, will all of these Hail Marys count for anything against what I've done? No. I don't think that they will.

I still haven't opened the bloody email. I did tell you about it, didn't I? Honestly, I'm sure it's nothing, but it is very odd for her to contact me out of the blue like this. And there's something so commanding about it. 'You need to know'. I don't see why it's up to her to tell me what I need to know. Maybe I should delete it.

I saw Mimi and the twins today. Popped in for morning tea. I was trying to be helpful. I wanted her to let me do something for her. Anything. A load of washing. Stack the dishwasher. Change

47

their nappies. But she wouldn't let me! In the end, I think I was
more trouble for her. Instead of resting, she was fussing over me,
making me a pot of tea and a slice of raisin toast, telling me to sit
down and relax. That wasn't the point!

But she insisted and, somehow, I couldn't insist back. It was
nice though, having a cup of tea made for me.

I wish you would bloody come back and make me a cup of tea
again.

Love,
Jill

Jill still hated how empty the house felt at night. You'd
think she would have grown used to it by now, but she
hadn't. However much she told her sons that she was fine,
that she was comfortable, happy, safe. She left strategic
lights on throughout the house when she went to bed.
The one above the stove in the kitchen. The desk lamp
in Frank's study. The mirror light in the main bathroom.
They created small glowing pools of warmth throughout
her home. Safe harbour.

But it wasn't the same as having Frank here with her.
She hadn't realised how much safer he'd made her feel,
how much she would miss holding his hand. His old,
wrinkly hand with the sunspots and the arthritic bumps.
She hadn't realised how much she'd miss the *intimacy* that
came with having a partner. In truth, they were barely
having sex anymore – yes, occasionally, but mostly they
were too tired and it took too much effort so they'd simply
cuddle together at night. And that was enough.

When Frank was here, they would sleep with the windows thrown open throughout summer, catching the

cross breeze to cool the house at night. But now she slept with the windows firmly closed and locked.

Pete had actually broached the idea of her moving in with them. She'd seen the panic in Mimi's eyes when he'd made the suggestion. It wasn't that they didn't get along. On the contrary, Jill was happy with the relationship she had cultivated with Mimi. She worked hard to avoid being too overbearing. But it was still an understandable reaction. Having your mother-in-law move in with you was a big deal. And in all honesty, Jill had no interest in moving in with them anyway.

If she lived with them in their home, she would forever feel like the outsider. The interloper in their lives. She would have to fit in with their schedules. Share their meals. After years of having her own space, she simply couldn't bring herself to start compromising again. Fifteen years she and Frank had been alone together, once all the boys had moved out. Fifteen years of bliss mixed with loneliness. It was funny how much as a parent you both looked forward to the day the last of your children flew the nest and simultaneously dreaded it.

Tony had been the last to move out, even though he was the eldest. But Jill was glad she'd had the extra time with him. She'd needed it.

Darren

He was in over his head. And the worst thing about it was it meant Steph had been right. He should have taken more time to answer. He'd said yes simply because he would do anything to make Charlotte happy. And now not only had he made a promise he was no longer so sure about keeping, he'd also invented a new girlfriend who Charlotte and Steph wanted to meet. He lay flat on his back on his bed, on top of the covers and still fully dressed, shoes included, and stared up at the spinning ceiling fan.

Thankfully Steph hadn't grilled him about the imaginary woman he was dating, but she'd mentioned her in front of Charlotte when they were leaving the bar. By that point, the three of them were all smashed. When Charlotte had gone to get celebratory drinks, she'd returned with a tray of shots and chasers.

'Are you kidding me?' Darren had said. 'You know it doesn't end well for me when I have shots.'

But Charlotte had pushed the shot towards him and her eyes had sparkled in that way they always used to when she was up to no good and he'd given in. From there it had been round after round until Charlotte was wiping snotty tears on his shoulder and telling him she would spend the rest of her life finding a way to repay him. The rest. Of. Her. Life. He'd managed to refrain from suggesting she repay him in the form of some kind of indecent-proposal-style deal – he was drunk, but he wasn't that drunk. Or that stupid.

It was as they were stumbling out onto the footpath that Steph mentioned the new girlfriend.

'We have to do this again,' Charlotte had been saying, or slurring, really. 'This was *fun*. We have to have all the fun before me and Steph are home being new mummies.'

'Yes!' Steph shouted a little too loudly. 'And Darren can bring his new lady friend!'

Charlotte had spun around on the spot and almost lost her balance. 'New lady friend? What new lady friend?'

Thankfully a cab had pulled up right at that moment and Darren had bundled the two of them into the back seat, promising to tell them all about his 'new lady friend' soon.

Now, as he lay very still, breathing deep and trying his best not to throw up, he pictured Charlotte's face as she'd looked back through the window while the cab pulled away. Was it just his imagination, or was it possible that she was jealous of him seeing someone new?

Jesus, he had to let that shit go.

He had to accept the facts.

He had to throw up.

He lurched his body upright and then clambered off the bed and stumbled to the bathroom, just making it to the toilet in time. When he'd finished purging his stomach of the copious amount of alcohol he'd drunk, he lay down on the cool tiles and made himself a promise.

You're going to get the fuck over Charlotte. You're going to find this imaginary girlfriend and make her real. And you're going to think properly about this promise you've made. Because if you can't follow through, you're going to have to man up and tell her.

Christmas Eve

The second driver slowed for a look, but he was in the far right lane and even after easing his foot off the accelerator, he was still going too fast to switch lanes and pull off onto the hard shoulder in time. Besides, was one of the cars a witness who'd already stopped to help? It didn't look crumpled like the others. Although . . . was there smoke coming from its bonnet? Too late, he was past.

But he did at least hit the call button on the centre console.

'Who do you want to call?' Siri asked in her weirdly stilted voice, the intonation always slightly off.

'Triple zero.'

'Calling Tristan mobile.'

'No. Stop. Hey Siri. HEY! SIRI! STOP!'

Tristan's voice filled his car. 'G'day mate, haven't heard from you in yonks.'

'Yeah, sorry, bud. Siri fucked up and called you by mistake. I was trying to call for an ambo. Just passed an accident on the freeway.'

'Far out. You need to go?'

'Nah, look, it's not worth it now. There's probably already a whole heap of people calling in about it and I think someone had already stopped. How are you anyway?'

He never bothered to check the news to see how things turned out.

3

Andrea

Andrea smiled as she walked towards her mother-in-law and sister-in-law at the outdoor tables of Bellbird Café. Mimi was leaning right back in her chair, her hands laced together over her stomach and a look of pure relief on her face. Her long curls were twisted up into a knot on top of her head in that effortless way that still somehow looked elegant. If Andrea had tried to do that with her hair, back when it was long, she'd have looked like there was a bird's nest perched on her head. That's why she always kept it short now – much easier to manage.

Meanwhile, Jill – who was probably the same height standing as Mimi was sitting – was hovering over the double stroller, one baby in her arms and her mouth twisting as she clearly deliberated how she might be able to pick up the other one as well. Andrea could see damp underarm patches developing on Jill's blouse as she struggled with the decision.

Andrea quickened her pace. 'Hey,' she said, 'you need me to grab . . .' She broke off as she tried to figure out which one Jill was already holding. 'James for you?' she asked.

Mimi grinned. 'Nicely guessed. Sure, you can pick her up, I don't think I burped her properly after her feed.'

Jill was still hovering with Elliot in her arms. 'She needs burping?' she asked, concern in her voice. 'Do you want to take Elle and I'll pick up Jamie?'

Andrea and Mimi exchanged a brief look. Mimi had commiserated with her in the past about the fact that, while well meaning, it was clear Jill assumed that being child-free meant she didn't know how to deal with babies.

'All good,' Andrea said as she reached into the stroller and scooped up James.

'Well, mind you keep her face in the shade,' said Jill.

'You know you'll get in trouble with Pete if he catches you changing their names,' Mimi said, arching an eyebrow at Jill.

'What? What did I say? I didn't change them.'

'Don't you play all innocent with me. Elle? Jamie? We all know you're trying to girl up their names. For the record, I don't care, I like shortening them to nicknames. It's Pete that keeps trying to stick to full names.'

'Still hung up on not getting his boys?' Andrea asked as she sat down, lifted James up over one shoulder and began to gently pat her back. Her small compact body was warm against Andrea's skin.

'Fuck yes,' said Mimi.

'Language!' Jill put one hand over Elliot's ear and they all laughed.

'You're the worst offender of us all,' Mimi said. 'Callie told me you were getting her to explain the meaning of WTAF to you the other day.'

'Not explaining. I knew what it meant. I just needed . . .

clarification. I didn't understand why there was an A in there.'

'Ah yes, what the *actual* fuck,' Andrea said. 'Where are Callie and Tara anyway? I thought this was meant to be a girls' lunch with *all* the girls.'

'Callie ditched us in favour of the beach with her friends and Tara has percussion lessons. She's doing extra at the moment because she's performing at a Christmas musical evening at the end of term.'

'I didn't know she was performing,' said Jill. 'When is it? I'll come.'

'Honestly, you don't need to,' said Mimi. 'It's not really a big deal. There's a whole heap of schools involved and she'll only be on stage for all of three minutes.'

'That doesn't matter! I'd love to come. Send me the details and I'll be there.'

Mimi shrugged. 'Your choice, but no pressure.'

A waiter interrupted them. 'Ready to order?'

'Oops, haven't looked,' said Andrea, leaning forward to pick up a menu with one hand while keeping James snuggled into her shoulder.

Mimi spoke at the same time. 'Bottle of the Margaret River cab sav,' she said. 'Three?' She glanced around at the others then continued without waiting for an answer. 'Yes, three glasses, please.'

The waiter nodded. 'I'll come back for your food orders.'

'Oh yes,' said Andrea, 'you're free from breastfeeding now, hey?'

'Hell yes.'

'Still,' interrupted Jill, 'it's an *early* lunch. Should we be having wine?'

'Wine-o-clock somewhere,' Mimi said.

'Fair enough,' said Andrea. 'Oh, Jill, did Tony remember to come and move those boxes up into the roof storage for you yesterday? I forgot to ask him if he did it last night.'

'No, but he doesn't need to. I can handle that.'

Andrea exchanged yet another quick look with Mimi while Jill had her eyes focused down on Elliot. They had aired their concerns with one another about how hard it was to get Jill to accept any help. Andrea particularly didn't like the idea of her trying to climb up to the roof space on her own.

'It's no trouble,' Andrea said. 'He works his own hours, he can drop by.'

'For that matter, so could Pete,' Mimi added.

'Nonsense. Pete needs to be at home helping you out with these babies. And Tony's on deadline for the next book. We don't want him working through Christmas, do we?'

'True.' Andrea paused. 'Jill, Tony said the other day that you're still happy to do the usual trip up the coast. Are you sure that's what you want? Because we'd all be more than happy to –'

'Absolutely,' Jill cut in. 'And this year we're going to make sure we have a set meeting point so that we all leave at the same time.'

'Of course, we can do that,' said Mimi.

Jill shifted her attention back to Andrea. 'How's the little one doing there? Have you managed to coax a burp out of her yet?'

As if on cue, James let out a loud croak.

Mimi gave Andrea a golf clap. 'Expert technique.'

Mimi was loving all of this time without having to hold, feed, rock or burp her babies. With her own parents back in England and no other family here in Australia, she had to rely on Pete's family for any outside help with the kids. And right now, Jill and Andrea had it all under control. They'd managed to get both of them to sleep; Andrea had even done a perfect transfer from her arms to the pram while Jill insisted James would wake the moment she placed her down.

Now, as Jill fanned the pram with a plastic menu to keep the girls cool, there was a look on her face that was a mixture between impressed and mollified that Andrea had done so well. Actually, Mimi noticed, there was something else there in Jill's expression. Underneath all of that. Something that had been beneath the surface throughout all of lunch. A hint of sadness perhaps? And her hair wasn't set as neatly as normal. Usually her shoulder-length, silver-streaked hair was blow-dried around her face. Today it was pinned back with clips, as though she'd done it in a hurry. Jill had been alone for almost a full year now and yet she always seemed to put up a steady façade of brightness and bravery around her family. Were the cracks finally starting to show? Was she ready to accept their support instead of worrying about everyone else for a change? Surely it had to happen eventually. Then again, Jill was a determined woman and as the matriarch of her family, an ex-principal and a mum of three boys, maybe she would never let those vulnerabilities show.

Either way, Mimi couldn't help but feel good that she'd

been able to eat her southern fried chicken burger and enjoy her glass or two of wine in complete peace. Bellbird Café was decked out in tinsel, and silver and gold stars hung from the huge outdoor umbrellas. A small Christmas tree covered with fake snow was set up in the corner. This was the time of the year she loved most. When everyone started decorating, the shops were bustling and people were giddy from long Christmas lunches with drinks. The one thing she did miss was having an office job where you got to enjoy the big company Christmas party. Working from home with Pete had its perks, but it didn't include enjoying the office culture of water-cooler gossip and work lunches and meetings.

'Hey,' said Andrea, 'can I get both your opinions on something?'

'Shoot,' said Mimi.

'I'm not overreacting when I say it's wrong to leave a child alone in an apartment, am I?'

'How old? Who? What? Why?' Mimi asked.

'It's my neighbour, and she's only six.'

'Oh, the one you've mentioned before. With the bad mum?' Mimi topped up her glass of wine and offered the bottle to Andrea and Jill, who both shook their heads.

'Yeah, that's her,' said Andrea. 'Tony and I were . . . *discussing* it after I went around there the other night to check on her. But you agree, right? It's not normal to leave a six-year-old alone in an apartment, is it?'

Mimi's mouth twitched. It was clear from Andrea's tone that Tony didn't agree. Should she get involved? Then again, she knew whose side she was on for this. Screw it. 'Definitely not normal,' Mimi said firmly. 'Six is very young. I mean, maybe for five minutes while you duck downstairs because it's a secure building, but apart from that, no, she shouldn't be left alone.' She paused. 'I take it Tony has a different opinion?'

'Sorry,' said Jill, holding up a hand. 'But I don't think I've heard the start of this story. There's a little girl in your building?'

'Oh, sorry, Jill, I thought I'd mentioned Violet to both of you last time we caught up, but I must have only told Mimi. Yes, she lives down the hall from us and the mother seems to neglect her a lot.'

'That's awful,' said Jill.

Andrea nodded. 'I think it's because she's a drug addict.'

'You haven't mentioned that before,' said Mimi.

'I wasn't sure at first. I used to think she was just a bit of a party animal. But one of the times I went over to check on Violet, Heather was passed out on the floor and there was powder on the coffee table. The worst part is, she'd told Violet it was sherbet, but that it was Mummy's special treat so she couldn't share. Imagine if Violet had decided to try some while Heather was sleeping it off?'

'Jesus,' said Mimi. 'And that wasn't a one-off, obviously, if you're saying she's an addict?'

'Well, I mean, I don't know if I'm exaggerating. But, no, it definitely wasn't a one-off – I've seen her high in the elevator before. I don't know how to classify an addict, but regardless, she definitely neglects Violet.'

'And what does Tony say?' Jill asked, reaching out to absentmindedly rock the pram even though the twins were still silent.

'He thinks it's not really any of our business.'

'That makes it difficult,' said Mimi. 'I guess he thinks he doesn't want to cause trouble. But if everyone turns a blind eye to this type of thing, then who's there for the kid, right?'

Andrea rapped her fist on the table. 'Exactly. So what am I meant to do?'

'All you can really do is keep watching out for the poor little girl,' said Jill. 'And if the situation escalates, you'll have to report the mother.'

Mimi took a large sip from her glass. 'Speaking of keeping an eye on kids, albeit bigger ones – have you run into Callie between classes at all?'

'I haven't actually. I miss teaching her. She could run rings around every one of my Year Eleven history students even when she was in Year Nine. Why do you ask?'

Mimi fiddled with her glass. 'I'm sensing a change in her lately and I wanted to see if you'd noticed anything. Maybe it's just irritation at having her life turned upside down with two babies in the house, I don't know.' Mimi turned to Jill. 'You spoke to her the other day; how did you think she was?'

'I thought she seemed great. She was cheerful, polite, patient with me when I asked her to explain all those internet acronyms. Maybe you're looking for trouble when there isn't any? Not all teens go through the difficult phase.'

'I know, and I really thought we *had* made it through the worst of the teen years without any major issues. But lately she seems . . . different. She gets hostile over the smallest things and she's never been quick to anger. It's so out of character. But no matter what I do, I can't reach her. If I'm honest, I miss her.'

'I can catch up with Callie between classes,' said Andrea. 'See if I can suss anything out.'

'Thank you. She's always been good with you.'

'Fingers crossed that hasn't changed.'

Two women walking by their table stopped just past the double stroller and then backtracked to take a look inside.

'Oh, my goodness, would you look at those sleeping angels!' one gasped.

'Adorable,' said the other. 'Twins?' she added.

Mimi took in a deep breath of irritation before plastering a smile on her face. 'Sure are.'

Andrea caught her eye and grinned.

'Hmm,' said one of the women, leaning down closer towards the girls. 'You don't think they might be a bit hot in there, do you? Their little faces look very pink.'

Mimi felt her body tense. 'Oh . . . well, I mean –'

Jill spoke over the top of her. 'Don't be ridiculous, they're perfectly content. And I think their own mother would know if they were too hot.'

The woman pulled back. 'Oh! Sorry, I wasn't *judging.*'

'Yes, well, it certainly sounded like you were.'

The two women had both completely lost their friendly smiles now. They said their goodbyes and moved along. As soon as they were out of earshot, Mimi and Andrea both burst into laughter.

'What?' said Jill. 'What's so funny?'

'Nothing,' said Mimi. 'That was so perfect, that's all. You said exactly what I always want to say when someone tells me how to parent but never have the guts to. Thank you.'

Jill looked rapt. 'Just looking out for my daughter-in-law,' she said.

'Should we get one more bottle of wine?' Mimi asked then.

Andrea winced. 'Oh hon, I don't think I can. I was thinking of heading off shortly.'

'Actually,' said Jill, 'I think I should probably drive your car home, darling.'

Mimi creased her forehead. 'What for? I would have only had a couple of glasses.'

'Ah, I only had one,' said Andrea. 'And I think Jill skipped the wine altogether.'

Jill nodded.

'So that means the rest of the bottle was all you. Definitely making up for lost time with the breastfeeding,' Andrea added with a laugh.

Mimi's faced reddened. 'I didn't even realise. Okay, if you wouldn't mind, Jill, that'd be great.'

'Of course. I caught the bus today anyway. I didn't want to worry about finding parking.'

Mimi glanced down at the twins and felt a prickle of guilt. Talk about bad mums. That wasn't a very responsible parenting move, was it?

Jill

Dear Frank,

I'm worried about Mimi. I don't know what it is. It's not as though there's anything specific. To anyone else, it probably looks like she's doing fine. She's not unhappy . . . She's not frazzled or unwell, the twins are well looked after and yet . . . something has

me concerned. Babies are hard. Being a mother is hard. But with
twins, it's intense. I'm scared she's not coping as well as it looks to
everyone else.

I guess all I can do is keep watching and checking.
Love,
Jill

Jill stood on the chair with a screwdriver in one hand and squinted up at the smoke alarm, trying to figure out how to open the damn thing. Why the hell had she always let Frank do these kinds of jobs over the years? She never would have considered herself helpless in any way. She ran a high school. She brought in a good salary and she dealt with their finances and stayed more or less on top of her own computer literacy over the years. And yet somehow, she'd still let herself fall into those archaic gender norms when it came to fixing appliances, changing lightbulbs, checking the oil in the car and the like.

It didn't help that she didn't have the time over the years to do these sorts of things. Not on top of running a household and raising three boys while holding down a full-time job. Frank was a wonderful husband, but he'd never been particularly progressive in terms of helping out with the house or the kids. That's not to say that he sat on the couch and refused to lift a finger. No, he would read the bedtime stories to the boys, and he'd do the drying while she washed up after dinner. But the bulk of the housework was her responsibility. So it made sense to let him take care of the lawns and the cars and the handyman jobs.

But right now, Jill was wishing she'd been the one to

do those sorts of jobs once in a while. At least then she'd know what she was doing with the bloody smoke alarm.

She reached up and attempted to push the screwdriver into the right spot and the chair wobbled beneath her. She probably should have gone and got the stepladder out of the garage rather than dragging a kitchen chair over, but she couldn't be bothered with the extra effort.

'Come on, you little bugger,' she muttered.

The screwdriver finally seemed to fit into place and she started twisting it, unwinding the screw. She pushed a little too hard and her hand slipped, causing her to lose her balance and make the chair wobble harder. Her hands flew down to grab the back of the chair and steady herself. Once she had her balance again, she stepped down off the chair and threw the screwdriver across the room.

'Fuck it!' she yelled. 'Fuck it all.'

4

Sunday 6 December

Darren

He kept telling himself that if he at least opened the Word document, eventually something would happen. Inspiration would strike. He'd force himself to sit in front of his computer for hours at a time. Don't get up, don't walk away, don't give up. But invariably his hand would stray to the mouse and next thing, fifteen tabs were open on his browser. Facebook. Twitter. Instagram. Goodreads. Amazon Kindle charts. Email – one Gmail account, one old Hotmail account. Online banking – may as well check his balance. VISA statement – better see when that's due. Google Maps – maybe if he checked out Street View for the suburb this book was meant to be set in, he'd get some inspiration. Google search results: biggest waves ever surfed – it was sort of research, sort of not. One video led to another. Hours passed. And not a single word written.

Today had been no different. He'd been in front of his computer since 9 am and still the Word document remained blank. Every now and then he'd type out a sentence, but minutes later he'd be backspacing. Delete. Delete. Delete.

He was beginning to believe what he was sure others must already know: he was a one-hit wonder. When he won the Esther Arlo Prize and his first novel was published, he thought he'd made it. He thought he was going to be huge. Bigger even than Pete, who was making a pretty solid living from his adventure stories. He and Pete had always loved reading and writing when they were younger, so it had made perfect sense when Pete got into writing in his early twenties.

What was strange was when Tony announced that he'd also written a novel – crime – and was 'joining the family business'. That had surprised Darren because Tony hadn't ever been much of a reader. He was smart and did well at school. Really well, actually. But his thing had always been maths or economics or computer studies.

Darren had spent *a lot* of the advance for the two-book deal they'd offered him within a few months. A new car, a few new electronics, several big nights out, and a large chunk was gone. But at the time, he was confident more would be coming. Royalties would start rolling in. Overseas book deals. Maybe he'd sell the film rights. It was just the way the publishers spoke about him, as though he was some sort of prodigy.

But then the book hit the shelves and he was given the sales figures for week one – ninety copies.

'Is that good?' he'd asked his agent.

Elizabeth's voice was gentle. 'It's not what we were hoping for.'

'Okay, but it's decent? For the first week?'

'Not exactly.'

He thought sales would pick up the next week, or the week after. They didn't. The publishers entered his book into the NSW Premier's Literary Awards and the Voss Literary Prize. It didn't make the longlist for either. A scathing review in the *Sydney Morning Herald* came out in week four from renowned critic, S. Carter. Standout words included: *pretentious, amateur, clichéd*. He hated S. Carter. He often harboured vividly violent fantasies involving S. Carter.

The publishers admitted that maybe they'd packaged it incorrectly. Maybe the jacket wasn't quite right. Maybe the tagline didn't represent the feel of the book.

He asked if they would change the jacket design for the smaller paperback. Apparently, there wasn't going to be one.

But they were hopeful they could turn it around with book two. *How is book two coming along?* they asked, more recently on an increasingly regular basis. They were keen to get it in so they could plan the publishing schedule.

'It's close,' he kept promising. Even though he was now two months past the original deadline with nothing but a bunch of half-written plot notes to show for his efforts over the past two years.

In the meantime, Tony's book had gone to auction and he'd somehow scored some of the biggest debut book contracts Darren had ever heard of. When it came out next year, the publicity was going to be huge. It was pretty much guaranteed to top the charts. In addition to that, Tony had recently mentioned how far along he was with *his* second book. 'Hit sixty thousand words,' he'd said, as though it was a race and he knew he was winning.

Darren knew jealousy was an ugly trait, but it was hard not to feel slightly put out when the brother who'd never been into English at school had eclipsed him.

He kept hoping that the right idea would spring to mind. But every time he touched his fingers to the keyboard, those words from the review would swim in front of his eyes: *pretentious, amateur, clichéd*. And he'd find himself breathing faster and faster until he'd snap the laptop shut, telling himself that tomorrow would be better. But so far, tomorrow hadn't delivered. No tomorrows had. Thankfully he'd slowed down on his frenzied spending and started stretching out the money from his advance so he could live off it while he tried desperately to get this book written. But if something didn't happen soon, he'd have to find himself an office job once again. It would be so humiliating after quitting his position to write full time.

As he tried yet again to force himself to type, a text message from Pete appeared on his phone. He snatched it up. Any distraction was welcome.

Got a spare five to meet me at Morrison Park?

Yep. See you there, he tapped out in response.

'Can I ask what the point is of bringing them to the park at this age?'

Pete leaned back against the park bench and surveyed his two sleeping babies in the pram in front of them. 'No fucking clue.' He paused. 'No. Wait. Fresh air. We're here for the fresh air.'

'Can't you get that in your backyard?'

'Technically, yes. Look, it's just habit, okay?'

'Yeah, fair enough.' Darren leaned forward, resting his elbows on his knees. 'Do you get chicks trying to pick you up when you're out on your own with them?'

'Nah. Everyone wants to look. Twins!' He waved his hands in mock celebration. 'Sometimes it's nice that they're interested but sometimes it's bloody annoying. But no one's hit on me. So no, you can't borrow them to pick up women.'

'I wasn't asking!'

'Yes, you were.'

A scruffy dog trotted past. 'I'd get a puppy if I wanted attention from passing women,' said Darren, nodding his head at the dog.

'Not one like that. It looks like it hasn't had a bath in years. Women would avoid you, not hit on you. Looks diseased.'

'Poor doggo.' Darren whistled and the dog immediately turned and bounded back towards them.

'Don't do that. Now it'll think you've got something for it.'

'Where's its owner anyway? You see anyone around?'

Pete didn't reply, he was too busy shifting the pram as the dog started sniffing at it. 'If that mutt gives fleas to my girls . . .'

'You're all right, aren't you, mate?' said Darren, clicking his fingers to get the dog's attention away from the pram and then scratching him around the ears. 'You're a good boy, aren't you? Who's a good boy?'

'I am,' said Pete. 'I'm a good boy.'

'Fuck off.'

Pete laughed then nudged him as he continued to scratch

the dog. 'Oy. Do not get attached to that thing. Trust me. You don't have time to look after a dog right now.'

'Says the guy with four kids to the single guy with none.'

'You know what I'm talking about.'

The tone in Pete's voice made Darren look up. He saw a mix of concern, sympathy, and maybe even a little panic in his brother's face. Pete was the only one who knew how bad things were with his current manuscript. Not because he'd confessed the truth to him, but because Pete had always been able to see through his bullshit.

'Any progress?' he asked.

Darren looked back down at the dog and kept scratching him, postponing his answer. Eventually he shook his head.

'What's going on? Tell me you haven't been out surfing instead of writing. You're not even that good at catching waves.'

'I'm not *that* bad. And no, I haven't been surfing. I've been sat in front of my computer every single bloody day.'

'Okay, so what's the problem? You wrote the first one so fast it was like a blur. I remember reading your original draft and you could tell you'd just bashed it out from the sheer number of spelling mistakes.'

'Jeez, thanks.'

'No, but that's not the point. It was good. The *story* was good. That's what you need to do this time. You need to get out of your head and just smash it. Stop over-thinking it and trying to get it perfect. Just write.'

'That's not how *you* do it.'

'Yeah, but that's because you and I work in different ways. You work best when you switch off. Tell me you're not still letting that one shitty review affect you.'

Darren looked up and around the park again as a breeze rustled the trees and cooled his skin. 'Seriously, do you think this dog is lost?'

'I don't know, maybe.'

Darren leaned down and picked up a stick from the grass. He waved it in front of the dog. 'Want this? You want this?' He threw it across the park and the dog cocked his head to the side and stayed put. He seemed to be giving Darren a look that said, *What did you throw it away for?*

'You're supposed to fetch it.' Darren checked around the dog's neck. 'No collar,' he said.

'You're going to take the damn thing home, aren't you?'

'No. First I'm going to take it to the vet and check if it's chipped. *Then* I'm going to take it home.'

Pete threw up his hands. 'Yeah, all right, maybe it'll give you inspiration.'

'Did you hear Tony's already over halfway with his second book?'

'Don't compare yourself to Tony, that's not going to help.'

'But don't you think it's weird? Writing was always *our* thing. And then out of the blue he's written a fucking masterpiece.'

Pete sighed. 'It is bloody good, isn't it?'

'Right? How the hell did he pull that out of his arse?'

'Cut him some slack. It must have been hard seeing both of us get published if all along he liked writing too. You know he's always felt a bit on the outer with us.'

'Yeah, but that's not our fault. He never wanted to hang out with us growing up. We used to offer him a turn on

Street Fighter and he'd look at us like playing games was beneath him. We'd invite him to come out on the street for cricket and he'd tell us to get lost. Like, how is it our problem if he wasn't interested in anything we were?'

'I know, he did make it hard,' said Pete.

They fell quiet for a moment as Pete rocked the pram and Darren picked up another stick and attempted to get the dog interested in fetching it.

'Hey,' said Pete, 'I assume Mum's told you the Christmas trip is going ahead?'

'Yeah, I heard. You think it's a good idea?'

'I don't know, but if that's what she wants . . . By the way, she's said we're all going to drive in convoy, stick together. So we have to all leave at the same time.'

'No worries.'

'Okay, I'm gonna take the girls home. Any other news before I go?'

Darren looked up at the playground. At the swings and the slide. For a moment, he pictured a kid playing on the equipment. That same kid he'd been seeing every time he closed his eyes ever since Charlotte and Steph had asked him their big favour. The slightly odd-looking kid with the big ears and translucent skin. Only she wasn't looking so odd anymore. She was starting to look kind of sweet. Endearing in her own way. He wasn't sure why he could only imagine having a daughter. Maybe it was because he had all those nieces so it felt normal to picture a girl. He imagined telling her not to worry when the other kids picked on her for having big ears. He imagined telling her to tell them to stick it. He imagined pulling her up by the hand and dusting off her knees when she fell off the swing.

He squeezed his eyes shut and shook his head slightly to brush the image away.

'Nah,' he said. 'No news from me.'

Mimi

Mimi stood outside Callie's bedroom door and gave her whole body a small shake. This was ridiculous. This was her daughter! Her first-born. Why was she nervous? *Come on*, she thought, *pull yourself together and just knock*.

She lifted her fist and rapped on the door.

For a moment, there was silence and then, 'WHAT?'

Mimi had to give her credit. It took skill to inject that much attitude into one single syllable. She pasted a smile on her face, opened the door and stepped inside. *Don't show fear, don't show fear.*

'Hey,' she said brightly. 'I was thinking we should go out and do something. You, me and Tara, have some time to ourselves seeing as Dad has the babies.'

Callie was sitting on her bed, her eyes on the phone in her hands. Her bedroom was a strange melding of the little girl she'd once been and the woman she was soon to become. Her favourite stuffed bear still had pride of place on her pillow, but the walls were covered with posters of indie films Mimi had never heard of. Several of the book series Callie had read as a twelve-year-old were still stacked on her bookshelf, but next to them were scattered lipsticks and bronzers and concealers. Mimi didn't even know the right way to use bronzer – something to do with contouring?

Callie didn't look up. 'No, thanks,' she said.

A part of Mimi wanted to accept her answer and turn right around and leave her be. Avoid any potential argument. But that would be taking the easy way out. Tentatively, she stepped further into the room.

'Come on. It'd be nice to do something together. We haven't had time with just the three of us in ages.'

Callie finally looked up at her. She tucked a strand of hair behind her ear, and as Mimi observed her more closely, she noticed dark shadows under her eyes. Maybe she wasn't sleeping very well at the moment. Could it be the twins disturbing her through the night?

'Do something like what?' Callie asked.

An opening! Mimi hastened to come up with an answer that might appeal. 'The movies? Escape the heat?'

Callie made a face and returned her attention to her phone.

'Okay, we could just go out for coffee.'

'Don't really feel like it.'

Mimi racked her brain. 'Oh! We could go to one of those chocolate cafes.'

Callie shook her head. 'Yuck.'

'Yuck! Who says yuck to chocolate?'

'I do,' Callie said, shooting a look of irritation at her.

Tara appeared in the doorway. 'What about chocolate?' she asked.

'Nothing,' said Mimi. 'I was just trying to think of something fun for the three of us to do together.'

'I have an idea. Let's make a TikTok,' said Tara, her eyes bright.

'You have got to be kidding me,' said Callie. 'There is

74

no way I'm making a TikTok with my mum and my little sister.'

'Come on, please!' Tara begged.

'Wait, what's a *tick tock* again?' Mimi asked, pronouncing it carefully. 'Is that like Snapchat?'

'Jesus, Mum, could you be more basic?' Callie threw her phone down and started scratching savagely at the inside of her left wrist. 'Can you two, like, get out of my room, please?'

Mimi hesitated. She wanted to push back. She wanted to walk over to Callie, sit down on the bed, take her hands into her own and get her to make eye contact. She wanted to wrap her arms around her and say, 'What's happened? Where have you gone? What did I do wrong?'

But she sensed that she'd already been frozen out and if she kept pushing, she'd only make it worse. She took Tara's hand and they backed out of the room and closed the door.

'Will you make a TikTok with me?' Tara asked.

Mimi shrugged. 'Sure,' she said.

Andrea

'Feel like heading to the bedroom?'

Tony spun around in his chair, away from his computer to face Andrea. He cocked his head to the side and stroked his neatly shaped beard. Several seconds passed.

'I was kind of hoping for a more enthusiastic response than that,' she said. She'd been sitting on the couch, reading a book while Tony worked, but the book wasn't really holding her attention and her mind had begun to drift. A lazy afternoon of sex had slowly become rather appealing and she'd wondered if this could be her chance to get things back on track. But perhaps not, judging by Tony's lack of response.

Tony laughed. 'Sorry, I didn't mean to hesitate. It's only because I've been making some good progress.'

'But it's Sunday. Come on, you need a day off.' God, she hoped she didn't sound too desperate.

'I know, I know. I'm so sorry. I would, but I fell behind on my word count this week.'

Tony kept a whiteboard above his desk where he had all his days planned out with a word count he had to hit both daily and weekly in order to reach his target by the deadline. As far as Andrea knew, neither of his brothers worked that way, but she supposed it was one of the side effects of transitioning from accounting into writing.

The day she'd met Tony she'd borne witness to his admirably organised approach to life. Their meeting place was a little unusual – the pain relief section of the chemist. Andrea had been looking for something to help her get through a migraine she could feel coming on. She'd assumed the man standing to her right looking at the children's Panadol must have been a dad. He'd glanced sideways when she let out a tut of frustration as she tried to decide between brands, her mind already starting to cloud over as the migraine took hold.

'Sorry,' she said. 'Didn't mean to do that out loud. I just can't think.' She rubbed her hand against her forehead.

'Don't be sorry,' he said. 'Maybe I can help.' He'd stepped towards her and picked up a couple of boxes off the shelf. 'You've got a headache?' he asked. 'This one is really good for targeting specific pain. But are you feeling sick as well?'

She'd given him a wry smile. 'Are you a doctor or something?'

'Not even close, I'm an accountant. I just like to store useful information like this. Never know when it might come in handy.'

'Well, I'm feeling everything bad right about now. Killer migraine.'

'Got it,' he'd said, putting the first box back on the shelf. 'You should go with this one. Easy on the stomach.'

She'd reached out to take the tablets from him but then her vision had begun to blur and she'd stumbled.

He'd stepped in closer to steady her. 'Hey, are you okay?'

'No . . . Not really.'

He'd guided her to the waiting area seats near the prescription counter and told her to hold on. She'd expected him to palm her off to staff, but instead, a minute later he returned with a box of tablets and a bottle of water that he'd purchased himself. He'd pressed two capsules into her hand, unscrewed the cap off the water and passed it over.

'I double-checked with the pharmacist. These are definitely the best for migraines,' he'd said. 'Combination of both paracetamol and ibuprofen. I'll sit with you until it kicks in.'

Her previous boyfriend, Angelo, had been a drummer in a local band who practised late into the night. On one occasion when she'd been suffering a bad migraine, she'd begged him to take a break at 1 am so she could sleep.

He'd sneered at her and told her to spend the night at her own place if she was going to be that soft.

The glaring contrast between Angelo and this stranger in the chemist was startling.

She shook her head. 'You don't have to do that. Don't you need to get medicine home to your kid?'

'I don't have kids.' He looked momentarily confused. 'Oh! The children's Panadol. No, I was picking that up for my brother. My niece has a cold. But it's all good; it wasn't urgent. I can stay.'

In the end, she'd felt too sick to argue and too grateful for the company. He sat by her side and made quiet small talk, and when she'd finally felt well enough to move, she admitted there was no way she could drive. He'd insisted on booking her an Uber using his own account.

The following day when she was feeling well again, she'd racked her brain as she tried to remember the guy's name so she could somehow track him down and thank him for his help. He'd introduced himself as he sat chatting with her but her mind had been so fuzzy she'd struggled to take it in. Tony . . . Leyton? Lennon? Levett? Finally, it came to her: Tony Lewis. A Google search revealed hundreds of Tony Lewises, but she narrowed it down by adding the word 'accountant' to the search window. Eventually she recognised his face on a LinkedIn result. She sent him a message and, after chatting back and forth, they'd agreed to meet up for a coffee. A coffee date led to a lunch date, a lunch date led to a dinner date, and the relationship progressed from there.

She wouldn't call it love at first sight or anything like that. It was more a case of her attraction growing for him each time he showed her she was worth more than being stood up or dumped via text. Each time he made her realise she deserved better than cheap dates or late-night booty calls. He'd helped her to realise that she'd been gravitating towards men who made her feel worthless because *she'd* believed she was worthless. Because that's the way her own parents had made her feel.

Now, Andrea leaned her elbow on the back of the couch. 'That's unusual for you to fall behind. You're so strict about following your whiteboard.'

'I know. But I've had a few bad migraines.'

Andrea had to hide her smile. One of the things they'd spoken about that day in the chemist was how awful migraines could be and how irritating it was when people who simply had everyday, run-of-the-mill headaches claimed they were suffering from a migraine. As she'd got to know Tony, she soon realised that he was one of those people. But she'd let it slide, finding it cute when he massaged his temples and complained about his bad migraine. Maybe it was because it took her back to the day they met when he'd taken such good care of her.

'That's no good,' she said. 'Well, I'm glad you're getting back on track today.' She stood and wandered over to him. 'Can I see a little of what you've written?'

He snapped the laptop shut. 'You know you can't,' he said, but he was smiling as he stood and pulled her towards him.

She hadn't seen a single word of *Don't Breathe* before he announced he'd been accepted by a literary agent. In fact, she hadn't even known he'd been writing it. And he said he didn't want to jinx things by changing that with the second book. She wasn't allowed to read it until he was done.

'Just one page,' she said. 'One paragraph. Come on, the book I'm reading is boring. I want to read another Tony Lewis classic.'

He ran his hands through his thick, dark hair. It was a strong point of contention that as the eldest brother, Tony still had all his hair, while Pete, two years younger, had started going bald in his mid-twenties. There was a family bet around whether Darren would keep his hair.

Tony leaned forward and wrapped his arms around her waist and then reached down to squeeze her butt. 'I have a better idea,' he said.

'I thought you were too busy.'

'Changed my mind.'

Christmas Eve

Sixty seconds ticked by before a third car came upon the accident. This time, the car slowed up immediately and crossed over to the left lane before pulling onto the shoulder and coming to a stop, fifty metres beyond the crash site.

The driver jumped out and slammed the door behind him before sprinting back towards the crumpled cars.

'Shit,' he said as he looked from one car to the next. 'Shit, shit, shit.'

He patted his pockets and realised he'd stupidly left his phone in the car. He wavered for a moment, torn between heading straight to one of the victims to help them and running back to retrieve his phone so he could call for emergency services. Two more cars flew by, neither of them stopping to help. He felt a flash of irritation, although he supposed it was difficult to pull up in time when you were doing 100 kilometres per hour. Especially as it was dark and the crash was right after a bend.

He decided to check on the first car before he did anything else.

5

Monday 7 December

Mimi

'What the . . . ?' Mimi stretched her arm down the side of the seat, her fingers searching for the lever to slide it back. Her breasts were practically squashed against the steering wheel. She remembered why it was so far forward as she finally managed to move the seat back. Jill had driven her car home after lunch on Saturday. She'd had to pull it all the way forward just to be able to reach the accelerator.

Tiny, fierce Jill.

The woman was an enigma. She could swing from being intensely protective of her sons to throwing them under the bus if she thought they weren't doing the right thing by their wives or partners. When Charlotte broke it off with Darren, she'd been certain that Darren must have done something terrible to cause it. Poor Darren. Mimi thought it was pretty clear that the guy had had his heart broken, that Charlotte's decision had been a huge shock. But there was Jill, quizzing him on why he'd let her get away. Eventually Pete had stepped in and run interference, patiently explaining that Darren was in no way responsible for Charlotte realising she was gay and suggesting that Jill ease up on the guy.

With the twins, she constantly checked in to make sure Pete was doing his part. *Is he helping you in the night? Because you know you have to give him a good hard nudge to wake him up. Once when Darren was a baby I shoved Frank so hard he fell out of bed. He stopped sleeping through the cries after that. Not that he was any help to me with the babies.*

Yet other times she was in their corner when it wasn't always warranted. They'd all heard the story of how she'd jumped the fence at one of Tony's soccer games when he was fourteen and on the ground, clutching his ankle after a tackle that everyone else said was clean. In fact, Darren swore Tony had taken a dive. But there was Jill, bolting across the field. Everyone thought she was headed for Tony to see if he was okay, next thing she was lunging at the player from the other team, intent on knocking him down.

She was banned from the games after that.

Mimi had appreciated the lift home on Saturday, but she was embarrassed. She could have sworn they'd all been sharing that wine equally. It's just that it seemed to go down so smoothly lately. She'd been hoping that after twelve months of not drinking, she might now be a bit of an easy drunk. That one or two glasses would have her feeling pleasantly tipsy, saving both money and calories. Instead, it was like she was instantly a seasoned drinker again. Annoying and unfair. She wanted to have that nice wine buzz in the evenings after the kids went to bed. Something to take the edge off as she tried to become accustomed to life as a family of six instead of four.

When Tara was born, it was as though she was exactly what their family had been waiting for. She closed an open circle. She just . . . fit. But with the twins, everything felt out of sorts. Disjointed. Callie was irritable all the time. Tara had matured overnight. That should have been a good thing, but instead it had Mimi sometimes yearning for the old Tara. Her baby, who still wanted four songs and five cuddles at bedtime. Now she read to herself and switched off her bedside lamp before Mimi had come in to say goodnight. Mimi kept hopefully offering her the old songs but Tara would wave her away and reassure her that she didn't need them anymore.

You might not need them, but I think I do.

James and Elliot were cute babies, but recently she'd come to the awful realisation that they still hadn't tugged at her heartstrings in the same way Callie and Tara both did as babies. It was painful, it made her feel like a failure as a mother. Weren't you supposed to instantly bond with your children? That was the way it had been with her other two. It was as though the twins kept her so busy, so on the go, there simply hadn't been time to slow down and fall in love with them. Sometimes, when they were both screaming in the middle of the night, each one of them demanding her immediate attention, she'd catch herself thinking things. Nasty things.

You know I never actually wanted you two?

It had only happened a few times. And every time she would shake the thought away and mentally slap herself. Stop that. Don't *think* things like that. That's why it was so nice when she was finally able to start drinking again. The wine helped to soften those nasty feelings. She just needed to be more careful not to accidentally drink entire bottles when she was supposed to be driving.

Now as she pulled up at a red traffic light, she twisted around in her seat to look back at the twins. They were in rear-facing capsules but Pete had installed mirrors so she could see their faces. James was fast asleep. Elliot was awake, her eyes darting about. Mimi prodded at her own chest with her fingers. *Come on then, heart, wake up and feel something.* A car beeped its horn behind her and she gave them the finger before turning back around and pressing down on the accelerator. The light could only have been green for an instant. Impatient fucker.

Mimi used to like parking and walking in for the school pick-up. There were several mums she liked catching up with. But it had been Tara's idea to meet her at kiss-and-ride in the afternoons. 'So you don't have to get the twins out,' she'd said helpfully.

Mimi was about to turn down towards the queue when she made a last-minute decision to find a parking spot instead. Screw it, it wasn't that hard to put the girls in the double stroller. She wanted to say hi to the other mums. Annoyingly, when she did finally find a spot and haul the stroller out of the boot, she discovered Elliot had now fallen asleep too. How had that happened in less than two minutes? Too bad. She was parked now. She scooped the girls out one at a time. Elliot stayed asleep; James woke and started whimpering. As she strapped them in, she noticed heavy dark purple clouds gathering over the school. *Great, was it going to storm?* She hadn't heard anything on the weather report about rain. Hopefully it would hold off until after they'd all made it back to the car. Although it was Murphy's Law that if an afternoon storm was going to hit, it would hit at school pick-up.

She pushed the heavy stroller up the hill towards the school gate. With any luck, she'd catch Tara before she ran down to the kiss-and-ride line. Although that would depend on how many parents stopped her to take a look at the girls on the way.

When she finally did reach the old meeting spot, thankfully managing to call out to Tara and stop her as she was sprinting by, she'd been pulled up no less than six times by well-meaning parents. Their admiring looks had been accompanied by the usual comments. *Here's double trouble. These two mustn't be letting you have too much sleep. Adorable, aren't you lucky? Are they identical? Boys or girls? Or did you hit the jackpot and score one of each.* For fuck's sake, it was as if having babies was a lottery where getting a pigeon pair was the main prize.

Finding herself standing next to the usual school mums after all that felt like a monumental achievement. Tara was already expertly comforting James while her best friend Chloe looked on with a hint of longing on her face.

'I see that look,' said Leesa, Chloe's mother. 'And I can tell you right now this baby factory is closed.' She drew a circle around her stomach and Mimi laughed.

'You know I thought mine was closed too, right?'

'Yes, but there's no chance with me. Angus already got the . . . you know.' She motioned scissors with her hand.

'The what?' Chloe asked, looking up at her mum. 'What did Daddy have?'

Leesa dropped her hands. 'Nothing, honey, never mind.'

'I call my dad Dad now,' Tara told her friend. 'And Mum is Mum.' She didn't sound judgemental but rather encouraging, like she thought it was probably time they both dropped the mummys and daddys from their vocabulary.

Chloe looked unfazed. 'I'll always call mine Mummy and Daddy.' There was that note of certainty to her voice that only eight-year-olds who believe their life decisions are already set in stone can affect.

Mimi felt a pang of jealousy. She wanted Tara to keep calling her Mummy. She missed the innocence of it. She also missed that certainty in your own decisions that Chloe had just displayed. *Hold onto that, kid. Although maybe don't call your parents Mummy and Daddy when you're thirty.*

The girls returned their attention to the twins and Mimi and Leesa were able to continue chatting.

'So yeah, he's had the snip, therefore no chance of getting knocked up over here. I don't know how you did it.'

'Well, when a man and a woman love each other very, very much . . .'

Leesa whacked her arm. 'Shut up. You know what I mean. I don't know how you made the decision.'

Mimi tipped her head to one side. 'Foolishly?' she suggested. 'Rashly, stupidly, miserably?'

'Stop! You're not miserable. Look at you, you're glowing.'

'No I'm not.'

'Okay, well, you're dressed, you're out of the house and you're making fully formed sentences. What more do you want?'

'Where do I start? A nanny. A chef. A personal trainer. A full night's sleep.'

'We all want that shit. I'll just settle for a G and T this arvo. It's gotta be Friday somewhere, babe.'

'Err, no it hasn't. Nowhere in the world is it Friday right now.'

'Don't kill my buzz. The only bloody reason we put a pool in our backyard is so that I can sit by it and drink G and Ts. Don't take that away from me.'

'So, you're a gin woman? I don't think I knew that.'

'It's a new thing. Wine wasn't cutting it for me anymore.'

'Oh really? Now this is something I was needing to discuss with someone. Exact same thing's been happening to me lately. I think a couple of glasses of wine will take the edge off and it's like I'm drinking water. What the hell?'

'I know, right? Trust me, switch to gin. Fewer calories than wine, stuff some lime in it, you'll feel like you're on a beach somewhere. Perfect summer drink.'

'I'm sold. I'll buy some on the way home.'

'Better yet, come around to mine after school when it is Friday. Bring Tara for a play with Chloe. We can ignore the kids and pretend we're on a beach together.'

'Sounds bloody fabulous.'

A fat drop of rain hit Mimi's shoulder then. 'Dammit,' she said, 'I was hoping to make it back to the car before it started raining.'

'Oops,' said Leesa. 'You need a hand with the twins?'

'No, I'll be right. Thanks anyway.'

By the time Mimi and Tara had dashed back to the car, pushing the stroller in front of them, the rain had started teeming down. They were both soaked, but at least the twins were safe and dry under the shield of the pram. Tara was laughing, delighted at being caught in the sudden summer storm. She helped her mother transfer the babies into their capsules and then they both jumped into the car and Mimi started laughing too; Tara's good mood was infectious. Oh well, at least it had cooled them down.

On the drive home, Mimi considered stopping at a bottle shop to grab some gin, as per Leesa's suggestion, but Elliot was asleep yet again and somehow it felt like dragging twin babies and an eight-year-old into a liquor store to buy spirits would be . . . unseemly.

Hold off for Friday with Leesa, she told herself. *Much more fun than drinking alone.*

Andrea

The bell for the end of the school day had already rung when Andrea remembered her promise to Mimi. She was supposed to check in on Callie. The problem was that her day was always so busy, there was never a chance to seek out a student who wasn't in one of her classes.

She wondered if she could catch Callie before she got on the school bus. Although then she'd be chatting to her in front of all the other kids lined up, and Callie probably wouldn't thank her for that.

Then again, she'd always got along really well with her niece, so maybe it was worth a try. She left her things in the classroom and strode out to find her.

By the time she reached the bus bay, she'd been stopped by two teachers wanting to talk to her about swapping around their lunch duty for the rest of the week and a Year Eleven student complaining about the mark she'd given him on his history assignment. She arrived just in time to see Callie's bus pull away.

She stood still for a moment, glancing up at the gathering storm clouds as she watched the bus disappear over the hill and heard a low rumble of thunder. Ah well, there was always tomorrow, and it looked like she needed to get back inside before the sky cracked open.

Walking back to her classroom, she laughed to herself at the sheer audacity of Jayden Scott, the student who'd been complaining about his mark. He was a good foot taller than her and it was clear he thought he could intimidate her with his height as he stood over her, earnestly explaining that his mum had promised him a car for his birthday if he kept all his marks above eighty per cent. Senior students often made the mistake of underestimating her, based on her size. She was quick to show them she was no pushover and Jayden was no exception. Besides, knowing Jayden, Andrea was pretty sure the mum had made the deal knowing that it was a safe bet. She wasn't sure if that made it a genius move or terrible parenting.

Then again, should she be judging anyone's parenting skills, not being a mother herself? She knew a lot about kids − spending six hours a day, five days a week with them − but did she know what it was like to make those tough parenting decisions?

As she walked, she tried to imagine what sort of a parent she would have been had she and Tony not made the decision to be child-free. Would she be the type to make a bet like that with her son? Would she have the same problems as Mimi was having with Callie, and have to ask someone else to help her reconnect with her teen daughter? Would she be a good mother?

Not if she modelled herself on the only mother she'd ever known growing up, she wouldn't.

'You look deep in thought.'

Andrea looked up to see Kelly Tao – a teacher from the maths department – smiling at her.

'Not really,' she lied. She liked Kelly, but didn't know her well enough to start opening up about her difficult childhood. 'Two weeks until the end of term,' Andrea added to switch the subject. 'Are your kids bouncing off the walls too?'

'You bet,' said Kelly, adjusting her thick bright turquoise glasses as they slid down her nose. 'I'm counting the bloody hours until break. Oh, Christmas drinks this Friday – see you there?'

'Ah, I think so,' said Andrea, keeping her voice non-committal.

'Come on, of course you're coming,' she insisted. 'All right, I'm heading out. I've had enough of today and I've got my kids back from my ex this week. I promised I'd take them to the pool this arvo.'

'Good luck with that, it's about to storm.'

Kelly wrinkled her nose. 'Yeah, small issue there. Hoping it will pass quickly.'

Andrea said goodbye and continued on to her classroom. It would probably be another couple of hours before she escaped herself; she was still finalising her end-of-year reports. That was a bonus of choosing to be child-free – when she stayed late at school, there was no guilt because she wasn't spending time with her kids or breaking promises to take them places.

She'd made the right choice.

Jill

Dear Frank,

What if there are more sins than I even realise? There are times when I wonder . . . where I'm afraid I might have . . . missed something along the way.

I will tell you one sin. Did you know that I kissed Alan McIntosh when you and I first started dating? It's funny, I kept it a secret at the time because you hated Alan and I knew it would make you so mad. But my plan was always to tell you eventually. I thought we would laugh about it together. Instead, I'm sharing it in a letter and it's not the same at all.

By the way, it wasn't my fault. We were roller-skating and I lost my balance. He caught me, and before I knew it, he'd leaned in and kissed me! Cheeky sod. I don't know what made me think about that.

I broke a tea cup today. One of my favourites. It was because I made myself a cup of tea and then forgot about it. By the time I remembered, it had gone cold. So I picked it up and threw it across the room. The cup broke into three sharp pieces and now there's a brown stain on the carpet in the shape of Tasmania. I liked that cup. You know the one. From the set that Andrea bought me for my birthday three years ago. White with pretty purple butterflies.

What a silly thing to do! You would have looked at me like I'd gone mad if you'd been here to see it. Although if you had been here, I wouldn't have done it.

Come back, would you?
Love,
Jill

Jill sat at the kitchen table, watching her son unclip the smoke alarm and replace the battery with ease. It turned out you didn't even need a screwdriver. There was a clip you pressed on the side. She was both thankful and irritated. He'd also changed two lightbulbs for her, tightened up a leaky tap in the main bathroom, moved the boxes up into the roof space and cleared the weeds from her veggie patch. He'd made it back inside from the garden just as an afternoon storm had hit.

'You know, Mum,' said Pete as he replaced the cover on the smoke alarm and then stepped back down the ladder without a single wobble, 'if you moved out of this place into something new, something smaller, the smoke alarms would be hardwired in and you wouldn't even have to worry about this type of thing.'

Jill sipped her tea and eyed him over the top of her cup. 'That's great,' she said, placing the cup back down on its saucer. 'Except that I don't want to move anywhere else. Come and drink your coffee before it gets cold.'

Pete folded up the stepladder and stowed it back away in the garage before coming to join her at the table.

'But why not move into that village where Wayne and Barb went? Wouldn't it be nice to have them as neighbours again?'

Jill made a face at him. 'Don't talk to me like I'm a toddler who needs to be cajoled. I told you, I don't want to move.'

Pete rolled his eyes. 'I wasn't treating you like a toddler, I was trying to help. Mimi told me you nearly fell off the chair trying to change those batteries the other night.'

Jill immediately wished she hadn't mentioned her near

miss to Mimi. She'd only been making conversation, revealing some of her own vulnerabilities in the hopes it might help Mimi to do the same.

'I didn't nearly fall, I was exaggerating.'

'Ah yes, exaggeration is something you're well known for,' Pete said sarcastically. 'Just make sure you call me next time you need something like that done. I'm happy to help, Mum. Seriously, any time.'

Jill softened. 'Thank you,' she said. Then she beamed at him. 'And that's why you're my favourite son.'

Pete gave a bark of laughter. 'Don't be ridiculous, we all know Tony's your favourite.'

'What are you talking about? No, he's not. I was only kidding anyway, of course. I don't have favourites.'

'Yes, you do,' said Pete, slurping his coffee. 'It's okay, Darren and I always accepted that Tones got favourite status cause he was your first. We forgave you long ago.'

'But, honestly, I don't favour him.'

'Sure you do.'

Pete was grinning at her and for a second, Jill felt an urge to reach out and slap his grin away. She shivered. What an awful, strange thing to think.

'Stop it!' she said, 'That's not true. Not one bit.'

Pete held up his hands. 'All right, calm down. If you say it's not true, it's not.' But the tone of his voice was clear – he absolutely did not believe her.

Excellent, thought Jill, *yet another one of my failings.*

At least she'd have something different keeping her awake tonight.

Christmas Eve

A woman was slumped in the driver's seat. A thin line of blood trickled from her hairline down around the side of her face to her chin.

'Oh God,' said the Good Samaritan. This was so far beyond his capabilities. He'd done a first aid course for work about five years ago, but he'd never had to use it. He didn't even know where to begin.

'Are you . . .' He wasn't even sure she was conscious. 'Are you okay?' he asked, realising as he said it that it was the most ridiculous question he'd ever asked in his life. Of course she wasn't okay.

The woman's head lolled to the side and then her eyelids flickered. *Thank God*, she was conscious. She started to mumble something and he leaned in closer to listen.

'My husband,' she said.

'I'll call him for you,' he said in a rush. 'Don't worry, I'm going to get help and I'll get your husband for you as well.'

'No,' she said. 'No, no.' She pointed to the passenger seat. 'My husband. He's gone.'

6

Wednesday 9 December

Andrea

Tony took two wineglasses out of the cupboard but Andrea shook her head. 'Not for me. I'm still working on these reports. If I have a glass of red, I'll be asleep on the couch in half an hour.'

'You're no fun,' Tony mocked. He put back one of the glasses and picked a bottle off the wine rack, lifting it up to look at the colour in the light. 'Are you sure? I have a feeling this one's going to be good. Perfect drinking age.'

Andrea considered suggesting he save it for a special occasion then, but realised that was pointless. All the wine on their rack was 'special-occasion worthy'. It was really quite extraordinary how quickly and comfortably Tony had adapted to a lifestyle of wealth.

'Don't tempt me,' she said. 'I'm trying to stay strong. If I don't get these reports finished tonight I'll be screwed.'

'Fair enough.' He poured his glass and then walked over and massaged the back of her neck with one hand while he sipped his wine.

'You okay? You seem stressed.'

'Yeah, I'll be all right. Just worried about . . .' She trailed off and he dropped his hand from her neck.

'Andrea, no. You have to stop thinking about her. She's a neighbour. She has a mother. She's not your responsibility.'

'I know but –'

'But what? You can't do anymore than you've already done. If social services don't see fit to interfere then I don't see how you can.'

'But you agree, don't you? The way that mother treats her is wrong.'

Tony rubbed his chin. 'I guess, but I don't know. I'm not a parent.'

'Tony! Come on, you know enough to know that you don't leave a six-year-old alone in an apartment. You know enough to know that you don't pass out in front of your kid or leave drugs out for them to find. That's not rocket science.'

'Yeah, okay. But still, maybe that was a one-off. Maybe she's getting help. Maybe the last time you went over there she really did only duck out for groceries. I'm just saying, we don't know the full story and she's asked you to back off.' He paused. 'Tell me you weren't round there this afternoon?'

She couldn't keep the guilty look off her face.

'Wait, is this why you're behind on your work? Because you were playing mum to the next-door neighbour?'

Andrea bristled at the words, 'playing mum'. That wasn't what she was doing. She was being a caring neighbour, that was it.

'I only went to check on her. And I'm glad I did. She was alone. Again. And she told me Heather gave her a fifty-dollar note for the canteen for lunch today instead of packing her any food.'

'So what? At least she made sure she didn't go hungry.'

'Well, what about the fact that she was alone again?'

'How long was it for?'

Andrea felt her cheeks flush. 'Okay, it was only a short time – while she grabbed a parcel from the post office.'

'There you go! The post office is only two blocks away.'

'But there have been other times where she's gone out. Like properly out for the night and there's a gap before the babysitter shows up. What kind of a mother doesn't wait!'

'Are you sure that wasn't some kind of miscommunication with the sitter?'

'Why are you defending her? Trust me, the kid is lonely. And too skinny.'

'She hardly looks malnourished.'

'How would you know? When did you see her last?'

'I don't know; I'm sure I've seen her in the lift from time to time. Either way, I can't say I've ever noticed her looking unhealthy. I just think you might be looking for more problems where there aren't any.'

'Maybe. I don't know.'

They fell silent and Andrea wrestled with herself internally as she tried to decide if Tony had a point or not. Yes, it was true that, once again, Heather had only ducked out for a short time this afternoon . . . but why did she keep doing it? Why did she keep leaving her daughter unattended?

Or did Andrea feel so strongly about it because of the way her own mother had treated her? Because there had been no one around to step in and check on her when she was left alone for hours at a time?

Once again, the thought crossed her mind. *What kind of a mother would I be?*

But it was a moot point. She and Tony had made the decision. The 'what do we both want' conversation had come up after only a few dates, but that was to be expected when you met someone in your mid to late thirties – you needed to find out fast if you were on the same page. Tony had been easygoing to begin with. He probably didn't want to have kids, but he could be swayed if she was really keen. She'd been leaning towards a no, but had agreed that she was pretty much the same – she could potentially be swayed if he was desperate for children.

And so their relationship had progressed. They'd moved in together. Tony had proposed after only six months and initially, when she'd seen the sparkle of the diamond as he knelt down in front of her, her instincts had said, no, it's too soon! But then he'd made his speech. *I'm going to take care of you. I'm going to treat you the way you've always deserved to be treated. No one else could ever love you as much as I love you.*

The strong, independent woman inside of her was ashamed to admit those words spoke to her. No, she didn't *need* a man to take care of her – but at the same time, after having had one too many men treat her so badly, she craved what he was offering. So, she'd ignored the doubts and said yes. Besides, relationships rarely recovered from a rejected proposal and she wasn't ready to let him go. What if she never found someone who cared for her so deeply again?

About a year into the marriage, she'd realised that their 'probably not but some day maybe' stance on kids had shifted to 'definitely not' without them ever having really talked about it again. It was clear in the way he answered questions from well-meaning friends or relatives. *No, we've decided not to have children. We just feel it's the right choice for us.* And Andrea would nod in agreement, even as a voice inside wondered, *but when did we decide for sure?*

And then there was the issue of their sex-life. Even if they had decided to have children, it would be a bit hard to create life when things had slowed down so rapidly in the bedroom. Her attempt to rekindle the spark on Sunday afternoon had ended up fizzling after they'd headed to the bedroom. A back massage that was meant to be a sensual appetiser to the main event had instead resulted in Tony snoring into the pillow. She'd tried hard not to be offended and had hopped in the shower for her own solo event while Tony napped the afternoon away. He'd woken in the early evening, bleary eyed and apologetic.

'Oh, fuck it,' said Andrea. 'Pour me a glass of red, would you?'

Tony headed back to grab the bottle and another glass and then filled it almost to the brim. He placed it in front of her. 'Sorry,' he said. 'I'm not meaning to antagonise you. I just don't want you to end up in a war with the woman next door.'

'I know,' said Andrea. 'Maybe you're right, maybe I am overreacting.'

Tony sat down next to her at the table. 'Can I help with the reports?'

'Ha, you're very sweet but that's impossible. You know what I do need help with though? Figuring out what to do with the kids for the next week and a half. It's always so hard finding ways to keep them engaged when school's almost done for the year and the exams are all over.'

Tony swirled the wine in his glass. 'Hmm, I always enjoyed playing a few rounds of hangman during the final weeks of the term.'

'Oh, very helpful.'

Tony suddenly sat up straighter. 'Actually,' he said, 'I *can* help you!'

'With the reports?'

'No, with the kids. I could come in and chat to your English class.'

Andrea was taken aback. 'Chat to them about what?'

'About being a published author!'

Andrea smiled. Considering Tony's book wasn't even out yet, she wasn't sure how much he'd have to tell them. But she could see the spark in his eyes. He was excited by his own idea. She supposed he could discuss his writing process. She did her best to match his enthusiasm.

'Of course! I can't believe I've never thought of that. They'd love to hear from a published writer.'

He looked worried then. 'Although . . . I don't really know how to talk to high school kids, what if I don't know what to say to them?'

'You talk to them the same way you'd talk to anyone about writing. They prefer it when you treat them like adults.'

'All right, I'll do it,' said Tony, as though Andrea had been the one asking. 'But can you do something for me?'

'Sure.'

'Try . . . just *try* to pull back a bit on visiting the neighbour, okay? It's really not our business.'

'Okay. I'll try.'

Mimi stood in the hallway, torn for a moment about which direction she should be heading in. In one bedroom, her teen daughter was raging and had just thrown something against the wall – she was yet to find out whether it was something breakable or precious. In another, her middle daughter was sobbing uncontrollably. Usually this would be a divide and conquer kind of thing. Pete would take one daughter while she took the other. But he had his hands full downstairs with the twins.

In the end, she decided it made more sense to go to the daughter who would allow her to help.

She entered Tara's room and sat down by her on the bed. Tara immediately threw herself across her mother's lap, crying so hard her body shook.

'Oh darling,' said Mimi, rubbing her back. 'I'm so sorry. It's my fault.'

Tara stopped crying long enough to turn her tear-stained face up towards Mimi. 'It's not,' she said. 'It's her. It's always *her*. She hates me.'

Mimi tried to choose her words carefully. 'I know it feels like that, but I can promise you, she doesn't. She's your big sister and she loves you. It's just that sometimes being a teenager can be hard and you say things you don't mean.'

Tara started crying again and Mimi stroked her daughter's hair and wished she'd been smart enough to anticipate all of this.

When she'd made the TikTok with Tara on the weekend, she hadn't even considered it might come back to bite her. She'd had a lot of fun learning the dance together with Tara. They'd fallen about laughing each time one or the other of them got a move wrong, and it had taken a good hour or two to finally get the choreography right. Eventually, they'd nailed it and uploaded it to Tara's account along with a few of the bloopers. Mimi knew Tara was a little young for any kind of social media apps, but they'd let her have TikTok because she loved making videos, and they'd set her up with a private account with restricted access. She was only allowed to accept followers that she knew.

The problem, apparently, was that she'd accepted follow requests from a few of Callie's friends. And those friends had shown the video to some other friends and eventually someone at school had made fun of Callie for her mum's 'pathetic' dance moves.

Callie had screamed at both Tara and Mimi. *Why do you have to be so embarrassing? Why can't you be more normal? You guys looked so stupid.* Lovely things like that. Mimi had wanted to strangle her for hurting her sister's feelings so badly, but at the same time, she remembered the pain that came with embarrassment in high school. Callie had a really great group of friends, so it wouldn't have been one of them picking on her, it would have been someone outside of her circle who'd decided to be nasty. Why did some kids have to be such arseholes?

She heard footsteps and looked up to see Pete standing in the doorway. 'Twins are both changed and I put them in their rockers,' he said. 'Want me to see if I can tame the beast?'

'Oh God, yes.'

'Damn, I was hoping you'd tell me I could take over here.'

As though in response, Tara burrowed her head further into Mimi's lap.

'Nope, this one is all mine. Good luck.'

Pete gave a look of mournful resignation and headed off.

'Should we FaceTime Nan and Pop?' Mimi tried once he was gone. 'See if they've had any snow yet? Apparently, they've had an early cold front come through and they're predicting a proper white Christmas for once. Should be the right time to call London.'

Tara shook her head. 'Not right now,' she said. 'Can we talk to them later?'

'Sure. Tell you what,' said Mimi, 'you can share some of my secret ice cream after dinner tonight and we can call them then.'

Tara sat up and looked at her. 'You have secret ice cream?' she asked.

'Yep, I keep it hidden under the peas. No one ever looks there.'

'Are you going to share it with Callie as well?'

'Nope. Just you and me.'

Tara smiled. 'Okay,' she said. 'But can I still cry a bit more?'

'Sure, if you still need to cry, that's fine by me.'

Tara returned her head to Mimi's lap.

Pete pulled back the covers and climbed into bed. 'You know Tara told me about your secret ice-cream stash when I said good night to her earlier?'

'One second,' said Mimi, staring at her phone, 'I just

have to finish watching this video of a donkey helping a flock of ducks cross a road.'

'Facebook is a magical place.'

Mimi finished the video and put her phone down on her bedside table. 'That sneaky little thing. She was supposed to keep that to herself.'

'You're a good mum,' he said. 'I could tell she was very proud of knowing something that I didn't know.'

Mimi screwed up her face. 'I don't feel like a good mum. I feel like a shit mum. You at least got Callie talking to you. She still wouldn't even let me into her room tonight.'

'I think that's only because she felt bad and she didn't want to have to admit to you that she'd overreacted. Especially after she'd been through it all with me.'

'What did you say to her to get her to calm down?'

'I don't even know really. I mostly made dumb dad jokes until she couldn't take it anymore and she had no choice but to crack a smile.'

'Nice work.'

'Thanks, had to pull out some of my best material. She's promised to try and make it up to Tara tomorrow, so we'll see how that goes.'

'I can't believe one daggy dance could cause this much trouble.'

'You know I haven't even seen the video in question. Give me a look.'

Mimi picked her phone back up, found the video and passed it over.

Pete watched it with a smile twitching at the corners of his mouth and then he looked sideways at her.

'What? What's that look?'

'I don't think it's daggy,' said Pete. 'I happen to think you look pretty damn sexy.'

'Oh stop, I do not!'

'I'm serious,' said Pete. 'You've got some moves, woman.'

Mimi grabbed the phone back off him. 'Stop making fun of me!'

'I'm not! I'm telling you, I've always liked the way you dance. You've got nice . . . hip movements.'

Mimi finally stopped arguing and smiled back at him. 'Really?'

'Seriously.'

She rolled over onto her side to face him. 'You want to, you know . . . do stuff?'

He raised his eyebrows. 'What kind of stuff would you be talking about?'

'You know what kind of stuff I mean.' She reached down under the covers to make her intentions clear.

They'd only had sex two or three times since the twins were born. First there was all the waiting for Mimi's body to be ready again, and then with the constant interruptions throughout the night, it meant that every minute of potential sleep had been too precious to give it up for sex. But suddenly Mimi was feeling too turned on to give in to sleep. She'd liked seeing that look in Pete's eyes as he talked about the way she danced. It was nice to feel desired again.

'Ah,' he said. 'Well now see, I did wonder if that was the sort of stuff you were talking about, but I didn't want to get my hopes up in case I was wrong.'

'Go ahead and get them up,' she said, stroking her hand around the outside of his boxer shorts.

'Oh, they're up,' he said. 'I think you can feel that for yourself.'

Mimi laughed and flicked the waistband of his shorts. 'You are such a dork,' she said.

'I know,' he replied. 'That's why you love me.'

Darren

After the twelfth time retrieving the ball from across the living room, Darren had to accept it – he was playing fetch with himself. The dog was simply watching.

'I'm telling you,' said Darren. 'This is *fun*. This is something all dogs love. I throw the ball, you grab it and bring it back.'

He tried one last throw and when the dog still didn't move, he gave up and left the ball where it was.

'Okay,' he said. 'We'll try again tomorrow.'

On that first day at the park, he'd taken the dog straight to the vet to check for a microchip. The dog had one, but the details hadn't been updated in five years and the only phone number on file was disconnected.

'He doesn't look like he's been properly cared for in a long time,' the vet had commented. 'So I'd say he didn't just escape from a yard. I reckon he's been wandering the burbs for a while.'

'Any guess on breed?' Darren had asked.

'Likely a mix. The spots on his paws might indicate a bit of cattle dog in him.'

'So how does this work? Can I just take him home?'

'You truly want to keep him?'

'Yep.'

The vet tapped his fingers against his chin. 'Here's the thing. I'm not supposed to release him straight to you. He's meant to go to the pound and then you could follow up later. Try to adopt him through the proper channels.'

'Come on, mate. You said yourself he hasn't been looked after. Let me give him a good home.'

'I do know the local pound is nearing capacity . . . All right, take him with you but maybe do your due diligence – check Facebook's lost dog pages, keep an eye out for posters. You can put up your own post that you've found him if you want.' He gave the dog a scratch behind the ears and the dog leaned into him. 'Although like I said, even if he has just escaped from someone, whoever it was neglected him, in my opinion. So maybe don't try too hard to find them.'

Darren had booked him back in for a more thorough check-up and to get all his shots and worming and flea tablets up to date. He'd also asked for a card for a good groomer so he could get him cleaned up as well.

He'd been torn about whether or not to put up a post on social media saying he'd found the dog. What if the vet was right and he had a shitty owner who'd been neglecting him? But then, what if he had a loving family who'd lost him years ago and were still searching?

Although if that was the case, how bloody hard was it to update the poor mutt's microchip details?

In the end, he snapped a blurry photo of the dog, put

it in a few different Facebook lost and found pets groups with minimal details, and added that the dog was safe and had a new home now if no one claimed him. He was crossing his fingers that no one came looking.

He was well aware of the likelihood that his sudden attachment to this dog was a knee-jerk reaction to everything that was happening with Charlotte. *I'm probably substituting this dog for the imagined baby I'm handing over,* he thought to himself. Which was ridiculous, because it wasn't as though he'd been pining for a child in his life prior to Charlotte asking him for this favour.

Or maybe the dog was a procrastination technique. Something else to concentrate on so he wasn't staring at an empty Word document.

Or maybe that was all bullshit and he just liked the damned dog.

'All right,' Darren said now, patting the dog's head. 'If you're not going to play, I'm giving up and playing with this instead.' He picked up his Xbox controller and turned on the console, then reached for his headset on the coffee table. Hopefully one of his mates might be online for a game of *Call of Duty*.

He was about to put the headset on when he noticed the mangled microphone.

'You bloody didn't?' He looked down at the dog who immediately turned away as though pretending he wasn't paying attention.

'Oy, did you chew this? You know how much this headset cost me?'

The dog continued to look the other way.

'*Fuuuuuck,*' said Darren, tossing the headset back onto

the coffee table. 'Now what am I supposed to do with my night?'

The dog stood up, walked over to him and rested his head on Darren's knee.

'All right,' Darren said. 'Apology accepted. I guess I'll try and do some writing instead.'

Christmas Eve

Had the woman's husband been thrown from the car? Out of the corner of his eye, the man saw lights and he turned to look back down the freeway. Headlights were approaching. *Help*. He couldn't do all of this on his own. He hadn't even looked at the other cars yet.

'Stay there,' he said completely needlessly to the barely conscious woman. 'I'll be right back.'

He turned away from the car and took a few swift steps towards the side of the road and then started waving his arms, trying to flag the next car down. He wasn't going to let another one fly by without helping.

Thankfully, the car slowed and then pulled over sharply. He jogged over as another man started to get out of his car.

'Thanks for stopping. This is bad. It's really bad. And I'm an idiot and left my phone in my car. Can you call triple zero?'

The other man reached into his back pocket and pulled out his phone. He looked up at the accident as he started to dial and then froze.

'That's my mum's car,' he said.

7

Friday 11 December

Mimi

She'd knocked on the door twice but there was still no answer and no sound of movement from inside the house. Tara shifted from one foot to the other. 'Mum, why aren't they answering?' she asked.

'I don't know,' Mimi said. 'I'm sure they're here.'

They better be there. They'd walked over, and even though it was only a fifteen-minute walk, in the summer heat it had been sweltering. The air was also hazy today, with a hint of a smoky smell to it. There must have been a bushfire somewhere, maybe in the Blue Mountains or up the coast. That was worrying; summer had only just begun. Mimi wanted to fall face-first into Leesa's pool. As if on cue, she heard a splash.

'Ah,' she said. 'They're already out in the pool. Come on.'

They headed around to the side gate and Mimi reached up and over to find the latch to let themselves in.

'Hellooo,' she called out as they headed through. 'We knocked!'

'Oh, sorry!' Leesa jumped up from the daybed by the pool. She was wearing a black bikini, a huge floppy sun-hat and an open flowing white kaftan. Mimi couldn't help but be impressed by her well-defined abs; she wasn't sure she'd ever discover the existence of her own abs again after four babies.

'I always forget that I can't hear from around here. Come in, come in.'

Leesa let them through the pool gate and Tara immediately stripped off to join Chloe in the pool.

'Jesus,' said Leesa, giving Mimi a kiss on the cheek. 'The sweat is dripping off you. Come sit, I have everything we need out here.'

There was a bar fridge next to the daybed, stacked with bottles of wine and tonic water, cans of soft drink and a tray of strawberries, blueberries, watermelon and soft cheeses.

'Wow, you really do have everything we need.'

'Once I'm settled on this daybed, I don't want to have to move. It's close enough to watch the kids, but far enough not to get splashed. And also, the more sloshed I get, the further down the cushions I slide.'

'Ha, very nice. I brought champagne,' Mimi added, pulling the bottle out of her bag. 'Should still be cold.'

'Perfect, we'll start with that then move on to the gin,' said Leesa, taking the champagne from her and twisting the wire cap off the top before starting to turn the cork. 'Tara can have a sleepover if you like.'

'Now that's very tempting. But I didn't bring PJs or anything like that for her.'

Leesa faced the bottle out towards the pool as the cork popped and it flew in an arc before landing on the surface of the water. Both girls made a dive for it.

'All good,' said Leesa as she poured their drinks and

put the champagne away in the bar fridge. 'Chloe can loan her some. Besides, it'll alleviate my guilt. You've had the twins for several months now and I haven't done a thing to help you out. Bad friend,' she said, slapping her own wrist before picking up the two champagne flutes and handing Mimi one.

'Nah, you're good. Mums who are on their third and fourth kids aren't meant to get help. It's the new mums who need to be fawned over.'

'Yeah, but the rules change for twins.'

'Anyway, you brought me a casserole. Remember? And you sent flowers to the hospital. You've done plenty.'

'Still, let me have Tara stay tonight. Chloe will be ecstatic.'

'All right, well, I'll take you up on the offer, but only because I'd be an idiot to turn you down, not because you've been a bad friend – you're a great friend. Look, you're giving me Friday drinks. Brilliant.'

'Okay good, guilt alleviated.' They fell quiet for a moment as they relaxed, sipped their drinks and watched their girls.

'Did you hear about the fire in the mountains?' Leesa asked eventually.

'Ah, so there is a bushfire. I thought the air seemed hazy today.'

'Yep. Apparently there was a storm out there, so it was started by lightning.'

'That's awful.'

'I know. And it's already spread from Blackheath down to Katoomba. They're saying they're expecting another bad fire season this summer. Although I don't know if it could get any worse than last year.'

Mimi thought back to last Christmas and felt an involuntary shudder run through her body.

Leesa gasped. 'I'm an idiot. I didn't even think. I'm so sorry, I shouldn't have brought that up.'

Mimi shook her head and placed a reassuring hand on Leesa's arm. 'Don't be silly. You're fine. *I'm* fine.'

'Yeah, but sometimes I really don't think.'

'Honestly, it's okay.'

'How is everyone since . . . you know?'

'Yeah, not too bad, I suppose. Christmas will be hard, but you know how it is – it's not like you can sit and wallow. Life keeps going on around you, so you have to get on with it too, otherwise you'll get left behind. Jill's insisting that we still go up to Robin's Nest on Christmas Eve. I guess that's a good sign.'

'Robin's Nest?'

'Oh sorry, that's the name of their holiday house up at Nords Wharf.'

'Ah, I see.'

'Anyway, I think the twins were a welcome distraction for pretty much everyone this year.'

'Speaking of those two, who's looking after them this arvo? Callie?'

Mimi almost spat out her champagne. 'Ha! Now *that's* hilarious. You think I'd leave Callie in charge of two newborns?'

'What? She's sixteen, isn't she? Some kids give birth at sixteen.'

'Don't say that! And trust me, she's a *young* sixteen. She's had zero interest in helping out with the babies. I'd sooner leave Tara in charge than Callie. No, Pete's home on dad duty.'

'Ah yeah, I always forget you have a work-at-home husband. That you two have some sort of weird relationship where you can spend all day and all night together.'

'Yeah, yeah, we're freaks of nature. We should set up a glass window, charge admission. Come and gaze upon the married couple who spend all their time together.'

'Oh, people would pay.'

Mimi laughed. 'You know, in all honesty it's not *that* weird.'

'Yeah, I know, I'm just jealous because I know if it was me and Angus, we'd murder one another within two weeks.'

'You would not.'

'We would too. And it would be violent. I'm talking gory horror film stuff. How's work going anyway? You two have a new book coming out any time soon?'

'We're working on one, but we've been slowed down by the twins. And I'm really struggling to draw anything. I'm stuck on this stupid monkey that's supposed to be cute and cheeky and instead he keeps coming out looking rabid and deranged. I don't know what's wrong with me.'

'I do,' said Leesa. 'You need a break!'

'*Muuuum,*' Chloe called from the pool. 'We're hungry, can we have snacks?'

'Open your mouths,' Leesa called back. 'I'll throw blueberries at you like you're seals.'

'Mum! No!'

'Okay, okay, fine. Go in and get some packets of crisps. See how much water you can drip on my clean kitchen floor on the way.'

Mimi laughed again and took a large sip of her champagne, enjoying the way it fizzed in her throat as it went down. 'You're one of the cool mums, you know that, right?'

'Hell yeah, I know it. Come on, now's our chance to jump in the pool while they're not there to annoy us. Quick!'

Jill

Dear Frank,

There's a smoke haze throughout Sydney today. A nor-easterly wind brought it across this afternoon. I was onto the news quick smart to see what was going on. And then I went to double-check the Ventolins in the house before I realised. There's no point checking them anymore, is there? And then I cried.

You know I used to love summer, don't you? It used to be my favourite season. When I was younger, before I met you, I used to catch the bus to go swimming at Bondi every Saturday and Sunday throughout the summer. Now I can't even put my head under the water unless I want an ear infection.

But this year, as soon as we got that first sweltering hot day, right back in September – don't try and tell Australia it's still only spring, it doesn't care – I felt . . . weakened. And I've only felt weaker and weaker ever since. Not that you'd know to look at me. I'm good at projecting the image I choose. I've been doing it for a long time. But today, well let's just say I was glad that I was alone when I smelled that wisp of smoke on the air. Because there was no way I was hiding my initial reaction. Do you know I almost vomited? The smell might have been mild, but I could still feel the burn in my throat.

*Is it going to be like this every summer from now on? Every
time I smell smoke? Every time I hear about a bushfire?*
Love,
Jill

The smoke was already making her feel uneasy so it was
probably no wonder she jumped when the doorbell rang.

She opened the door and widened her eyes when she
saw Callie standing there, tears streaming down her face.

'Callie! What's wrong? What's happened?'

She hung her head. 'Nothing,' she said. 'Nothing's
happened.'

'Well, but then . . .' Jill realised it was stupid to stand
there in the doorway, questioning the poor girl. 'Come
on, come inside.'

She ushered her into the lounge room and they sat side
by side on the couch.

'Nothing's happened?' Jill clarified.

Callie shook her head.

Jill put an arm around her granddaughter. 'What's going
on, then? Why are you crying?' She paused. 'How did you
get here? Do Mum and Dad know you're here?'

'I caught the bus straight from school. I texted Dad and
told him.'

'Okay, good. Now talk to me, tell me what's wrong.'

Callie scratched hard at a spot on the inside of her arm.
'No,' she said. 'I'm keeping my mouth shut.' And there
was a fresh wave of tears.

Jill looked back at her, horrified. 'What on earth do you
mean? Keeping your mouth shut about what?'

'I . . . I didn't mean anything. It was nothing.'

'No, it was something. Talk to me.'

'Grandma, please.' She continued to sob and Jill thought it best to stop pressing.

'Can I get you something?' Jill tried eventually. 'A cup of tea?' It felt like a ridiculous suggestion, but she didn't know what else to offer.

'Okay,' said Callie.

Jill gave her a quick squeeze before standing up, grabbing a box of tissues to place surreptitiously in front of Callie, and then hurrying away to the kitchen to boil the kettle. Maybe by the time she came back with the tea, Callie would be ready to talk.

Jill realised as she made the tea that this meant Mimi had been right. Something was going on with Callie; she shouldn't have been so dismissive of her daughter-in-law's concerns.

Ten minutes later, Callie's tears were finally starting to subside. Jill had almost finished her own cup of tea, but Callie's had pretty much sat on the table in front of them untouched. Jill had done her best to make conversation, nattering on about the weather or Christmas or about it almost being school holidays.

'Do you actually like tea?' Jill said eventually.

Callie gave a small smile. 'Not really,' she said.

'Sorry, I should have thought to offer you something else.'

'No,' said Callie, 'it's fine. I don't need anything.'

'Are you ready to tell me what's got you so worked up?'

'It's . . .' Callie faltered. 'It's like . . . I don't even know who I am anymore. I've turned into such a huge bitch.'

Jill stayed silent, giving Callie the room to speak.

'I'm mean to everyone and I can't seem to help it. Like,

sometimes it's as though I'm watching from the outside and I can see myself saying these horrible, awful things and hurting Tara and hurting Mum . . . but I can't stop myself. And I hate it, I hate myself, I don't want to be that way.'

'Okay, well, the fact that you feel bad about saying something nasty means that you're not a bad person though, doesn't it?'

Callie fidgeted. 'Does it? I mean, wouldn't it be better if I wasn't a bitch in the first place?'

'Don't forget being a teenager is hard. It's normal to lash out sometimes. And it's always the people you love the most who you hurt the most. You've got all these hormones –'

Callie cut her off. 'It's *not* hormones.'

'Okay. I only meant –'

'This isn't just normal teenage stuff. I went through all of that already, when I was like thirteen or fourteen. This is different. This is more than that.'

'Callie,' Jill said carefully, 'has something happened? Something at school, maybe? Earlier, when you arrived, you said you were keeping your mouth –'

Callie spoke over her again. 'Sorry, I was being stupid. My music teacher convinced me to sing at the concert that Tara's performing at on Friday, and it's this big secret. That's all I meant. I'm just nervous about it. No one knows I'm doing it. Not even Mum and Dad.'

Jill sensed this wasn't at all what had been on her mind earlier, but she needed to be delicate with her granddaughter. It would be better to bide her time.

'That's exciting, your voice has always been so lovely. I've missed hearing you. It's been such a long time – I never understood why you stopped.'

Throughout primary school Callie had always been a part of the choir, and in Year Seven, she'd had a decent role in the school musical. Frank and Jill had often gone along to see her perform. But as she'd hit her teen years, she'd started to grow shy about her talents.

'I didn't stop . . . not altogether. I just didn't like doing it in public anymore.'

'What's changed your mind now?'

Callie's eyes slid sideways. 'I don't really know.'

'Well, I'm glad you're doing it. And stage fright is completely normal. I think nerves can even help you perform . . . or something like that. I'll admit performing isn't really my thing. Would it help if you practised for me? I can promise to be completely objective.'

Callie laughed. 'You really think you can be objective?'

'Absolutely, Scout's honour.'

Callie looked like she was considering it but then she changed her mind. 'Nah,' she said. 'I'm not really in the mood for singing.'

'Fair enough. Hey, do you want to play a game of Rummikub? You used to love that.'

'Sure, that sounds good.'

Jill mentally congratulated herself for coming up with a good idea and went to collect the box of numbered tiles.

They sat and played for a good half an hour, chatting about other things. About the twins. About school. About singing. Each time Jill asked a question she tried to keep her voice casual. Tried to make sure it didn't sound like she was probing too much.

'Tell me something,' said Jill as she placed a row of tiles on the board that cleared four of her highest numbers and left her with only two tiles to get rid of. 'What does "OK boomer" mean?'

Callie almost snorted with laughter. 'OMG, Grandma. Where do you hear these things?'

'I think someone said it on the radio.'

'Right,' said Callie. 'Well, the main thing you need to know is that it's an insult. So, if anyone says "OK boomer" to you, you tell them to fuck right off. Got it?'

Jill made sure she didn't baulk at Callie swearing. A little while back, she'd told her that she was allowed to swear in front of her whenever she wanted. It was important for kids to have rules at home, but with their grandma? That was when they were allowed to express themselves without judgement, when they could completely relax. And today in particular, Jill wanted Callie to feel relaxed, to feel safe, to feel like she could open up if she wanted to.

The truth was, Jill already knew exactly what 'OK boomer' meant. It had been explained when she'd heard it on the radio. Some shock jock had been lamenting the fact that kids these days had no respect for their elders. But Jill disagreed. Kids these days were just trying to navigate life in an online world. And she knew it made Callie feel good when she got to explain new things to her grandmother. Kids liked it when they got to feel wise . . . smarter than their elders. Too many adults seemed to think they had to remind kids about all the things that they *didn't* know yet. They felt like they had to bring them down a peg or two, that they had to prove they didn't have all the answers or life experiences yet, that they weren't wise, that they had so much more to learn.

But as far as Jill was concerned, they already *knew* that!

They might not act like it, but deep down, they did. They knew that they hadn't seen it all or done it all. They weren't idiots! And they were insecure about the things they didn't know yet. Insecure and scared. So why not let them feel like they had it all figured out sometimes? Why not give them that boost they needed to feel smart, to feel valued?

Obviously, there were some teens who could use the odd take-down, but not Jill's granddaughters.

Eventually, as Jill finished their third round by placing her last two tiles on the board, she asked carefully, 'Callie, is there something else that's upset you? Something apart from the stage fright?'

Callie stood abruptly. 'I better go. I told Dad I wasn't going to stay long. He wants me home in time for dinner.'

Jill hesitated. Should she keep pushing, try to find out what else what upsetting Callie? But if she pushed too hard, then she might push her away. Maybe it was better to leave it at that, so hopefully Callie would feel comfortable coming back and chatting again.

'All right, darling. I'll give you a lift home.'

Darren

Darren was hedging his bets. He was sitting in a booth at The Oaks Hotel, keeping an eye out for any single girls while simultaneously swiping through Tinder matches on his phone. He needed a date for tomorrow night. Charlotte and Steph wanted to take him out for dinner to say thank you and it was also going to be the opportunity for them to get into the details of how this would all work. *Bring the new chick*, Charlotte had added to the end of her last message. It was likely a hopeless mission. Even if he did manage to pick up, the chances of convincing someone to join him on a double-date tomorrow night were slim. But he had to at least try.

If Charlotte didn't already know everyone in his life from when they were together, he would have asked a friend or maybe even one of his sisters-in-law to pretend for him. Actually, maybe not – he couldn't imagine getting either Mimi or Andrea to play the part of his date. They were too much like actual sisters to him.

He also had his laptop open on the table in front of him, a blank Word document on the screen. Every now and then he'd glance over the top of his phone at the empty white screen and it would feel like it was mocking him. He wondered if having the laptop made him look more or less appealing. Did he look ostentatious or conscientious?

Who was he kidding? There was no way he was going to get struck by inspiration here. He looked back at his phone and hesitated on a brunette with a killer smile. She reminded him of Charlotte. He swiped left.

He wondered if Doggo was doing okay back at home. At the moment, that was all he was calling him – Doggo. He couldn't bring himself to give him a proper name yet, not until he knew for sure that someone wasn't going to come out of the woodwork and claim him.

A shadow crossed the table and he looked up to see a woman standing in front of him, holding two beers.

'This is going to sound like a pick-up line,' she said.

'And okay, that's because I am trying to pick you up. But it's also true. I bought a beer for my mate and then he totally ditched me. And so now I've got two beers and I'll look like an alcoholic and a complete loner if I sit up at the bar on my own with these. So, you want one?'

Darren grinned. There was nothing sexier than a girl with confidence. She had blonde hair piled up on her head in a messy bun and huge bright pink hoop earrings.

'Love one,' he said.

She smiled back at him and he became aware of deep dimples in her cheeks. He shifted slightly and motioned for her to join him. She put down the drinks and slid in next to him.

'About time,' she said. 'You were like the sixth person I offered this beer to. It's probably gone flat.'

He laughed, before picking it up for a test sip. 'It'll pass,' he said. 'Number six, hey? What did all the other blokes have on me that I didn't?'

'Oh, not much. Just better looks, nicer clothes, more charm. You know, the usual.'

'Surprised I even made the cut.' He was liking this instant banter.

'Well, like I said, it was you or sit by myself.' Her eyes sparkled at him in a way that suggested she very much wanted to be sitting right here next to him. And then she shifted a little closer. She wasn't the type to waste any time. Even better.

'I'm Darren,' he said, figuring they ought to at least know one another's names before the flirting went any further.

'Sage,' she replied.

'Pretty name.'

'It is until you find out it's short for Sagittarius.'

'Really? As in the star sign?'

'Yep. And even worse, I was born in August, so it's not my actual star sign. I'm a Leo.'

Darren laughed. 'So how did that happen?'

'My parents' names are Maureen and Graeme. Apparently Mum always hated growing up with such a boring name. And then she got caught up in the whole hippy thing and she never grew out of it. So, here I am. Sagittarius for a first name, Moon for a middle name.'

'Love it,' said Darren, clinking his beer against hers. 'It's the cutest name I've ever heard.'

'You wouldn't be saying that if they'd gone with Libra. Imagine if I had to get about with the same name as a tampon brand.'

Darren laughed. 'I reckon you'd make it work. So they wouldn't be a fan of my name then. Can't get much more boring than Darren.'

'Yeah, but it's a classic, isn't it? Dazza. Perfect Aussie name.'

'True.'

'Anyway, I don't think you need to worry about what my parents think of your name. I'm not exactly planning on taking you home to meet Mum and Dad.'

They chatted back and forth as they drank their beers, the flirtatious banter continuing. He noticed she was a toucher. She would put her hand on his arm or press her leg against his as they talked. On their third round, he decided to level with her.

'You know how you were up front about that extra beer you needed to get rid of? I'm going to be upfront too.'

'Go for it,' she said.

'I've got dinner tomorrow night with an ex and her new girlfriend. I need a date because I lied and told them I was already seeing someone. Any chance you want to take on the role?'

Her mouth dropped open. 'Are you for real?'

He cringed. 'Uh, yeah. I know, I know, it's asking a lot. But I'm seriously desperate.'

'I'll tell you what, grab us another round and I'll think about it.'

'Done. Take all the time you need.'

Darren jumped up from the table and Sage called after him, 'Can you get a bowl of fries or something too? I'm starving.'

He grinned and nodded.

A few minutes later he returned to the table with the drinks and a number for their food. 'I ordered chicken wings as well, to sweeten the deal.'

'Nice move. All right, first things first, where is this dinner tomorrow night?'

'The tapas bar on Keely Street.'

'Okay that's good, close by, I wouldn't have to travel. Now, why did you lie about already having a girlfriend?'

'Umm, because I'm a coward and a dickhead.'

'I like your honesty. Next question, is this your way of trying to get me to see you again or do you genuinely need a one-off date? Because I'm not interested in a relationship. I like keeping things casual.'

'That's absolutely fine by me. Casual is perfect. It really is a one-off date so I don't get caught out.'

'But what happens when your ex expects to see you with a girlfriend again next time?'

'I'll say we broke up.'

'Hmm. Your ex and her partner – are they fun? Interesting? Will I have a good time at this dinner?'

'Last week they got me blind drunk on shots. Does that answer your question?'

'It might. I like people who can put a few drinks away. Okay, I'm in. I have no plans for tomorrow night, so why not?'

She leaned in then and kissed him, long and slow.

'What did I do to deserve that?' he asked when she eventually pulled back.

'Right place, right time,' she said with a shrug.

He wondered if he should tell her the purpose of the dinner with Charlotte and Steph but reconsidered. He seemed to have met the unicorn of women. Sexy, confident and willing to help out on a weird sort of half-date. That information could come later, he didn't want to push his luck.

Andrea

Andrea had realised that the main reason she'd remained non-committal about Christmas drinks was in case Violet needed her. And she'd also realised that that was ridiculous. For God's sake, she wasn't the child's mother. Tony was right, it wasn't her business and she couldn't keep interfering. Yesterday after school she'd lingered outside

Heather's apartment to listen in and make sure everything was all right. A voice had come from behind her. 'Can I help you with something?'

She'd turned around to see Heather walking towards her from the lift, hand in hand with Violet. They looked like a perfectly normal mother-daughter duo.

Andrea had muttered an excuse and slunk away, embarrassed.

So now she was out at a bar with a group of teachers from school for what they liked to call 'the unofficial Christmas party'. This was the one without the principal and department heads. It meant they could let their hair down even more than usual. Not that anyone especially had any issues with the heads of the school, it was more that it was hard to completely relax with your bosses around.

She was up at the bar, ordering a round of drinks, when she spotted a familiar face across the room. Her brother-in-law, Darren, sitting in a booth with a gorgeous blonde woman.

Andrea smiled. They were looking very cosy and she was glad for him. He hadn't seemed to have had much luck with women since Charlotte. Usually Andrea would have gone over to say hello, but she didn't want to interrupt.

She collected the tray of drinks and headed back to her friends.

'Who was that you were checking out?' Kelly asked as she reached the table.

'What are you talking about? I wasn't checking anyone out.'

'I saw you looking over at some cute guy.'

'What? No! That's my brother-in-law!'

'Seriously? He's hot. You sure you picked the right brother?'

'Hey!'

Kelly laughed. 'I'm kidding. Tony's great. I'm just saying . . . man, that brother.'

Andrea laughed despite herself. 'Yeah, all right, calm down. Looks like he's hitting it off with someone over there anyway.'

'Okay, but if it doesn't work out, introduce me.'

'No way. You'd chew him up and spit him out. And he's already had his heart broken.' Andrea knew that Kelly had dated a slew of men since breaking up with her husband and while there was absolutely nothing wrong with that, she still didn't want Darren to be one of the men left in her wake.

'Pfft,' said Kelly. 'Any other cute brothers then?'

'The other one's taken.'

One of the drama teachers, Greg, sat down next to Kelly. 'Who's taken?' he asked.

'Andrea's being mean with her brothers-in-law,' said Kelly.

'I'm not being mean! Pete has four children, including twin babies!'

Greg took a large sip of his wine and then waggled his finger at Andrea's stomach, while giving her an over-exaggerated wink. 'Is that a little secret something of your own starting to brew in there that I can see?'

Andrea felt her whole body tighten at the same time as Kelly made a loud choking noise. 'Are you fucking joking, Greg? You don't ask a woman that!'

Andrea gave a tight smile. 'Mmm,' she said. 'Super appropriate, Greg.'

'What?' he said, letting his wine slosh around in his glass and some splash over the side. 'Why can't I ask? A few of us were thinking it.' It was clear he was more than a little tipsy.

Andrea stood up. 'I'm just going to the bathroom,' she said, acknowledging Kelly's sympathetic look with a small nod of her head.

In the bathroom, she stood side-on in front of the mirror and eyed her belly. She'd been enjoying herself, grazing from a shared cheese platter with her drinks and hadn't noticed that her stomach had become bloated. Obviously, something she'd eaten wasn't agreeing with her. She tugged at her top, pulling the material tight and then ran one hand gently around her stomach. With her small frame, any bloating really did make her look pregnant. Usually it didn't bother her and for a moment she wondered if she'd overreacted, but then Kelly came barging through the door after her. She quickly dropped her hands and turned to face Kelly.

'Fucking Greg,' Kelly said. 'He is the king of putting his foot in it. Are you okay?'

Andrea smiled. 'Yeah, I'm fine.' She paused. 'I know you're probably thinking that maybe I can't have them or that I'm self-conscious about my body but honestly, I'm not and –'

Kelly cut her off. 'No. I'm thinking that it's no one else's business! And more importantly – honey, you do *not* look pregnant to me.'

Andrea glanced down at her stomach again. Yes, she

did. Kelly was being kind. But there was something so invasive about the way Greg had questioned her just now. She realised with a surge of horror that she was about to cry.

Kelly must have noticed, because she took two swift strides across the bathroom and pulled Andrea into a tight hug. 'He's a dick,' she said. 'I might go back out there and throw my drink at him.'

Andrea gave a half-laugh, half-cry. 'No don't,' she said. 'It'll be a waste of a perfectly good merlot.'

They pulled apart and Andrea wiped at her eyes with the sleeve of her top. 'You know what's stupid?' she asked.

'What's that, honey?'

'It's that Tony and I decided not to have kids, right? And I was pretty much okay with that. But the thing is, part of me always thought we might revisit it. A part of me always thought, one day, he'll sit down and ask me *why*? He'll say, "Andrea, why don't you want to have kids?" And then I'd spill it all. Everything about my fears of not turning out like my mother, and then . . . and then . . .' She stopped and stared at Kelly. 'Oh my God,' she said. 'I can't believe I just started blurting all that stuff out at you. I'm so sorry. I think I've had too many drinks.'

'Don't be sorry! We might not be super close but that doesn't mean I can't be here for you.' Kelly paused, then said gently, 'And you thought he'd reassure you, right? He'd tell you that you wouldn't turn out like your mother?'

Andrea nodded. 'I know. It's stupid. It's just that, he knows about my childhood, about my mum. So, I suppose I thought he might figure it out for himself.'

'I get it,' said Kelly. 'I know what it's like when you're

wishing that your partner would say the thing you want them to say. But the problem is, they're not mind-readers. So, if you don't open up, they won't know to ask. Trust the woman who's already been through one bad divorce, okay?'

'That's a fair point. You know, I'm just not sure at what point we made that final definitive choice. I'm not sure when we completely closed the door, all I know is that it's closed.'

'But is it? I mean, if you don't want it to be, shouldn't you at least talk to him about it?'

'I don't really know what I want. But when idiot Greg asked me just now, there was a part of me that wanted to be able to say yes. To be able to make this happy announcement. But that's so ridiculous. I mean, where did that thought even come from?'

'Probably from your fucking ovaries,' said Kelly. 'Women's bodies are excellent at taking control at the most annoying times.'

'Stupid biological clock. I've probably left it too late anyway. I'm almost forty.'

Kelly shook her head. 'There's still time,' she said. 'If it's something that you want, there's definitely still time. Now, you know what I think?'

'What?'

'To start, I think we need more drinks and that they should be bloody Greg's shout. And then I think maybe you need to have a conversation with Tony.'

'I know,' said Andrea. 'You're right.'

Christmas Eve

Darren thrust his phone at the stranger. 'You make the call,' he said. 'I have to get to my mum.'

He sprinted over to the crumpled Volvo and leaned into the driver's side. 'Mum, *Mum*? Are you awake? Are you okay? Can you hear me?'

Her chin was resting on her chest. He couldn't tell if she was breathing. He heard the other man talking on his phone from behind him.

'Four cars,' he was saying. 'Looks really bad. Oh right . . . M1 freeway. Umm, I think we're just a few kilometres before the Gosford exit.'

Darren turned around to look at him. 'The Peats Ridge Road exit,' he corrected.

'Oh right, yes, sorry. The Peats Ridge Road exit.' He shifted the phone away from his mouth for a moment. 'She said her husband is gone,' he said to Darren, pointing at the passenger seat. 'I'm worried he's been thrown from the car; we need to look.'

Darren straightened up.

'What the hell? She was driving alone. My dad's dead. He died a year ago.'

8

Christmas Eve – a year ago

Jill

'So, I called to let him know there was a parcel collection card here for him and you know what he said? He said, could you pop by the post office and pick it up for me? I mean, could you believe the nerve?'

'Well, why do you get involved with these things? They've never done nothing for us.'

'Because it's the neighbourly thing to do. And they've never done *anything* for us, dear.'

They'd come out to a café for breakfast and had lingered over their coffees, avoiding joining the last-minute rush in the shops as people grabbed their final food and shopping for Christmas tomorrow.

Frank dipped his spoon in cappuccino froth, positioned it like a catapult and flicked it across the table at Jill. 'I ain't changed the way I talk for fifty years and I ain't about to change it now, woman.'

Jill picked up a serviette to wipe the froth off the front of her top, but she was smiling. She would never admit it, but she actually liked it when Frank did childish things like that. It made her feel like they were teenagers again.

Although if she'd been wearing her silk blouse she might not have been so amused.

Her own parents had always hated the way Frank spoke. Not to mention his table manners. The fact they disapproved was one of the reasons Jill had pursued Frank in the first place. Growing up on the Upper North Shore meant Jill's parents weren't too keen on her dating a boy from the west. They never did stop looking down on him – even after he built his own construction company from the ground up.

In the end, he was worth more than Jill's parents had ever been, yet whenever he came to visit, they continued to speak to him like a poor farmer boy who might steal the silverware, right up until they'd both passed on. To his credit, he let their barbs fly right by, never biting.

The good thing was that Frank had always been determined to treat his own sons' girlfriends with kindness and respect. Mimi and Andrea were welcomed into the family with wide open arms. As was Darren's girlfriend, Charlotte – and fingers crossed that boy would get off his backside and pop the question to her soon too.

'You're not going to pick up the parcel for them?' Frank asked.

'Well, I could hardly say no.'

'Yes, you bloody well could. It's Christmas Eve. You're busy enough as it is. How do you always end up doing so much for other people?'

'I'm nice. That's how. I offered to keep an eye on their mail while they were away.'

'Which ones are we talking about again? The young ones on the left?'

'It would be nice if you remembered their surname, they've been living next to us for five years now.'

'It *has not* been five years since Wayne and Barb moved out.'

'It has.'

'Don't see why they had to move into a bloody retirement home.'

'Don't go saying that to them. They call it a "lifestyle resort". And Barb says they're very happy there.'

'Bullshit. Wayne loved that house.'

'Wayne couldn't get up the stairs anymore.'

'Bullshit,' Frank said again.

'I guess we should get moving,' Jill said, knowing there was no point continuing this line of the conversation – Frank would only continue to argue. 'We still have to go to the post office, pick up the ham from the butcher and buy one last gift for Tara *and* we want to be on the road by four.'

'Darl, you're bloody dreaming.'

'We can get it all done if we move it now.'

'No, not about getting it all done, about driving up the freeway. The Mount White fire, remember? I reckon the freeway will be closed this arvo.'

'No, it won't. Don't say that! The Christmas plans will be ruined if the freeway is closed.'

'No. The kids have the backup plan. Christmas at Tony and Andrea's.'

'We are not having Christmas in an *apartment*. It's too small! We're going up to the Nords Wharf house like we always do. It's not Christmas if we're not there.'

'Darl, it's still bloody Christmas wherever the hell we are.'

'But if we're not at Robin's Nest . . . Frank, you know how important it is to spend Christmas there.'

Frank gave her a sad smile. 'Yes, love. I do.'

'There you go,' said Frank, taking one hand off the wheel to jab at the radio. It was several hours later and they were well on their way up north. 'Did you hear that? They've closed the freeway behind us. We were probably one of the last ones through. We're bloody well fucked.'

'Don't swear!'

'Fucken fucked,' said Frank, and she knew it was just to annoy her more.

'We are not . . . *fucked*.' Jill placed the appropriate amount of reverence around the word. 'As long as the kids got through before they closed it, we'll all make it to Nords.'

'You're bloody dreamin'. You think any of that lot were on the road yet? Darren's never been on time in his life. Pete will still be packing the car full of the girls' stuff and Tony . . . well, I guess Tony's usually a bit more punctual. But I still doubt he and Andrea will have made it. Now we'll be stuck up there unable to get back and they'll be stuck down in Sydney unable to come up. How's that going to work for your Chrissy Day plans, love?'

'They'll have got through,' Jill said, feigning confidence.

'God, you're obstinate, woman.'

'I'm not, I'm positive. I have a can-do attitude. I'm optimistic and decisive. I'm –'

'All right, all right,' he said, laughing as he cut her off and patted her thigh. 'I get it. Actually, can I tell you something?'

'Yes.'

'I wouldn't mind having Christmas morning just with you. I know, I know,' he said, waving his hand in her face and letting the car veer slightly when she started to open her mouth. 'Blasphemy,' he continued. 'Worst thing I could ever say. Not wanting to spend it with the kids and the grandkids, and of course I do want to see them. But do you ever miss the days when it was just us?'

'But, it's always just us, now. We're constantly on our own.'

'Yes and no. I know they're busy with their own families and a lot of our day to day is just us. But then when it comes to the big things, the events, it's people everywhere and noise and nonsense and I can't concentrate on anything any of 'em are saying anyway.'

'So, get a hearing aid. I keep telling you, it'll help.'

'It's not my bloody hearing, woman. It's them.'

Jill laughed. 'Oh yes, it's never you, is it?'

'Nope. It's them. They all talk over the top of each other. Picture waking up Christmas morning with just the sounds of the bush. Drinking cups of tea in bed without being dragged out to the living room because the girls can't possibly wait till a decent hour to open their presents but Grandma and Grandpa have to watch.'

'Isn't watching them open their presents the loveliest part of the day? Doesn't the look on their beautiful faces make it all worth it?'

Frank made a noise of indifference. 'Take it or leave it.'

'Bullshit,' said Jill, making Frank snort. She might not swear often but he was always amused when she did.

'Yeah, all right,' he said. 'It's a bit of bullshit. But if they *didn't* make it through, this is our bright side, all right?'

Jill smiled. 'All right.'

They were quiet for a few minutes, and then they both seemed to realise the same thing at the same time.

'Is it getting . . .' said Jill.

'Smokier,' said Frank. 'A lot smokier.'

It seemed to happen in an instant then. One minute they could see for metres and metres in front of the car, the next they were engulfed in a thick, black cloud.

'Where the hell did that come from?' Frank slammed on the brakes.

'You can't stop here! It's a freeway. What if someone hits us?'

'Well what do you want me to do? I can't see a bloody thing.'

She could hear a note of fear in his voice and that frightened her more than the eerie, heavy black smoke around the car. Frank didn't scare easily.

'Creep forward,' she suggested. 'Maybe we can ease onto the shoulder.'

He did so and as the car edged forward and to the left, they both started to cough. 'The smoke's getting into the car,' said Jill.

'No kidding, Sherlock.'

'Don't make fun of me!' There was a hysterical edge to Jill's voice. She started flicking all the aircon vents closed.

'I think we're pulled over,' said Frank.

'Now what do we do? Do we call triple zero?'

'Just wait a minute. Maybe it'll clear as fast as it came. I don't see flames, do you?'

'I don't think so. I'm not sure.'

They both coughed again but Jill noticed a wheezier sound to Frank's cough. 'You don't sound good,' she said.

'I sound the same as you do.'

'No, you don't, you sound breathless, Frank. Where's your Ventolin? Tell me you brought one with us.'

'I don't need any flippin' Ventolin.'

'And you say I'm obstinate. Did you pack one? Is it in your bag?'

He started coughing again but this time it was a longer, wheezier cough, and when he finally stopped it had left him gasping for air. Despite the vents being closed, the smoke was seeping into the car. Jill's eyes were starting to smart and the back of her throat was beginning to burn.

'For God's sake, Frank. Is there one in your bag? You need it.'

He looked sideways at her, and there was terror on his face. 'I think there might be,' he finally said. 'In the boot.'

She immediately reached for her door handle. 'I'll get it for you.'

He grabbed her arm with a vice-like grip. 'Like hell you will. You're not going out there. I'll get the stupid thing myself.'

By now they both could feel the heat. There was a fire nearby, and it was getting closer.

'You can't,' said Jill. 'You can't go out there.'

'Well I'm not letting you.' He still had a hold of her arm. But then another coughing fit overtook him and his grip weakened. She took her opportunity, throwing open the car door, wrenching her arm free and stepping out into the plumes of smoke. She slammed the door shut behind her, not wanting to let anymore of the smoke into the car and into Frank's lungs. The heat draped over her like a heavy, thick blanket and for a second she couldn't think which way to move to get around to the car boot. Her eyes were streaming and her nostrils and throat burned.

She was an idiot. She should have tied something around her face. The car, that's how she'd find her way. By feeling the car. She tugged at the collar of her top to pull it up over her nose and mouth and then she reached back for the car. The metal was hot under her fingertips. She touched it lightly and followed it towards the back, then felt around for the car boot latch. Finding it, she tried to press the button but found that her fingers didn't seem strong enough. Her entire body was weakening. She hadn't noticed how much she'd started struggling for breath, how much her chest was heaving. She'd been too busy concentrating on finding her way around to the boot.

But now her vision was tunnelling and her legs were heavy. She tried again to release the boot latch. Her fingers fumbled. She squeezed her eyes shut tight against the sting of the smoke and held one arm over her nose and mouth as she tried again. Finally, she felt the button yield and the boot started to open. She stumbled backwards as it lifted and then when it was high enough, she collapsed in on top of the bags, her hands searching, feeling canvas and leather. Zippers and clasps. There was no way she was ever going to find her way into the right bag, search through the contents, get hold of the Ventolin that might not even be in there.

That's when she heard two things at once.

From the front seat of the car, Frank's voice. 'Jill, love, are you all right? Tell me you're alive.'

She managed to choke out a response. 'I'm ... here ...'

And then the second thing. The whine of a siren. A fire truck was coming. They would be saved.

9

Saturday 12 December

Jill

Dear Frank,

I stayed in bed until late again this morning, but you can hardly blame me. I still can't seem to sleep. So, I lay there and rested, and I imagined you were still here with me. I imagined I could hear the drone of the mower while you did the lawns, or that you were fixing the engine of the old Holden Commodore in the shed or pottering around downstairs, and any moment you'd appear in the doorway and say, 'For goodness sake, woman, get out of bed – you're retired, not dead!'

Yes, but you are, my dear.

And you're not coming back, are you?

It's stupid that I post these letters, isn't it? Do you know where I send them? Up to Robin's Nest. So silly, as if you're up there having a holiday. As if this Christmas when I arrive, you'll be there waiting for me. But you won't, will you? Because you're gone. In those first few months I kept thinking, okay, that's enough now. You can stop being dead. You can come back. I've done my grieving and I've had enough of it and you can bloody well come back.

But you didn't. You wouldn't. Didn't matter if I cried. Didn't matter if I yelled and screamed and swore. Nothing would make you come back. I keep asking you questions as though one day you'll write back and give me all the answers. For instance, that damned email. 'You need to know'. What am I meant to do with that, Frank? I should have deleted it the moment it arrived. She has no right to tell me what I need. But for some stupid reason I've held onto it and it just keeps niggling at me.

I'm going to have to make sure I'm the first one to arrive at the house this Christmas. I'll need to run in there quick smart and grab the mail before they see all the letters. They'll think I've gone mad if they find them. Letter after letter addressed to you. And what will I do with them? Open them up and read them? Tear them to pieces? Burn them?

Each time I write the words 'Robin's Nest' on the front of the envelope, I think back to the day I had the plaque made up for the house. I wasn't sure what you'd think when you saw it. I was worried you might be upset. But instead you touched your fingers to it and you smiled. The boys still don't know why I chose that name. I wonder if I'll ever tell them.

The closer it gets to Christmas Eve, the harder it is to breathe. The harder it is to hold on. The harder it is to hide the pain.

I know it was my fault, love. I know it was my stubbornness that killed you. I know I should have listened. I know you'd still be here today if I wasn't so hung up on stupid traditions. And I know that no number of Hail Marys will ever make up for it. They won't make up for that and they won't make up for any of my sins.

But you know what you could have done? You could have hung on. You could have held on for only a few minutes more. Or you could have carried your Ventolin with you, right there in your front bloody pocket where you always kept a ballpoint pen. Or stored one in the glovebox. Or any one of a million places.

You could have fought for it. You could have let them save you. They came, Frank! They came to rescue us. And I thought everything was all right. I thought, well this will be a real lesson to us, won't it? I thought, imagine what the kids will think when we tell them what almost happened.

But no. They couldn't save you, because you were already gone.

Do you know I always carry a Ventolin in my handbag now? Ever since that day . . . I put one in there and everywhere I go, I make sure it's there. I constantly double-check. That's silly, isn't it? It's too late now. I'm continuously checking the bushfire app and the weather app too. It was the wind that got us. It caused the fire to suddenly change direction and jump the freeway.

And anyway, I'm making excuses, trying to find a way to place the blame somewhere else. But we all know the truth, don't we?

None of that was what mattered. What mattered was that I made us drive up that freeway.

There's no other way of looking at it.

I killed you.

Mimi

Before she'd even opened her eyes, she could feel her skull pulsating as though it was trying to burst its way out of her head. Her eyelids fluttered and she tried to swallow but her tongue was furry and her throat was dry. What the hell had she done to herself?

The previous night came back to Mimi in flashes. She and Leesa giggling like schoolgirls on the daybed, finishing off the bottle of champagne before moving on to the gin, Leesa pouring the drinks without a measure. They would have been double shots for sure. *'No need to measure, hon, no one's driving anywhere.'*

Mimi rolled over and the pulsating skull turned into a heavy pounding. She pressed the heels of her hands into her eyes. She couldn't remember the rest of the night. How did she get home? Where was Tara? Did she come home too? No, she had a sleepover at Leesa's. *When* did she get home?

'Good morning, sleeping beauty.'

Mimi kept her hands over her eyes and tried to talk but her voice came out raspy and she felt her stomach lurch. Ignoring the pounding head, she leapt out of bed and raced towards the ensuite to throw up.

'That bad, is it?' Pete called after her. 'Sucks when you haven't had a hangover in more than a year.'

When she was done emptying the contents of her stomach and had washed her face, she stumbled back out to the bedroom and collapsed on the bed, ignoring the look of glee on Pete's face.

'Why are you so happy to see me in pain?'

'Golf day, August, remember?'

'Ah.' He'd come home plastered after a golf day with his brothers a few months back. Mimi had been furious with him for getting so drunk when she was so close to her due date. The next day she'd taken great pleasure in watching him suffer through his hangover.

'I told you then there'd be a day when the tables would turn.'

'Yeah, well, my gloating was justified that time. You might remember I went into labour literally two days later.'

'Hush. Don't ruin this for me. I've been waiting for you to wake up so I could ask you this – what do you remember about coming home last night?'

'Oh no. Nothing. Why? What happened?'

Pete clapped his hands together – actually clapped them like a delighted child.

'God, it must be bad.'

'Are you ready? Edna had to pull you out of her rhododendron bushes and escort you to our front door.'

'She fucking did not.'

'She fucking did too.'

Edna was their seventy-year-old neighbour who'd already complained twice about the sound of the twins crying, three times about Callie and her friends picking flowers off her rhododendron bushes when they walked past her driveway, and too many times to count about Tara learning to play the tuba. In Edna's defence, they'd all wanted Tara to stop learning the tuba last year.

'You texted me about eleven to say you were walking home. I offered to come get you but you sent me an all caps message telling me you WANTED TO WALK. Apparently, you fell into Edna's garden and couldn't get back up again.'

'I'm mortified. I'll never be able to look her in the face again.'

'Nope, you won't. She did helpfully mention that matured rhododendron bushes are available at Flower Power for when we replace the one you crushed.'

'I crushed it? Come on, I mean I know I put on weight after the twins . . . !'

Pete laughed. 'I think it was more the thrashing about

you did trying to get back up. I wish I'd seen it; I'm imagining you as a giant turtle.'

Mimi leaned in close and held a finger up to his face. 'Never, ever use the word giant to describe me, ever again.'

He grabbed her finger and kissed it. 'You know I only get away with it because you're smoking hot, right?'

'I think I'm going to be sick again.'

This time he guided her to the bathroom.

'What's on for today?' Pete asked as he placed a bacon and egg roll from Pinky's takeaway down in front of Mimi.

She was sitting at the kitchen table massaging her temples and thanking the gods that Pete had taken the twins for a walk in their stroller around the corner. Returning with the girls fast asleep and a bacon and egg roll were the cream and the cherry on top. She didn't deserve the guy.

'Oh damn,' she said. 'I was meant to line up at Aldi this morning for the bike accessories special for Tara. What time is it?'

'Err, it's midday.'

'I'm a terrible mother,' she said, picking up the roll and taking a huge bite.

'No, you're not. I could have gone and got it.'

'Ha. We all know I'm the Christmas shopper in this house. Remember the iPhone 8 incident?'

'Of course I do. Between you, Callie and Tara, I'll never be allowed to forget it. So, you reckon all the bike gear will be sold out?'

'It's likely. But I should still go and check it out.'

'Want me to?'

'Honestly, my preference would be to go myself and leave you here with the twins, if you don't mind?'

'Nope. Why would I mind? I get to chill on the couch and play Xbox. When are we expecting Tara home?'

'That's a good question. I can't remember what I organised with Leesa.'

On cue the doorbell rang.

'Speak of the devil,' said Pete, jumping up with far too much energy and enthusiasm. 'I'll get it.'

Mimi eased herself up from the table and followed Pete to the door, carrying the bacon and egg roll with her.

She was relieved to see Leesa looking just as dishevelled as she felt. She was wearing oversized dark sunglasses and when she spotted the bacon and egg roll in Mimi's hand, she almost fell through the door, grabbing at it.

'Give me that,' she said. 'I need a bite.'

Tara weaved through her parents. 'Are the girls awake?' she asked.

'Yep, they're lying on the blanket in the lounge room,' said Pete.

'You don't expect me to give this back, do you?' Leesa asked, taking a bite of the roll.

'Yes, yes I do.' Mimi tried to wrestle it back from her friend before Pete intervened.

'Here, I'll go and cut it in half for you two.'

They followed him into the kitchen and Callie appeared from the stairs. 'Can I smell bacon?' she asked.

'She lives!' said Pete. 'Thought we'd never see you today.'

'Whatever. Mum only just got up. Can I have some bacon?'

'Yeah, check if we have any in the fridge and we'll cook it up. I think these two are going to need more anyway.' Pete nodded his head at Mimi and Leesa, who'd both collapsed at the table.

'What's wrong with them?' Callie asked.

'Hung over,' said Pete.

'Pete! Don't tell her that!'

'Why?' said Callie. 'You think it's going to encourage me to drink? Don't worry. There's no way I want to look as bad as you do right now.'

'Wow, thanks,' said Mimi.

'Silver linings?' Pete asked.

'Solid parenting,' said Leesa, and she fist-bumped her friend.

A little while later, after Leesa had left, Mimi approached Callie's bedroom door tentatively. She'd seemed in a bright enough mood earlier so Mimi wanted to make the most of it. She knocked and waited.

'Yeah?'

Okay, that was a good start. She didn't sound annoyed.

Mimi opened the door and poked her head in. Callie was sitting at her desk on her computer. One of Callie's favourite YouTubers was on the screen in front of her, strumming a guitar and singing mournfully at the camera with big doe eyes.

'I'm going out to try and find that bike basket for Tara. Want to come with me?'

Callie tapped the spacebar to pause the singer, who froze with her mouth in a perfect, round O. 'Weren't you supposed to get that first thing this morning?'

'Yeah, I was. But I kind of stuffed up and slept in.'

Callie gave her a half-smile. 'Oops.' She glanced back at her computer and was quiet for a moment, as though she was contemplating her decision. Mimi held her breath: *please say yes, please.* But as she watched, she saw Callie's shoulders slump. 'No, thanks,' she said. 'I'd rather stay home.'

As Mimi turned away, something occurred to her. She hadn't heard Callie singing for months. Even when she'd given up performing in public, she still couldn't help belting out ballads in the shower or absentmindedly practising scales under her breath as she sat in front of the television. Mimi couldn't believe she'd taken this long to realise the sound of her daughter's beautiful voice had vanished from their home. She supposed the void had seamlessly been filled with newborn wails.

Honestly Mimi, what kind of a mother are you?

Darren

He met Sage out the front of the restaurant and hesitated as he wondered whether to kiss her hello. She was looking gorgeous in a printed knee-length dress with her blonde hair hanging in a long loose plait down her back. Last night he'd ended up taking her back to his place for a damn fine evening of sex, before she'd slipped out in the early hours of the morning without saying goodbye.

He'd wondered if she would even show up tonight, but he had no way of calling to confirm. They hadn't swapped phone numbers at any point. If she hadn't been here, he supposed he would have had to confess to Charlotte and

Steph that there was no girlfriend. But here she was, waiting for him as planned.

Eventually he settled for an awkward kiss on her cheek. 'Thanks again for doing this,' he said.

'It's no big deal,' she said. 'It's a free dinner with a good-looking guy. But then this is it, right? You're not going to expect me to keep playing pretend-girlfriend with your family or the rest of your friends, are you?'

'Absolutely not. It's a one-off so I can save face. But, uh . . . there is one thing I probably should have mentioned about tonight.'

'Ah. Here we go.'

'The reason for dinner . . . it's because my ex and her new girlfriend want me to donate my sperm to them. Might make for some uncomfortable dinner conversation.'

Sage burst out laughing. 'Is that all? I thought you were going to say you were all swingers or tell me your ex is still in love with you or something like that.'

He couldn't stop the look from crossing his face.

'Ah. *Is* she still in love with you?'

'No, not in the slightest.'

Sage nodded. 'I get it now. *You're* still in love with her, aren't you?'

Darren winced. 'Sorry,' he said.

'No need to be,' Sage said brightly. 'I should have realised that was the obvious thing. Why else would it be so important for you to show you've moved on?'

'Okay, cool. You know you're, like, really fucking awesome, right?'

'Yep. Come on. Let's put on a show.' She grabbed his hand and started to pull him towards the entrance, then stopped. 'Wait, am I on board with the sperm-donating thing or am I going to need a bit of convincing?'

He laughed. 'You can play it however you like.'

'Got it.'

He clocked two things when he walked inside and approached the table where Charlotte and Steph were already sitting. First, Steph was clearly surprised to see him with an actual woman by his side, and second, Charlotte wasn't. Something definitely flickered across her face. Could it be she was the tiniest bit jealous? Or was he projecting his own feelings onto her?

The initial looks cleared from both of their faces when he introduced Sage and they sat down, everyone warmly greeting one another with either kissed cheeks or handshakes. Sage broke the ice smoothly by telling the same story she'd told him the previous night about her name and making both Charlotte and Steph laugh.

They ordered drinks and a selection of tapas to share and then Steph got straight down to business.

'So, you're all good with this . . .' she motioned between herself, Charlotte and Darren, 'arrangement?'

Sage grinned. 'Oh look, it's definitely a new one for me! But honestly, things are still so new between Daz and me. And who am I to get in the way of a couple creating life? To be honest, I think it's amazing that he's doing this.'

Darren was impressed with how easily she was slipping into character as his girlfriend. He couldn't have met a more perfect person to play the role.

Charlotte nodded. 'It is, it really is. We're so grateful. And thank you for letting him.'

'Oy,' said Darren. '*He* can speak for himself! No one's letting me do this. I happen to be the one making the decisions.'

'Of course!' said Charlotte. 'Sorry.'

She looked more contrite than he'd expected and he felt bad. He'd only meant that as a joke. He realised that Charlotte was still nervous, and wondered if she thought he might change his mind. And he understood this meant he really couldn't back out – not without crushing her heart, which was something he could never do.

'So, there are some details we need to go over with you,' said Steph. 'Here's the thing, we can't afford to go through a clinic or anything like that – it's too expensive. So, we need to look at doing this another way.'

Darren choked on his drink. 'Holy shit. Do you want me to sleep with you?'

'No!'

Darren let out a breath of air, while Sage helped him out. 'And here I was worrying that things were going to get weird.' They all started laughing.

'Okay, so what we mean is that we need you to provide us with a donation,' said Charlotte, 'and then Steph would be inserting it herself at home . . . you know, turkey-baster style. I mean, not with an *actual* turkey baster. There's this special type of syringe –'

Darren held up his hands. 'Yep, that's all I need to know. No more details required.'

'Well,' said Steph, 'one more thing you need to know is that for this to have the best chance of working, we need to do it at the right time. And the sample needs to be . . . umm . . . fresh. So, we might have to call on you with short notice to create one quickly.'

'All good. It's not like my work isn't flexible.'

'Oh, and the only other thing we need is for you to get a bit of a health check-up. Charlotte already knows your family is pretty clear of any major genetic diseases, but it'd still be good if you could get the all-clear that there's nothing we need to worry about.'

'Too easy. Like I said, work is flexible, so I can get that done.'

'How is the next book going?' Charlotte asked.

He glanced sideways and was relieved to see zero reaction from Sage that he was a writer. Their conversation hadn't extended beyond flirtation the previous night, and they hadn't even asked one another what they did for a living. She really was smooth.

'I'm making progress,' he said.

'Really? That's great. So that means you've stopped letting that horrible review get to you?' Charlotte glanced at Sage. 'Did he tell you about that? the *SMH* absolutely slaughtered him and it really knocked his confidence. He got stuck for ages.' She turned back to Darren without giving Sage a chance to reply. 'So, you're close to delivery now?'

'Pretty much.'

'How exciting. Your agent must be so happy. She always said you were a star.'

'Yeah, for sure.'

'I'm really proud of you. I know this one was giving you so much trouble.' Charlotte gave him a hard look. 'You know you're bloody talented, right? You always have been.'

Darren noticed that both Steph and Sage were being left out of the conversation. Sage was giving all of her attention to her drink, stirring it fairly vigorously.

He decided to shift the conversation away from his writing. 'How's your work going?' he asked, turning to Steph and trying to remember exactly what it was she did for a living. Something to do with project management for a shipping company, he thought vaguely.

'Boring,' she said flatly.

'Ah.'

'What do you do?' Steph asked, turning to Sage.

Darren found himself turning to her with interest himself, trying to guess what the answer might be. He wouldn't be surprised if she said she was an actress, considering how great she was at playing his girlfriend tonight.

'I'm a ballet dancer,' she said.

'Really?' said Darren, unable to stop himself.

Charlotte gave him a funny look. 'Didn't you already know that?'

'Well, I mean, yeah, of course –'

Sage cut in. 'He's surprised because I don't usually describe myself that way. I'm usually too embarrassed to say it straight out because I only recently made company. Same way as I'm guessing Darren would have been embarrassed to tell people he's a writer when he was first published.'

'Yeah, I was definitely like that,' Darren said quickly.

They were interrupted then as two waiters appeared at the table with various dishes of food.

The conversation continued on, punctuated with eating and passing dishes around and comments on how amazing the deep-fried cauliflower was, or suggestions that they order another plate of the meatballs. Throughout, Sage regaled them with stories of training as a dancer throughout her childhood and how she never thought she'd be able to make dancing her career.

When the evening eventually came to an end and Charlotte and Steph had left, Darren took Sage's hand and kissed it. 'You were bloody amazing tonight,' he said.

'Thanks. It was fun, actually . . . getting to be someone else . . . spend a night pretending.'

'Yeah, it was, hey?'

'Anyway, thanks for dinner. Good luck with the whole donation thing.' She pulled her hand out of his and started to turn away.

'Hang on, wait, I don't have your number.'

'So? This was a one-off thing, remember?'

'Yeah, but . . . what if we wanted to . . . you know, maybe catch up again?'

Sage screwed up her face. 'Nah, I don't think that's a good idea. But it was great meeting you.' She started to move away again and then she stopped. 'Hey, listen – before you do this whole donation thing, maybe just make sure you really do think it through, okay? Don't do it for the wrong reasons.'

She left then before Darren could respond, climbing into an Uber that he hadn't even noticed her order. He stayed standing in front of the restaurant, thinking about what she'd just said.

Don't do it for the wrong reasons.

Was that what he was doing? But Sage didn't even know him. And now he was never going to see her again. Which was fine, obviously. She was only ever meant to be a pretend girlfriend for one night.

He was glad Doggo would be waiting for him at home.

10

Sunday 13 December

Jill

Jill smiled down at the small girl next to her in the lift. The little girl grinned up at her and, almost immediately, her mother yanked on her hand, pulling her in close. The girl's face dropped and Jill was taken aback. She tried to catch the mother's eye, hoping to let her know she wasn't a threat and that she was only trying to be friendly, but the mother wouldn't look her way. A moment later, the lift doors opened and the woman and her daughter stepped out and headed down the hall. Jill followed behind and then passed them to reach Tony and Andrea's apartment.

She knocked and after a few seconds Andrea opened the door. 'Jill! I didn't know you were coming by. We were just . . .'

Tony appeared behind her with keys in hand and Jill realised they were heading out. How could she have been so stupid to think she could just drop by for a cup of tea and expect them to have nothing on?

'Sorry,' Jill began, 'I shouldn't have –'

'No, this is perfect!' Andrea said. 'We're going out for a late brunch. You can join us.'

Jill glanced at Tony, wondering if he was as enthusiastic about this idea as Andrea was. But he didn't look annoyed.

'How did you get through the security door downstairs, Mum?'

'Oh, someone else was coming in at the same time. A mother and her little girl next door.' As she said it, she realised who they must be. The girl that Andrea had been worrying about. Perhaps that explained the mother's attitude in the lift. Was she simply unfriendly to everyone?

'Heather and Violet,' said Andrea. She looked as though she wanted to say something else, but Jill saw her glance sideways at Tony and then smile brightly. 'Are you happy to go straight back out again?'

'Of course,' said Jill. 'But I don't want to impose. You don't have to have me along.'

'Don't be ridiculous,' said Andrea.

The three of them walked together to a nearby cafe with waterfront views. It was the type of place Jill would only think to book for a special occasion, but Tony mentioned they went there every weekend for brunch. She had to admit, it was a great spot; there was a pleasant breeze off the water that took the sting out of the sun's hot rays.

Jill noticed that Andrea had been quieter than usual on the walk. She wondered if there was something bothering her.

'How's school?' she asked when they were sitting down. 'I always found the kids got a little out of sorts in those last few weeks before the end of the year.'

Andrea nodded. 'Oh yeah, they definitely lose their concentration. Actually, Tony's offered to come in tomorrow and chat to my senior English class about writing for that exact reason. I needed something different to keep them occupied.'

'Really?' Jill glanced across at Tony. 'You should ask Pete for some tips. He's done a few talks to schoolkids.'

'Pete talks to primary schoolkids,' Tony said. 'I'll be right.'

'Yes, but he could still help you out. He's been doing it for such a long time now and he's developed a great presentation. Why not give him a call?'

It was so brief that Jill almost missed it, but before responding, an ugly scowl crossed Tony's face. 'I said I'll be fine.'

Jill kept her voice pleasant. 'I'm sure you will,' she agreed.

She thought about Pete's comment last week, when he'd casually mentioned that Tony had always been the favourite. It was a shame he wasn't here to see this exchange. She wouldn't be surprised if right now Tony made the opposite claim. Since revealing that he'd written a novel, Tony often seemed defensive about the potential comparison between himself and his brothers. Should she have somehow picked up on his interest in writing when he was younger? Had she fostered a love of English in Pete and Darren but completely missed it in Tony?

She was tired of having these constant self-doubts about her sons. She'd thought about Pete's comment a lot over the past week. Eventually she'd come to a conclusion about why Pete thought she'd favoured Tony. It wasn't favouritism that he'd picked up on. It was over-protectiveness. As her eldest child, she'd treated him differently, worried about him more. She'd been anxious about letting go of the apron strings.

But she'd had her reasons.

Andrea

Tony turned the page, shook out the newspaper, then folded it over and smoothed it out. Andrea knew it was his habit to read the paper at brunch, but she'd still been surprised to see him open it up while Jill was with them. It seemed a little rude. They'd finished eating and Tony had grabbed the paper off the stand by the counter after he'd ordered himself a second long black.

Andrea felt guilty. Clearly Jill had come to see them because she was in need of company. Andrea couldn't imagine what it would be like to lose your life-long partner in such tragic circumstances. She often wondered if they ought to talk about Frank more. Of course, Andrea had only known him for a relatively short time in the scheme of things, but during that time she'd grown to really enjoy his company. He was generous and welcoming. The kind of father-in-law anyone would love to have. The kind of *father* she would have loved. She wished she'd had more time with him. But she was never sure if bringing him up was the right thing to do or not. Would it upset Jill or Tony if she casually started chatting about him?

Either way, Andrea didn't feel like they'd been the best company throughout brunch today. Her own mind had kept wandering to her conversation with Kelly last night.

Jill seemed to take Tony reading the paper as her cue

to depart, and she started reaching for her handbag. 'I might leave you two to it. I've interrupted enough of your time.'

'You don't have to go,' said Andrea. 'Are you sure you don't want a refill of tea?'

'No, I'm fine. I really should get on with my day anyway.'

Tony put down his paper. 'It was good to see you, Mum. I'm glad you dropped by.'

Jill reached into her bag and pulled out her purse. 'How about this one is on me?' she said.

'Absolutely not,' said Tony. 'We've got this.'

Andrea was relieved that Tony was redeeming himself. She stood up with Jill. 'I'll walk you back to your car,' she said. 'Leave Tony to have his coffee.'

They walked back towards the apartment block in silence, until Andrea said carefully, 'Jill, how are you, really? I know it must be so hard with the anniversary coming up. I'm sorry we weren't better company for you just now.'

Jill looked sideways at Andrea. 'You're very kind,' she said, 'but I'm okay. You two were lovely company.'

Andrea scoffed. 'No, we weren't. I was distracted and Tony read the bloody paper! I often want to talk with you about Frank . . . I want to tell you that I miss him. I know I didn't know him very long, but I really did think he was a wonderful man. I'm never sure if I should . . .'

Jill stopped, turned and pulled Andrea into a quick but tight hug. 'Thank you,' she said. When she stepped back, her eyes were glassy. 'You know those boxes I needed put up into the roof?'

Andrea nodded.

'I'd finally packed up some of Frank's things, but I couldn't bring myself to give them away. Isn't that silly? Putting them away as though he might come back and need them again, one day. I feel like a fool.'

'Jill, I would never call you a fool. I think that's absolutely understandable. You should keep Frank's things for as long as you want.'

They started walking again. 'How about you?' said Jill. 'What was keeping you distracted today?'

Andrea pushed her hands into her back pockets and looked away, thinking. Next thing, the words had tumbled out before she could stop herself. 'Do you think Tony would be likely to change his mind about having kids?'

The shock on Jill's face was evident, and then it immediately turned to sympathy. 'I'd wondered who was behind the decision to stay child-free.'

Now it was Andrea's turn to be surprised. 'He's never spoken about it with you?'

'No. I guess I tried to ask . . . back when you two first met and it looked like you were becoming serious. But he rebuffed me. And then it seemed like it was a decision you were both happy with.' She paused. When she spoke again, her voice was kind. 'Have you changed your mind?'

'I don't even know,' said Andrea. 'Sorry, I shouldn't be asking you about this. I'm putting you in a difficult position.'

'You're not,' said Jill. 'I'm glad you feel like you can talk to me. I know you don't have a very . . . close relationship with your mother.'

Andrea laughed. 'That's putting it mildly.'

They reached Jill's car, parked in one of the outdoor visitor spots, and stood next to it.

'I wish I could give you an answer about Tony,' said Jill, 'but I don't know what's behind his decision not to have children. All I can say is, talk to him. If you're no longer sure about what you want, then it's important to talk it through. You don't want to be left with regrets. Trust me.'

'I know,' said Andrea. 'I'm just not sure how I'm going to even bring it up. I think it's going to really blindside him.'

Andrea looked across the carpark and saw someone familiar. 'Actually, Jill, do you mind if we return to this another time? I've just seen someone I want to catch.'

Jill nodded. 'Of course.'

They said their goodbyes and Andrea saw Jill into the car before turning and hurrying after the man she'd seen. It was Violet's driver and he was alone. She wanted to ask at least one more person about Violet's wellbeing before she really backed off, as per her promise to Tony.

'Excuse me,' Andrea called out as she got closer.

He turned around and smiled warmly at her. 'Help you?' he asked.

'Umm, I hope so. This might sound a little weird, but I know you work for Heather and I was wondering . . .'

The guy's expression changed and he laughed. 'Work for Heather?' he said. 'No, not exactly.'

'Oh. Sorry. I thought . . . I thought you were her driver.'

'Is that what she calls me?' His eyes went skyward. 'For the record,' he said, 'I'm a firefighter, not a chauffeur. Not that there's anything wrong with being a chauffeur. I don't mean to sound elitist or something.'

Andrea was thoroughly confused. He wasn't Heather's chauffeur yet he drove Violet to and from school every day. Why would he do that? Then her eyes widened. 'Are you Violet's father?' she asked.

'Ah, I'm not . . . no . . . but it's complicated,' he said. 'Sorry,' he added, 'do you mind telling me why you're . . .'

Andrea realised she was questioning the man with no explanation at all.

'No, I'm sorry! I shouldn't have just started quizzing you. I'm Heather's neighbour. I've sort of got to know Violet and I was hoping to ask if you . . .' Andrea broke off, embarrassed. This was harder now that there was this weird ambiguity around his relationship with Heather and Violet. But he was standing there waiting, so she was going to have to spit it out.

'If you ever had any . . . concerns about Violet,' she finished.

'Ah,' he said. 'That depends. Do you have a couple of hours to spare?' He glanced down at his watch. 'Actually, I don't have time to spare right now myself. I'm going to be late for my shift. Listen, could I get your number and take this up with you again another time?'

'Yeah, of course. My name's Andrea, by the way.'

'Shaun,' he replied, offering her his hand.

She noticed he had a good, strong handshake without squeezing too hard. The combination of his warm handshake and friendly manner put Andrea right at ease.

They exchanged phone numbers and before turning away he looked her right in the eyes. 'I'm glad someone else is there for Violet. I reckon she needs lots of people on her side. Thank you.'

II

Monday 14 December

Darren

'Look at *you*!' said Darren, crouching down to welcome Doggo as the groomer brought him out from the back. 'Aren't you a handsome fella? Aren't you a good-looking doggo?'

The dog's matted fur had all been clipped away and his coat now looked shiny and new. The groomer had also left him with a fluffy ball at the end of his tail, which was perhaps a bit of an odd choice considering he wasn't a poodle, but Doggo managed to pull it off.

The woman above him cleared her throat and Darren stopped fussing over the dog and stood up. 'Sorry, I didn't realise how he'd look. He's like a completely different dog.'

'Yes, well, maybe don't leave it so long next time before you get him groomed.'

Darren clenched his jaw, about to defend himself to the judgemental groomer, but before he could a younger woman sprang up from behind the counter.

'Claudia! He didn't! This is the guy who found a stray and *took him in.*'

Claudia blushed. 'Oh, right. Sorry. I shouldn't have assumed.'

'All good,' said Darren. He paused then added a little stiffly, 'You did a great job with him.'

It wasn't until he was on his way out of the grooming place that he remembered he'd been planning on dropping into the medical centre for the health check-up that Charlotte and Steph wanted him to have. He'd meant to do it while Doggo was being groomed but instead he'd taken a long walk, convincing himself that the walk would clear his mind. That ideas for his book would fall into his lap. They hadn't.

Never mind, he'd have to find another time for the check-up. Charlotte and Steph had only just asked him on the weekend, surely they wouldn't be calling him for a donation right away, would they?

Anyway, the main thing was that Doggo had been taken care of. He would have been uncomfortable under all that matted fur. It was already a hot summer. He wasn't sure if it was his imagination, but it seemed like there was a difference in the way the dog was walking now, more pride in his trot, whereas before he'd seemed kind of mopey as he walked along.

'I know exactly how you feel,' Darren said, looking down at him. 'I'm the same after I get my hair cut. You own that swagger, buddy.'

He looked up in time to see an older woman staring at him, a bemused look on her face as she passed. He nodded politely at her, not the least bit embarrassed to be caught chatting with a dog as he walked along.

'What should we do today, Doggo? Visit the park?' His phone started vibrating in his pocket and he pulled it out to see Tony's name on the screen. Unusual. He and

Tony got along well enough when the family got together, but with Darren and Pete being the closer brothers, Tony didn't often call out of the blue.

'What's up, mate?' Darren said as he stopped under the shade of a tree and answered the call.'

'Quick favour. I'm on my way to talk to Andrea's class about writing. You've done these things in the past, haven't you?'

'Yep, a couple.'

'Have you got some notes you can shoot through to my email for me? I just need something to get me started.'

'Yeah, I should have some stuff saved. Not a full speech, just a few dot points.'

'That's fine, perfect.'

'Okay, I'll send it through to you now.'

'Thanks, appreciate it.'

Darren hung up and searched through his Dropbox account on his phone. He found a document that should give Tony a few basic pointers and emailed it through. It wasn't often that Tony asked for help with anything. He generally preferred to come across as completely self-sufficient. It was nice to feel needed by his eldest brother for a change.

Right, what to do now? He could drop by to Pete's place. Although Pete would only hassle him about the fact that he should be writing. He mentally ran through a list of his mates, wondering if any of them might be available to catch up. But it was a weekday – they'd all be working. Sometimes Jono or Raj could duck out and catch up for lunch, but they needed notice.

He found himself wishing he could show Doggo's haircut to Sage. She'd been pretty taken with the dog when she'd come back to his place on Friday for their one-night stand. She'd be impressed with how good he looked now. But then on Saturday night after dinner, she'd vanished into that Uber without a second glance. He knew she didn't want anything serious, but it still would have been nice if they could have hooked up one more time. Now there was no way he could contact her.

He found himself heading towards The Oaks, the pub where he'd met Sage, telling himself it wasn't because he was hoping to run into her again, but more because he wanted a cold beer, and also wanted to avoid going home to stare at a blank document on his laptop.

He remembered his conversation with Pete about using a dog to pick up women. But he wasn't really that much in the mood for talking to strangers.

'Let's hope The Oaks welcomes dogs,' he said to his companion as they walked.

Thankfully The Oaks was very welcoming to dogs – provided they sat outside. Doggo had settled himself on the ground in the shade of Darren's table, his tongue hanging out as he panted until someone from the bar brought out a dish of cold water for him along with Darren's Corona.

He'd only been there about five minutes when a voice from behind him exclaimed, 'Darren?'

He swung around, grinning. It wasn't Sage though, it was Claudia, the groomer he'd just picked Doggo up from. The one who'd prejudged him.

'Sorry, it is Darren, isn't it?' she asked.

'Yeah, hi.'

'Listen, I wanted to apologise again about earlier. I really shouldn't have jumped to conclusions. It's lovely what you've done, taking in a stray instead of just handing him into the pound. I really admire that.'

Darren shrugged. 'It's really no big deal.'

'No, no, it is. I know for a fact the local pound is at capacity at the moment. If he'd ended up there, you just don't know what might have happened to him. It's so hard to get people to adopt older dogs.'

'Thank you,' he said.

'Can I ask you a question? How come you haven't named him yet? Jane at work told me "Doggo" is just his nickname.'

Darren dropped his eyes, slightly embarrassed. 'Well ... I'm worried that his original owners might still turn up and –'

'And you don't want to have named him and made him yours and then have to give him up?'

'Yeah, I guess so.'

'That's actually really sweet.'

'Or really soft,' he said.

'Nope. Sweet,' she said firmly. She went to move away from his table but then she stopped. 'I don't suppose I could join you for a few minutes, could I? Jane's supposed to be meeting me here but she got held up.'

Darren smiled. He supposed she'd more than made up for her earlier gaffe. And now that he was looking at her through different eyes, she was pretty hot.

'Sure,' he said.

'Callie! Callie! Slow down.' Andrea had to run to catch up with her niece. It had been an entire week since she'd missed her at the bus stop and she'd been feeling guilty about her promise to Mimi. So it was a relief to spot her on her way towards the library this afternoon.

Callie finally swung around to face her as she caught up with her at the library entrance.

'Oh hi, Aunty Andrea. Sorry, I didn't hear you.'

Andrea was still catching her breath. She was perplexed; there was no way Callie hadn't heard her, she'd shouted from a short distance and the quadrangle was clear and quiet, with most of the kids gone for the day now the last bell had rung. On top of that, there was a dullness to Callie's voice that was unusual. Maybe Mimi was right to be concerned.

'I feel like I haven't seen you around school in ages. How are things going?'

'Fine. But I'm running late for my study group.' She nodded towards the library door.

Study group? That seemed unusual; it was almost the end of term.

'Oh! Sorry. I don't want to keep you,' Andrea said, trying to hide her disbelief. 'But can we catch up some time, Callie? Maybe have a coffee together after school one afternoon? Like I said, it's been ages. I miss having you in my classes.'

Callie had been keeping her eyes on the ground, but now she looked up and stared Andrea straight in the eyes.

When she spoke, her voice had turned icy. 'Actually, I'd rather not, thanks.'

Then she turned and pushed her way through the library doors.

Andrea was left staring at the closed door. What the hell was that? She'd always felt sort of proud of her relationship with Callie, she made her feel like the cool aunt. Even at high school, where it would have been perfectly reasonable for Callie to ignore her out of embarrassment at being related to one of the teachers. She'd often told Andrea that she *was* one of the coolest teachers at school. One of the teachers that most students were happy to have. *They like the way you talk to them*, Callie had said. *And the way you actually listen. Not all teachers do that, some of them think you have nothing worthwhile to say.* Why would that suddenly change now? Did she have a new group of friends who thought it was uncool for her to be friendly with her aunt? Although if that was the case, why would she seem so angry with her? None of her friends were around right now to witness the interaction.

Andrea waited for a moment and then headed into the library. She scanned the room. As she suspected, there were no study groups. And Callie was gone. She must have walked straight through the library and out the side entrance.

Andrea was definitely going to have to try to chat with Callie again another time. See if she could get her to tell her what was wrong, find out if Andrea had done something to upset her.

At least Tony's talk with the class had gone really well today. She'd expected him to simply tell them a bit about who he was, how he'd become a writer, that sort of thing, and then they could ask questions. Instead he'd come in really well prepared with discussion points that sparked all sorts of interesting debates and intelligent conversation among the class. He had them talking about Roland Barthes' theory of the Death of the Author, debating books versus movies, and he'd taught them about intertextuality. The kids were completely engaged, and while you could tell they didn't all want to show it, they were also impressed by Tony's success.

Tony himself had also seemed pleasantly surprised with how well it had all gone. 'Maybe I should do more of these talks,' he'd said as he was leaving and then he'd pulled her in close for a deep kiss on the lips, which was more than a little awkward in front of her students. Several of them had whooped and whistled, others had groaned in disgust or made charming vomiting noises. When she'd broken away from him, embarrassed, he'd laughed like he knew exactly what he was doing. 'Sorry, Mrs Robinson,' he'd whispered, waggling his eyebrows at her. 'Oh, ha ha,' she'd replied.

He'd also suggested they go out somewhere special for dinner tonight, so it was clear he was on a bit of a high. Andrea had agreed, but she was hoping to have enough time to duck in and check on Violet this afternoon before they went out. Even though she'd promised Tony she would pull back, having Shaun suggest that Violet needed people to look out for her had bolstered her. Shaun hadn't contacted her yet, but she was hoping to hear from him soon. He'd seemed so caring and genuine when he'd told her he was glad she was looking out for Violet, it had made her feel validated. And she was curious to find out the full story of his connection to Heather and Violet.

Mimi

'Hey Mum, can I ask you something?'

Mimi put the book she'd been reading face down on the coffee table and turned to look at Callie. She tried hard to keep her voice steady as she replied. If Callie was finally ready to talk, she didn't want to jeopardise it by sounding too eager. 'Of course, you can ask me anything.'

'Could you please take me out for a driving lesson? I want to make sure I can take the test for my green Ps as soon as I turn seventeen, like the second it happens.'

Oh. It was nothing to do with having a chat after all.

'I thought you only liked it when Dad took you out,' Mimi said cautiously.

'Whatever, if you don't want to take me, you don't have to.'

God, that girl could turn in an instant lately. Mimi scrambled to reassure her. 'What? No! That's not what I was saying. I was surprised, that's all. Come on, grab your stuff. Let's do it.'

'Okay . . . Thanks, Mum.' Callie's voice was still flat despite Mimi having agreed to take her out. Maybe they would have a chance to chat in the car.

Callie headed off to put on her shoes and it was only as Mimi stood up that she noticed the half-empty glass of wine on the coffee table next to the book she'd put down. Dammit. She'd completely forgotten that she'd just been enjoying a few vinos while she was reading. Even though she wasn't the one driving, she was still supposed to be under 0.05 as the instructor. How many had she had? Too many to take Callie out?

Callie reappeared with her shoes on, keys jangling in her hand. 'Ready to go?' she asked.

Mimi hesitated, searching for an excuse. But if she told her the truth, that she'd forgotten she'd had a few drinks and couldn't do it after all, Callie would be so disappointed. And lately she could lose her temper at the smallest of things. Mimi didn't want to set her off.

Maybe it was fine. Surely, she'd only had one or two, hadn't she?

'Yep,' she said. 'Ready to go.'

Andrea

A two-minute look-in just to be sure and then she'd be able to relax at dinner tonight. Andrea held still at the door, trying to listen and judge whether or not Heather was home. After a few seconds of listening though, she couldn't be certain so she knocked and then stood back to wait. A moment later, the door swung inwards and she saw a beaming Heather wearing a blue and white checked apron with flour down the front, a spatula in her hand.

Heather's expression darkened when she saw who it was. 'Can I help you?' she asked, her voice clipped.

Violet appeared behind her mother, a look of pure glee on her face, a smear of chocolate icing on her cheek. 'Hi, Andrea!' she exclaimed.

'Oh hi. Are you . . . doing some baking?'

'You came by to ask if I'm baking?' said Heather, moving her body just slightly so that it was clear she was blocking Violet from stepping around her and getting any closer to Andrea.

'What? Oh . . . uh, no. I came by to . . . ask if I could borrow a cup of sugar.' It was the first thing that came to mind and even though Heather would be able to see through it – a cup of sugar, what a bloody cliché – it was the best she could do. If she admitted she was there to check up on Violet, Heather would probably explode. Maybe it would even ruin the clearly happy moment mother and daughter were finally sharing for once. She should never have knocked. Tony was right when he said she needed to stay out of it.

'But I can see you're busy so don't worry about the sugar,' Andrea said, backing away from the door.

'Okay, great,' Heather said.

Andrea saw two things as the door shut in her face. A look of smug superiority on Heather's face and a look of sad confusion on Violet's.

Mimi

When she saw the red and blue lights in the distance, her stomach plummeted. An RBT set up in the precise point where they often were on a Friday evening or sometimes a Saturday morning, catching people who'd had too much the night before and didn't realise it was still in their system. Would they breath-test both of them? Or just Callie as the driver? What were they doing there on a Monday night? Who was out drinking on a Monday? *I suppose I was*, she thought, feeling angry with herself.

'Stay calm,' she murmured.

'I *am* calm,' Callie snapped. 'I know how an RBT works.'

Mimi didn't bother to explain that she'd been talking to herself. If only Callie had listened to her when she'd tried to talk her into turning off the Pacific Highway back at Greenwich Road. 'Let's do the circuit down near River-view,' she'd suggested.

'No way, I've done that heaps. I need more practice on main roads,' Callie had argued.

And now here they were, about to get breath-tested. Mimi was mortified at the thought of being caught out teaching her teenage daughter to drive with alcohol in her system. But still, would anything register? One or two glasses, she was sure she couldn't have had more than that.

Three cars in a row in front of them were waved in for testing. And then it happened. The police officer out on the road stepped back and waved them on by with a slight nod of his head. Mimi could have kissed him. Although then he might have smelled the wine on her breath. The relief was so palpable she was certain Callie was going to be able to sense it from her.

Okay, she thought to herself as they drove by, a good ten kilometres under the speed limit, *this is your turning point, Mimi. Stop drinking so much on a week night so that nothing like this ever happens again.*

Although, at the same time, she was still considering the possibility that had she been tested she would have been perfectly fine. Under the limit. After all, she *felt* fine. It was just that annoying niggling feeling of not knowing exactly how much she'd had. So, maybe she didn't need to stop drinking altogether during the week; after all, she did still need that little bit of relaxation with a glass of wine in the evening, and what was so wrong with that? Instead, what she needed to do was keep better track of it, so that next time Callie asked her to take her out, she would know with certainty how much she'd had.

'Mum, are you even listening to me right now?'

Oops, Callie had been talking and she'd been letting the drone of her daughter's voice wash over her while she indulged in her own thoughts. So much for her plan to connect with Callie as they drove. Instead she was completely ignoring her. What a fantastic mother she was.

'Sorry, honey, what did you say?'

'I said I'm going to take a right up ahead so I can do that set of roundabouts. I have to get used to indicating when I'm exiting the roundabout. You know both you and Dad never do it.'

'Yes well, that's because it's stupid and pointless.'

'Mum! It's the law!'

'That doesn't make it a good idea.'

'*Mum!*'

'Sorry, sorry. Yes, you're right, I should try and start doing it myself. Okay, hop into the right lane so you're ready to turn.'

Callie indicated, checked her side mirror, checked her blind spot and then glided smoothly across. Mimi found herself wondering if Callie may actually be a better driver than her already. She was definitely better than Mimi was at her age. She'd failed her test four times. And whenever she changed lanes, she would always panic that another car was going to appear out of nowhere so she'd wrench the steering wheel and jerk the car across, usually swerving into oncoming traffic and then having to immediately wrench the wheel back the other way to straighten up. In the worst of her four failed tests, the instructor's head had banged against the passenger window on one of the jerky lane changes. 'Let's call it a day, shall we?' she'd suggested in a slightly strained voice.

They turned off the Pacific Highway and approached the first of the six roundabouts stretched out ahead of them.

'Okay, slow up a little,' said Mimi, 'so you can make sure your right side is clear as you enter the roundabout.'

'It's fine, I can already see it's clear.'

Mimi found herself pressing her foot against an imaginary brake on the floor as they sailed through the roundabout. Admittedly, it was clear and Callie was still keeping the car smooth and within the lane, while simultaneously remembering to flick on the indicator as they exited. But Mimi still thought they could have slowed down a bit more.

'You know I'm the one who's meant to be instructing you, right?'

'Yeah, but I know what I'm doing. Like I said, I just need to make sure I've clocked up the right number of hours.'

She approached the second roundabout at the same speed and flew through it yet again.

'Callie, you can still take my advice. I know you've got really good at looking ahead and being aware of what cars are around. But there are people around here who sometimes fly out of the side streets. If you're going a little slower, then you can be ready if someone does that to you.'

'Seriously, I'm fine, I know what I'm doing.'

Mimi threw up her hands in frustration. 'So, what am I here for then? Just to be a fully licensed body in the car?'

'Exactly!' Callie seemed to have missed the sarcasm in her mother's voice.

They were heading for the third roundabout and Mimi could see that Callie's smooth run thus far was giving her a false sense of overconfidence. This time they really were going a little too fast.

'Callie,' she said, her voice tightening, 'slow down, please. I'm serious. You're going to take this bend too fast.'

'I'm not!'

'You *are*. Slow down.'

They were about to enter the roundabout when Mimi saw it. A car flying into the roundabout from the right, just as she had feared. Callie realised her mistake too late and wasn't going to react in time. Mimi grabbed the hand brake and wrenched it up. The wheels locked up and they skidded to a hard stop, the back of the car kicking out to the left. The other car continued on through the roundabout and Callie and Mimi sat still, breathing hard.

'Mum,' she began, 'I'm so –'

'Out,' Mimi said. 'Out of the car. I'm driving home.'

Callie didn't say another word. She scurried out and the two of them swapped seats. Then they drove quietly towards home. Five minutes from their street, Mimi pulled over. 'Out,' she said again.

'What? Are you making me walk home?'

'No. I'm putting you back in the driver's seat. You need

to get back on the horse. But, one rule – you bloody well listen to me from now on, got it?'

Mimi might not have wanted to antagonise her daughter, but she also wasn't going to pull any punches when it came to her safety.

Callie nodded. 'Okay, I will. Mum?'

'Yes?'

'I'm really sorry.'

Mimi paused for a moment, trying to plan the best thing to say. She was relieved that Callie wasn't blowing up at her and she wanted to take advantage of her being more reasonable for a change.

'I am too. I should have been taking you out more often instead of letting Dad do it all the time. And I shouldn't have relaxed and acted like you were already an experienced driver. I think because you really are so much better than I was at your age, I wasn't teaching you the way I should have been. But the thing is, we all make mistakes and I don't want your mistake to make you feel like you can't do this, because you can and you *are* good. You just need to be a little more cautious still.'

Callie smiled. 'Thanks, Mum.' She leaned across the seat and hugged Mimi, and Mimi was so surprised she almost didn't hug her back. But then she wrapped her arms around her daughter and squeezed her tightly. It felt like she had the old Callie back, so she whispered in her ear, 'I'm always here for you. You know that, right? Anything you need.'

She felt Callie's upper body lift as though she was taking in a breath to speak, but then she pulled out of the embrace and turned away. 'I know,' she said softly.

Callie absentmindedly scratched hard at a spot on her thigh and Mimi placed one hand over the top of hers to still her. 'I've noticed you scratching a bit lately, is your eczema coming back?'

'No,' said Callie. 'It's nothing.'

Then Callie was jumping out of the car, ready to take the driver's seat again, and Mimi couldn't help but feel like she was still losing her.

Darren

He and Claudia had been drinking together now for a couple of hours and there was still no sign of her colleague, Jane, but it seemed Claudia wasn't concerned. He wondered if she might have surreptitiously texted her and told her not to come.

If so, that meant it had turned out to be true. Dogs were great wing-men when it came to picking up women. Or wing-canines, he figured it should be. He just hadn't expected it to be the dog's actual groomer that he'd be picking up. He also hadn't expected to be drinking this much on a Monday. He'd initially assumed that Claudia was only here on her break and that she'd be headed back to work at some point. But she'd explained that it was the end of her shift and she had nowhere she had to be. She'd given him one of *those* looks when she'd said it.

She wasn't coming on quite as strong and straightforward as Sage had the night he'd met her, but it was still clear that she was interested in taking things further. What was going on with him lately? He'd had zero luck meeting women since Charlotte, and now, two women in the space of a week had hit on him.

The question was, did he want to take Claudia home? Especially when a part of his mind was still drifting off every now and then towards Sage.

This was ridiculous. Sage had been clear about what she wanted, or more specifically, what she didn't want. Which meant he needed to put her out of his mind.

He looked at Claudia. 'Do you want to get out of here?' he asked.

'Love to.'

Christmas Eve

Darren turned back to Jill. Had she taken such a hard knock that she'd lost her memory? Why had she told the other guy that Frank had been in the car with her? Maybe it was the initial shock and her mind would clear in a minute. She lifted her chin and Darren reached in to steady her. 'Take it easy, Mum. Everything's going to be okay.'

'My fault,' she mumbled.

'Don't worry about that right now. It doesn't matter whose fault the accident was.'

'No . . . not the accident . . . the email . . .'

Jesus, she really was confused, he had no idea what she was on about. He could still hear the man on the phone behind him; he was describing Jill's injuries.

'An older woman, she definitely hit her head. No, she's awake.' Then Darren heard him say, 'I don't know about anyone else, I haven't even made it over to any of the other cars yet.'

Darren had been so focused on his mother that he hadn't thought about the fact that there were other people who might need his help.

He took a small step back from his mum's Volvo and looked around at the surrounding carnage.

His eyes widened.

12

Tuesday 15 December

Andrea

There was no way she could ignore the raised voices out in the hall. And Heather's voice was unmistakable. 'Oh my God,' she was squealing, 'you are *such* a slut.'

It didn't sound like it was being said in anger though, there was more of a playful tone to her voice. But she was loud. And it was late. Into the early hours of Tuesday morning already. Tony was in bed, fast asleep. But Andrea had stayed up, unable to sleep. She was sensing a migraine might be coming on and she'd been sitting out in the dark living room, drinking herbal tea and trying to relax.

Dinner had been . . . interesting.

Tony had been in such a great mood after the talk with the English class. They'd gone out to an expensive restaurant at Cockle Bay Wharf where he'd suggested they do the seven-course degustation menu with matching wines. Quite the celebration for a Monday night. Andrea had managed the pre-dinner visit up the hall to Heather's place without Tony noticing that she was attempting to interfere again and she had resolved to keep a more distant eye on Heather and Violet. The woman was baking with her daughter. She couldn't be all bad, could she? And if

Shaun was really that worried, he'd have contacted her quite quickly, wouldn't he?

The problem came when she decided to finally take both Kelly *and* Jill's advice and talk with Tony over dinner about the new feelings she'd been having around parenthood.

'I know we closed the door on this a long time ago . . . but can we maybe revisit the idea of having a child?' she'd blurted out over the fifth course.

Tony had frozen with his fork halfway to his mouth; she'd seen his Adam's apple jerk as he swallowed. 'Wow, this is pretty far out of the blue.'

'I know, I know, I'm sorry. I'm not saying this is something I even necessarily want, I'm only saying that I want to talk about it again.'

'Okay,' he'd said, nodding. Then he'd given her a piercing look. 'I know where this is coming from.'

'You do?'

'Yes. This is because you've been getting so carried away playing mum to Violet and now it's made you broody.'

Andrea had flinched at his tone. At his words. He was being nasty. He'd never been nasty to her like that before. And this was the second time he'd called her involvement with Violet 'playing mum'. There was something so patronising about the way he said that.

She'd taken a long sip of her wine. 'Umm, no actually,' she said. 'That's not what this is about.'

'All right, what is it about?'

'You know what? Maybe we should forget I said anything.'

And in a flash his face changed and he'd reached across the table to take her hand. 'I'm really sorry. I shouldn't

187

have said that. I think I was taken aback and I lashed out. That was immature of me.'

Andrea chewed on the inside of her cheek. For a moment, she wanted to tell him to shove his apology. But then she softened at the genuine guilt in his eyes. 'Apology accepted. And just so you know, this isn't about Violet. I know it might seem like I'm being mothering towards her, but I'm really not. I simply want to look out for the kid.' Andrea hesitated. 'The same way I wish someone had looked out for me.'

Tony was still holding her hand and now he squeezed it. 'I can't believe I've never thought about it that way. I'm an idiot.'

'You're not an idiot. I should have opened up more. Obviously I have all these unresolved feelings inside, which isn't healthy. The truth is, I think that's why I told you I didn't want kids when we first met. Because of my mum. Because I was scared that . . .'

'That you'd turn out like her?'

Andrea nodded and tears threatened again, but she bit down hard on her lip. She wasn't usually such a teary person and crying in front of Kelly the other night had been bad enough. This wasn't the type of restaurant you started blubbering in.

'For the record, you wouldn't,' said Tony. 'I know you've only told me bits and pieces about your mum. You've always hated talking about her. But even from that, I can tell that the two of you are worlds apart. You're your own person. An incredible teacher, a beautiful aunt, an amazing wife.'

He stopped and Andrea saw the hesitant look in his

eyes. He was finally saying all the things she'd wished he would say. But there was something else coming.

She managed a small smile. 'Why do I feel like there's about to be a "but"?'

He let out a long, slow puff of air. 'I don't want there to be a "but", I really don't. It's just that . . . as much as I know you would be a wonderful mother, I don't know if I could get there. I can't explain why, I just never pictured myself as a father.'

'I understand. It's unfair of me to ask this of you – especially when we'd already made the decision. Although . . . can I ask . . . when *did* we make the decision? I mean, I know when we got together we thought probably not. But at what stage did it become definitive for us?'

Tony shrugged. 'I don't know, I just thought we'd basically been on the same page since day one. And not to sound harsh, but we're not exactly spring chickens. I figured as time went on, we were happy with things staying the way they are. Are you not happy anymore?'

Andrea was thrown by the question . . . and even more so when the answer didn't come instantly. Was she unhappy? She thought about all the ways Tony seemed to have changed since they'd married. About his cruel snipe a moment ago about her 'playing mum'.

But then she thought about the way he'd asked her all the right questions just now. The exact things she'd been desperate for him to ask. Besides, marriage wasn't meant to be easy, was it? A good relationship was something you worked at. So what was her answer?

'No,' she said, 'it's not that. I'm still happy. I just wasn't sure if I'd made the wrong choice about kids. Or made the right choice but for the wrong reasons. That's all. But I still want to be with you.'

Tony smiled. 'How about this? I know we don't have long left if we *were* to have kids, but could you give me a bit of time to think things through? Maybe . . . I don't know, I'm not saying yes . . . but maybe I could work through some feelings. See if I can find a way to come around to the idea of me as a dad. Can we leave it for a short while and revisit again? See how both of us feel in a few months?'

'Of course. That's completely fair.'

Throughout the rest of dinner, they turned to lighter subjects. Tony was a little more subdued than he'd been after his successful chat to the high school students, but generally speaking, things were comfortable enough between them.

After Tony had gone to bed and she'd felt those tell-tale signs of a migraine coming on, Andrea had sat and replayed the conversation from dinner. It wasn't a yes and it wasn't a no. But that was okay, because she wasn't certain if she wanted to change her mind about having children anyway. It was probably the best possible outcome. Time for both of them to keep thinking. And most importantly, she'd discovered that the door wasn't completely closed. She wondered if she should have also taken the opportunity to talk about their sex-life. Or more specifically, their lack of a sex-life. But one step at a time. It might have been a bit much to bring it all up at once.

Now though, all thoughts of tonight's talk were driven from her mind as she stood up and went to the front door, which she opened just enough to peek out and look down the hall.

'No, you're a slut! You're the sluttiest of all of us,' another woman was shouting. Heather was half-stumbling down the hall from the lift with two other women. All three looked completely trashed and wore towering high heels and skin-tight short skirts. Andrea kept watching as they reached Heather's front door and Heather started fumbling with her keys, jabbing at the lock and missing. She dropped her keys and one of the other women kicked them out of her reach when she bent over to pick them up, before hooting with laughter at her own hilarious joke. 'Try and pick them up now, skank!'

Heather tumbled to the floor in a fit of laughter and then Andrea saw the front door open on its own. A young woman stepped out into the hall. 'Uh, hi, Mrs Pickerell,' Andrea heard her say.

'Oh,' said Heather, looking up at her. 'You're still here?'

The woman edged out into the hallway. 'Violet's asleep. I'll . . . I'll get going then.' She moved hastily down the hallway and into the lift.

At least Heather had booked a babysitter. Andrea was about to close her own door when she heard Heather squeal again.

'Holy shit,' she cried, 'it's my mini-me! My mini-slut! Mini-slut, how are you, baby?'

Andrea felt the heat rising up her neck. Obviously Violet wasn't fast asleep as the babysitter had thought. The idea of Heather calling that precious small girl a slut made Andrea feel sick. So much for the perfect mother she'd seen earlier, looking like she was right out of a meme of a 1950s housewife in her checked apron as she baked a cake with her daughter.

She watched as Heather crawled through the doorway on her hands and knees. One of the other women placed a stiletto heel on her bum as she crawled. 'Giddy up, bitch, mama needs another drink.'

'Or a little something else,' the third woman trilled. She produced a small plastic bag of powder from her handbag and waved it in the air. 'Found it!'

The heat flushed across Andrea's face now. Those three women were going to go in there blind drunk, sky high, and then keep taking drugs right in front of Violet. Enough was enough. She had to do something.

She pulled her door all the way open and strode down the hall to Heather's apartment. She caught the door just as it was about to close and pushed it in. Heather was lying on her back on the floor; her skirt was riding up and she was giggling to herself. One of the other women was already sprawled across the couch and the third had knelt down and was intently searching through her handbag. None of the three women had even noticed Andrea walk in. Violet was standing by the door and the look on her face broke Andrea. It was a look of pure resignation.

Andrea reached out and took hold of Violet's hand. 'Hey, sweetie,' she said. 'Would you like to come and have a sleepover at my place tonight?'

Violet's eyes darted towards her mother, then she motioned for Andrea to come closer. Andrea crouched down in front of her to listen.

'I want to,' Violet whispered. 'But sometimes when Mummy comes home after her special nights out I have to watch her. In case she gets a little bit sick.'

'Is that what she's said to you?' Andrea asked.

Violet nodded.

'Well, how about this? Tonight, it looks like your mum has two friends with her, so maybe they could watch her this time and you could have the night off.'

A small smile twitched at the edges of Violet's mouth. 'You think that would be okay?'

'I think it would.'

Heather rolled over on the floor and seemed to finally notice Andrea's presence in her apartment.

'Oh hey,' she said. 'Look, girls, it's the stupid bitch I was telling you about. The nosy cow. Hello, nosy cow, moooo.' She snorted at her own joke then reached out for Andrea's ankle. 'What the fuck are you doing in my apartment, nosy cow?'

'I'm taking Violet back to my place,' Andrea said, trying her best to keep her voice firm, even though she wasn't sure if Heather and her two friends might suddenly pounce on her with their French-tipped talons and rip her to pieces for interfering. Andrea pulled her leg away and her ankle slipped out of Heather's weak, drunken grip.

Heather stared at her, and for a moment Andrea thought she was in for a fight. But then Heather dropped her gaze. 'Fine. Whatever. I don't give a shit.'

At the same time, the woman who'd been searching through her bag pulled out a credit card and tapped it on the coffee table.

'*Yesss*,' said Heather. 'Line it up.' She turned back to Andrea. 'Fuck off, nosy cow.' Then she fixed her eyes on Violet. 'And you can fuck off too, little cow traitor.'

Violet's eyes filled with tears and Andrea grabbed her hand again and took her quickly out of the apartment.

Out in the hall, Andrea knelt down in front of Violet and wrapped her in a hug. 'Don't listen to her,' she said firmly. 'She doesn't know what she's saying right now. Don't even think about it. I'm going to take you back to my place and you can sleep in the giant bed in our spare room. And if you want, you can have Monkey with you tonight; have I ever told you about Monkey?'

'No,' said Violet.

'Monkey was my most favourite toy when I was a kid. When I grew up and started thinking I didn't need toys anymore, I could never bring myself to give Monkey away. So I kept him. And he came with me when I moved out and when I travelled overseas, and when I got married. And now he lives on the window seat in my living room so he can look out at the view. But he could probably use a good cuddle. Want to look after him for me tonight?'

'Yes, please.'

Andrea stood up and led Violet down the hall back to her place.

Jill

Dear Frank,

I can't seem to stop writing to you. I keep telling myself it's pointless. These letters aren't going to magically find their way to you. But the problem is, I still want to tell you things. So I keep pretending.

It's two in the morning and I've been lying here in bed trying to fall asleep since eleven. Three hours staring at the ceiling in the half darkness, thinking about all the things I've done wrong throughout my life — my mistakes, my inadequacies, my sins. Maybe I'd fall asleep easier if I made it pitch black, but I still can't bring myself to turn off those lights. I need those islands of warmth throughout the house so the darkness doesn't completely close in.

Sometimes during the day I can cope with the lack of sleep. I can pull myself together with cup after cup of tea. But other times, I'm like a walking zombie and I don't know how I make it through the day.

I opened the email. But then I read the first line: 'Jill, I tried to tell you this once before.' And I thought, who the hell do you think you are? So I closed it again.

Tomorrow . . . well I suppose it's today now, isn't it? Anyway, today I'll be going out to lunch with Mimi and Andrea again. Andrea organised it. That was sweet of her, wasn't it? I think those daughters-in-law of ours are trying to keep an eye on me. But I'm more worried about them.

Poor Andrea. I wish she'd talked to me sooner, but knowing she had that difficult relationship with her mother, I never wanted to overstep. I didn't want her to think I was trying to replace her mother. But I should have tried harder. Because now I'm worried, what if it's too late for her? And what if it's our Tony's fault? I did try to ask him once why he didn't want children. But he wouldn't talk to me so I didn't push it. Was that wrong of me?

And Mimi. Is she coping with those twins? Or is she hiding her struggles? And there she was, telling me that something was going on with Callie and I brushed it off! But it looks like I was wrong. Now I don't know what to do. Do I go to Mimi, tell her that Callie came to see me, that she almost confided in me? Or would that be the wrong thing to do because then I'd be betraying Callie's confidence?

Tony. Back to Tony. Our eldest. My precious Tony. The one
I worried about the most. You knew why, didn't you? Why I was
so scared I might lose him. That's why you didn't stop me from
smothering him so much when he was young.

But now what have I created?

And what have I ignored?

Andrea

'I wonder if you were planning to tell me about the small
child asleep in our spare room?'

Andrea opened her eyes and blinked a few times, slowly
taking in the words.

'Ah yes,' she said as her brain registered. 'Sorry, I meant
to wake up before you.' She'd taken a long time to fall
asleep last night. She'd felt so unwell with that potential
migraine coming on, and then she couldn't stop worrying
about poor Violet. So when sleep had finally come it had
dragged her down with a vengeance.

'Why? So you could sneak her out before I knew she
was here?'

'No! So I could warn you. There's a good reason, by
the way.'

'It's okay, I figured there would be. What happened?'

Andrea sat up and explained what had occurred the
previous night, keeping her voice low in case Violet had
woken.

'You know what I would have done if it were me?'

'What?' said Andrea, bracing herself for the irritation
that would follow when Tony said she should stay out of it,

or that she should have called the authorities rather than bringing Violet back here.

'The exact same thing,' said Tony.

Andrea's body relaxed. 'About time you were on board.'

'Yeah, yeah. I'll admit I really didn't think things with Heather were as bad as they clearly are. The way she behaved last night sounds awful. I'm sorry you had to see that.'

'I'm glad I saw it, otherwise I wouldn't have been there to get Violet out of the situation.'

'That's true. What are we going to do next?'

'Well, for now I'm going to go next door and collect Violet's school uniform, then I'll get her ready for school and take her to meet her driver.'

'Want me to come next door with you? Give you some back-up in case things get heated with Heather?'

'Nah, it's okay. I can manage Heather.'

'All right. Well, if there's anything you need me to do, just say the word.'

Andrea gave Tony a kiss; she couldn't believe how much better it felt finally having him on her side about all of this. She climbed out of bed and headed to the other bedroom to see if Violet was awake.

Andrea had been preparing for a battle when she went next door. She was ready for Heather to scream and swear at her for taking her daughter back to her apartment for the night. But she wasn't prepared for this.

Heather had just *apologised*.

Heather had just thanked her.

Heather was looking contrite and grateful and . . . actually, she was looking depressed. Really, really depressed.

Andrea had already brought Violet over, helped her get ready for school and sent her off with Shaun – the chauffeur who wasn't a chauffeur. Shaun had caught her eye as he was taking Violet by the hand and mouthed at her, *thank you, I'll call you soon*. So that was good to know that he was still planning on contacting her.

Now, she and Heather were sitting opposite one another in Heather's apartment. The women from the previous evening were nowhere to be seen. Heather's hair was wet from the shower and she was wrapped up in a robe. Andrea realised it was the first time she'd seen her without makeup and she looked younger. More vulnerable. Softer. There was a large red pimple on her chin and, somehow, it was making her seem more . . . *human*.

'I know what you think of me,' Heather said, her eyes down on the carpet as she spoke. 'But the thing is . . .' She paused. 'The thing is, you don't really know me. I know I've made some really bad mistakes, but that's not all I am.'

Andrea was having a hard time reconciling the woman in front of her with the woman who'd called her six-year-old a slut last night. She was also finding it hard to be forgiving.

Heather looked up and stared straight at Andrea. 'I know I'm a shit mum,' she said. 'But I don't want to be.'

'Okay,' said Andrea. 'I guess you might want to start by not taking drugs in front of your child.'

Heather looked back down. 'I don't need you to patronise me,' she said.

'And I don't need you to get snide with me again. You realise I could report you to social services for what you did last night? To be honest, I probably should.'

'I didn't end up taking those drugs last night. After you left, I realised what I'd said to my own daughter. My so-called friends were sitting there laughing about it and suddenly it was like . . . I hated them. I hated myself. I kicked them out and I flushed the drugs, okay? And then I slept it off.'

She twisted the edge of her robe between her hands and said, 'So don't. Don't call social services on me.' Then her voice cracked. 'Please. Give me another chance?'

'It's not the first time though.'

'I know. But I'm telling you, I'm trying. I want to be better. And look, I won't have a go at you anymore if you want to keep checking in on us. I get it. I get that you care about Violet and I get that that's more important than me feeling . . . intimidated by you.'

Andrea cocked an eyebrow. 'You're intimidated by *me*?'

'Yes. You make me feel inadequate, okay? Are you happy now?'

Andrea stopped herself from replying *yes* and instead shook her head. 'All I want is what's best for Violet. I'm happy to help out where I can.'

Heather looked up again and met Andrea's eyes. 'Thank you,' she said.

Darren

He answered the phone to a voice so bright and bubbly that he could hardly understand what she was saying.

'Charlotte? What did you say? Slow down, would you?'

'Sorry! I'm just excited. Steph's ovulating, so we were

kinda sorta hoping we might be able to come over and get a donation from you. Any chance that might be okay?'

'Oh! Right. Umm, I see.'

'Sorry. Are you in the middle of something? I'm being so selfish right now; I shouldn't have assumed you'd be free.'

'No, no, it's not that. It's just that . . . I didn't expect it to be so soon.'

He could hear Charlotte sucking air in through her teeth and then, when she spoke, there was a note of guilt to her voice. 'I know. To be honest, Steph thought we should wait until her next cycle. Give you more time, seeing as we only discussed it all properly on the weekend. But I'm too excited to wait and I told her it would be okay. I'm so sorry, is this not okay?'

He hated hearing her sound disappointed.

'Of course it is. Totally. Let me just . . . organise myself.'

'I don't suppose you've had the chance to drop in to the medical centre yet for the check-up, have you?'

Darren scrunched his face for a second, then he put on an upbeat voice. 'Sure did, all good.'

'Awesome. Oh, and did you remember to ask for specimen jars when you were there?'

'Ah, yeah. Let me just find them.'

'Okay great, we'll see you soon.'

Darren hung up the phone and rubbed his face with his hands. What the hell had he got himself into? And why had he lied to Charlotte? It was totally understandable that he wouldn't have had the time to get to the doctor yet. Why not just be honest with her? It shouldn't really matter though, it wasn't like the doctor was going to find any health issues.

Right, he needed to get himself sorted before Charlotte and Steph arrived. That meant he needed to get himself into the mood. Obviously, he wanted to have the donation ready to give them when they arrived. Because there was no way he could do that in the bedroom while the two of them sat out in the living room waiting for him. Fuck, this was weird.

It took a good ten minutes to get his mind to stop wandering; in the end, Pornhub on his phone did the trick. Then, when he was just starting to get into it, the dog managed to push the bedroom door open and wander in.

'No, mate, we don't have that sort of relationship,' he said, shooing him back out of the room and closing the door more firmly.

Then when he'd almost reached his climax, he had a last-minute panic when he realised he'd forgotten about the jar. Shit, what could he use that would be appropriate? Obviously he didn't have the proper specimen containers because he'd never made it to the doctor. He wrapped a towel around his waist and made a mad dash for the kitchen where he found an old, clean jam jar. That would have to do.

When the knock at the door came he was thankfully done. The jar was in a brown paper bag – it just seemed wrong to have it out on display.

He opened the door to a beaming Charlotte and stood back to let her in. For a moment, his mood lightened. No Steph! She must be waiting at home for the donation to be delivered back to her. But then she appeared from the hallway. He gave her an awkward nod, not quite able to meet her eyes with the knowledge hanging between them of what he'd just been doing. 'Right, cool. So . . . I guess I'll grab it and you guys can be on your way.'

'Actually, we can stay for a bit,' Charlotte said, continuing to beam at him.

'Ah, okay, come on in.'

Charlotte strode inside and Steph followed, giving Darren a look that landed somewhere between a smile and a grimace. He understood how she felt.

Charlotte turned and looked at him expectantly.

He stared back at her.

'Any chance of a coffee?'

'Oh! Right, sure thing.'

'Only for me. Steph is off the caffeine for now. Thanks, babe.'

Darren's neck muscles tightened as he headed for the kitchen. Man, he wished she'd quit calling him babe. He had started the coffee machine when he heard a shriek from the living room. 'What? What's wrong?' he asked, sticking his head out of the doorway.

'Sorry,' said Charlotte, 'I got startled. You have a dog now?'

'Oh yeah, sort of.'

'What does "sort of" mean?' Steph asked.

He leaned against the doorframe while he waited for the coffee machine to finish and then explained about finding Doggo and potentially taking him in.

'Huh,' said Charlotte. 'I guess it makes sense – you never could get one while we were together.'

'Oh yeah, true.' He turned back into the kitchen.

He'd actually completely forgotten about Charlotte's allergy, but she was right, he had mentioned wanting to get a dog once before – a long time ago near the start of their relationship. She'd apologised and said she was allergic. It hadn't even crossed his mind when he'd met the dog in the park.

'Do you need me to put him out on the balcony or something while you're here?' he called out as he took down two mugs from the cupboard, automatically choosing Charlotte's old favourite one with the ugly leopard-print pattern. He'd never liked that cup and yet he couldn't bring himself to throw it away.

'No, no,' Charlotte called back. 'I'll be okay as long as I don't get too close.'

As he poured milk and sugar into Charlotte's coffee – he preferred his own strong and black – he wondered if Charlotte was the real reason he'd formed the attachment with the dog. A bit of a subconscious moment of acceptance that Charlotte wasn't coming back? Or even a subtle *fuck you* to her?

Of course, when he returned to the living room with the two coffees it was just in time to see the dog jumping up to rest his paws on Charlotte's lap.

'Oy, get down,' he said.

'I got it,' said Steph. She snapped her fingers at him and patted her own lap and the dog obediently left Charlotte in favour of Steph.

'How'd you do that?' Darren passed a coffee over to Charlotte and blew across the top of his own cup to cool it down. 'He hasn't followed a single instruction I've given him. Wouldn't even play fetch for me.'

'Dogs like me.' Steph's tone was unabashedly confident.

'So anyway,' said Charlotte. 'We have a favour to ask.

Could Steph use your bedroom to . . . you know . . . do the deed now?'

Darren had just taken a sip of his coffee and now he coughed as he choked on it. 'You're doing it here? I thought you were taking it home?'

'We would,' said Charlotte. 'We absolutely would and that was the original plan, but Steph's parents and her brother are visiting from Melbourne. They're all staying at our place so it's a bit crowded back there. On the way here, I started thinking this might be the easier solution. She needs to do it quite fast – the sperm will only last for about an hour. Sorry, I know it's a little strange. Do you mind?'

Darren bit the inside of his cheek. 'No problem,' he said as at the same time a voice in the back of his head was muttering, *Why the fuck did you ever agree to this? This whole thing is getting weirder by the minute. Your ex-girlfriend's new girlfriend is about to stick a syringe filled with your jizz up her clacker in your bedroom, and you and your ex will sit out in the living room drinking coffee while it happens. How the hell did you get yourself into this?*

Steph stood and for a moment they stared at each other awkwardly until Darren got the message.

'Oh right, the jar.' He put his mug down on the coffee table and grabbed the brown paper bag from the side table by the front door and handed it over. 'Umm, enjoy?' he said. Then his face reddened as Steph quirked an eyebrow at him. 'Sorry,' he said, 'I didn't know what else to say.'

'All good,' said Steph. She leaned forward and whispered quietly. 'Mate, this is pretty fucking weird for me too.'

Darren smiled. 'Thanks, Steph.'

To be honest, he hadn't really considered that from her point of view the whole thing was just as fucked up. He wondered for a moment if Charlotte had pushed her into the idea of using him for the donation, if Steph would have preferred to have found someone a bit less entangled in their lives.

Steph headed into the bedroom and then two seconds later she stuck her head back out the door. 'Really?' she said. 'A strawberry jam jar?'

'Oh yeah, sorry. Is that okay? I couldn't remember what I'd done with the proper containers,' he lied.

'Darren!' said Charlotte. 'Jam?'

'At least it wasn't mayo!'

Charlotte threw a cushion at him, which he caught, while Steph shook her head.

'You're a shocker,' she said. 'But yes, it'll do.' She disappeared back into the bedroom.

'Ah, should I maybe turn on some music or something?' Darren asked.

Charlotte narrowed her eyes at him. 'What, you think there'll be sound effects?'

'Jesus, Char.'

Charlotte laughed. 'Sorry, I'm just stirring you. Hey, tell me the jam jar was clean, right?'

'Yeah, yeah, it was clean.'

He switched on the stereo and picked one of his Spotify playlists at random, then sat down on the other couch and patted the spot next to him for the dog, who just ignored him and walked away.

'He's a work in progress.'

'I see,' said Charlotte. 'What's his name?'

'At the moment, Doggo. I'm getting to a proper name, once I know for sure I'm keeping him.'

That's when they were interrupted by a shriek and Darren twisted around in time to see that the dog had once again managed to push his bedroom door open. As it swung inwards he could see Steph, lying on her back on his bed with her legs up in the air.

'Oh Jesus, Jesus Christ, Jesus fucking Christ.' Darren slapped his hands over his face and turned away at the same time as Charlotte leapt up and raced to close the door.

'I am so fucking sorry,' Darren called out, his hands still over his face. 'I didn't see anything, not a thing.' They all knew it was a complete lie but he didn't know what else to say.

'Maybe I'll stay in there and lean against the door,' said Charlotte.

'Good idea,' both Steph and Darren said at the same time.

The dog trotted back over to Darren and jumped up onto the couch where he curled up next to him and fixed him with innocent eyes.

'You little bastard.'

Andrea

'The Oyster Bay Pinot Gris?' The waiter held out the bottle with a slight flourish and Andrea nodded.

'That's the one,' she said. She'd never quite understood the need to make such a fuss of presenting the bottle of wine that you'd ordered. Showing the label, pouring a sip for a taste as if anyone would ever send back a wine bottle with a screw cap. Although she supposed there were some wankers out there who did sometimes turn it down.

Almost immediately, she remembered that Tony had once sent back a bottle of French rosé on one of their earlier dates, and she felt bad for thinking that way. When he'd done it, she hadn't thought he was a wanker. She'd thought he was brave to point out that it was corked and ask for a replacement.

'You're fine to pour,' Andrea said as the waiter started to pull the bottle back after pouring just a splash in the glass. The waiter nodded and filled the glass before placing the bottle back into the ice bucket.

Mimi and Jill were both running late and Andrea had decided she couldn't wait for them before getting started on a drink. She needed it after everything that had happened in the last twenty-four hours. She and Mimi had planned this lunch after both agreeing that they needed to keep a closer eye on Jill and make sure she was doing okay. On Tuesdays, Andrea didn't have classes after lunch and, while she would usually use the time to do marking, being days from the end of the year meant she could give herself the afternoon off.

She felt her phone buzz in her pocket and pulled it out, expecting it to be a message from either Mimi or Jill, letting her know they were on their way. It wasn't, it was from Shaun.

Sorry I didn't contact you sooner after we met on the weekend. Things have been busy. But thank you so much for stepping in with Violet last night. Sounds like you were there for her right when she needed you. Can we meet up and talk properly? Any chance you're free for a drink on Friday night? No pressure.

She registered a tiny flip low in her stomach. That was weird. She supposed it was just that she was pleased she was going to learn the full story about Shaun's connection to Heather and Violet. Although . . . drinks on a Friday night. Was that leaning into date territory? Did she need to clarify with Shaun that she was married? As soon as she'd had the thought she felt silly. A guy like Shaun wouldn't have any interest in her. She dismissed her concerns and wrote back that Friday night was perfect and he replied with details of a bar where they could meet.

She was glad that she'd have something to do this weekend. With school finishing up this week, spending Friday night home alone would have felt a bit anticlimactic. Tony was going to be out at Christmas drinks with his publishers and she'd been disappointed that the invite hadn't extended to partners.

She looked up to see Mimi weaving her way through the tables towards her. She had one baby strapped to her chest.

'Umm, Mimi,' said Andrea as she reached the table. 'Did you forget one of your babies?'

'Ha,' said Mimi. 'No, James is at home with Pete. Divide and conquer. One twin each. From now on James is his and Elliot is mine. If we ever split up, it'll be like *The Parent Trap*.'

'Wait, what?'

'I'm kidding! James was a bit sniffly, that's why I left her with Pete.'

Mimi started unstrapping Elliot from her chest and

then passed her across to Andrea before sitting down and plucking at her top. There was a damp mark where Elliot had been pressed against her. 'What's going on?' she asked. 'You don't sound like yourself.'

'I know, sorry,' said Andrea. 'I'm a bit distracted. More issues with Heather, the mother down the hall. I ended up having Violet stay at our place last night; there was no way she could stay at home with what was going on at her place.'

'Really? What happened?'

Andrea gave Mimi a brief rundown of the previous night's events while jiggling a slightly fussy Elliot in her arms.

'Yeah, okay, fair enough. That does sound pretty bad,' said Mimi when Andrea was done explaining.

'Okay, but here's the twist. When I went back round there this morning, Heather *apologised*. She said she wants to make a change, wants to quit drugs for good and be a better mother. She even said she doesn't mind me getting involved anymore.'

'No way. That's a big turn around.'

'I know!'

'Well, congratulations, my dear, it looks like you've really got through to her. You know what?' Mimi added. 'I know you guys don't wants kids, but I have to say, I think you would make an excellent mother with the way you've looked out for that kid.'

Andrea didn't know what it was – if it was the kindness of Mimi's words or the shock of her saying that so soon after she'd discovered that perhaps being a mother was still a possibility, but she instantly burst into tears.

'Oh no! I'm so sorry, I've said the wrong thing!'

'No, no.' Andrea shook her head. 'You haven't – that was a lovely thing to say. They're happy tears . . . sort of . . .' She sniffed and Mimi rummaged through her bag for a tissue and passed it over.

'Do you want me to grab Elliot back?' Mimi asked.

'No, I'm good.' Andrea took in a deep breath. 'It's that I'd started thinking lately . . . wondering if I'd made a mistake . . . wondering if I did want kids.'

Mimi's eyes widened. 'I had no idea.'

'I know you didn't and that's why you don't need to be sorry. I broached it with Tony only last night. And while we haven't exactly made a decision, it's back on the table.'

'Wow. That's great news.'

'Well, I don't know if I'd go that far. Like I said, it's back on the table, but it's far from a sure thing. We're both going to take some time to think it all through. See what we really want.'

Mimi hesitated for a moment. 'Not to play devil's advocate, but what happens if you two both think for a while and then arrive at opposite conclusions?'

Andrea grimaced. 'I don't know.'

'Can I ask you something? What was behind your decision not to have children? I mean, originally . . . I guess I always wondered. You're so great with kids, with your students, with your nieces . . .' Mimi looked nervous as she waited for the answer, as though she was worried she may have overstepped the sister-in-law boundaries.

Andrea took in a deep breath. Even though Tony knew about her childhood, she'd always avoided sharing the details with the rest of his family. She wasn't really sure why, perhaps it was the desire to project a certain image to everyone else. An image of strength and complete competence. But perhaps if she'd been more open about her past, about her fears, she wouldn't be in this situation. She wouldn't have realised so late that she might actually want to have kids.

She looked back at Mimi and answered with certainty. 'Because of my own mother.' Then she looked back down at Elliot and stroked her wisps of hair, her voice now turning soft. 'I know I've never said much about my family; you guys all just know that I'm pretty much estranged from them. But the full story is that my upbringing was absolutely awful, to put it plainly. My dad wasn't around and my mum didn't care one bit about me or my older brother. My brother took off as soon as he was old enough, and he didn't bother to stay in touch with me either.'

Mimi leaned forward, her face pained. 'God. That's terrible. I'm so sorry.'

'Yep. And Mum always made me feel like I was a burden. She was more interested in blaming me for existing, for ruining her life, than actually loving me.'

'Was she . . . a drinker? Or into drugs or something?'

'Gambler. So, there was never much money for annoying expenses like, oh, you know, food? I got out of there as soon as I could, too. I did try to track my brother down, but he didn't want to have a relationship with me. I think I was too much of a reminder of Mum and he wanted to shut that part of his life out altogether. Anyway, I got a job, I found myself a share house and I worked my way through university and promised myself I'd have a better life than the one I'd had with her. But I was still terrified that if I became a mum, I'd be just like her. I mean, even though I got my life together, for a long time my childhood really influenced my relationships. Until I met Tony, I'd only ever dated complete arseholes. Guys who treated me badly because that's what I was used to. Tony was like a breath of fresh air after those men.'

Andrea finally looked up from Elliot and across at Mimi. 'That's my fun story,' she said. 'Delightful, isn't it?'

Mimi stood and moved around the table to put an arm around Andrea. 'I wish I knew the right thing to say.'

'You don't have to say anything. Thank you for listening.'

'Of course. I'm here for you any time. For the record,' said Mimi, returning to her seat, 'you're not your mother. From everything you've told me about her, you're bloody nothing like her. And I don't know if you want to hear this or not, but I want you to know that if you do end up having kids, you'll be an absolutely incredible mother.'

'Thank you,' said Andrea, trying hard to stop the tears from spilling again.

Mimi looked as though she wanted to ask more questions but was stopped as Andrea glanced up and spotted Jill. She quickly wiped her eyes and tried to reset the expression on her face. She didn't think she could go through all of that again right now with Jill as well.

'Here comes Jill,' she said. 'You mind if we keep this between us for now?'

'Absolutely.'

'Hey, watch her ask where your other baby is the moment she arrives.'

Mimi grinned then sat back and pasted a neutral look on her face until Jill arrived at the table, her eyes on the wine.

'Someone needs to pour me one of those,' she said, before sitting heavily into the third chair. Then she fixed her gaze on Elliot in Andrea's arms. 'Wait,' she said. 'Where's the other one?'

Mimi

Between Jill and Andrea, there was no chance of embarrassing herself by drinking too much at lunch today and having to be driven home by her mother-in-law, like a shameful teenager who'd had one too many Passion Pops. The two of them were steamrolling through the wine and Mimi could barely get herself one glass. Not that she'd intended to have anymore than one today. She was being extra careful with how much she drank when she knew she had to drive.

Obviously Andrea needed a drink after opening up about her childhood and her fears. And on top of that, now that she thought she might want children, her husband needed time to think. What was going to happen if he eventually came back and said no? No wonder the woman wanted to drown her sorrows. But neither of them entirely understood the reason for Jill's need to indulge in a fairly extensive spot of alcohol-induced escapism. When they asked her what was wrong, she brushed them off and said everything was fine.

Mimi had decided not to press her. After all, it was less than two weeks until Christmas. If the anniversary of her own husband's death was approaching, Mimi would probably be drinking excessively too. Meanwhile Andrea was continuing to race Jill to the bottom of the wine bottle. The best Mimi could do was pour them several glasses of water so they wouldn't both have headaches tomorrow.

It was when Jill signalled the waiter for a third bottle that Mimi decided to try one last time to get Jill to open up.

'Are you okay, Jill? You know you can talk to us, right?'

Jill fixed her eyes on Mimi's face and then they dropped to Elliot who was back in Mimi's arms, fast asleep. 'Do you two think I'm a good mother?' she asked.

Mimi leaned forward. 'Of course you are,' she said at the same time as Andrea's perhaps a little too effusive exclamation. 'Are you kidding, you're a great mum!'

'Why do you ask?' Mimi said.

Jill poured herself another glass of wine and took a large drink before responding. 'Oh, I don't know. Just something on my mind.'

'What's going on?' Mimi pressed. 'Something has you rattled.'

But Jill's face was shutting down again. 'It's nothing, I was being silly. But there is one thing I should tell you. Callie came to see me last week after school. I wasn't sure if I should say anything, if it would make it worse if I betrayed her confidence, but I realised it's more important that you know. She was very upset about something. I think you were right that there's something going on.'

'Oh,' said Mimi.

Andrea clapped her hand to her mouth. 'I forgot to tell you that I finally got the chance to try and talk to

Callie too. It was only yesterday but with everything else going on with Violet next-door, it feels like it was days ago. Umm, it didn't go well.'

'Damn, really?'

'Yeah. It was like she was really angry with me, but I don't know why.'

'And what did she say to you, Jill?'

'Not a lot. But she was crying and I felt like there was something she wanted to tell me, but she didn't know how.'

Now Mimi felt like crying herself. *What an emotional bloody lunch. If Callie wouldn't talk to her parents, wouldn't talk to her grandmother and wouldn't talk to her aunt, who would she talk to?*

Darren

'Didn't think I'd be hearing from you so fast.'

'Oh yeah, why's that?' Darren sat down on his couch and put his feet up on the coffee table. Calling Claudia had been a spur of the moment idea. After seeing his ex-girlfriend's new girlfriend's vagina as she was about to insert his sperm into it, he was kind of keen to do something to take his mind off it.

'Because I got the sense that you were only after a one-night thing after I left your place this morning.'

God, imagine if Claudia had still been there when Charlotte had called asking to come around. Now *that* would have been awkward.

'What gave you that idea? I asked for your number, didn't I?'

'Yeah, but you know you didn't offer me any breakfast, right? I assumed asking for my number was an obligatory move.'

'What? I offered you breakfast!'

'Mate, you pointed at the kitchen, that doesn't count.'

'Ah. Sorry, sometimes I can be a bit useless. But now you know I really did want your number.'

'So, what can I do for you?'

'I was thinking you might want to meet for a drink.'

'A drink?' He could hear the disappointment in her voice and he realised she was probably hoping he would invite her out for a proper date. Maybe dinner.

Darren sat up and took his feet back off the coffee table. 'I mean . . . how about dinner? Tonight?'

'Dinner sounds nice.' He could almost hear the relief in her voice. 'Where did you have in mind?' she asked.

He really should have planned this better. He said the first one that came to mind – the tapas bar where he'd taken Sage to meet Charlotte and Stephanie.

'I love that place. Do you want to meet there?'

'No, no. Give me your address and I'll pick you up. Seven, okay?'

'Seven is great.'

After she gave him her address he hung up the phone and wondered if he was actually looking forward to tonight. If he was honest, the answer was no. He'd been looking for a way to distract himself from everything else in his life. But he wasn't really up for doing the whole proper date thing. For having to put on his best show and make conversation and flirt. He just wanted sex.

Actually, what he wanted was sex with Sage. What the hell was wrong with him?

Mimi

She was feeling fairly morose as she pushed Elliot through the shops in her pram. She'd sent Jill and Andrea home in an Uber each and now she was trying to get some Christmas shopping done. But she was struggling to focus. Initially, she'd felt quite proud of herself for remaining sober despite there being three bottles of wine on offer throughout lunch. But now, after hearing that both Jill and Andrea agreed something wasn't right with Callie, she was wishing she'd had a few glasses. She was also a little irritated that Jill hadn't told her about Callie coming to see her sooner. Jill knew she was worried, she should have called her right away.

She supposed that's why when she passed the bottle shop she felt like she kind of deserved something for herself. A bottle of gin to keep at home so she could enjoy the odd summer drink ... not as many as she'd had with Leesa when she'd ended up in Edna's rhododendron bushes, but enough to help her relax. For instance, a treat this afternoon to congratulate herself for *not* drinking wine over lunch.

And then later that afternoon, there was a voice inside her head telling her it wasn't the smartest move as she poured the gin into the half-empty bottle of diet lemonade. But there was a louder voice, telling her it was fine,

she was just being sensible. Making things more conveni-
ent. Mixing a drink each time would be annoying.

She was confident no one would drink from that bottle
because no one else in the house liked diet soft drinks.
And she wasn't doing it to be secretive, she just wasn't sure
what Pete would think if he saw her mixing up a gin now
and then during the week. Besides, it wasn't like she'd lie
outright if he asked her what she was drinking.

Anyway, apart from one small drink today, she'd try to
save the rest for Friday.

So, the thing was, she didn't have a problem.

Christmas Eve

Darren stared at the other cars.

What the hell?

Wasn't that Tony's Lexus? Tipped on its side? And Mimi's SUV?

It couldn't be. He stumbled back further from Jill's car to focus properly on the other crumpled vehicles. It *was*. That was Pete and Mimi. That meant the twins would be in the back.

And the fourth car. That was Andrea's convertible. With Andrea passed out alone in the driver's seat.

What had happened here? How had his entire family ended up in this horrific mess?

What was he meant to do now? Who did he go to?

That's when he heard the screams start up. A horrible guttural sound. A sound of pure pain and anguish.

13

Wednesday 16 December

Darren

He was in a crappy mood when Doctor Clermont called him in for his appointment. His date with Claudia last night had sucked. And that was his fault. He should never have asked her out, not when he knew he wasn't genuinely interested. Obviously, his lack of interest had shone through in his weak conversation game and she'd grown progressively more irritated throughout the night. Eventually she'd faked an emergency phone call and ditched him just before the desserts came out.

He was left with mini lemon-meringue pies and liqueur-dipped strawberries – neither of which were his choices – and found himself staring at the table where he'd sat with Sage the night she'd pretended to be his girlfriend. He needed to get her out of his mind. She'd been clear that she wasn't interested in anything more with him, so why was he wasting his time thinking about her?

And now this doctor's appointment was another waste of his time – time which could be spent working on his book. But he felt guilty about lying to Charlotte and was keen to tick this off so he could stop feeling bad.

Of course, the reality that even if he was sitting in

front of the computer he still wouldn't be able to get a single word written was beside the point right now. He was pissed off at the world and ready to take it out on anyone. He supposed the upcoming anniversary of his dad's death wasn't helping. And as Christmas loomed, it was becoming harder and harder to keep the grief at bay. He bloody well missed him.

He followed Doctor Clermont into her office and she motioned for him to take a seat, smiling warmly at him as she sat down at her desk. 'What brings you in today?' she asked.

'I need a check-up. I'm donating my sperm to a friend.' He'd tried to say it with a casual, confident air, but of course his voice went up on the word sperm. Sometimes he felt like he'd always be an awkward fourteen-year-old boy on the inside.

'Ah, I see. That's very generous of you.'

He shrugged. 'It's no big deal.'

'I'm sure it is to the friend you're donating to. All right, let's start with your history.'

Doctor Clermont began asking him questions about his past health issues, which were minimal – a hernia when he was a teenager and eczema when he was a kid. She quizzed him on his family medical history, his current relationship status and sexual activity, and asked him if he'd sought legal advice.

He hadn't realised there would be so many questions.

She was printing out a pathology request form for his blood and urine tests when she leaned forward abruptly and said, 'That mole on the side of your neck. Has that always been there?'

Darren was taken aback. She must have sharp eyes, he hadn't even noticed her glance at him. 'I don't know. Maybe?'

'It's the colour that has me concerned. Can I please take a closer look?'

'Yeah, of course.'

Darren turned sideways, allowing her to examine him. Eventually she said firmly, 'I'm going to do a shave biopsy. Basically, it means taking a small scraping so I can send it off for testing, okay?'

'Now?'

'Yes, the sooner the better.'

Darren felt his shoulders tense. Growing up under the hot Australian sun had meant he'd let himself get sunburnt several times as a kid. And even though there were always plenty of warnings about sun safety and skin cancer, it was one of those things that you never really thought would happen to you.

He turned back to face her. 'Should I be worried?'

'Not yet,' Doctor Clermont said, her voice becoming kinder. 'Let's wait and see what we find.'

'Fair enough.' Darren still wasn't thrilled about the whole thing. This was meant to be a routine check-up, nothing to worry about.

'Before we do it, one last question about your good deed. The friend you're donating to, how close are you?'

Darren squirmed. 'It's my ex and her new partner.'

'Your ex?' Doctor Clermont's composed demeanour slipped for a moment and she adjusted her glasses. 'I see.'

Her composure returned. 'And you feel entirely

comfortable doing this? Because this isn't a decision you should take lightly.'

'Absolutely.'

'All right, well, it's still important that you talk to a counsellor about what you're doing, even if you think it's no big deal. Especially based on your previous relationship with the recipient.'

'Got it,' said Darren.

'Right, let's get back to this mole.'

By the time Darren had finally left the doctor's office, his mind was whirling with thoughts of skin cancer, Sage, legal documents and the image of his sperm doing its thing inside Steph right now. He actually felt a little queasy.

Mimi

Mimi supposed she should have read the room. Checked on her daughter's mood first. Yes, there had been an altercation during the last driving lesson – but at least it had ended with that lovely hug. And so she'd been hoping to replicate that closeness. Perhaps Callie would open up to her and tell her whatever it was that had made her so upset the day she'd gone to see Jill.

Instead, an innocent offer to take her out for another driving lesson after school had resulted in tears – Mimi's, not Callie's.

Tara sat up on a stool at the kitchen bench and drummed her hands across Mimi's back – her attempt at a comforting massage. 'Want me to go and talk to her for you?' Tara asked.

Mimi laughed. 'You are the sweetest,' she said. 'But no. You'll only get your head bitten off as well. Sorry,' she added. 'I shouldn't be crying in front of you.'

'Why not? You always say tears can be good for you.'

'True. But this is putting me between you and your sister and that's not fair.'

Mimi honestly hadn't meant to burst into tears. It must have been a combination of the shock of Callie's response and how cutting her words had been.

Callie had walked in the door from the school bus and Mimi had jangled the car keys in front of her almost immediately. 'Fancy a lesson with your favourite mum?' she'd asked brightly.

'Favourite?' Callie had scoffed. 'Do you seriously think I'd want to have a driving lesson with you ever again? I *hate* that you're my mother and I *hate* this family.'

Mimi had been bewildered. It was a slap to the face, as if that special moment in the car when they'd hugged had never happened. Then Callie had let out a growl of rage, thrown her school bag across the room and stomped upstairs, where she'd slammed her bedroom door before turning on loud music.

Pete appeared in the doorway. 'What's happened?' he asked.

'Callie made Mum cry,' said Tara.

Mimi wiped her eyes. 'No, I'm being silly. Obviously she had a bad day at school and she took it out on me. I shouldn't be taking it so personally.'

'No way. She was really mean, Dad,' said Tara, thumping away at Mimi's back harder than ever. 'I think you should tell her off.'

'Uh . . .' Pete looked unsure. 'Should I go sort this out?' he asked.

'I don't think it's a good idea right now,' said Mimi. 'I think we should let her have some time to calm down. Maybe try later?'

Pete let out a puff of air. 'Sure thing. I can try later.'

They heard a cry from one of the twins who'd been asleep for their afternoon nap and both Pete and Tara immediately moved towards the stairs.

'We'll get them for you,' Tara said. 'You relax.'

'Tara,' said Mimi, 'is there any chance you can stay this way forever?'

She glanced sideways for a moment. 'I can try?'

They disappeared upstairs and Mimi was left alone in the kitchen. It was only Wednesday. *How* was it only Wednesday? How was she supposed to make it through to Friday?

One drink, she thought to herself. *Just one drink from my special lemonade bottle to cushion the senses.*

Andrea

She knew she was doing the wrong thing, but her curiosity was too strong. Tony was in the shower and he'd uncharacteristically left his computer open. The Word document was right there on the screen.

He must have left it open because he thought she'd still be out. She'd headed up the hall to visit Heather and Violet and told Tony she'd be a little while. After Heather's break-through and admission that she did need help yesterday morning, Andrea wanted to make sure she kept the momentum going in case Heather suddenly turned on her again. She'd taken a packet of Tim Tams to share with them and pasted a bright, friendly smile on her face when she'd knocked on the door.

Heather hadn't been rude, but she hadn't exactly been thrilled to see Andrea either.

'I thought we could share these?' Andrea had said, waving the Tim Tams hopefully.

Heather had moved back to let Andrea inside. They'd stood awkwardly, Heather's arms folded tightly across her body as they made stilted small-talk, Violet watching the two of them with cautious optimism.

But when Andrea tried to move towards the couches, Heather had snatched the biscuits from her and said, 'Sorry, but can we do this another time? I'm just a little tired.'

So Andrea had returned home. Disappointed that it hadn't been a meaningful chat, but hopeful enough seeing as Heather had mentioned there being another time. She supposed this was going to be a more long-term process than she'd imagined.

When she'd spotted the open computer and heard the sound of the shower running . . . it had been too much to resist. Tony hadn't even let her in on the general plot idea for this book and all she wanted was a quick peek to see what it was like.

She slipped into his chair and checked the page number so she could make sure she returned to the right place after she'd had a look. Then she scrolled back to the beginning of the document and read the title.

Don't Breathe Twice, by Tony Lewis.

Okay, interesting. So, it was going to be a direct sequel. Catchy title, she supposed, if a little kitsch.

She started to skim read, wanting to take in as much as she could before Tony got out of the shower. But after a moment or two, she found she had to stop, go back and re-read it.

What the hell was this? It was nothing like his first book. Obviously she wasn't expecting it to be polished, being his initial draft, but this was far from the quality of *Don't Breathe*. The sentence structure was all over the place. The description was clunky and the dialogue was awkward. This had to be a joke. Maybe he'd left this decoy document open on purpose, knowing she might look? She scrolled through the pages, but it was more of the same. And there was too much material here for it to be a decoy. She read a character description that caught her eye: 'Detective Bonnie had legs up to her armpits. And breasts that a man could bury his face in. Her blue eyes sparkled like sapphires above her ruby red lips.'

Andrea wanted to gag. *Don't Breathe* was smart. The characters were well drawn and the writing far from this clichéd example. What the hell had happened? She started to read more but then she realised the sound of the shower had stopped. She quickly scrolled through the pages, returning the document to its original place. Then she hurried over to the front door, opened it and slammed it shut.

'Andrea? That you?' he called.

'It's me,' she called back.

A moment later he appeared from the bathroom, a

towel wrapped around his waist. 'You're back sooner than expected.'

'I know. Heather claimed she was too tired for me to stay.'

'Sorry, honey. That's a shame.'

She saw his eyes stray to the computer. Then he wandered over to it and gently closed it.

Christmas Eve

The Good Samaritan, the first person to stop at the accident, was relieved to hear that the woman's husband hadn't been thrown from the car after all. The scene in front of him was overwhelming enough as it was. The idea of having to search through it all for someone else – potentially even a dead body – was terrifying.

And the emergency dispatcher on the phone kept asking him difficult questions. He was frightened he might get one of the answers wrong.

The second guy to stop, the one who said it was his mum's car, had asked him to stay with his mother, keep an eye on her while he figured out which car to go to next.

'Sir, did I hear you say someone was missing from one of the vehicles?' the dispatcher asked now.

'Oh,' he said. 'No, sorry that was a false alarm. No one was thrown from the car.'

This time, though, his answer was wrong.

14

Friday 18 December

Mimi

She was feeling rather delightfully giddy as she shuffled sideways along the row past the tucked-up knees of various parents and grandparents. Pete had driven so Mimi had been able to do the one thing she and the other mums had always joked about doing – watch a very long school performance while mildly pissed.

To be honest, she didn't really know how serious any of the others were whenever they made that joke as they sat through a shopping centre choir performance or an extra-long awards assembly when your child wasn't getting any awards. Usually they all made hilarious quips about needing a hip flask to get through it. And while she hadn't gone so far as to bring along a hip flask, what she had done was pour herself a few glasses in quick succession from her 'lemonade bottle' before they headed out.

She had wondered when she mixed her second bottle this morning if she'd gone through that first one a bit too quickly. Especially as the plan had been not to drink until tonight. But it had been such a tough week. And she had noticed that this time the ratio was more like two-thirds gin to one-third lemonade rather than the other

230

way around, but that was only because it had been going down a little too easily previously. Making it stronger would probably mean she'd pour fewer drinks.

Anyway, a few drinks would make tonight's musical performance much more bearable. And she was allowed to feel that way because Tara was only going to be on stage for all of two minutes, playing the triangle in the very back row of the band. For the remaining two hours and fifty-eight minutes (God willing it didn't go over three hours), they'd be watching other people's children from other schools sing, dance or play musical instruments and Mimi was bloody well allowed to be half-baked for that.

Plus, they had a babysitter for the twins, Callie was at a friend's house, and after the musical tonight, Tara was heading to a sleepover with one of her friends from the concert. So, Mimi had minimal parenting to do.

She flopped down into a plastic chair and Pete landed heavily beside her, catching the edge of her skirt under his thigh. 'Never enough room,' Mimi whispered as she tugged it out from under him.

'That's because these chairs are made for child-sized butts,' said Pete, not bothering to whisper.

'Shh,' she hissed with a giggle. 'You can't say butts in a school hall.'

He elbowed her in response. 'You're the one who's whisper-shouting.'

'Am not.'

'Are too. You sound drunk. Actually . . . you *smell* drunk, woman. Take a mint, for God's sake.'

Uh oh, did he know about her lemonade bottle? It had

felt like he was watching a little closely as she'd poured her drinks before they left home.

'Did you sneak in a cheeky glass of wine?'

Ah. 'Umm, yeah, I did . . . sorry.'

'No need to be sorry . . . well, except for the part where you didn't offer me one.'

'I know, I'm such a selfish bitch.'

'The worst.'

'I can't believe your mum didn't want to sit with us.'

'I know! She spotted that single seat in the front row and she was like a vulture. Like, thanks, Mum, don't worry about us.'

The crowd around them started to quieten down as a teacher took to the stage to introduce the first act – the Year Four choir from Gordon East Public School performing 'A Million Dreams'.

Oh! thought Mimi, *I like this song!* She and Tara had watched *The Greatest Showman* together three times after it came out on digital. Mimi settled into her seat to enjoy the song along with her pleasant buzz. The Year Four choir was followed up by two Year Six girls from St Thomas performing a liturgical dance, then the Sacred Heart marching band (who marched in place on the stage).

Mimi sat through most of it with her eyelids gently drooping as she waited for Tara's turn.

'Next up, North Sydney Public School ballroom dancers dancing to "A Million Dreams".'

Lovely, her favourite song again.

'And now we have the Fort Street Public School swing band performing "A Million Dreams".'

This time there was a quiet tittering from the audience.

By the fourth time the same song was announced, the parents laughed raucously and Mimi had stopped feeling so fond of it. Her thighs were sticky with sweat and she kept shifting uncomfortably in her seat.

Finally, it was Mowbray Public School's turn and the Year Three band set up on the stage. Mimi sat up straighter and tried to spot Tara, but she was barely visible at the back of the stage. However, Mimi did make sure to tune her ears specifically into the triangle and noted that Tara did a fabulous job dinging it rhythmically. She'd have to congratulate her on her timing later on.

When Tara's band cleared the stage, Mimi wondered if it would be entirely inappropriate for them to sneak out and wait outside rather than watch the rest of the show. She was considering suggesting it to Pete when she heard a familiar name being announced.

'Now we have Callie Lewis and Jordan Zhang from Redmond High performing a duet of "Shallow".'

Mimi turned to look at Pete. 'What the hell?'

He looked as surprised as she did. 'There's not another Callie Lewis at Redmond is there?' he asked.

She shook her head. 'I highly doubt it.'

They watched as their daughter and a young boy walked onto the stage and stood in the middle under a spotlight.

Mimi's stomach was somersaulting; Callie hadn't sung in public in years. Mimi had always adored the sound of her voice. She'd been so disappointed when Callie had said she didn't want to try out for the school musical in Year Eight. As had the drama teacher who'd been counting on her for one of the main roles.

When had she decided to perform in public again? And why hadn't she told them she'd be doing this?

The acoustic guitar intro began and Mimi pressed her palm to her chest as she saw the boy reach across to take Callie's hand, give it a brief squeeze and then let it go. Callie gave him a sweet smile in return. It was a gorgeous interaction, but who was this boy? Mimi had never heard her mention him before.

Jordan's part was first. His voice was rich and smooth. Mimi found it hard to believe he could possibly be sixteen like Callie. Meanwhile, Callie swayed slowly, her eyes trained on Jordan as she waited for her turn.

Finally, Callie lifted the microphone to her lips and started singing.

Mimi grabbed hold of Pete's hand and sucked in her breath as Callie's voice gently rose and fell with the opening lyrics of her part of the duet.

Holy shit.

Her voice was even better than Mimi remembered. Callie had always been pitch perfect, but there was something more to her voice now. Mimi didn't have the musical knowledge to define it, but she could recognise beauty when she heard it. It was somehow soulful and delicate all at once. Mimi was bursting with pride.

My girl can really *sing.*

Pete squeezed her hand and she tore her eyes away from Callie long enough to glance sideways at him. His eyes were shining.

She's incredible, he mouthed.

I know.

They refocused on the stage and Mimi sensed that the

rest of the audience was as spellbound by the pair as they were. Callie and Jordan's voices complemented each other perfectly.

When the song finished there was thunderous applause from the audience. Mimi almost leapt to her feet but stopped herself. They were amazing singers, but standing ovations were taking things a tad too far for school hall performances. She was tipsy, but she hadn't lost all control of her senses.

Callie and Jordan were the final act of the night. The principal wrapped up with a respectably short talk and then the lights were back on and the crowd was all standing.

Mimi turned to Pete. 'Why did she keep her performance a secret?'

'No idea. Maybe she was nervous.'

'But why keep it from us? We're her parents.'

Pete shrugged. 'Teenage girl prerogative.'

'You kept Callie's talent under wraps, didn't you?' said a parent Mimi only vaguely recognised.

They were standing outside the hall along with hundreds of other parents and family members all waiting to collect their children. Mimi tried to chuckle good-naturedly and bob her head in a noncommittal sort of way while not giving away the fact that she'd had no idea Callie would be singing tonight. She hadn't found Tara or Callie yet among the crowds of students and families spilling out into the covered walkways and quadrangle.

She touched Pete's elbow. 'You seen the girls yet?'

'No,' he said. 'But there's Mum.'

They moved through the crowd to greet Jill who was positively radiating joy. 'Wasn't Callie incredible?' she said as they reached her. '*I knew* she'd be wonderful.'

Mimi's head snapped towards her. 'You knew she was going to be singing tonight?'

Jill's face dropped and her voice faltered. 'Well . . . I mean, she only mentioned it to me very, very recently.'

Mimi opened her mouth to reply but Pete spoke over her. 'There are our girls.'

He pointed through the throngs of parents and children and Mimi craned her neck to see. Tara and Callie were both moving through the crowd towards them. They all met up and Mimi's eyes roved between her daughters. She wanted to gush about Callie's voice, but originally, tonight had been all about Tara. She leaned down and pulled Tara into a tight hug. 'Fabulous dinging on that triangle,' she said.

Tara hugged her back and then pulled away. 'Thanks, Mum, but did you hear *Callie*? She was awesome!'

'I know! She was amazing.' Mimi turned to Callie and saw her daughter duck her head, embarrassed.

'Why didn't you tell us you were going to sing?' said Mimi. 'Sweetheart, your voice has grown so much. It was absolutely beautiful.'

Callie chewed on her lower lip. 'Thanks. Sorry I didn't say anything. I – I wasn't even sure I was going to go through with it up until the last minute.'

Mimi stopped herself from saying, *but you told your grandmother.*

'Well, I'm so proud of you. It was an incredible performance.'

'Hundred per cent,' said Pete, reaching out to high five her.

Mimi saw Callie exchange a quick look with Jill. Something seemed to pass between them, but Mimi couldn't quite figure out what it was.

Then Callie said quietly, 'I wish Grandpa could have been here, too.'

'So do I,' said Jill. 'He would have been enthralled by your voice.'

Pete shoved the knuckle of his index finger into his eye. 'I agree,' he said, his voice turning a little hoarse.

'And her boyfriend was really good too,' Tara piped up, somehow completely missing the poignant moment between the family.

Mimi remembered the tenderness between Callie and Jordan at the start of the performance. She'd been so taken by Callie's voice that she'd almost forgotten about it. She tried to sound casual as she spoke. 'So . . . Jordan's your boyfriend?'

Callie shoved Tara. 'He's not my boyfriend,' she said. 'He's a boy and he's my friend. Tara just doesn't get the distinction.'

'I do too!'

Mimi couldn't help but feel relieved. It wasn't that she'd have a problem with Callie having a boyfriend, it was more that she didn't want there to be yet another thing Callie had kept from her.

'Anyway,' said Callie, 'you guys mind if I go? I need to find Peyton.'

'Already?' Mimi had so much more to say. She wanted to talk with her about her decision to sing in public again.

Find out where she'd gained the confidence when in every other respect, it felt like she'd been retreating from the world. She wanted to ask her about Jordan. What if Tara *did* have it right and he really was her boyfriend? And if not . . . was that something she wanted? When had Callie stopped talking with her? Confiding in her.

'Yeah, I'm meant to be staying at her house tonight, remember? Oh! There, she is. Peyton, wait!' Callie called out. 'Can I go, Mum?' she added.

'Of course,' said Mimi. She couldn't stop her. Even if she did, Callie wasn't going to talk.

Callie gave Jill a quick hug. 'Thanks for coming, Grandma.' Then she leaned into Tara and whispered something. Tara giggled. She glanced at Mimi and Pete. 'See you tomorrow,' she said.

Mimi noticed ruefully that, apparently, Callie only had the capacity to give out the one hug.

And then she was gone.

Andrea

It was a combination of things that had her betraying her husband's trust. Over the past forty-eight hours, Tony's manuscript had been swimming through her mind. She kept turning it over and over, trying to figure out why it read so differently from his debut. One minute, she'd dismiss it as normal for a rough draft. The next she had flipped. No. It would be impossible to turn what she had read into anything remotely reminiscent of *Don't Breathe*. Something wasn't right.

But then this morning, she was cleaning out her desk ready for the summer holidays and noticed a student's A+ essay stuck between some folders. She remembered the meeting with the student's parents. Showing them the essay. 'I'm sorry,' she'd said, 'but I simply can't reconcile this work with anything else Sasha has handed in this year.'

Sasha's father had been perplexed. 'What are you saying?'

But Andrea had seen the look of resignation in the mother's eyes.

'She means Sasha didn't write this,' the mother said. 'She's had someone else do the work for her.'

As Andrea stared at the essay this morning, it struck her. The difference between Tony's two books was just as stark as the difference between Sasha's usual work and her essay.

She means Sasha didn't write this.

But that was a high school student cheating on an assignment. Surely, she couldn't be coming to the same conclusion about her husband? It made no sense. If Tony's new book was the true quality of his work, how had he managed to get someone else to write *Don't Breathe* for him? Who would write a knockout novel like that and then let someone else release it under their name? And why wouldn't Tony get them to also write the next one?

Maybe she was missing something. Maybe she was completely wrong, jumping to unfair conclusions. Throughout the day, she'd wrestled with the question of whether she should confront him. Admit to having looked at his manuscript and share her concerns about its quality. In the end, she couldn't do it. She needed to know more before she broached it with him. She needed to investigate this further. So, she waited until he'd headed out to meet with his publishers. She had half an hour before she had to leave herself to meet up with Shaun. When she'd mentioned to Tony that she was going to be having drinks with Shaun, she'd wondered if he'd be a little jealous at her meeting up alone with another man. But on the contrary, he'd seemed quite cheery about her having her own plans for the night.

See, she'd thought to herself. *Even Tony knows you wouldn't be Shaun's type.*

Once Tony had left, she'd headed for his iPad. She couldn't look at his computer again, he'd have left it password protected. But the iPad didn't have his manuscript on it, so he didn't keep it as closely guarded. And this time, it wasn't the document she wanted to look at. It was his email. She wanted to look back through his correspondence with his publishers. See if he'd provided them with any snippets of his new book and if they were registering similar concerns. Or maybe even go right back to the email when he sent his original draft of *Don't Breathe* to them. Check the quality of that work. Anything that might explain all of this.

She knew that looking at his private email was crossing a line, but she was desperate for an answer. She sat down on the couch with the iPad and opened up his inbox. Then she began scrolling back through the emails.

She soon found emails that went back and forth between Tony and his publishers, but none that shed any light. It looked like they were in the dark on details of his second book too. In a few of the emails they'd requested a synopsis but he'd given them the run-around, telling them he couldn't share any notes on the plot yet because he was writing without knowing exactly where the book was going, but reassuring them that he was on track and happy with what he had so far.

Really? Andrea thought. *You're happy with that?*

She scrolled further. Right back to before *Don't Breathe* was submitted to an agent. And that's where she saw it. A bolded subject line that grabbed her attention. Late last year. An old email from Tony's dad. About a week before Christmas.

Sender: Frank Lewis

Subject: Writing opinion

She opened it and read at speed.

G'day mate. Reckon I could ask you a favour? I feel like a bit of a wally saying this, but I thought I'd give this writing thing a crack. It's probably complete rubbish, but I thought seeing as you're the more analytical son, it might be better to show it to you first. I know you'll be straight with me if it's no good. Reckon Pete or Darren would pussyfoot around my feelings. I dunno, your mum's said a few times that she thinks your brothers got their creative streak from me cause I always liked to tell tall tales, but that could be bullshit. Anyway, I haven't told anyone else about this so I'd appreciate it if you could keep it under your hat. Let me know what you think.

Cheers mate,

Dad

Andrea's skin turned cold as she clicked on the attachment and opened it up. *Don't be it. Please, God, don't be it.*

She read the title: *Don't Breathe, by Frank Lewis.*

When she walked into the small hole-in-the-wall bar in the city and spotted Shaun sitting at a table in the corner waiting for her, that same flutter appeared in her stomach. What was going on? Okay, so she was attracted to him. But who wouldn't be? He was good-looking. Well-built. Friendly, warm and caring. It didn't mean anything. And it probably didn't help that it felt like she and Tony hadn't slept together in forever. So, her libido was up a notch – that was no surprise.

Besides, she was in a strange, jittery mood after her shocking discovery about Tony's betrayal of his father. Of course her stomach was fluttering. She was confused and upset. She was afraid that her husband was not the man she'd thought he was.

She needed to pull herself together and focus on the reason she was here. This was about Violet. Nothing more. Hopefully a few drinks would settle her nerves and she'd be able to put everything else out of her mind for the time being.

But then she reached the table. Shaun stood up and greeted her with a warm smile and a kiss on the cheek. A kiss where his lips seemed to linger just a fraction too long. And a single thought flashed through her mind: *I'm in trouble here.*

Darren

He sat on the cool sand with his elbows resting on his knees. One piece of his broken surfboard was next to him. He assumed the other half had washed up further down the beach. The ocean was ink black in front of him but he could hear the waves continuing to crash, always relentless. He wondered what the time was. Maybe around nine?

'I wouldn't head out there now, mate,' another surfer had called out to him as he'd jogged down to the shore this afternoon with his surfboard under his arm.

'I'll be right,' Darren had replied. He'd tried to project an air of confidence. He didn't feel like being told what to do today.

'Don't say I didn't warn you,' the surfer said.

Okay, so the dude who'd attempted to caution him had been right. Darren wasn't experienced enough to cope with the rough conditions. He'd caught two, maybe three waves before the ocean started to batter him into submission. Next thing, his surfboard had been ripped from his arms. He assumed it had been destroyed on the rocks; he hadn't stayed to watch it happen, he'd been too intent on making it back to the beach alive. At least he was a strong swimmer, otherwise he probably would have been smashed to pieces on the rocks too.

'That was pretty fucking dumb,' he muttered to himself. He should have gone out for beers with his mates instead of coming to the beach. When Raj had messaged to say drinks were a go this arvo in the city, he'd hesitated before replying. There was a small white bandage on the side of his neck from where the doc had sliced out her sample. The guys would probably notice, they might ask him what he'd done to himself. He didn't feel like answering. They would shrug it off, tell him it'd be fine. But for some reason that wasn't what he wanted to hear.

What other conversation topics would come up? Usually Charlotte. *You still hung up on her?* Again, he didn't feel like answering. Maybe he was, maybe he wasn't. Maybe he was hung up on someone else now. Either way, there was no chance he'd confide in his buddies that he couldn't stop thinking about a chick he'd only slept with once. And he didn't want to tell them about his donation to Charlotte and Steph either.

Eventually he stood up and brushed the sand off his wetsuit. 'Pull yourself together, ya dickhead,' he said.

Back home, he changed and messaged Raj to make sure the night hadn't wound up. *Still going strong bro*, the reply came back. He was about to head out the door and join them, when he stopped and turned back. He walked into the kitchen, opened the cupboard above the stove, took down the mug with the leopard-print pattern and dropped it into the rubbish bin. Then he strode out the door.

15

Wednesday 23 December

Mimi

Her intention was never to lie about it. And certainly not to blame anyone else. But the problem was Jill's reaction. Mimi felt immediate shame.

The past few days had passed in a whirl of Christmas shopping and planning for the annual family trip to Nords Wharf. As Christmas approached, the reality of this being the first anniversary of Frank's death became more palpable and it felt as though everyone was on edge. Mimi had been a little shocked to discover she'd finished another pre-mixed bottle of gin and lemonade. But then she'd figured she'd needed it and she'd filled up the bottle in the fridge again. Callie still wouldn't talk to her and Mimi was fed up and scared. This time the ratio favoured the gin quite a bit more.

If only she'd paid closer attention when Jill went to the fridge. She should have remembered that Jill liked diet lemonade. But she was busy strapping Elliot into the double pram ready to take the twins for a walk, and by the time she looked back up, Jill was putting the glass to her mouth, and next thing she was spitting her drink out into the sink.

'What's in this?' she said, wiping her mouth.

Mimi straightened up. She was trying to figure out how to respond when Jill filled in the blanks for her. 'This tastes . . . *alcoholic.*'

Jill looked revolted. That's when Mimi threw her own daughter under the bus.

'That's Callie's bottle of lemonade,' she blurted out. Almost as though Mimi were a younger sibling dobbing in her big sister to Mum and Dad.

Obviously, she should have come clean, admitted it was her own. Explained that it was simply a matter of convenience. That no one else drank diet lemonade and she'd started pre-mixing so that she had the odd drink ready to go. But Jill was so horrified that the words wouldn't come. So, instead Mimi rearranged the expression on her face. Pretended that this was coming as a surprise to her too.

'Are . . . are you sure it's alcohol?' she asked.

'Taste it,' Jill said, thrusting the glass at her.

Mimi took a sip and tried not to let the feeling of contentment show as the gin slid down her throat. Instead she screwed up her face. 'Oh, umm, yeah. I think you're right.'

Jill took the glass back and had another sip. 'This is strong,' she said. 'It's not just a little nip in there. Mimi, do you think this is what's been going on with Callie lately? The reason she's been agitated? Down?'

Mimi hesitated. She didn't know quite how to respond. She was grateful that Pete had taken both Callie and Tara out. They'd gone to see Darren so the girls could meet his new dog. Apparently, he was going to get the girls to help him choose a name for him.

James started whimpering from the pram and Mimi jumped on the distraction. 'Let's start the walk so the twins settle down and then we can talk properly.'

'Good idea,' said Jill. She picked up the lemonade bottle. 'Shall I tip this down the sink?' she asked.

'I guess so,' said Mimi. And she tried not to let the disappointment show on her face as she watched her gin disappear down the drain.

Darren

'Can we take him for a walk?' Tara looked up at Darren with pleading eyes.

'It's fine with me but it's up to your dad,' said Darren, turning to look at Pete.

Pete pointed at Callie. 'You take care of your little sister and you take care of the dog, got it?'

Callie rolled her eyes but she looked pleased. Both of his nieces hadn't stopped patting Doggo since they walked in the door. Darren gave them the lead and they clipped it on and headed out the door without a backwards glance.

'Nice to see Callie not entranced by her phone for a change,' said Pete once they were gone.

'Maybe you guys need a dog too.'

'Yeah, not bloody likely. We're a tad busy. All right, tell me what this email said.'

Darren flopped down on the couch and ran his hands through his hair. The email from Elizabeth, his literary agent, had come through that morning and he hadn't known who else to talk to about it. Now, he pulled his phone out, opened the email and passed it over to Pete. 'Read it for yourself,' he said.

There was silence while Pete read, then he eventually spoke. 'Yeah, all right, this isn't ideal.'

Darren laughed. 'That's putting it mildly. If I don't deliver by March I'll have to repay the advance. I'm fucked.'

'Okay, yeah, it's not great. But it's also not impossible.'

'Pete! You don't get it. I don't have anything. Not a single word down on paper.'

'But you have ideas, right? Hold up,' Pete interrupted himself. 'You just got a Facebook message from someone. Here.' He passed the phone back.

Darren swiped on the message and the first thing he saw were two capitalised words at the top: *LOST DOG!!!*

His body tensed as he read the rest of the message.

Hi Darren,

I saw your post on the Lost and Found Pets North Shore Facebook page and it looks like you've found my beloved dog, Freddie! I'm so excited, I couldn't believe it when I saw the photo you shared, I thought I'd never see him again. Could you please call me on the number below so we can arrange to meet? I can't wait to see Freddie. You've seriously made my year for me.

Thank you so much!

Tia

Darren felt like punching something. He wished he'd never put the Facebook posts up. He should have known some fucking flake would come out of the woodwork to claim the dog. Doggo was better off with him. Hadn't the vet said he hadn't been well looked after? His fur had been overgrown and matted. He was underweight and he had fleas. And he'd been wandering around that park, lost and alone.

So why hadn't Tia been searching for him? Why hadn't he seen any lost dog posters or Facebook posts for him? She didn't deserve to have him back.

His thumb hovered over the trash can icon above the message. He could pretend he'd never received it. Maybe it had been accidentally deleted. Maybe he could block her profile and take down the Facebook posts and just pretend.

But he knew he couldn't do that. Because what if this Tia woman had a perfectly good explanation for everything? And what if she really did love and miss this dog? Which might mean the dog was missing her too.

He moved his thumb away from the delete button and put the phone down on the couch next to him. 'It's about the dog,' he said to Pete. 'Seems like someone wants to claim him.'

Pete let out a sound of disappointment. 'Mate, I'm sorry.' He put a hand on Darren's shoulder. 'You all right?'

Darren's body jerked under his brother's touch. 'Not really.'

'You know that's a good thing, right, reuniting a dog with its owner? You did a really good thing.'

'Yeah well, I feel shit. And also . . .'

'Also what?'

Darren stopped. He'd been about to tell Pete about the mole on his neck. He'd taken the bandage off now, so it was no longer noticeable. Not that his mates had even mentioned it when he'd joined them on Friday night anyway. But the doctor still hadn't called with his results and the longer he waited, the more he felt certain it was going to be bad news. He changed his mind and instead he blurted out, 'I met someone.'

He squeezed his eyes shut. Why the hell had he gone with that when he could have said any one of a thousand other things? *And also, I had a crappy night's sleep. And also, I've got a shocking headache. And also, I'm waiting to find out if Charlotte's girlfriend is pregnant with my baby. That one would have been a good conversation-starter.*

He hadn't even been thinking about Sage . . . but then, maybe he had. Because he'd remembered how much he'd wanted to show her Doggo after he'd been groomed but hadn't been able to. And now he was realising he was about to lose his dog as well.

'Yeah?' Pete's eyes brightened.

But Darren shook his head. 'It's not a good thing. I met this woman but turns out she's not interested.'

Pete gave him a look. 'Not much we can do about that unfortunately.'

'Ha. I'm just sick of everything at the moment.'

'Well, you know what you need to do?'

'What's that?'

'Use it. Use all of it. Channel everything you're feeling into your writing. You've got to get out of your damn head and stop fucking around. Put that bloody Sagittarius woman out of your head and write.'

Darren flinched. 'How do you know her name?'

'Huh?'

'The woman I was seeing? How do you know her name?'

'What? I wasn't talking about her. I was talking about the reviewer. From the *SMH*.'

'But that's a guy. S. Carter wrote that review.'

'Talk about sexist stereotypes, buddy. S. Carter isn't a guy. It's a woman. She goes by her first initial because she hates her name – Sagittarius.'

Jill

It was throughout the walk that Jill had caught onto the truth. Mimi's stilted voice made it obvious. There was no way that bottle belonged to Callie. It was Mimi's. And for some reason, she was hiding it. And hiding alcohol was never a good sign. She'd bloody well known that Mimi was going to find it hard with the twins. Why hadn't she insisted on helping more? Jill had decided not to call her out on her lie yet though. For whatever reason, Mimi wasn't ready to talk and Jill didn't want to force her. After all, she knew what it was like to avoid something, considering the fact she still hadn't reopened that email. She knew she would have to read it eventually. But it could wait, at least until after Christmas. For now, she needed to keep an eye on Mimi. Maybe up at Nords Wharf they would get the chance to chat.

Back at home, Jill had opened her suitcase on her bed and started packing her neatly folded clothes into it when the doorbell rang. She opened the door and found Andrea standing on the porch, a strange, sad look on her face.

'What is it?' Jill said immediately. 'What's wrong?'

'It's Tony,' Andrea said. 'He's been lying to me. Actually, he's been lying to all of us.'

They had sat and talked for over an hour. Their cups of tea had gone cold. The plate of biscuits Jill put down in front of them remained untouched. To begin with, Jill had been disbelieving. She was certain there had been some sort of mix-up. But eventually, Andrea had got through to her and she understood. Tony had stolen his father's book.

'But how was Frank writing it without me even knowing?' Jill had asked, more than once.

'I can't answer that,' Andrea had said. 'But maybe he was embarrassed? Scared that he would fail and so that's why he kept it to himself. I'm sure his plan was to show you eventually.'

The hard part had been deciding what to do about it. Should they confront Tony? Should they talk with Pete and Darren? Should they find a way to give Tony the opportunity to own up to it?

In the end, they'd decided to do nothing for now and to discuss it further, up at the holiday house. Jill wanted a little time to think it all through.

They stood out on Jill's front porch to say their goodbyes. Andrea wrapped her arms around herself and shivered despite the warmth of the late afternoon sunshine. A light breeze was snaking its way around her body but instead of finding it refreshing she felt like it was giving her a chill.

'Do you want a cardigan to take with you, love?' Jill asked.

'I think it's more of an emotional shiver.'

'I'm not surprised.'

'Do you mind that I brought this to you, Jill? I'm so sorry, I didn't know what else to do.'

'Absolutely not,' Jill said. 'You did the right thing. He's my son and I deserve to know.'

'Remember how I asked you if you thought Tony would be open to having kids?'

'Yes.'

'I brought it up with him before I discovered this . . . news. He said he was happy to think about it.' Andrea looked down at her feet and then back up at Jill. 'Now I'm so confused. I feel like I don't even know who he is anymore. What kind of man does something like this? Who steals from their late father?'

Jill looked past her, out towards the quiet street. An unreadable expression on her face. She looked like she was about to say something and then seemed to change her mind. She shifted her gaze back to Andrea. 'I honestly don't know,' she said. 'But we'll figure this out.'

'All right, I'd better get going. I should check in on Heather and Violet when I get home. I haven't been able to catch her over the past few days.'

'Good luck,' said Jill.

Andrea drove home feeling frustrated that they hadn't come to a conclusion about confronting Tony. But she supposed it was fair that Jill needed the time to digest. The problem was that it had already been percolating in Andrea's mind for the past few days. Tony would surely know something was wrong with her. She wasn't a good enough actress to hide her emotions completely.

Although it helped that she had her own guilty feelings to balance things out.

16

Thursday 24 December – Christmas Eve

Mimi

'Did you check the oil and water?'

'Yes, even though we got it serviced last week, I double-checked.'

'And they were sure it didn't need new tyres?'

Pete smiled. 'Yes, hundred per cent. What's going on?'

'It's a big drive for Callie, that's all. And it'll be dark as well.'

Jill had suggested they leave quite late to miss the afternoon Christmas traffic. She wanted to make sure their convoy could stay together without other cars cutting in.

'Yes, but we'll be right there with her, so it's all good. Don't stress.'

Mimi turned to see Callie dragging her suitcase from the bottom of the stairs towards the front door. She shot her mother a look. 'You don't think I can do it?' she asked.

Mimi closed her eyes. *Of course, she'd happen to come down right as they were talking about her.*

'I absolutely think you can do it. You're a great driver. I was only making sure the car is fine, that's all.'

Pete moved past Mimi towards Callie and lifted the case for her. 'Here, I'll take it out for you. I'm assuming by the weight you've packed enough until Christmas next year?'

'Ha, ha, Dad.'

Andrea

Andrea re-read the note in her hand. She hadn't told Tony about it. Instead she'd lied and said she needed to dash out and buy one more gift before they headed off. That it would be better if he just got on the road without her and that she'd catch them up in her own car. She needed him to leave first because she had an idea and she didn't think he'd be so keen on it.

He'd hesitated before agreeing; it was clear that he wanted to ask her what had been wrong these past few days. But even if she and Jill hadn't agreed to wait until later to deal with Tony stealing Frank's book, today wasn't the day to do that. Not on the anniversary of his father's death.

In the end, it was easy to get Tony to agree to go ahead without her. Everyone knew how important it was to Jill that her sons met up at the service station before the freeway so that they could drive together.

Andrea was glad she'd been the one to spot the note under the door, with its large, careful handwriting and misspelled words.

Dear Andrea,

Please may I spend Chrissmas with you? Today mummy tole me santa issnt real. But I know he is becose I sat on his lap at the shops.

So mabey he will still come if I am at your place. And I miss haveing
monkey wen I go to sleep.

Love Violet

Its tenderness struck her hard and she knew she needed to do something. She was beginning to wonder if Heather's claim that she wanted to change had been faked for her benefit. Maybe it was simply a way to stop her from calling in child services. Ever since Andrea had attempted to drop in with the packet of Tim Tams a week ago, Heather seemed to be avoiding her. She couldn't let Violet have a miserable Christmas. If she reasoned with Heather, maybe she could get her to agree to her idea.

Darren

Don't forget to take the Doyalson Rd exit when you come off the freeway, otherwise you'll end up halfway to Newcastle again. Better yet, hurry and leave so you can catch us up on the road. Love you.

Darren clenched his teeth as he read the message. How long had they been going to the Nords Wharf house? Obviously he knew which exit to take. He'd missed it once . . . *years* ago. It took all of his self-restraint not to write back: *Or how about I just give the whole fucking thing a miss this year?*

Of course, he wasn't going to do that. It was the first anniversary of their dad's death. As much as Darren had a whole heap of shit going on in his own world, he wasn't going to be an arsehole to his mother, even if he would have preferred to be alone right now.

He was going to have to leave a bit later than the others because he was waiting for Tia to turn up and claim her dog. He planned to ask her to show him photos of her with Freddie before he let him go with her, just to be certain she was the genuine owner.

At first, he hadn't understood why his mum had been upset that he was going to be running late and couldn't travel in the convoy as per her plan.

Pete had had to spell it out for him. 'Last year we all drove separately and Mum and Dad ended up caught on their own. That's why it's so important to her.'

And then Darren had felt like a dick for not realising. Of course, that made sense. But unfortunately, he'd already agreed to let Tia come and collect her dog. He promised he'd do his best to catch up. But at least Jill wasn't going to be alone. Pete and Tony were both running on time to meet her at the designated spot before they got on the freeway.

He tapped out a reply to his mum. *No worries, thanks for the reminder. Love you too.*

He crouched down in front of Doggo and gave him a scratch around the ears. 'You don't look like a Freddie to me, just saying.' He paused. 'And you would have had a bloody awesome time up at Nords. This Tia chick better take you for lots of walks and feed you the good stuff.'

Doggo sniffed at his face then licked his cheek.

'Thanks for that, mate. You know you're the only one who knows my shitty news? And now you're just going to leave me all alone with it.'

Doggo licked him again.

'Your breath stinks, you know that?'

The potentially bad news had come in the form of a phone call a few hours earlier. And it was one of the reasons he was in a such a foul mood. He almost hadn't answered it, seeing it was from an unknown number. But then he'd relented and picked it up.

'Hi Darren, this is Angela from the Fig Street Medical Centre.'

This was it. The call about that bloody mole on his neck.

'Doctor Clermont asked me to book you in for a follow-up appointment. When are you available to come back in?' the cool voice of the receptionist had continued.

'Why?' he blurted out. 'Is there a problem with my results?'

'Unfortunately, I don't have that information. But let's get you booked in and Doctor Clermont will be able to explain.'

He'd made the appointment and was frustrated to discover that because of Christmas, he wasn't going to be able to see the doctor until late next week. He wished they'd just tell him the results over the phone instead of making him wait.

But really, considering his track record with bad news these past few days, skin cancer wouldn't really come as a surprise.

Doggo continued to pant in his face.

'Your breath really is disgusting, buddy. But I guess Tia can get your teeth cleaned for you now.'

The vet had suggested a proper teeth cleaning was in order for the dog after Darren had found him, but after paying for his shots, check-up and groom, the expensive dental procedure hadn't quite been in his budget just yet.

And according to the email he'd received from his agent the other day, it probably wasn't going to be in his budget any time soon. There was no way he'd be able to get a manuscript delivered by March. Two months to write a book that was currently nothing more than a blank Word document was impossible. Not when he had zero ideas, motivation or inspiration.

And he needed to find out if Sage was the same Sagittarius who'd written that review. Although it seemed more than likely. Sagittarius was hardly a common name. So had she lied when she said she was a ballet dancer?

Within the space of four weeks he'd lost his career and his dog and had most likely been deceived by the woman he thought he might have really liked. Not to mention he'd handed over a sperm donation that, if he was honest with himself, he really hadn't wanted to give. No wonder he wasn't surprised to hear that his doctor wanted to see him.

'Where is this so-called owner of yours anyway? You'd think if she was desperately missing you she'd at least be on time.'

If she didn't turn up within the next ten minutes, maybe he could still chuck Doggo in the back of the car and take him up to Nords with him.

Of course, that was when there was a knock at the door.

Jill

There wasn't a single bushfire burning right now anywhere between home and the holiday house. And yet Jill had checked and double-checked the bushfire app over and over again this morning.

Her friend Marjory had phoned her the other day to see how she was feeling about the trip. 'Are you certain you don't want to change your plans?' she'd asked. 'I bet your family wouldn't mind.'

But Marjory didn't understand. Jill had to take this trip again. She had to get there safely this time. It was the only way she might start to feel okay again.

And besides, Marjory didn't know why it meant so much to Jill to spend Christmas every year at Robin's Nest. No one else did. Not with Frank gone.

Jill took her suitcase out to the car and checked the bushfire app one more time. Still nothing.

Everything was going to be okay.

As long as they just stuck together this time.

And perhaps up at Nords, she might finally get some damn sleep.

Andrea

Despite her determination that she wasn't going to let Violet have a bad Christmas, Andrea was still feeling nervous as she knocked on Heather's door. She was going to have to be clever with the way she presented her proposal. Find a way to make it really appeal to Heather.

As it turned out though, she needn't have worried. It was Violet who opened the door. Her face lit up as she saw Andrea. 'Did you get my note?'

'Yep, sure did. Where's Mum, honey?'

Violet's eyes dropped to the floor. 'Gone out,' she said.

'When did she say she'd be back?' As determined as Andrea was feeling, she still knew that she needed to talk to Heather first.

Violet chewed on her bottom lip, her eyes still fixed on her own feet. 'Not until tomorrow.'

'Wait, what? Are you sure? She said she'll be out *all* night? On Christmas Eve?'

Violet nodded. 'She got cranky with me because I told her I didn't believe her about Santa. She said I'd see for myself when I woke up tomorrow and there were no presents because there was no Mummy to give them to me.'

Andrea felt as though flames were coursing through her body, burning her from the inside out. How dare Heather treat her child this way, how dare she leave her all alone for Christmas.

The woman wasn't fit to be a mother.

Andrea crouched down in front of her. 'Sweetheart, I'm so sorry she said those things to you. But I'm going to fix it. You know how you wanted to stay at my place tonight?'

Violet nodded.

'Well here's the thing, I'm going away to a holiday house up near a beautiful lake for Christmas. Would you like to come with me?'

A voice at the back of her head was telling her that she was taking things too far. That taking Violet away up the coast was basically kidnapping and that she should find another solution, another way to make Christmas magical for her small neighbour. But the rage she felt at Heather was drowning out any sense of reason. Besides, Heather had told Andrea she wanted her to step in and help out.

Violet finally tore her eyes away from her feet to look at Andrea. 'Yes, please,' she said.

Then she launched herself at Andrea for a hug that nearly caused her to topple backwards. In all the time she'd known Violet, the most physical affection the child had ever instigated was to hold Andrea's hand. The unexpected hug told her she was doing the right thing.

'Okay, go and pack some clothes into your backpack and I'll write a note for your mum.'

Darren

When he opened the door, his eyes widened. 'What are you doing here?'

Sage stared back at him. 'That's a good fucking question.'

'What do you mean?'

'I mean I don't really know why I feel like I need to do this . . . but for some reason, I do. There's something I have to tell you.'

Darren knew then and there what it was she wanted to say. 'You're not a ballet dancer, are you?'

Her eyes flickered in surprise and then she nodded. 'How did you know that?'

But he didn't answer. Instead he held her gaze and asked, 'Sage, are you S. Carter?'

To her credit, she didn't look away and her voice was steady when she replied. 'Yes.'

He didn't know if he was furious or devastated or if he just didn't care anymore. It had been one thing after another and he was fed up.

'Listen,' said Sage. 'I didn't know it was you when I met you in the pub that day. And later when I found out you were a writer and I realised I'd reviewed your debut, I thought it might be best if we didn't see each other again.'

He held still, trying to figure out how he was feeling, knowing the truth. Betrayed? Tricked? But was that fair?

Eventually, he spoke. 'Thanks for coming to tell me,' he said. 'But why? What made you feel like you needed to?'

'I don't know! It's like you got under my skin or something. I started to feel guilty. And I wanted to see you again.'

'You mean, now you want to date or something? I thought you were only interested in casual sex?'

'I am! I was. I don't know . . . I'm just confused. Playing the part of your girlfriend that night, like I said, it was fun pretending to be someone else. Maybe I would like to see you again . . . Is that something you'd want?'

Darren groaned. 'Oh, now you think you're interested in something more? Now that I can see there's no way it would work. I mean, surely you get that, right? You hated my book, and my writing is who I am. It's me. And considering you shat all over it, that kind of makes things pretty awkward between us. So how would we date?'

'Look, I don't even know if that's what I'm saying, okay? It's just that I liked you. Or, I *do* like you, so I needed to talk to you. To tell you the truth. I'm sorry you felt hurt by my review, but it wasn't personal.'

'Yeah, well, to me, it is personal. Like I said, my book is me.'

Right then a woman approached from the lift. She was

tall with blonde hair tied back in a slick ponytail and heavy makeup. 'Darren?' she said.

Sage looked at the other woman and then back at Darren. 'Ah, I see.'

'Sage, wait, that's not what this is.'

'All good.' Sage held up her hand as the other woman looked back and forth between them. 'You and I were never a thing, you're free to do as you please.'

'No, I mean, she's here for the dog!'

'Oh,' said Sage. 'You found Doggo's owner?'

Darren nodded. 'Seems like it.'

Her face fell. 'Darren, I'm really sorry.' She still backed away though. 'But I should go either way. Let you sort everything out with the dog.'

'Sage, hang on,' said Darren.

'Here,' she said, pulling a card out of her back pocket and passing it across. 'If you do decide you want to talk sometime, this is my number. But you're probably right, it'd never work.'

Then she turned and left at a brisk pace down the hall.

Meanwhile, the other woman was stepping forward. 'Sorry,' she said, 'did I cause a problem there?'

'No, no, it's fine. You're Tia, right?'

'Yep.'

Darren stood back and let her in. Doggo was curled up on the couch, seemingly oblivious to the drama unfolding at the front door.

Tia held her arms open wide and squealed out, 'Freddie! Come here, boy!'

The dog lifted his head and tilted it to the side, surveying Tia with what Darren would say was a suspicious look in his eyes. Then he stood slowly, jumped off the couch and trotted over to her. Not exactly the bound of a pining dog who'd just been reunited with his long-lost owner.

Tia knelt down and started hugging him. 'Oh my God, you don't understand how happy I am to see this big boy. I've missed him so much. Thank you for finding him.'

She stood up and Darren saw that she'd seamlessly clipped a lead onto Doggo's collar without him even noticing while she'd been crouched down hugging him.

'How much do I owe you?' she asked.

'What? There's no fee! I *found* him and looked after him. I wasn't doing this for a reward.'

'Okay, well if you're sure.' She was already starting to move towards the door.

'Hang on!' Darren stopped her. 'How do I know he's really your dog? And when exactly did you lose him? You know he was in a really bad state when I found him. And how did you even recognise him from the post I put up – it wasn't that clear a picture.'

'Yes, I know, it was hard to tell from the photo, but a dog owner just knows, you know? And besides, now I'm face to face with him, of course I know he's mine. He's my Freddie!'

'But when did you lose him? Why didn't I see any posters or posts of you looking for him?'

'Honestly, it was a long time ago. I'd given up hope. And I live over in Marrickville. I have no idea how he ended up so far from home, but that's why you didn't see any posters – I never would have expected him to end up here.'

'Well, do you have any proof that he's your dog? Photos you could show me?'

Tia's face changed, her smile dropped and she fixed him with a cold stare. 'Are you kidding me? You want proof? He's my dog! I've been through hell wondering where he is and if he's okay. How about the way he ran right to me when he saw me?'

'He didn't exactly come racing towards you.'

'Are you for real? Now I'm glad I didn't give you the reward, you don't deserve it. Here I am, searching everywhere trying to find my dog. How do I know *you* didn't kidnap him in the first place?'

'What? Why the hell would I kidnap him and then put up a post saying I'd found a lost dog?'

'Maybe to try and make money from rewards?'

'I didn't want your stupid money!'

'Look, whatever, I'm getting out of here. You're an arsehole, giving me the third degree after everything I've been through.'

Tia stormed towards the door and Darren followed after her. 'Hang on, you never showed me any photos.'

He reached out a hand for her and she spun around and roared at him. 'Don't you dare even think about touching me. If you lay a hand on me, I'll call the cops and tell them you're stopping me from leaving your apartment.'

Darren pulled his hand back, bewildered. Tia opened the door and pulled the dog through it. Then she strode off down the hall with Doggo at her heels. He probably thought he was off for a nice walk; he wasn't even looking back at Darren. But then at the lift, Doggo turned, cocked his head and barked.

A second later, they were gone.

'We can put the roof down if you want?' Andrea offered. 'Feel the wind in our hair while we're driving up the freeway.'

They'd just hopped in the car in the undercover carpark and were about to get moving. The sun was setting but with the temperature being in the high thirties today, it was going to be a warm evening. Andrea's Mercedes was a late nineties model and it was pretty rundown, but she loved her old convertible. Even when Tony had offered to buy her a new, top of the range Land Rover, she'd declined. She was too attached to the Mercedes.

'Yes, please,' Violet said from the back seat. 'It's hot in here.'

'Watch this.' Andrea pressed the button and they both looked up as the roof retracted and folded itself neatly away. 'Pretty cool, hey?'

Violet nodded and Andrea started to back out of the parking spot. A twinge went through her body. Should she really be doing this? Taking a child that wasn't hers? Could she be arrested for kidnapping? But she'd left a note. And really, wasn't she protecting an unattended child? Well, maybe she could make that argument if she took her straight to the police station. But that's not what she was doing. So yes, most likely she could be arrested for kidnapping. But she wasn't willing to leave Violet alone on Christmas Eve. She wanted to give her a magical Christmas with a real family, like she deserved. So, fuck it, she'd deal with the consequences later.

In the end, she'd only left about twenty minutes after Tony and, knowing he'd be stopping at the service station to meet his family, buy snacks and fill up the car, it was likely she'd catch him up on the freeway.

Mimi

'Looks like we're the only ones here.' Pete was cleaning the windshield with a squeegee while Mimi filled the tank. Callie and Tara had gone into the shop and both twins were wide awake in the car, their little hands reaching out and legs kicking jerkily. As the petrol pump clicked off, Mimi noticed James looked in danger of crying. Why did babies take such offence to the car being stationary for all of five minutes?

'Not like us to be on time. I feel strangely proud.' Mimi put the petrol hose back on the cradle and opened the back passenger door to make soothing noises at James.

'Usually Tony's first cab off the rank.' Pete finished with the windscreen and headed round to the side of the car where Mimi was still trying to keep James from crying.

'Speak of the devil.' Mimi nodded towards the entry to the service station as Tony's shiny Lexus turned in, the last dying rays of sunshine reflecting off the bonnet. He pulled up behind them.

'Here's Mum too,' Pete said as Jill's Volvo followed Tony in and parked near the shop entrance.

'That's good, cause we've gotta get going before this one loses it.' Mimi then glanced across at Elliot and saw her bottom lip starting to tremble. 'Scratch that,' she said. 'We need to get moving before they both lose it.'

Jill

Jill sat still in the car for a moment after parking at the service station. She'd waved merrily to Mimi and Pete as she drove in, but now she was finding it hard to get out of the car. To actually face them.

Would anyone say anything? Would they acknowledge the significance of the day? Of the drive? Or would they avoid it for fear of upsetting me? Of course, they all had other things to deal with on top of remembering Frank.

Mimi and her secret bottle of lemonade.

Mimi and her troubles with Callie.

Callie and that sadness she was hiding within.

Andrea and her discovery about her husband.

Tony and his terrible betrayal.

Tony, the son who perhaps wasn't the person she'd thought he was.

Yes, they might all be feeling the pain of Frank's loss, but they also had other things on their minds.

Jill pasted a smile across her face and climbed out of the car.

As she walked towards her sons and daughter-in-law, she found herself staring at Tony. She had thought that, this being the anniversary of Frank's death, she shouldn't say anything about the stolen book. That she should wait. But as she stared at him, she began to wonder if she was wrong. If this was the exact time for her to

challenge him. If she owed it to Frank to confront their son today.

She made a decision.

Mimi

She had one hand resting on Elliot's chest, her body awkwardly stuck halfway into the car as she tried to soothe her. *Hurry up*, guys. It was taking forever for them to get moving. To start with, Jill had pulled Tony aside for a quiet word. Mimi had no idea what it was all about, but the conversation had looked unusually intense. Then they'd all disappeared inside the shop to pay for the petrol and snacks.

Finally, Callie came out of the shop and Mimi could see actual sympathy on her face when she saw her predicament with the twins. *Goodness, she actually does give a shit about me.* Callie headed to the other passenger door, opened it up and leaned in to help soothe James.

'Thanks, hon.'

Callie's eyes flicked up to look at her mother and then straight back down at James again. 'That's okay,' she said.

Mimi frowned. What was it that she'd seen in her eyes just now? Irritation at having to help out with the babies? Or something else? Something more like . . . despair?

She was about to ask her if everything was okay, if maybe they could just *talk*, when Tara came running out of the shop and across to the car.

'Oy,' Mimi said. 'Look both ways first, missy. This is a service station, cars everywhere.'

'I checked,' Tara protested.

'I didn't see you check.'

Tara ignored her. 'Guess what?' she said. 'I'm going in Uncle Tony's car.'

'Are you now? And is Uncle Tony on board with this?' she asked at the same time as Callie snapped, 'No you're not.'

Tara looked between them. 'Yes, I am,' she said to Callie, before turning her attention to her mum. 'He asked if I wanted to.'

'You can't,' said Callie.

'Why not?' Tara asked.

'Yeah, why not?' Mimi put in, curious.

'Because she just bought herself a whole heap of chocolate. And she'll get it all over his expensive leather seats.' Callie gave Tara a withering look. 'When you eat chocolate you're like a toddler. A baby. You make a huge mess of it; you're embarrassing and it's gross.'

'Callie!' Mimi said. She could see the hurt on Tara's face. It was amazing the way sisters could always hit each other right where it hurt most. Mimi knew Tara hated being called a baby, especially now when she'd been feeling so mature helping out with the twins. She also knew there was some truth to what Callie had said, and true jibes hurt the most. Somehow Tara always seemed to let chocolate melt all over her hands while she was eating it, ending up with it smeared on her chin and cheeks like a two-year-old with an ice-cream cone. Mimi kind of loved that about her – a girl who was so entranced by chocolate that everything else fell away. She could relate.

In the end, the only comeback Tara could muster was,

'You're horrible, I hate you,' before turning and running back across to the shop – once again not checking for cars.

'Callie, did you have to do that?'

Callie lifted her chin. 'What?' she said. 'I was only saying the truth.'

Mimi watched Tony emerge from the shop as Tara was about to walk in. The two of them stood speaking for a minute.

'Mum . . .' said Callie.

'What is it?' Mimi snapped.

'Never mind,' Callie whispered.

Mimi sighed. She could almost cry. She hadn't meant to let the note of impatience creep into her voice but she was disappointed that Callie had upset Tara, and she was desperate to get moving so the twins would settle down. 'Callie, I didn't mean –' she began.

But then Tony and Tara appeared next to them. 'I *am* going with Uncle Tony,' Tara sang happily.

Callie slammed the car door shut. 'I'm going with Uncle Tony too,' she said.

Tony gave her a nod and a smile. 'That's the way,' he said.

'Oh? Are you sure? But you were going to drive! Get in your night freeway practice. And I was thinking that if Tara was with Tony, maybe on the way up we could talk?'

'What would we even talk about?' Callie said, and then she headed behind their car to Tony's Lexus. Meanwhile James had burst into tears after the loud bang of the car door. *Thanks for that, Callie.*

Jill and Pete came out of the shop next and walked over to them. Mimi glanced from Jill to Tony, who was leaning against his car. Were they avoiding eye contact? She wanted to ask what their chat had been about, but it was going to have to wait.

'We really need to go,' Mimi said. 'The twins are losing it.'

'I'm good to go,' said Pete. 'Petrol's all paid for.'

'All right,' said Jill. 'Stick together, everyone.' She headed off to her own car, and Mimi turned back to her family, who were all hovering between their car and Tony's.

'Right,' Mimi said. 'Time to go. Last double-check. Who's going in which car?'

'I'm going with Uncle Tony,' Tara said firmly.

'So am I,' said Callie.

'But what about driving?' said Mimi, in a final desperate attempt to get Callie to stay with them.

'Why don't you grab your learner plates,' said Tony, tossing the keys to Callie. 'You can drive my car instead.'

17

Same day – Christmas Eve

Andrea

Andrea had attempted to make conversation with Violet for the first fifteen minutes of the trip, but eventually she'd lapsed into silence – it was far too hard to chat properly with the combination of Violet's tiny voice trying to reach her from the back seat and the roar of the wind with the roof down. Anyway, Violet seemed content to sit quietly and watch the darkening world go by.

The problem with the silence though, was that it was giving Andrea too much time to think. Tony and that damned stolen book. The same question had been running through her mind for the past several days: *How could he do that? To his own father? And if he could do something like that, what else was he capable of?*

This was the man she'd asked to have a child with her. And in a few months' time, they were meant to be revisiting that conversation. If he came back to her and said, *yes, let's do this*, would she still want to? Should she be considering bringing a baby into this relationship?

Then there was her own guilty conscience. But she quickly brushed that away. It was a mistake. Best to pretend it never happened.

Finally, Violet. The line she was crossing by taking her up the coast. The more she thought, the more she was realising that she'd done a very, very stupid thing. You could be arrested. *You could lose your job. The job that you love.*

She should have forgotten about the holiday and simply stayed with Violet in her apartment. That way the child still wouldn't have been alone for Christmas but Andrea wouldn't have been breaking the law.

She was probably going to have to turn around. She wished she'd come to her senses before getting on the freeway. Now she'd have to wait until the next exit before she could turn back. The hard part was going to be explaining to Violet that she couldn't take her on a fun Christmas holiday after all; that instead she was taking her back to her cold, unwelcoming apartment. Back to her cruel, uncaring mother.

Just picturing spending Christmas Eve in Heather's apartment, waiting for her to stumble in drunk or high the next morning and kick her out, made Andrea's skin crawl. She pictured Violet waking up on Christmas morning hoping for love and gifts and festivities. Saw her disappointment when her mother instead gave her nothing but snipes and jibes.

She couldn't do that to her. Who knew what was going to happen with Violet next? If Heather wasn't serious about turning things around, then Violet might eventually be taken away by social services. Andrea would continue up the coast and wear the consequences, no matter what they were. It was worth it to give Violet this experience.

Andrea glanced up in the rear-view mirror at Violet.

She couldn't tell if she looked happy or not. 'Everything okay?' Andrea called.

She saw Violet nod.

'Honey,' Andrea said, still having to raise her voice to be heard over the wind. 'Do you know your mum's mobile number?'

Violet looked nervous. 'Why?' she asked.

'I just thought . . . maybe I should try and call her, you know, explain about all of this.'

'But you left her a note.'

'I know I did. But it would be better if I had her permission.'

Violet shook her head. 'I don't know it,' she said.

'What was that?' Andrea called. Violet's voice had been whipped away by the wind.

'I said I DON'T KNOW IT!'

Andrea was surprised. She'd never heard Violet raise her voice.

'Okay,' said Andrea, 'It's no problem. No big deal.'

She looked in the rear-view mirror again and could see that Violet was embarrassed by her own outburst. She was biting her fingernails furiously and Andrea wondered what that was all about.

Mimi

Elliot continued screaming for the first twenty minutes of the journey and it felt like twenty hours. Or twenty bloody days. And somehow, miraculously, James had fallen asleep – as though her sister's screams were some

276

kind of soothing lullaby. Mimi wished the sound of a baby screaming had that effect on her. Instead, she was on edge and had a throbbing headache. When Elliot finally gave up and went to sleep herself, Mimi thought the silence would be like heaven. But instead it felt suffocating, as if there was tension in the air between herself and Pete, even though there was absolutely no reason for it. Everything was fine between them.

Maybe it was because of the way Callie had sniped at her before they left the servo.

'Hey, do you mind if we pull over and swap when we take the exit?' Pete said, breaking the silence.

'Why?' Mimi asked. 'We'll almost be there by the time we leave the freeway.'

'I know, but I'm bloody tired and sometimes it's that last stretch of a trip where you really get weary.'

Mimi shifted in her seat, trying to figure out what she could say, how she could get out of driving without seeming like she was being a bitch. The truth was, there was no way she should be driving. Not after the couple of drinks she'd had right before they'd left home. Although, then again, it wasn't like it had really affected her. She wasn't *feeling* drunk. But no, after that time she'd taken Callie driving and they'd passed the RBT, she'd promised herself she would never take that risk again. And the twins were in the back. Taking the wheel when she was over the limit would be grossly irresponsible.

But what was more irresponsible? Letting a tired person, who was actually saying they felt too tired, keep driving? Or driving herself despite being potentially over the limit when she *felt* perfectly sober.

She hadn't been planning on having anything to drink today. But then Callie had made that crack about Mimi not thinking she was a good enough driver, and the bottle had seemed to call out to her. The plan had been for Pete to sit up front while Callie drove, and Mimi to sit in the back with Tara and the twins, so there'd been no danger in her having a quick drink. Just a little something to help her relax before a long trip with four children.

Obviously, her sneaky lemonade bottle was now gone, thanks to Jill pouring it out yesterday. And to be honest, she'd wondered if that was yet another wake-up call. A reason to stop hiding the gin in the fridge. But the problem was, she still *wanted* it. She still wanted that way to relax. That way to escape. And so, she'd hid in the pantry and poured herself a quick shot.

She was only going to have the one. But it went down easy. So, she poured a second shot. And then, as usual, it took longer than expected to get everyone out the door and into the car, to pack all the bags and the boogie boards and the esky. So there'd been time to sneak back for another one. A generous pour for that shot. Then a final glass on the way out the door – one for the road. It had given her a pleasant but short-lived buzz.

That's what seemed to happen these days. She'd developed such a tolerance for alcohol that in order to get any kind of feel-good effect from it, she had to pretty much skol a few drinks in quick succession and then she'd get her happy buzz. But the buzz would always wear off too quickly and leave her feeling irritable, headachy, sticky-mouthed and stone-cold sober again.

'Are you really that tired?' Mimi asked.

'Kind of,' he said. 'I mean, I was the one who got up to the twins last night. At three and again at five.'

'You did not, they slept through the three o'clock feed.'

'Ah. No, they didn't. You did.'

'Why didn't you tell me?'

Pete shrugged. 'Was saving it up for the credit when I'd need it most.'

'But I didn't even hear them!'

'Like I said, you slept through it. In fact, you snored through it.'

'I did not. I don't snore.'

'Oh yes, you do. Like a freight train. Ask Tara, she heard you.'

'Tara woke up as well?'

'Yeah. If I'm completely honest, she was the one who woke me, otherwise I probably would have slept through the two of them crying as well. We're such excellent parents.'

'But why did she go to you instead of me?'

'She said she tried to wake you first but you just rolled the other way, so she gave up and came to me.'

'Huh. I had no idea.' Mimi shifted uncomfortably in her seat. She didn't like the idea that Tara had tried to wake her and she hadn't even realised. She'd shared a bottle of wine with Pete over dinner last night and then, after he'd gone to bed, she'd had a few gins on her own.

'So?' said Pete.

'So, what?'

'So, have I met the requirements, madam? Will you take over driving for me?'

'Oh. Right. Umm.' She hesitated. What was the right thing to do here? Admit she'd been drinking and face

279

Pete's judgement for skolling down spirits in the middle of the day or continue to lie, and trust that she really did feel perfectly sober?

Darren

He was more likely about half an hour behind the others rather than the fifteen minutes he'd claimed once he finally got moving. There was still a part of him that wanted to head in the opposite direction and run away from everything, from everyone. But he couldn't do that to his mum. Not knowing what she must be feeling with this being the one-year anniversary.

He couldn't stop thinking about Sage. About her turning up out of the blue. He wanted to know how their conversation would have gone if Tia hadn't shown up. He wanted to call her and talk. Because what if there *was* a way it could work between them?

She didn't know him from a bar of soap when she wrote that review. And then when they slept together, again, she had no idea she'd been the one to destroy his self-esteem and thereby his career. So how could he blame her for any of that? She was a critic with an opinion. She had every right to say what she wanted about his book. He was the idiot who'd taken it to heart, who'd let those words control him instead of shaking them off.

What if he was being a self-important dick and he and his writing were not one and the same as he'd claimed so self-righteously?

In all honesty, he wanted to ask her out on a date. A real

one. He wanted to tell her that it didn't matter if she didn't like his writing, because he liked her.

But then he remembered several things at once.

Number one, she still wasn't sure if she even wanted a relationship.

Number two, everything between them had been based on lies . . . or half-truths at least.

Number three, his life was currently in tatters, so he was hardly a catch.

He turned onto the Pacific Highway and was relieved to see less traffic than usual. His mum was right about leaving later and missing all the Christmas travellers. Maybe he wouldn't be as far behind the others as he thought. He wondered how Doggo was doing, back with his original owner. Was he happy? Did he miss him? Then he felt like an idiot for wondering. He was a dog. An animal. He'd probably forgotten Darren the moment he was out of sight.

His phone started ringing, interrupting his Spotify playlist. He hit the answer button on his steering wheel. 'Hello?'

'Darren, hi, it's me, Sage.'

She sounded out of breath, her voice didn't have the usual smoothly modulated tone to it. He instantly felt worried.

'Sage? How did you get my number? What's going on? What's wrong?'

'I have him. I have Doggo for you.'

'What? What are you talking about? He just went back to his owner.'

'I know . . . Hang on . . . let me just . . .'

He heard barking and then the sounds of Sage soothing the dog.

'Sage! What's going on there?'

'Sorry, I was just making sure he's okay . . . and getting my breath back . . . so I can explain.'

Darren waited, letting her take in a few deep breaths, then she spoke again. 'I followed her. That woman who took him. I had this weird feeling about her . . . this vibe. One of my colleagues at the paper has been working on a story about people who steal dogs for these illegal dog-fighting rings. Sometimes they just break into backyards and take them . . . but sometimes they pose as pet owners and collect lost dogs.'

'Wait, are you saying that . . .' Darren's chest had tightened. His knuckles turned white as he clenched the steering wheel. He couldn't finish the sentence.

'I know. I know, it's horrible. Awful. But it's okay, I've got him for you. I followed that woman after she left your place, around the corner, to a van. I knew I was onto something as soon as I saw the two guys jump out of the van and reach for the lead. She was about to hand him over and they were giving her money.'

Darren wanted to punch something. He'd known there was something weird about that woman, known he shouldn't have let her take Doggo. He felt sick. If Sage hadn't been there . . . the idea of what could have happened to his dog.

'What did you do? How did you get him off them?' His thoughts now turned to Sage, and the realisation that she may have put herself in danger to get his dog back . . . that she could have got hurt. That he hadn't been there himself to back her up.

'It's a long story and you're on the road. But just know that I've got him, that I'm glad I carry pepper spray, and that he's safe and the cops have those arseholes' number plate. I'll look after him till you get back.'

'Fucking hell, Sage. You're amazing. I love you.' The words came out before he could stop himself. To be honest, it was true. Right now, he did love her, because she'd rescued his dog and it was the kind of thing you'd say to a mate when they did something incredible for you like that, but he didn't love her in *that* way! How was she going to take it?

There was silence for a moment and then she laughed. 'You talking to me or the dog?' she asked.

He laughed then too, relieved. 'So how *did* you get my number?'

'I'm a journalist, remember? I can find out anything.'

'Impressive.' He paused. 'Sage, can I please take you out to dinner when I get back? To say thank you?'

There was another pause, and when she responded he could hear the smile in her voice. 'Sounds good.'

Andrea

Violet had always been shy. Quiet. But this was different. Every time Andrea glanced at her face in the mirror, she felt more and more concerned. Something was wrong. Maybe she was regretting coming with Andrea? Maybe she was afraid?

Andrea really had made a terrible mistake. She had to take her back.

'Violet,' she asked, raising her voice to be heard above the roar of the wind. 'Would you like me to take you home?'

She watched Violet's reaction in the mirror, saw her face slide from surprise to sadness to . . . relief.

'It's okay,' said Andrea. 'We can take the next exit and go back.' She would get her home before Heather even knew about the note she'd left. And instead, she'd deal with Heather the right way – through the authorities. Not through kidnapping her daughter.

Violet nodded. Then she spoke and Andrea had to concentrate hard to hear her.

'What's that, sweetheart?'

'I said I told you a lie.'

'What do you mean?'

'Mummy didn't say she would leave me alone all night.'

Oh no. 'She didn't? What did she say?'

'She said she was only going to have a nap for a little bit.'

'Wait . . . are you telling me your mum was still at home when I took you?'

'Yes.'

'Violet! Why did you tell me she was out?'

Violet's voice sounded teary. 'Because she was mean to me. And you're always nice and I wanted to be with you instead.'

That's when Andrea's phone started ringing.

Mimi

'I can't drive,' she said. Then she clenched her jaw as she waited for Pete to ask her why.

'No worries. If you're not up for it, it's not the end of the world.'

Oh. That was unexpected. But instead of relief she was feeling something else . . . disappointment? That was odd. She hesitated. 'Don't you want to know why?'

'I figured you're tired too.'

'But you got up to the girls last night. I didn't. Why should I be tired? Why should I have any *right* to be tired?'

He glanced sideways at her. 'I don't know, maybe you didn't sleep as well as I assumed.' He paused. 'Is everything okay?'

'No! It's not okay. I'm not okay. I'm awful. I'm a horrible, awful person who sleeps through her babies crying in the night and then can't take over the driving for her amazing husband who's tired because I'm a fucking drunk.'

Pete let out a bark of laughter. 'Mimi, what are you on about? You're not a drunk!'

'But I am! Don't you get it? That's why I can't drive right now, because I threw back half a bottle of gin before we left. That's why I didn't wake last night, because I had five shots before bed. Haven't you noticed? Haven't you smelled it on me? Haven't you wondered why I've been constantly pouring myself drinks from that lemonade bottle? Aren't you worried? Aren't you wondering what the fuck is wrong with me?'

'Wait, what? You drank half a bottle of gin today?'

'Well . . . no, I'm exaggerating. But God, I don't know, I drank a lot. And now I can't drive. That's bad. It's irresponsible. It's weird. Don't you think it's weird? Don't you think there's something wrong with me?' Mimi's voice was rising hysterically.

'Okay, can we slow down here? I think maybe you're getting carried away. One bad night with too many spirits and then a bit of hair of the dog the next day doesn't make you an alcoholic, honey.'

'You're not hearing me! It's not one bad night. It's worse than that, it's ... it's ... I don't know ... It's me escaping ... me wanting to escape from my life.'

'Wait, the lemonade bottle? You've been hiding alcohol in a lemonade bottle in the fridge?'

'Yes! That's what I'm trying to say here – I have a problem. I'm drinking and hiding it, drinking and lying about it. Blaming our teenage daughter. There's something *wrong* with me.' She put her face in her hands and rubbed at her skin in frustration.

'Blaming Callie? I'm confused.'

She dropped her hands and looked at him guiltily. 'Your mum drank from the same bottle yesterday. I kind of ... lied and pretended it was Callie.'

'You didn't?'

'I did.'

'Okay, okay, I get it. It's bigger than I first thought and I'm sorry, I didn't mean to downplay it, to dismiss you. I thought you were just feeling bad about a few big nights and that you needed me to reassure you.'

Now he reached a hand across and squeezed her thigh. 'And yes, lying isn't great, in fact, it's pretty crappy, because I always thought we never lied to one another – about anything. Except for that time you told me I looked good in those cycling pants –'

'Pete!'

'Sorry! I digress. But here's the good thing – you've told me the truth now, which means we can fix this. Because it means that you want help. You want to fix it. So, we're

going to do it together. And we're going to start with figuring out exactly what it is that you're trying to escape
from, okay?'

Mimi let out a long, slow breath. She'd told the truth.
They were going to fix it. Everything was going to be okay
again. And this horrible stage in her life was going to be
a small blip. A tiny moment where things had started to
take a dark turn, where things could have got much, much
worse. Where she really could have spiralled, done something awful, something she might have regretted for the
rest of her life. But instead, they were going to rescue her.

Her phone started ringing.

Jill's name was on the screen. Mimi looked at the phone
with surprise. Jill didn't normally call while she was driving. She said she found hands-free too difficult.

'It's your mum,' Mimi said before answering the call.
'Jill? Is everything okay?'

'Mimi, I think I know what's been wrong with Callie.'

'What? What do you mean?'

'I . . . I think it's got something to do with Tony.'

18

Same day – Christmas Eve

Jill

The first time something a little unusual happened with Tony, Jill brushed it off. After all, he was only young. He didn't mean anything by it. He thought it was a game. It was the middle of winter and she'd let all three boys have friends over after school. They'd all gone off to their various rooms to play.

But after only half an hour, Darren's little friend Tamara had come to see her.

'Mrs Lewis,' she'd said, 'I don't like the game we're playing.'

'Oh dear, is Darren not letting you have a turn?' Jill was used to playground politics from school.

'Not Darren. Tony. He keeps squashing me and I don't like it.'

'Squashing you? Goodness, what game are you playing? Where's Darren?'

'Tony told Darren he couldn't come in. I don't know what the game is, he made it up.'

Later, he had explained the game to Jill. 'I was the good knight and she was the evil witch and I had to stop her from escaping.'

'And how did you do that?'

'Well, I had to lie on top of her so she couldn't escape.'

Jill had carefully explained to Tony that Tamara hadn't liked the game. And that it wasn't okay for him to lie on top of anyone and hold them down, and especially not someone much smaller and younger than him.

Tony had said okay, and that was the end of it. Jill didn't mention it to Frank.

But then a couple of years later there was a phone call from the boys' school. There had been an incident with Tony, and Jill needed to come in. As the principal of another school, it had felt very strange to be on the other side of the desk.

It turned out that a girl had complained that Tony had slapped her leg on the school bus that morning. Even worse, Tony was twelve, the girl was only nine.

When Jill tried to talk to Tony about it, he told her it was because she'd ripped his favourite basketball card. But then the story changed when Jill found the card unharmed in his school bag. 'She was mean to me, Mum,' he'd said. 'She called me names.'

But eventually, Jill got to the truth. 'I told her I liked her,' he said. 'I asked her to be my girlfriend and she said she would. But then when I tried to kiss her she pushed me away. So, I hit her.'

It wasn't that Jill had let it go. She roused on Tony, told him it wasn't okay. She told him he couldn't try to kiss someone without their permission, that rejection was never an excuse to harm anybody. She gave him the old mantra: *Boys must never hit girls.* Of course, no one should ever hit anyone, but sometimes it was hard not to fall back on those deep-rooted parenting conventions.

But she still put it down to him being a child, making immature choices and mistakes. Even as a voice niggled at her that it was a little odd for him to want a much younger student to be his girlfriend.

And again, she didn't tell Frank. She knew he felt very strongly about boys mistreating girls and that he would have come down much harder on Tony, and that wasn't necessary. Not when she'd already dealt with it herself. Tony needed love and support, not a swift kick up the backside.

Over the years it kept happening. Little incidents. But each time, they were small enough to dismiss. High school romances that ended badly.

She was a complete bitch, Mum.

Tony! Don't use that word!

There was a rumour that Darren once mentioned but could never explain – the girls in his grade called Tony the 'creepy Lewis brother'. Jill had never entertained the idea that they meant creepy in *that* way. She just thought it was because he was a bit awkward.

There was the time in his late teens that she found the magazine under his mattress. She knew it wasn't unusual for a teenage boy to be looking at porn. With the things she'd found over the years from her high school students, she'd pretty much expected it. But the strange part was the ripped pages from a Kmart catalogue stuffed between the pages of the magazine. On one side of the catalogue page were grown women modelling lingerie. On the other side, small girls dressed in cute summer dresses.

She didn't put two and two together. She never imagined it was the other side of the page he was looking at.

Or maybe there was a part of her that did suspect but it was too horrific to even consider. So she told herself it couldn't possibly be the case and she pretended never to have seen it.

Then Edie had come along. Tony's long-term girlfriend in his late twenties. And for a while it seemed like everything had settled down. Jill believed she would never have to worry again about people calling her eldest son creepy or strange. Edie was lovely. Intelligent. Pretty. If she could fall in love with Tony then surely everything was fine with him. When they broke up after two years, Jill had been so disappointed. And then she ran into Edie in the shops. 'I was so sorry to hear you'd gone your separate ways,' Jill had said.

Edie had given her a piercing look before suggesting that she might want to ask Tony for the real reason they'd split. 'You have a blind spot when it comes to him, don't you?' she'd said. 'In your eyes, he can do no wrong. Try asking him about his favourite internet sites, see what your precious golden child has to say about that.'

Jill had backed away from her. What a ridiculous thing to say! Tony had told her they broke up because Edie wanted to focus on her career. That she wasn't ready to settle down.

Jill never told Tony about her run-in with Edie at the shops. And she never asked him what internet sites Edie might have been referring to. But perhaps that was because she was afraid of what the answer might be.

She hadn't thought of Edie for years. Not until four weeks earlier, when the email had arrived.

Sender: Edie_Simmons398@gmail.com
Subject: You need to know

The email that she kept refusing to read, because how dare this woman who didn't really know her son send her an email out of the blue with the intention of trashing him all over again? But today, two things had happened to make her realise she no longer had a choice.

The first was when she pulled Tony aside, asked him about his book.

'Just be honest with me, Tony,' she'd said. 'Did you steal your book from your father?'

The expression on his face told her the answer. But then instead of apologising, instead of asking her to understand, he told her to let it go. He told her it was done and there was no going back.

'How could you do this?' she'd asked him. 'To your dad? He loved you! He trusted you. Andrea told me you two are reconsidering having children. Imagine how you would feel if your own child did something like this to you?'

He'd snorted. 'Well that's a pretty unlikely scenario considering I've had a vasectomy.'

It was yet another slap to the face. And Tony must have realised he'd said more than he meant to, because then he stepped towards her, and she became acutely aware of how much taller he was than her. He spoke quietly. 'Don't breathe a word of that to Andrea. I'm letting her have her hope for now, got it? Just keep your mouth shut.'

She knew she shouldn't be afraid of her own son. She was his mother; it was still her responsibility to pull him into line. She should tell him that he'd splintered her heart when he'd betrayed his father. But there was something in the way he spoke that caused her skin to prickle and the words wouldn't come.

And then the second thing happened.

After they'd all said their goodbyes and were about to get moving, Jill had climbed into her car and looked in the rear-view mirror. She hadn't known that Callie and Tara were going to ride with Tony. But as she watched her two granddaughters climb into his car, she saw the look on Callie's face.

A look of pure fear.

And the words that Tony had said when she'd confronted him came slamming back against her.

Keep your mouth shut.

And then Callie's words, the day she'd turned up at her place in tears.

I'm keeping my mouth shut.

The two phrases tumbled around in her mind. The expression on Callie's face. The fear in her eyes. The anguish in her voice when she'd sobbed and sobbed at Jill's place.

Who told you to keep your mouth shut, Callie? Who told you that? And why? What were they making you keep quiet about?

Why hadn't she pressed harder that day?

It all came back to her then. Each and every incident over the years. She sifted through them and as she delved deeper, she began to understand. She began to see them all in a different light.

It finally hit her.

Tony was not the person she thought he was.

She'd scrabbled to pick up her phone and open the email. She read it at speed. By the time she was done, it was too late to do anything about it. Both Pete and Tony's cars were already pulling out of the service station.

She'd driven along the freeway, trying to figure out how to fix this . . . how to fix everything. And slowly, somehow, Frank materialised on the passenger seat next to her.

Why didn't you tell me about any of this, love? His voice was soft, not angry like she'd thought he would be.

'Because I never knew for sure. I had my concerns . . . but I thought it was nothing more than . . . some unnatural thoughts. I thought he'd grown out of it. I never believed he would actually . . .'

You still should have shared it with me. We're partners. We always will be.

'I was afraid,' she told him. 'He's still our son. And I didn't know what you might do.'

He reached across and touched her hand on the steering wheel. *Yes, you do. You know what I would have done.*

'You would have done the right thing.'

Jill, are our granddaughters in danger?

Tears streamed down Jill's face. They blurred her vision. 'They might be. Tony might have . . . I think there's a chance he's already harmed Callie.'

He squeezed her hand. *Do the right thing, be brave.*

She phoned Mimi.

Mimi

A sick feeling was rising up inside Mimi. When she spoke again, her voice had become hard.

'Jill,' she said, 'what does that mean?'

'I don't . . . I'm not . . .' Jill stumbled over her words.

'Jill!' Mimi cut through her waffling. 'You need to be

straight with me right now.' She could feel Pete glancing at her sideways, shocked at the tone she was taking with his mother, but Mimi didn't care. This was her daughter, she needed to know what was going on.

'I don't think Callie and Tara should be alone with him in his car.'

'Why, what has he done?'

'I think he might have . . .'

'Jill, for God's sake, he might have what?'

'I can't . . . I don't want to say it. Don't make me say the words.'

'Oh my God, Jill, do you mean . . .'

Jill let out a sob and the line went dead. Mimi held still for a moment, breathing hard as she attempted to process exactly what her mother-in-law had just said. Surely, she couldn't mean Tony was capable of actually hurting the girls. He was Pete's brother! He was their uncle. But then, at the same time, the implication was clear. Why would Jill make that up? She wouldn't. It made no sense.

Mimi twisted around in her seat. 'Where's Tony's car?' she snapped.

'I think they're behind us, why? What's going on?'

Mimi turned back to her husband. 'We have to get the girls away from Tony.'

Callie

Callie knew the moment Tara said she wanted to go in Tony's car that she couldn't let that happen. Not by herself. She'd almost spilled it all out to her mother then and there. But she didn't know how . . . she didn't know what to say.

And then there was the fear – what if no one believed her? Tony would deny it. He'd say she was making up stories. What if they all looked at her like she was a lying, conniving slut? So the only solution was to go along with Tara. Safety in numbers.

It had only happened a few months ago. The twins were brand new and Andrea had suggested that Callie and Tara come and hang out at their place so that Pete and Mimi could have some time alone with the babies.

'You two can swim in our complex's pool,' Andrea had said.

Callie had been keen, excited. She liked spending time with Andrea, and their harbourside apartment was amazing.

The problem came when Callie was done with the pool and had headed upstairs to change. Tara wanted to keep swimming so Andrea had stayed with her.

Callie hadn't been concerned when her uncle Tony had followed her into the spare bedroom. She'd thought he must have needed to grab something and that then he would leave her to change. But instead he'd closed the door behind him and stood staring at her without saying a word. Long enough that she started to feel uncomfortable.

And then he moved towards her. Instinctively, she stepped backwards.

'Don't be scared,' he said. 'It's just me.'

'Uncle Tony,' she said. 'What are you . . . what are you doing?'

'I think you know what I'm doing.' He stepped right in

close and the back of her legs hit the bed behind her. She tried to move around him, but he put his hands on her upper arms. 'I've seen the way you look at me,' he said.

She shook her head, bewildered. 'No, I don't look at you like anything . . . I don't mean to . . .'

He shoved her back onto the bed. 'Yes, you do,' he said as he climbed on top of her. 'So I'm going to give you exactly what you want right now.'

That was when she started to cry, when she started to fight. 'Don't! Please! Get off me.'

Then there was the bang of the front door of the apartment and he sprung away from her. Before he left the room, he leaned in quickly and whispered, 'Keep your mouth shut if you don't want everyone to know you're a slut.' And then he was gone.

Callie was left alone in the spare bedroom, her pulse racing and her chest hurting as she struggled to slow her breathing.

She couldn't understand it. This was her uncle. Why would he touch her that way? What had she done wrong?

She was left with one certain thought: this was her fault. She must have led him on somehow. Was it the way she acted? The way she spoke? The way she dressed? Dammit, why had she worn that stupid bikini instead of a one-piece today? She had to do better, she had to be more careful.

From then on, she made sure she was never again left alone with Tony.

Now as Callie drove down the dark freeway, she struggled to stay focused on the road. Having him right there beside her made her skin crawl and her stomach convulse.

She kept scratching at her neck, her chest, her arms, harder and harder each time. Her nails digging into her flesh. Her entire body was screaming at her to get as far away from him as possible, but there was no way to widen the gap between them. And every time he moved, she would flinch.

She was praying that he wouldn't dare do anything with the two of them there in the car with him.

'You're a great driver,' said Tony. 'Really smooth.'

Callie didn't respond.

'She went through a stop sign with Dad once,' Tara supplied from the backseat.

Tony twisted around. 'Oy, you dobbing on your big sister?' he said.

Callie saw him wink at Tara and she wanted to reach across and scratch his eyes out.

'Yes,' Tara said with a giggle.

Don't laugh at him, Callie wanted to say. *He's revolting.*

'Hey Tara,' said Tony, still facing the back. 'I hear you give great back massages to your parents. Reckon I can get one when we get up to Nords? My shoulders have been killing me.'

Callie felt bile creep up her throat. 'No!' she said at the same time as Tara said, 'Yeah, sure!'

Tony turned back to the front and reached out a hand to pat Callie's thigh. 'You okay, there?' he asked. 'You're sounding a little stressed.'

She wanted to bat his hand away but she didn't know how to do it without upsetting Tara. Tears stung the back of her eyes. 'I'm fine.'

She thought of Jordan. Sweet Jordan who had tried to kiss her for the very first time last week after the musical evening. He'd found her outside after she'd said goodbye to her family, when she was about to head home with Peyton. After she'd whispered to Tara that yes, actually, he was her boyfriend but be chill about it, please! Making Tara laugh.

Sweet Jordan who'd grabbed her hand and pulled her away from Peyton. 'Can we talk . . . just for one second before you have to go?' he'd asked.

Peyton had smirked and then darted away to give them privacy.

Lovely, kind Jordan, whose features had become stunned and then hurt when, moments later, she'd lurched away from him. 'Don't touch me!'

Jordan, who was meant to be her first kiss. All her friends thought it was hilarious that she'd never kissed a boy. Most of them had kissed boys when they were fourteen or fifteen. Some had kissed several! Some had taken it further. But Callie had waited. She'd thought it was all going to be okay when Jordan leaned in towards her. She'd thought she could push down all those repulsive thoughts of Tony. But instead, the moment he'd placed one hand on her waist, something had zipped through her body. And it wasn't a nice feeling. It was a nasty feeling.

Callie had chosen to sing that night because she'd thought it was going to be her turning point. The idea came to her when Peyton called her a wuss after she'd originally turned down Jordan's request to perform a duet together. 'OMG, why wouldn't you?' Peyton had groaned. 'If I had a voice like yours, I'd want everyone to hear it. Come on, Callie, be brave!'

That word had played on Callie's mind for days. She

didn't feel brave. She felt weak. She felt powerless. And she hated it.

She'd walked up to Jordan at school and told him she was in. And then she'd gone straight to the girl's bathroom and thrown up.

Be brave, she'd told herself as she sat in front of the toilet and wiped the corner of mouth after she'd been sick. *Just be brave. Then maybe . . . after you've done this . . . you can be brave about anything.*

Maybe you can tell someone. Maybe you can tell Mum.

But now everything she had with Jordan had been ruined. And she didn't feel brave. Not even a little bit. All because of *him*.

Tony turned around once again to talk to Tara and while his attention was elsewhere, Callie's eyes shot around the car, as she tried to figure out what to do, how she could stop him if he went too far again. If he tried to touch her. If he tried to touch Tara.

Her eyes fell on the cigarette lighter in the centre console. Tony still wasn't looking. She pushed it in to start heating it.

Andrea

Andrea wanted to cry. She had answered the phone to the sound of Heather's wild voice: 'WHERE THE FUCK IS MY CHILD?'

She'd tried desperately to explain what had happened. But she had no idea if she'd talked Heather out of calling the police or not. She'd assured her, over and over, that she was absolutely coming back with Violet, that she knew she'd done the wrong thing, that she'd only been trying to take care of her. That there had been a huge misunderstanding with Violet about where Heather was. But Heather had just screamed and screamed at her.

As soon as they reached the next exit, she would turn around. Would the police be waiting for her when she arrived back at the apartment block?

Oh God, what if there was already an amber alert out for Violet? She really had screwed up everything. She'd have no credibility when it came time to try to explain to the authorities that Heather had been neglecting her daughter.

She realised she'd better get over to the left lane ready to take the next exit. As she started to check around her before changing lanes, she saw a familiar Lexus in her side mirror. Was that Tony's car? Had she caught up without even realising it and passed right by him? Yep, there was Pete and Mimi's seven-seater and in front of them, Jill's Volvo. She started to indicate so she could move across and slot in between them. They were going to be confused when they saw her take the next exit.

'Andrea,' said Violet from the back seat, her voice so quiet that Andrea could hardly hear it.

'Yes, hon?'

'I'm sorry I told you a lie.'

'I know, it's okay, this isn't your fault. We'll sort it all out.'

'You can have one of my lollies if you want?'

Andrea smiled and glanced in the mirror. 'Nah, it's okay, you save those for yourself,' she said as she saw the small girl unscrewing the lid off a container and tipping something into the palm of her hand.

'Hang on,' said Andrea. 'What kind of lollies are those?'

'Mummy's lollies,' said Violet.

Andrea's eyes flew to the rear-view mirror again but she couldn't make out what Violet was holding. She twisted around in her seat for a better look. At the same moment as she spotted the small white tablets in Violet's hand, one fell onto the floor and Violet immediately unclicked her seatbelt. 'Dropped one,' she said.

'Violet, wait . . .'

Violet lifted her hand to her mouth and Andrea reached back to try to catch her arm. 'Violet! No!'

But she couldn't reach, had no choice but to take her eyes off the road for a split second. As she tried to grab Violet, the car swerved.

That's when she felt the huge jolt and slammed her foot onto the brake.

It was too late.

Jill

When the car to her right suddenly slammed into her driver's side, Jill had a moment of clarity. This was it. It was all over. Her sins had been tallied and God was coming to collect. No amount of Hail Marys could save her. There was no way to regain control, not at this speed. She was spinning out of control. All she could do was pray that her family following behind were somehow going to be able to veer around the crash.

Mimi

It seemed to happen in slow motion. Pete's eyes widening. Him shouting and pointing as the convertible came from the right to hit Jill's car right in front of them. They saw Jill's car spin out of control as Pete slammed on the brakes, but it was too late. There was no way they could avoid hitting them.

And then everything went black.

Callie

It was like the world had exploded right in front of her. One second she was strategising, trying to figure out how she was going to keep Tara and herself safe from Tony, and the next, her parents' car in front of her was slamming into her grandma's and everything was rushing towards them.

She thought that when she hit the car in front, everything would stop. But it didn't. Instead, they were flying through the air. Flying and spinning and tumbling. Like someone had picked up the car and put it in a giant tumble dryer.

In the end, she squeezed her eyes shut tight and waited for it to all be over.

Darren

There was no need for the guy on the side of the road to wave his arms at him, to flag him down. Of course he was going to stop. The crash scene before him looked horrific. But it never occurred to him that it might be his own family involved. That something had happened to cause their careful convoy of cars to seemingly implode.

After stumbling back from his mother's car, realising that there were three more cars filled with members of his family that needed his attention, he was frozen in place for a moment.

Who the hell was he supposed to go to first?

19

Mimi

'Mimi! Mimi! *MIMI*! Are you with me?'

She couldn't seem to focus on his voice because she couldn't hear him over the screaming. But then he shook her and her mouth snapped closed and the screaming stopped. *Silence.* She said the first thing that came to mind. 'Sorry!' As though her manners were kicking in on autopilot, as though she'd been caught doing something unseemly in public – throwing a tantrum, shouting at the top of her lungs for no reason.

But there was a reason. A very good reason. She looked up to see Darren leaning into the car, his eyes full of terror.

'It's okay,' he said. 'But, can you move? Can you get up? I need your help.'

'I think so,' she said. She turned sideways to look at Pete. He had a huge raised lump on the side of his head and a gash down his right arm. But he was awake, staring straight ahead with a dazed expression on his face. She was about to ask him if he was okay when she became aware of something: The silence. There was still silence. It was eerie . . . why was it eerie? What was it that she wanted to hear? And that's when it hit her. Why couldn't she hear . . . crying?

Her thoughts flew to the back seat. To her babies. Her twin girls. What the hell was she doing just sitting there when she didn't even know if her babies were okay? They should be crying. They should be wailing at the top of their lungs. Her motherly instincts were finally kicking in and all she could think was, *Please let them be okay, please, please let them be okay.*

'The babies,' she said, and she climbed out of the car, pushing past Darren to move around to the rear door to yank it open. Both girls were still strapped into their capsules and, incredibly, both were wide awake but quiet. The two of them staring up at her, as though nothing had happened. As though everything was perfectly normal. She started patting her hands over them, checking their little bodies, their arms, their legs. She started crying.

'They're okay,' she said to Darren. 'They're both okay.'

'Thank God,' he said.

There was a cough from the driver's seat and Darren darted around to the other side.

Mimi felt guilty for barely having checked on Pete, but her first priority had been those two tiny humans whose lives depended solely on her. If she'd failed them, she never would have been able to forgive herself.

Now that she knew they were all right, she dashed around to her husband. He still looked stunned and confused and she felt a rush of love and sympathy for him, but she couldn't stay to help him. He was conscious . . . he was alive. And Darren was with him.

'I'm going to find the girls,' she told him. 'Stay with the twins.'

Pete was groggy but he understood. He nodded. 'Go.'

Mimi stumbled back from the car and looked around, squinting through the darkness as she tried to properly take in the scene around her for the first time. To one side – Jill's Volvo. A stranger next to the car with a phone to his ear. She looked the other way and saw the crumpled convertible – the car they'd watched slam sideways into Jill. And then she recognised it. That was Andrea's convertible. And there was Andrea slumped over the wheel. Mimi's stomach turned. Andrea needed help.

But then she saw it – Tony's Lexus, tipped on its side. Callie's small form hanging in the driver's seat, held up by the seatbelt. She ran.

Jill

Jill was still trying to make sense of it all. To understand what had happened. She started to work her way back and piece it all together.

She remembered leaving the service station.

She remembered seeing that look on Callie's face. That look of terror that filled her with guilt and made her heartsick.

She looked sideways and remembered seeing Frank sitting there next to her. For a moment she was confused, her brain was muddled. But then the last twelve months slotted back into place in her mind. Frank hadn't been there at all.

And then she remembered realising that she had to act. Calling Mimi.

And then.

And then . . .

The car smashing into her. Her reckoning.

But it wasn't her reckoning, was it? Because she was still alive. And that's when she started to think about her family. Because they'd all been travelling in convoy, hadn't they? They'd been right behind her. So . . . where were they? Darren had been here, briefly, but where had he gone? And why hadn't anyone else stopped?

That's when it all fell into place in a rush. The impact after impact of more cars piling up after the first one had swerved into her. Her family hadn't stopped to help her because her family had been involved in the accident.

She needed to go and help them.

Darren

He'd wrapped Pete's bloodied arm up in a cloth he'd found on the back seat of their car. White with large yellow daisies. It must have belonged to one of the twins. It felt wrong to see the red patch blooming across the daisies. Pete still wasn't right, but he was looking more alert and Darren knew he needed to get to the next car.

'Listen, mate, I don't want to leave you, but . . . Andrea, she looks bad . . . and there's still no ambo yet. Do you think you'll be . . . ?'

His brother lifted his head and made eye contact with him. 'I'll be fine. I'll stay with the babies.'

Darren nodded and pulled away from the car. For a split second, he hesitated. What if he reached Andrea and found her . . . dead. She looked so still. So . . . lifeless. He was terrified. But then his body kicked back into gear and he started running towards the convertible. A glance at the damage on the car told him it must have rolled. The idea of it rolling with her strapped inside it made him almost gag. Could she really have survived that? And why was she alone anyway? Why had she and Tony brought separate cars?

When he reached the car, he placed two hands gently on her shoulders and then eased her back, pulling her away from the steering wheel. The moment he moved her, he cursed himself. Should he have kept her completely still? What if there was spinal damage and he was only making it worse?

'Andrea?' he asked. 'Andrea, are you with me? Are you there? Please, please wake up.'

There was no movement, and he couldn't tell if she was breathing. Where the hell was the ambulance?

Andrea

She was sitting at her desk at the front of the classroom, but she couldn't seem to get comfortable. She kept trying to shift her position, but her body was too heavy, her limbs wouldn't lift. Her neck ached. In fact, she couldn't even lift her head, which wasn't good. Not good at all. How was she supposed to keep an eye on what the kids were up to? They'd get away with murder if you let them.

Come on, concentrate, focus. Open your eyes. Just . . . open them! It was that simple. But her eyelids wouldn't comply; it was as though they'd been pasted closed with thick glue. She reached out in front of her, maybe she could find something on her desk to help pry open her eyes. But as she felt around, the desk seemed to slip out of her grasp, as though it was being pulled away, as though it were flying away from her – or was she flying backwards away from it?

Away from everything?

Mimi

Her heart was in her throat as she rapped her hand against the broken windscreen. 'Callie, Callie, can you hear me?'

Callie's eyes snapped open and locked with Mimi's. She started struggling against her seatbelt, her legs kicking. 'Mum, help me, help me.'

'I'm here, it's okay, I'm here.' She couldn't see through to check if Tara was okay and she was about to ask when she heard a second voice.

'Mum? Mummy?'

'I'm here, Tara, it's okay, baby, I'm here. I'll get you out of there.'

Mimi looked down at the front passenger seat. Tony was slumped against the window on the ground. It looked like he was unconscious. Seeing Tony brought it all rushing back. The phone call from Jill right before the accident. The implication of Jill's words even though she refused to say exactly what she meant.

What had that monster done to her daughter?

She started to kick at the bottom of the already cracked windscreen, away from where Callie hung sideways in the driver's seat and down near Tony. 'Hold on,' she said, 'I'm getting you out, just hold on.' Within seconds she had the frame of the windscreen loose and she was able to crouch down, get hold of it with her hands – the sharp edges cutting into her skin – and rip at it until it was pulled away enough for her to fit. She dropped to her hands and knees and started to climb in, going a little slower now. She didn't know how steady the car was, balanced on its side like this. What if she caused the whole thing to tip over onto its roof. Her entire body was trembling as she eased her way in. Her face came right up against Tony's before she could twist herself around and then carefully stand up inside the car, her legs brushing up against Tony's motionless body. The car remained still and Mimi exhaled, she'd made it.

'Tara,' she said, 'I'm going to get your sister free from her belt and then I'm going to climb back there and help you out, okay?'

'Okay,' Mimi heard her say in a small, scared voice.

'Are you hurt? Does anything feel . . . ?' She was going to ask her if anything felt broken but she couldn't finish the sentence. She changed her mind and just repeated, 'Are you hurt?'

'I think I'm okay,' Tara said. And again, her voice was so tiny that it shattered Mimi at her core. She was so used to her always sounding so firm, so sure of herself, so much more grown-up than her age.

She put her arms around Callie to support her and then pushed on the seatbelt release. She felt the weight of Callie's body in her arms and then braced her as she lowered her legs down until she was standing next to her on the smashed passenger-side window. Between Mimi, Callie and Tony, there was barely any room for them to move, and Callie's entire body was shaking against Mimi's.

'You're okay,' Mimi said to her, even though she didn't know if her daughter truly was okay. Nor if Callie was going to be able to climb out of the car while she was shaking so much; her legs were barely holding her up.

'You're going to be okay,' Mimi said again, more firmly. She needed Callie to believe it. 'Now, I want you to crouch down and climb out through the gap in the windscreen down there. Then I'm going to get Tara out.'

Callie nodded and started to lower herself and then she stopped. 'Mum . . . I have to tell you something. Something about Uncle Tony.'

At that moment, Mimi knew that there was no doubt about what Jill had been trying to say to her.

'Did he hurt you?' Mimi said.

'He . . . he tried to . . .' Callie's voice broke away. She couldn't say it.

Mimi took her daughter's face in her hands and looked her in the eyes. 'It's okay,' she said. 'You don't have to say it right now. We're going to talk about everything, but right now, I need to get you somewhere safe.'

She could see that Callie understood and she nodded. Then Callie dropped down and Mimi pressed herself back against Tony to give Callie the room to climb out. Once Callie had squeezed her way through, Mimi bent over and leaned through the two front seats to the back.

Tara was cowering down in the corner. She looked like she'd shrunk to half her size just from the way she had folded in on herself in fear.

'Is your seatbelt still done up?' Mimi asked.

Tara nodded.

'Okay, hang on, I'll get you out.'

Mimi reached back, found the button and unclipped her. 'Can you climb towards me?'

Tara shook her head. 'I can't,' she said. 'I'm scared.'

'It's okay,' said Mimi. 'I'm not going to let anything bad happen to you.' She pushed her way further between the front seats so that she could get hold of Tara. 'Put your arms around my neck. I'll pull you through.'

Tara made a small movement towards Mimi and that's when Mimi saw all the tiny cuts on her face and she wanted to cry. Her poor brave daughter, all cut up and telling Mimi she was okay. She was a warrior. And Mimi wished like hell she'd never let her go in a car separate from her.

'Come on,' said Mimi, 'grab hold of me. You can do it.'

Tara did as she was told and Mimi tried to ease her through to the front gently, so as not to hurt her. Tara let out a whimper. 'My wrist hurts,' she said.

'Stay strong. We'll look at it once you're out,' Mimi reassured her.

Once Tara was through, Mimi got her to crouch down ready to climb out like Callie had.

Tara glanced nervously at Tony, still unmoving in the passenger seat. 'Is he okay?' she asked.

'Don't worry about him now. I'm going to check on him next. But first we need to get you out.'

Tara began to crawl through the gap. She was almost out when she let out a squeal; Mimi was about to ask her what was wrong, what was hurt and then she saw it. Tony's hand gripping Tara's leg, pulling her back. He must have come to and grabbed at her in confusion.

'Let go!' Mimi bent over and shook his shoulder. 'Tony!

Let go!' His hand opened and Tara's leg disappeared through the windscreen. She was safe.

Mimi saw that Callie was waiting on the other side, helping Tara up to her feet. Her heart swelled with pride that she'd stayed to help. She would have understood if Callie had stumbled away from the car and collapsed, but instead she was holding it together to be there for her little sister.

'Go to our car, stay with the twins and your dad. I'll be right there, okay?' Mimi called out to them.

Callie had both her arms wrapped around Tara. 'Mum, get out of there. What if it . . . what if it catches fire or . . . or . . . explodes or something?'

'That's not going to happen,' she said firmly.

'But I could smell something in there . . . petrol maybe. Please, please get out.'

'I'm just going to help your uncle and then I'll get right out and I'll be with you, okay?'

Callie looked like she wanted to argue further but Mimi cut her off. 'Callie, listen to me. I need you to go to the twins. They're okay, but they need you. *Go*.'

Callie nodded and she and Tara backed away from the car.

Darren

He wasn't cut out for this – he hadn't updated his first aid in years. When would help arrive? Should he pull her out of the car? Lie her down to start CPR? Or was he not meant to move her? What if he did more harm than good? Why couldn't she just wake up or give him a sign that she was okay?

'Andrea, please, can you hear me? Open your eyes, please!'

He felt a hand touch his shoulder and he spun around to see his mum standing behind him, breathing hard.

'Mum! What are you doing? You're hurt, you need to wait for the paramedics.'

She shook her head. 'I need to help.'

'I don't know what to do, she won't wake up. And I haven't even been to the last car yet.'

'It's okay. I saw Mimi over there helping them.' She looked down at Andrea's still form and for a second her brisk demeanour slipped. 'Oh God, is she . . . ?'

'I don't know. And I don't know what to do.'

Jill seemed to snap back to attention, as though the fact that Darren was at a loss meant she had no choice but to pull herself together.

'We need to check if she's breathing.' Jill leaned over into the car, lowering her ear next to Andrea's face, and held still for a few seconds.

'I can't feel anything,' she said after a moment. 'Or hear anything. If she's not breathing then we need to start CPR.'

'But do we pull her out of the car? Lie her down?'

'No. We'll just put the seat back a little so we can tip her head back and do it here.'

'Are you sure? How do you know what to do?'

'I did a first aid course after we lost your dad. I never wanted to feel that helpless again. Trust me, I know what I'm doing.'

Darren felt a rush of relief; following someone else's

instructions was much easier than trying to figure out what he was meant to do alone. He yanked open the car door and reached down to the lever on the side of the seat so they could tip it back a bit.

Jill gently adjusted Andrea's head. 'Okay, Darren,' she said, 'you need to be the one to do it.'

'But I don't –'

Jill cut him off. 'My face is covered in blood. I can't do it. I'll talk you through every step. You can do this.'

Darren nodded.

Mimi

Once more Mimi bent over to look down at Tony. He reached an arm up to her.

'Help me,' he said, his voice coming out strange and wheezy.

Mimi caught his arm and pushed it back. 'First tell me the truth,' she said, her voice low, the rage burning inside as she looked him in the eye.

He looked confused. 'The truth?' he wheezed. 'The truth . . . about what?'

'About what you did to Callie.'

The look in his eyes told her the answer. He knew exactly what she was talking about, and before she could stop herself she started hitting him. Slapping and scratching and pummelling his face and his body. 'What did you do to my daughter?' she screamed at him.

He caught hold of her wrists to stop her but his grip was weak and she was able to wrench her hands free. She started crying. 'How could you? Your own niece, how could you?'

He shook his head. 'I never meant to . . . I couldn't help . . . I . . . I . . .' But there was nothing he could say to justify what he'd done and he knew it.

'I'm sick,' he said finally. 'I need help.'

'You don't need help,' Mimi said. 'You need to be in jail.'

'But don't you get it?' he said. 'Day after day after day, I stopped myself. I fought against these feelings. You think I don't know they're wrong? I know! I didn't want to do it. But it's not my fault, it's a compulsion. That's why I tried to get Andrea to stay away from the kid next door. I didn't want the temptation.'

'The temptation? A little girl? That's revolting.' Mimi wanted to throw up.

'Mimi, please. That's why I waited, don't you see? I waited.'

Mimi couldn't help herself. 'What are you talking about? What do you mean you waited?'

'Until Callie was older. Right? I never touched her before this year, I swear.'

Now Mimi thought she really might be sick. 'Jesus Christ, you're actually proud of yourself? You want me to be impressed? You're deluded. She's still your niece, you piece of shit. She's still a child. You can get yourself out of the car.'

'Mimi! Wait. I – I . . . can't . . . There's something sticking into me.'

She looked closer and saw a dark red stain across the bottom of his shirt, spreading out from his side.

'Please,' he said, reaching up once more to catch hold of her hand. 'Please . . . you need to help me.'

'Help you?' She was incredulous. All she wanted to do right now was hurt him, punish him; she wanted to get hold of whatever it was that was sticking into his side and twist it, push it in further, watch his face crumple with the pain. Hear him cry out.

She grabbed his hand and pulled it off her other wrist. Then she squeezed it, hard. She kept her eyes trained on his as she spoke.

'I will never forgive you for what you've done. I'm going to make sure you pay.'

He lowered his eyes. 'You – you . . . have to understand,' he began.

Mimi crouched right down, until her face was next to his. 'I don't have to understand anything,' she whispered.

She turned around to crawl back out.

'Mimi! You can't leave me here. Mimi!'

Jill

She was guiding Darren through the CPR, counting out the compressions and instructing him each time he breathed into Andrea's mouth.

She shifted her attention for a moment to see that Mimi was crawling back out of Tony's Lexus. Thank God. She'd been nervous seeing her inside that car while it was stuck on its side like that . . . scared that it might fall and she'd be hurt. Tony must be about to climb out after her.

In the distance, she heard the sound of sirens. Finally, help was coming. The professionals would take over and everything would be okay again.

'You're doing well, just keep going,' she said, 'the ambulance is almost here. Only a few more minutes and they'll take over from you.'

Darren glanced up at her. 'Do you smell smoke?' he asked.

Andrea

She was floating in a dark void. Her chest was tight but her limbs felt loose, light, free. Cool water was rushing over her skin. She lifted one hand and watched the small droplets of water fall from her fingertips. And as she watched the droplets fall, she saw something in them. Images. Tiny scenes in each one.

A small bottle being held in a child's hands.

Tablets on a palm.

Her own hand flinging out to knock the tablets into the air.

The tablets flying, floating, falling.

A little girl's face. Full of confusion and fear.

An unclipped seatbelt.

The crush of metal.

And now the little girl was flying through the air. Just like the tablets had been.

Her own hands, reaching out. Wanting to catch hold of her. Wanting to save her. Wanting to keep her safe.

Knowing that she had failed.

Violet. Violet flew out of the car.

You need to wake up, Andrea.

Christmas Eve

It's quite extraordinary how far a twenty-kilo child can fly through the air when thrown from a car. And if they land in the bushes and are unconscious, and it's dark and there is chaos all around . . . it's very difficult for anyone to spot them.

Especially if no one knows they're even missing to begin with.

That was the predicament that Violet was in as Darren performed CPR on Andrea.

As Jill tried to guide him through it.

As Tony's car was catching fire.

So, while six-year-old Violet's body was convulsing as it reacted to the drugs she had popped into her mouth, believing the only harm she had done was to sneak a few of her mother's sweets, no one was even glancing in her direction.

20

Same day – Christmas Eve

Mimi

She didn't see the flames take hold. After getting herself out of the car, she'd headed straight for her family. A stranger who'd apparently been the first to stop was putting pressure on Pete's wounded arm, which was bleeding through the thin muslin material that had been wrapped around it. Callie and Tara were huddled over one twin each, comforting them.

'We didn't know if we should pick them up or not,' Callie said as Mimi approached, 'or if they're safer staying in their capsules.'

The sirens were getting louder and another two cars were pulling over to help when someone shouted, 'That car is on fire – is there anyone in it?'

Mimi felt her shoulders stiffen. She couldn't bring herself to turn and look. But she saw Callie's head whip around and then Callie grabbed Mimi's arm and pulled her away from the rest of the family. 'Mum, that's Tony's car.'

Mimi closed her eyes. Oh God, what had she done?

'Mum,' Callie pressed, 'did Uncle Tony get out?' There was a waver to her voice.

'Umm, I-I'm not sure,' Mimi said, still refusing to turn around and face the scene. But the glow of the flames was entering her peripheral vision. Was she going to be able to live with the decision she'd made?

Callie stepped in even closer, forcing Mimi to look at her. They locked eyes. Right then, Mimi knew that Callie knew she'd abandoned Tony in his car. Callie held still for a moment, then she squeezed Mimi's hand and stepped back again.

Mimi turned to see Pete limping over to them. 'Mimi,' said Pete, his voice hoarse but desperate. 'Do you know if Tony got out of the car? We can't find him. Tell me he made it out.'

Mimi froze. This was her husband's brother, what was she going to say?

Callie spoke for her. 'He told Mum to go and help us and that he'd get himself out,' she said. 'But we didn't see if he did . . . there was too much else going on.'

Pete's face twisted in horror, then he turned and shouted out to the people who'd just arrived at the scene. 'We need help, we don't know if my brother's still in that car.'

Darren

There were people racing towards the car, but the fire had taken hold in an instant. Darren was doing everything he could to stay focused on helping Andrea, but at the same time, he was distracted. His chest was burning. His arms were aching. He'd never realised how much CPR took out of you. It felt so violent, pushing down on her chest with all his weight.

'Are you sure Tony got out?' he asked his mum.

'He must have,' she said. 'He would have climbed out right after Mimi.'

'But then, where is he? I can't see him anywhere.'

The reflection of red and blue lights flashed across Jill's face then and she squeezed his arm. 'Help is here, Darren. Everything's going to be okay.'

That's when a voice screamed out. 'I can see someone! There's someone still in this car!'

Jill

The paramedics were striding through the chaos, cutting a pathway of calm as they went. And the chaos was extreme. Strangers had surrounded Tony's car, but no one could get close enough to get to him; they kept being pushed back by the heat of the flames. Darren had started to cry as he continued to pump at Andrea's chest. Whether he was crying for Andrea or for Tony or for both, Jill couldn't say.

Pete was being held back by Mimi as he tried to run towards Tony's car, and Tara was sobbing into Callie's arms. The smells and sounds were overpowering. Voices screaming and crying. More sirens.

Jill's lungs were filled with smoke but it was different from that day when the bushfire had surrounded her and Frank. This time it mingled with the acrid smell of diesel and oil.

This is my family, she thought. *And this is my punishment. Did I bring all of this on them?*

Two fire trucks along with several police cars were pulling up now as well. Firefighters were jumping out of their trucks and unwinding hoses. A second and then a third ambulance arrived. Three paramedics had stopped briefly in the centre of the crash site and Jill was about to scream at them that they needed help, but then two of them made a beeline for Andrea's car.

One, a tall woman with a short ponytail, took a quick look at Andrea. Jill could see her eyes rapidly assessing, but her face gave nothing away. 'You're doing great,' she said to Darren. She turned to her partner and gave him some instructions. They were somehow brisk yet completely calm and he immediately started pulling equipment out of his bag. Then she placed a hand on Darren's back. 'Okay, mate, you can step back for me now. You've done an amazing job but we can take it from here.'

Darren stumbled backwards and collapsed on the ground, exhausted.

The second paramedic passed the first a pair of scissors and she sliced the front of Andrea's shirt open, then she held out her hand and was passed a large needle, which she inserted into Andrea's chest.

'Oh God,' said Jill. 'What are you doing?'

'I'm just going to decompress her chest cavity,' she replied, her voice so relaxed, she could have been saying, 'I'm just going to order myself a latte.'

A third paramedic, an older man with kind eyes, appeared in front of Jill. 'Ma'am, were you in this vehicle?' he asked her.

She stared back at him, seemingly stumped by the question.

'This car,' he said, 'were you travelling in it?'

She shook her head, her eyes returning to Andrea. The first two paramedics were now doing CPR again. 'I was driving that one,' she said, gesturing towards her Volvo.

He slipped a band around Jill's wrist with a yellow tag attached. 'Okay, can you do me a favour and go and stand by your car, and then someone will be over to take a look at your injuries.'

'No! I'm not –' Jill began, but the scene was suddenly flooded with light. She turned to see that tall lights had been set up around the site. For a moment they blinded her, but then her eyes adjusted. In the distance, she could hear the rhythmic sound of a helicopter approaching.

She looked back at Andrea's car, and that's when she saw it, lit up now by the strong floodlights. A small purple backpack with Disney Princess pictures on the front. It was sticking out from under the seat behind Andrea. Jill carefully stepped around the paramedics, reached down and tugged the backpack free.

She turned back to Darren, who was breathing heavily, leaning back on his elbows on the ground.

'Darren, why would Andrea have this bag in her car?'

He stared back at her with a look that told her he didn't give a fig as to why she had a small purple backpack.

Jill zipped it open and started pulling things out. 'Kid's clothes,' she said. 'A stuffed toy . . . This doesn't make any sense.'

'Mum, are you serious? Why the hell do you care what Andrea has in her car right now? Maybe they're gifts.'

Jill dropped the bag and held up a small white T-shirt with a giant blue star on the front. 'I've seen this before,' she said.

'What are you on about?'

'At Tony and Andrea's building . . . the little girl in the elevator.'

Jill swung away from Darren and grabbed the older paramedic by the elbow.

'I think there was a child travelling in this car. And I don't know where she is.'

Mimi

The word spread quickly that a small girl was missing and everyone needed to fan out and search. Mimi didn't entirely understand who she was or how she was involved, only that the police were trying to keep everyone calm and coordinate the frantic search so they had the best chance of finding her.

Mimi didn't know if it was the news there was child in danger that snapped Pete out of it, or if he simply finally realised there was no longer any hope of rescuing Tony, but he suddenly stopped struggling and slumped into her arms. There was a small explosion from the engine of the Lexus and the people who'd been trying to get close enough to pull him free had fallen right back, finally accepting there was no hope. The firefighters had their hoses out now, but it was too late.

Tony was dead.

And Mimi was to blame.

Darren

A part of him wanted to stay there where he'd collapsed onto the ground. He was worn out, physically and emotionally. The paramedics had strapped breathing equipment onto Andrea and were preparing to transfer her from the car to a stretcher. Darren was terrified that she wasn't going to make it.

And his brother was dead. The firefighters were hosing down the flames but there was no chance Tony could have survived.

But the news that a little girl was missing pushed him to his feet.

'It'll be the little girl who lives next door to Tony and Andrea,' Jill explained to him once others had fanned out to search. 'I don't know why, but I think she was travelling in Andrea's car.'

So Darren joined the search, half-thinking his mum must have it wrong. Why would Andrea have the neighbour's small child with her on Christmas Eve? It didn't make any sense. But if the child was there – and she'd been thrown from the car – then she could be anywhere. On the side of the freeway the ground sloped down away from the road and the bush was thick with undergrowth. And while the crash site was now lit up, it was still pitch black down there in the bushes. What if she'd hit the ground and rolled down the hill? How far could she have got?

He realised as he searched that a part of him didn't want to be the one to find her. What if she was dead? He couldn't cope with finding a dead child. Not after Andrea. Not after Tony.

But as it turned out, he was the one who saw it – a splash of pink in the scrub. He approached cautiously, and when he recognised it as a pink sneaker, on the twisted leg of a small child, he moved faster and dropped to his knees next to her. There was white froth at the edges of her mouth and her eyes were closed. But there was movement beneath the eyelids. She was alive.

'Here!' he yelled. 'She's here, I've found her!'

People crashed through the bush towards him as he touched a hand to her forehead. 'Help is coming,' he said. 'You're going to be okay.'

Then he burst into tears.

21

Friday 25 December – Christmas Day

Mimi

Maybe it was because the initial shock had worn off, or maybe it was because the two of them were alone together. Whatever it was, a switch had flipped and Callie was letting everything out.

They were together in a hospital waiting room – although neither of them had any serious injuries, everyone from the accident had been brought in to be checked. Pete, Tara and the twins had all been admitted: Pete for a head injury, the twins for observation, and Tara for facial lacerations and a suspected broken wrist.

A helicopter had landed in the centre of the M1 and Andrea had been airlifted to a different hospital. They'd tried to take Jill along with Pete for her own head injury, but she'd insisted on accompanying Andrea. Violet had been taken in an ambulance to a children's hospital.

Mimi and Callie had stayed with the rest of their family for several hours, but now they'd been temporarily ushered away. Tara and the twins were fast asleep and Pete was resting.

'Go and wash your faces and get yourselves a quick cup

of coffee,' one of the nurses said. 'Just take a breath for a minute. You can come right back when you're ready.'

They stepped into the visitor's room with the coffee machine and Callie spun on her heel.

'Why did all this happen?' she cried. 'Why did this have to happen to us?' She sobbed and yelled and raked her fingernails against Mimi's chest.

And then, 'Why did he do that to me, Mum? How *could* he? Why? Why?'

Mimi cried into her daughter's hair and held her tight, saying over and over, 'I don't know, baby, I don't know. It's not fair, none of it is fair, none of it.'

She didn't fight back as Callie clenched her fists and slammed them against her, all she could do was keep holding her. Keep telling her that it was okay, that she was going to be okay.

Eventually, Callie's sobs began to subside and her body collapsed against her. Mimi supported her as they moved across to a couch and sat down together. Callie lay down with her legs curled into her chest and her head resting on Mimi's lap.

'Why didn't you stop him, Mum?' she whispered. 'Why did you let him do that to me? He was going to rape me. If they hadn't come back when they did, I wouldn't have got away.'

Mimi clenched her jaw and squeezed her fist. 'I'm so sorry I failed you,' she said. 'But listen to me – I'm going to do everything in my power to protect you. I never want to let you down again.'

But Callie shook her head. 'No, I'm sorry,' she said. 'It wasn't your fault . . . I'm sorry, Mum, I shouldn't blame you for this.'

Mimi knew she'd never believe that. And she would never forgive herself.

Jill

Jill snatched up the phone the moment it started ringing. She hadn't been allowed in to see Andrea yet and she was desperate for any news. Darren had driven himself to the hospital to join her, but eventually he'd gone home to rest. Jill was refusing to leave until she had an update on Andrea. She was pacing the halls of the hospital, waiting for someone to tell her something, anything.

The reality that one of her sons was dead hadn't sunk in yet and she was forcing herself not to think about Tony, but instead to focus on everyone else.

'Mimi?' she said when she answered. 'Is everything all right?'

'Yes. We're all okay here. No serious injuries.'

'Thank God. I was afraid you were calling because something had gone wrong.'

There was a pause, and when Mimi spoke again, her voice had changed. It was cooler. 'Actually, Jill, there is something wrong.'

'What is it?'

'How did you know?'

'I'm sorry?'

'About what Tony had done. How did you know?'

There was a bench seat a few metres away and Jill walked to it and sat down heavily. She wanted to cry but that wouldn't be fair to Mimi, not right now. Mimi had called her for answers and Jill was going to do her best to explain.

'I didn't,' said Jill. 'But there was this email and I didn't want to open it. And then everything that had been going on with Callie. We were leaving the service station and I saw the look on her face and I just . . . I just knew.'

'What email?'

'It's complicated.'

'Then make it uncomplicated for me, Jill.'

'It was from an old girlfriend of Tony's. She contacted me out of the blue. Said she didn't want to keep it to herself. She said I had to know the truth about Tony.'

'Send it to me, I want to see it.'

'Of course I will.'

'How long?' Mimi asked then. 'How long have you suspected?'

Jill didn't know how to answer. She felt as though a part of her must have always known. But at the same time, how could she have known? Because she would never have put her own granddaughters at risk if she suspected there was any chance. So surely . . . surely she didn't know. Couldn't know.

Mimi's voice cut through the silence. 'Jill, for God's sake, how long?'

'I got the email four weeks ago. But I didn't open it until we were at the service station and I saw Callie's face.' Her voice cracked. 'Mimi, please. Is Callie okay?'

There was a pause and then a sob. 'No,' said Mimi. 'No, she's not okay. He put his hands on her, Jill, he tried to . . . he tried to rape my daughter. His niece. Your granddaughter. So no, she's not okay.'

The line went dead.

Jill sat still, staring at the floor, trying to hold herself together. Trying to make sense of it all. Then a doctor approached her.

'Mrs Lewis?' he asked.

Jill stood and wiped her cheeks.

'Yes, that's me. Please, how is she?'

22

Friday 1 January – New Year's Day

Mimi

Mimi lay in her bed staring up at the ceiling fan, watching the blades spin. Trying to follow one at a time, losing it, catching the next one. She would get up soon, but lately she found that she started most days this way. Taking a moment to ground herself before she could get out of bed.

Last night was the first New Year's Eve in almost twenty years that she hadn't had a drink to toast in the new year. Even when she'd been pregnant she'd always still had at least a sip of bubbles. But of course, last night no one celebrated. Maybe if they'd all made it out alive, they'd have been in the mood for celebrating. They'd have celebrated life. Strength. Survival. And of course, if Tony hadn't turned out to be a monster.

But instead, tomorrow they'd be burying him.

Pete knew the truth now. Not that she'd intentionally abandoned his brother in the car, that was a secret only she and Callie shared. No, he knew the truth about what Tony had done.

At first, Pete tried to argue that it wasn't possible, there must have been some kind of mistake. There was no way

334

his own brother could have done something so horrific. But Mimi had shut him down swiftly.

'There's no doubt,' she'd told him. 'And as hard as it is, you're going to have to accept it. Because Callie needs us and there's no way we're going to give her anything but our full support. And that includes our irrevocable belief and trust in her.'

Of course, she'd also shown him the email from Edie. Jill had forwarded it on to her as promised.

Jill,

I tried to tell you this once before. But I felt uncomfortable about coming right out and saying it, so I attempted to be subtle. That was a mistake. I could tell then that you didn't believe me and I knew that you weren't going to follow up on it. Since I saw you last, I married and had two children. As my eldest daughter grew, I found myself looking at her and realising how horrendous it would be if she ever came into contact with someone like your son. I saw that I would never be able to forgive myself if I didn't stand up for what was right.

The reason I broke up with Tony is because I caught him looking at child pornography on his computer. To this day, I still regret not reporting him to the police. But you might recall that I was younger than him, only twenty at the time. Tony could be very manipulative when he wanted to be. I was stupid enough to buy into his lies that it was his first and only time. He claimed that he came across the site by accident and it wasn't his fault. Deep down I knew it was rubbish. But I was a coward and instead of doing something about it I just got myself away from him.

While tracking you down to find your contact details, I saw through social media that you have grandchildren. So, please, for the sake of your grandchildren, you need to face facts. Your son is not the person you think he is. Stop protecting him and do something about it. Otherwise I will.

Edie Simmons

Since reading the email, Pete was no longer speaking to his mother. Mimi didn't blame him, she wasn't speaking to Jill either. Even if Jill didn't entirely understand what Edie had tried to tell her all those years ago, she still could have tried harder. She could have asked Edie to explain. She could have spoken to Frank, to Pete, to someone. She could have kept a closer eye on Tony. But since the day Mimi had met Pete, he'd always made jokes about Tony being the favourite son. And as far as Mimi was concerned, that was why Jill had been blinded to Tony's flaws.

Darren had been just as shocked as Pete to find out the truth about Tony. Mimi didn't know if he fully comprehended what it meant for her family, for Callie and her future, knowing what had happened to her. He didn't have children. So as much as he was furious about what Tony had done, he was more forgiving of the position his mother had been in.

The investigation into the accident had been gruelling. Question after question about who hit who and when. *Did you hear a bang before you felt the first impact? What did you see in front of you? Behind you?*

Eventually, it was concluded that Andrea's convertible was at the centre of it all, based on everyone's recollections of the order of events. But they didn't know what it was that had caused her to lose concentration and veer into the side of Jill's car.

The problem was, no one could ask her.
She was still in a coma.

Jill

Jill sat by Andrea's bed, holding her hand, willing Andrea's fingers to tighten around her own. But the doctors had been blunt about her prognosis. They'd explained that she'd suffered a traumatic head injury as well as a chest injury with a tension pneumothorax. Basically, a collapsed lung. Apparently, Darren had saved her life by persisting with CPR until help arrived. He'd kept her heart pumping until the paramedics could decompress her chest to release the air and allow her heart to beat again. But there'd been complications during surgery and she'd been placed in an induced coma to give her body a chance to recover.

Only one visitor was allowed at a time into the ICU, and Jill had to keep her visits brief. Each time she arrived, her breath would catch at the sight of her daughter-in-law's bruised face, sunken cheeks and the square patch where they'd shaved her hair on the side of her head.

'I found out today that Violet's going to be okay,' Jill told her now. 'She'd taken opioids . . . must have been right before the accident. She told the doctors that she thought they were her mum's sweets. Scary stuff. But she's recovering well. The drugs are out of her system and she's only been left with a few broken ribs and some nasty bruises from the accident. Kids can be very resilient, thank goodness. Apparently Heather has gone into rehab and Violet's

337

been placed in the care of her grandparents. So that's good news. She's safe and well.'

Jill looked at Andrea's face, hoping for some sign that she could hear her, that she was going to come back. But there was nothing.

'Will you forgive me?' Jill went on. 'When you wake up and hear about the horrendous things Tony's done? When you hear that a part of me always suspected something wasn't right? Will you forgive me for not speaking up sooner? Pete and Mimi haven't, and I don't blame them. But could you?'

She heard footsteps behind her and turned to see a nurse walking in.

'It's hard having that one-sided conversation, isn't it?' the nurse said as she headed around to the other side of Andrea's bed and started checking her vitals. 'But it's good that you're doing it. You just never know what she might be able to hear and take in.'

Jill nodded and tried to give the nurse a friendly smile. She wanted to say that a one-sided conversation was no problem at all for her. She'd been doing it all year in her letters to Frank with no chance of a reply. But she didn't say anything. She just waited quietly until the nurse had finished her checks and left.

Once they were alone again, Jill gave Andrea's hand a sudden and tight squeeze. 'Just wake up,' she whispered. 'I don't care if it means you have to face so much tragedy. That you'll have to learn you've lost your husband. Or about the terrible things Tony's done. I want you to wake up.'

There were more footsteps then and this time Jill turned to see Darren standing in the doorway watching her.

'Hey Mum, sorry to interrupt.'

'You're not interrupting,' said Jill. 'It's good to see you.' *And a relief to have someone in this family who's still talking to me.* 'I'll leave if you want to come in. We're not supposed to both stay in here together.'

'Any news?' Darren asked, jerking his chin towards Andrea.

Jill shook her head.

Darren

Darren nodded his thanks as Sage placed the beer down in front of him and then climbed onto the stool next to him.

'I really appreciate you coming with me,' he said. 'That was intense.'

'I hardly did anything to help.'

Sage had accompanied him to the hospital but she'd had to wait outside ICU while Darren visited Andrea.

'Yeah, but knowing you were there . . . it was nice.'

They had headed straight to a pub after leaving the hospital.

'What was it like in there?' Sage asked.

'Surreal. She's hooked up to so many machines. She looks . . . she looks terrible.'

'I'm so sorry.'

'And meanwhile there's Mum, convinced that she's going to wake up any minute. Mum has this wicked scar now, too. All the way from her forehead to here,' said Darren, tracing his finger down his face to his ear. 'It's because she wouldn't let them patch her up properly on the night of the accident. Kept batting them away, telling them to whack a Band-Aid on it and leave her alone.'

'She sounds tough.'

'Yeah, I guess she is.'

'You know what's funny?' said Sage. 'I thought things with you were already complicated enough when I found out you were in love with your ex and planning to donate sperm to her. And then I worked out I'd reviewed your book and I was like, *fuck*. But now . . . man, your family drama is off the charts.'

Darren snorted. 'Yep, that's us.'

'Sorry,' Sage added. 'I'm big on using humour to deal with bad situations, but you can tell me to shut up if you want.'

'No way.'

Darren had called Sage at 4 am on Christmas morning. She'd answered the phone groggily. 'Darren, I know you love this dog, but trust me, he's fine.'

'That's not why I'm calling.'

He'd gone on to tell her about the accident. About giving his sister-in-law CPR. About losing his brother. About finding Violet. He'd talked and talked while Sage listened in silence, letting him get it all out.

Eventually he said what he really needed to say. 'Sage, I like you. I really fucking like you. And I don't care if you hate my writing. Ever since I met you, I haven't been able to get you out of my head, and I think –'

Sage had cut him off, stopped him from letting the emotions from the accident carry him away. 'It's okay, Daz, I understand. You've been on my mind a lot too. Let's talk properly at dinner.'

Now, as they sat up at the tall bar table with their beers in front of them, Sage reached out and touched his hand. 'Hey, every family has issues, right?'

'I guess so. But this much? I mean, you don't even know the full story. My brother, Tony, we found out that he . . . he did something. Something horrific. I can't . . . I'm sorry, I don't think I can even say it.'

'You don't have to.'

'And now I don't even know who's going to turn up to his funeral tomorrow. It's the weirdest feeling in the world. I mean, who's going to speak? What are they going to say? Is it okay that I still want to be there?'

Sage's fingers closed around his hand. 'Look, obviously I don't know what Tony did and I'm not going to push you to find out, but I can see that it has you badly rattled. But as for going to his funeral, of course it's okay if you want to be there. This is about how *you* feel, not what you think others expect of you. He was your brother – if you want to say goodbye to him, you don't have to feel bad about that, regardless of what he did.'

Darren nodded. 'I guess you're right. I will tell you . . . eventually. I think I need to tell you, to be honest. I just can't right now.'

'There's no rush.'

They both picked up their drinks and sipped quietly for a few moments.

'Right,' said Darren eventually, 'let's talk about something else. Anything else. Tell me, how did you know so much about ballet when you were only pretending that was what you did for a living?'

Sage gave him a slightly sad smile. 'I was wondering if

you might ask me that.' She hesitated. 'It's what I wanted to be when I was young. What I thought I would be, actually. I was a dancer as a kid, right through to my teen years. I was really serious about it. But I had a fall when I was sixteen. Hurt my ankle. And bang, that was it, dream over.'

'Really? The injury was that bad?'

'It was. It got better eventually, but I missed out on some crucial stages in my competitions and my ankle was never the same. So that was that.'

'That's awful, I'm so sorry.'

'It's okay. I mean, yes, it sucked. And that's why it was fun to pretend that night with your ex, to imagine for a bit that I did get to pursue my dreams. But I'm fine. I like what I do. Though speaking of dreams, let's talk about yours.'

Darren made a face. 'Mine? Umm, I think mine are dead now too.'

'Explain. What's going on with your writing? Why haven't you written your next book?'

'Well . . .' he began.

'And if you say you can't write because of my review, I can tell you now that's bullshit.'

He rubbed his chin. 'Okay, I know I shouldn't let it affect me, but –'

'I'm serious,' she cut in. 'Using my review is like holding up a shield to deflect from something else. Because the truth is, you're a brilliant writer.'

Darren twisted his mouth in amusement. 'Ah, Sage, it's okay, you don't have to say that. We all know what you think of my writing.'

'No. You know what I thought of your first book.'

'Yeah, exactly. You hated it. Remember? Pretentious? Amateur? Clichéd?'

'Right, so those were the words that jumped out at you and you've let them define you. But did you even read the rest of the review?'

'Of course I did. The whole thing was negative.'

'Nuh-uh. You didn't read it properly. I re-read it myself after I realised who you were. And I agree – it was critical, for the most part. But not all of it. Here are the words that should have jumped out at you: *potential, joyous, sharp.*'

'What are you talking about? Those words weren't in there.'

'Yes, they were. Read it again for yourself if you don't believe me. So, tell me why you only focused on some of the words? And why you're using them as an excuse not to write again?'

'It doesn't matter. I've missed three deadlines and now my time's basically up.'

'Fuck your deadlines. Forget about that. Forget about your book contract. We're talking about *writing*. What made you write the first book? There was no deadline on that one, was there? No contract in place.'

Darren shrugged. 'I wrote it because I wanted to.'

'Okay, so what do you want to do now?'

'I still want to write.'

'And what do you want to write about?'

He traced his finger through the condensation on the outside of his beer glass. 'See, that's the problem. I should be –'

Sage interrupted him again. 'No, don't tell me what you

should be doing. Tell me what you *want* to do. That was the question – what do you want to write?'

Darren smiled. 'That's a bloody good question.'

'Okay, so why are you smiling?'

'Because I think I just thought of an answer.'

23

Monday 4 January

Mimi

'Okay, the kids are upstairs, time for you to tell me the full story. Why aren't you at your brother-in-law's funeral today?'

Leesa had brought two large takeaway iced coffees with her and they had taken them outside and sat down on the grass in Mimi's garden. The heat was sweltering even with the shade of a large umbrella over them, but they'd wanted to make sure they could talk in private without the girls listening in. Mimi could hear the whip-birds calling to one another in the bush behind the back fence. The familiar sound, along with the sensation of the grass beneath her feet, was helping to alleviate some of her disquiet.

Leesa knew most of the news. The accident, the fact that Andrea was still in a coma. And about Mimi's recent struggles with alcohol. But what she didn't know about was Tony, what he'd done. Mimi had called and asked her to come around and keep her company today, while Pete went to the funeral.

'Will you forgive me if I go?' he'd asked her the night before.

'Of course I will. He did something horrendous but you have a right to say goodbye to your brother. The question is, will you forgive me if I *don't* go?'

'I'd never expect you to be there in a million years. Honestly, I don't know if I'm going to say goodbye or to have some kind of last word with him, you know what I mean?'

'Yeah, I get it.'

Callie and Tara had stayed home as well. Callie obviously knew why; Tara didn't completely understand, but she accepted it. Mimi wasn't sure if Tara had been listening when Callie had begun to tell her about Tony in the car that day. Tara had never asked about it. But perhaps she'd sensed the tension between her sister and Tony during the drive, or perhaps she simply trusted her mother when she said they wouldn't be going.

Tara and Chloe were hanging out upstairs in her bedroom; Tara was excited to get Chloe to sign the cast on her arm. The twins were asleep and Callie was on the phone with Jordan. Callie had told Mimi all about Jordan. In fact, things had changed drastically between Mimi and Callie since the accident. They were maybe closer than they'd ever been. Callie had talked with her mum about everything from Jordan to singing to school friends. And of course, about Tony. She'd seen their GP and was scheduled for her first psychologist appointment on Monday. She'd told Mimi about the way she'd recoiled from Jordan's attempt to kiss her and Mimi had encouraged her to talk to him.

'You don't have to tell him anything that you're not ready to share,' she'd said. 'But if he's as good a guy as you say he is, I think he'll understand if you simply explain that you were scared.'

Mimi had also been able to ask Callie more about her surprise performance. 'What made you do it?' she'd said. 'Right when you were dealing with so much pain?'

'I did it *because* of the pain. I wanted to prove I could be brave, Mum.'

Her words had twisted Mimi's heart.

'You *are* brave, Callie. You chose to get in that car so that you could protect your little sister. Don't you understand? You're the bravest person I know. You're extraordinary and I am prouder of you than you could ever imagine.'

Leesa touched Mimi's hand now. 'Come on,' she said, 'you can talk to me.'

Mimi and Pete had already discussed the issue of who they'd tell about Tony. For the most part, it was up to Callie. But Mimi also needed a friend in all of this.

She took a deep breath and told Leesa everything.

When she was done, Leesa drew her into a fierce hug. 'Well, that bloody makes sense now,' she said. 'I wouldn't have gone today either.'

'So, you think I'm doing the right thing?' Mimi asked as they pulled apart.

'Absolutely.' Leesa picked up her iced coffee and stirred in the cream with her straw. 'And you're doing the right thing by Callie as well.'

The tears started then. 'But I didn't protect her,' said Mimi. 'I failed her. When she needed me most.'

'Oh honey,' said Leesa. 'This isn't your fault. There was no way you could have known, no way you could have prevented this.' She glanced across at Mimi's drink. 'Look,

I know you're doing a sober thing at the moment, but if I were you, I'd need more than caffeine and whipped cream right now. How long are you going to stick with it?'

'Ha. Very supportive,' said Mimi. 'I'm not sure. I'll aim for an alcohol-free January and go from there. I just don't want to get back to where I was before. Hiding spirits in the fridge and drinking to escape.'

'And what was it you were trying to escape from?'

'The twins.'

'Wow. You had that answer ready to go.'

'Yeah, well, I didn't know it at the time,' said Mimi, leaning back on the grass on her elbows. 'But I think I was resenting Pete for pushing me into expanding our family when I didn't know if I wanted to. No, that's not fair. I never pushed back properly. So maybe what I resent is that I didn't speak up when I should have.'

'And how do you feel about it all now?'

'Honestly, my connection with the twins only really kicked in when I realised they could have been hurt in that accident. It was like, suddenly I knew how much I loved them, how much I did want them . . . even if I didn't know that to begin with. My protective instincts for them finally switched on.'

Leesa bumped her foot gently against Mimi's. 'Well that's good news, right?'

'Yes and no. I mean, what kind of a shitty mum must I be if I couldn't connect with my babies until they were in a life-threatening accident?'

'Stop talking about yourself that way. You're a great mother with children who are loved and taken care of.'

Mimi shook her head. 'I don't feel like I am.'

'Is that Aunty Iris or Lorraine over there?'

Darren tried to see who Pete was pointing towards. He spotted a stooped over, white-haired woman with a walking stick.

'Iris?' he said. Then, 'Buggered if I know.'

They were standing outside the chapel and Darren could tell Pete was having as much trouble as he was knowing exactly how to feel. The service was over and it was clear that people were perplexed about why there was no wake arranged. It must have looked like his family didn't care very much, especially with close family members missing and the eulogy being delivered by the priest. At least no well-meaning but distant relatives like Aunty Iris-slash-Lorraine had come and queried them about it yet. Darren hoped maybe they'd assume it was because of Andrea still being in the coma.

'Hey, do you think people are looking at us strangely?' Darren asked.

'Yes, I do. I think they think we're pricks for not speaking.'

'And for not organising a wake. I was going to talk, actually. I started thinking . . . he was still our brother, right? I should say something. But then I thought about Callie and I felt sick.'

Pete stiffened.

'Sorry, I shouldn't have brought that up.'

'Don't be sorry. It's not like it isn't constantly on my mind already. I still can't wrap my head around any of it. How could he do something like that? I mean to anyone, obviously. But to his niece . . . to my . . . to my . . .'

349

Pete's voice was rising dangerously and Darren reached out to put an arm around him but he pulled away.

'I mean, *fuck*, you know? How could he? How fucking could he?'

In a sudden movement, Pete strode two steps to the side of the church and punched the brick wall. As soon as he'd done it, Darren could see the regret on his face. It would have hurt. And now more people were definitely staring.

Darren led him around the side, away from onlookers and pulled him into a hug. Then something happened that hadn't happened since they were kids – Pete was crying in his arms, his shoulders heaving. Darren held him tighter.

'I'm not crying for him,' Pete said. 'You know that, right? I'm not crying for that bastard. I'm crying for who he was, when we were younger . . . before all of this. And I'm crying for my daughter.'

'I know, mate, I get it.' And Darren started crying too.

Eventually, they both pulled themselves together and Darren snorted.

'What's funny?' Pete asked.

'Sorry, nothing. But I just thought, at least we know now he wasn't some sort of genius when it came to writing. Can you believe he stole Dad's book?'

'I know. Completely absurd. Can you believe Dad was a writer?'

'Nope.' Darren rubbed his hand around the back of his neck. 'I mean, he was in construction. I never thought he even had any interest in that type of thing. Why do you think he kept it from us?'

Pete shrugged. 'Nerves? You reckon that's where we got it from? The writing gene, so to speak?'

'Maybe? It's a bloody good book. Wish we could have had the chance to chat to him about it.'

'Me too.'

Jill

Dear Frank,

We're burying our son today. Parents aren't meant to bury their children, are they? But we already know what that's like, don't we?

Sometimes I wish I hadn't made it through the accident either. I don't feel like I deserve to be here. Knowing what happened to Callie . . . it cracks open my heart and it makes me sick to my stomach. I want to cry and scream and rage. I want to yell at Tony, but I can't, can I? If he was somehow here again though, the first thing I would do is grab hold of him and hug him tightly. Because as much as I'm furious with him, I still love him. I still want him back. He's still our son.

But he's gone. And who's left to blame? Me. Because I was his mother and I didn't see it. I was too protective of him to pick up on the signs. And if I had realised, I could have got him help. It didn't have to turn him into a monster. It didn't have to be that way. With the right support, he could have lived his life without ever hurting anyone. I'll never forgive myself for not saving Callie from the pain and the trauma.

That's why I've decided I've had enough of secrets. That's why I'm going to tell the boys another truth today. You should have

let me do it a lot sooner. But I understand why you thought we
shouldn't and I still love you very much.

   Love,
   Jill

She'd seen Pete punch the wall.

And watched as Darren pulled him away and put his arm around him. She'd wanted to follow, wanted to hug both of them, but it was a moment just for them. And besides, Pete was angry with her.

He'd been civil towards her when he arrived, even held her hand at one point during the service. And yet, Jill could still feel the iciness emanating from him. He was being a good son, but he was a long way from forgiving her.

People kept coming up to her, wanting to offer their condolences, their hugs, their sweet or funny anecdotes about Tony. But she was only going through the motions as she thanked them or hugged them back. Her body was stiff and her words were soulless. She was broken, not because she'd lost Tony this week, but because she was realising that she'd lost him a very long time ago.

Finally, the people started to thin out and Pete and Darren appeared from around the corner. She saw blood on Pete's knuckles and wanted to offer him a hanky to wrap around his hand, but didn't want to upset him by bringing it up.

'Do you want us to take you somewhere, Mum? For a coffee, something to eat?' Darren asked.

Jill glanced at Pete. He looked uncomfortable and it was clear he didn't want to but that he'd go along if she did. He was a kind son.

'That's okay,' she said. 'I think I'll just go home. Be on my own with my thoughts.'

The relief on Pete's face was painfully obvious.

'You sure?' Darren said.

'Yes. Thank you, though.'

Jill was about to walk away, but stopped. She twisted the order of service she was holding in her hands. It was time.

'There is something I think I should tell you though.'

Darren and Pete waited.

'I . . . I don't want anymore secrets in this family. Never again. So, I want you to know . . . to know that . . .' She was becoming flustered and she dropped the order of service on the ground. Could she really do this? After so long keeping this secret buried, could she really tell them?

Darren bent to retrieve the paper for her but Pete remained standing still, his body rigid.

'What is it, Mum?' he asked.

There was no going back.

'I want you to know that you boys had an older sister. Her name was Robin and she was Tony's twin.'

Robin. The girl that Frank had tried so hard to forget.

The girl that Jill could never let go.

Jill's greatest mistake. Jill's biggest regret.

Jill's first sin.

Because long before Jill had been responsible for killing her husband, she had been responsible for another death — her baby daughter.

Tony had had no idea he'd had a twin sister. And it was the reason Jill had been so afraid when she found out Mimi was having twins. She knew what those first few weeks were like.

How hard the sleep deprivation was, and the constant sound of babies crying. The pain of cracked nipples and the expectations on the mother who bore the brunt of the parenting.

She was terrified of Mimi ending up in the same dark place she had. Of course, everything was different now, and husbands helped out more. Sometimes she wondered how things might have been if Frank had been more hands-on with the babies.

But she couldn't blame him. She was the one to put Robin down to bed that day. She was the one to place her on her tummy. It was strange – Tony always hated sleeping on his stomach, but Robin loved it. She couldn't sleep any other way.

Frank tried to tell her it wasn't her fault. After all, no one knew any different back then. The advice about placing babies down to sleep on their backs didn't even come in until the nineties. But he wasn't there when it happened. He wasn't the one to fall so deeply asleep on the couch, unaware that anything was wrong. Wasn't the one who woke several hours later and wondered why she hadn't already been woken by one of her babies crying. Usually Tony slept soundly for hours, but Jill could always rely on Robin to wake her before too long.

Frank wasn't the one to walk into the bedroom and find Robin. Peaceful, so peaceful. Too peaceful.

A guttural scream had escaped her lips. An animalistic cry of pure pain. Pure anguish.

What about a mother's instinct? Why hadn't something kicked in? Made her wake sooner? In time to get to her baby girl? In time to rescue her.

For Frank, the easiest way to deal with the pain was to

never speak of her again. For Jill, that was excruciating. She wanted to tell stories of Robin's short life. She wanted to tell her boys about her cute little rosebud mouth. About her shock of thick dark hair. She wanted to talk about the colour of her eyes. She had bright blue eyes when she was born, but Jill would never know if they'd have turned brown like the rest of her boys'. She wanted to celebrate who Robin was. Have pictures of her up on the wall. She wanted to sing to her on her birthday when they sang to Tony. She wanted to *remember*.

But any time she mentioned her name, the profound pain in Frank's face tore her apart. So for Frank's sake, she stopped speaking about her. That meant the boys never even knew she'd been born. It also meant she gave all the love that was meant for two babies to one. All of her protection. All the time.

And maybe that's why she'd been blinded to Tony's flaws.

24

Wednesday 6 January

Darren

Darren was scared. It seemed ridiculous to feel afraid of a simple follow-up with the doctor after everything that he and his family had been through. For crying out loud, his brother was gone. There was a sister he'd never even known about. And here he was, sitting in the waiting-room, nervous to hear about a stupid mole.

To be honest, he'd prefer not to know the results. As long as he avoided hearing the truth, he could pretend everything was okay. But at the same time, he knew he needed to pull himself together and face up to it. He'd told Sage that the doctor had called him before Christmas, asking him to come back in. *Darren*, Sage had said, *you need to know.* She'd made him promise he would go and find out what was going on. Things were progressing well with them. Slowly, but well. And Doggo finally had a real name. Leo, after the star sign of the woman who'd saved him. It suited him. Although Darren still often called him Doggo.

'Darren Lewis.' Doctor Clermont gave him a friendly smile as she summoned him in for his appointment. He tried to tell if it was a 'I'm about to deliver terrible news' smile or an 'everything is fine' smile, but it was impossible to decipher.

He followed her into her consulting room and took a seat.

'You've been difficult to pin down,' she said, giving him a slightly stern look over her glasses. She picked up a piece of paper and placed it in front of him. 'Now,' she said. 'Here's the main reason I needed you back in.'

Darren braced himself.

'I forgot to get you to sign this form.'

He was still laughing at himself when he answered the call from Charlotte as he left the doctor's office. It turned out that the other reason the doctor had wanted to see him was to let him know his cholesterol was a little high, but nothing to really worry about as long as he cut back on saturated fats. Apart from that, he was generally healthy. The mole had been nothing sinister. He couldn't believe he'd put this off, imagining it was going to be the worst outcome possible.

'How are you?' Charlotte asked, her voice careful, reverent. She'd wanted to come to Tony's funeral but he'd asked her not to. He hadn't explained why but she'd respected his decision.

'I'm . . . I'm all right,' he said.

'Listen,' Charlotte said, 'I know this is the last thing on your mind with everything that's happened, but I have some news.'

'Oh yeah?' For a moment it didn't click, but then he understood. He'd been so caught up with his own life he hadn't even thought about the sperm donation. By the sound of her voice, he was about to be sucked back into her world. She sounded happy. Steph's insemination must have worked.

'The insemination didn't take,' she said.

Darren stopped short. 'Oh,' he said. 'I'm really sorry.'

'Don't be,' said Charlotte. 'We've had a talk, and we've decided this is for the best. It turns out Steph was never comfortable with asking you to donate, but she didn't speak up because she knew it was what I wanted. She finally came clean and we're going to get the donation from someone else. She has a family friend who's willing and it's just going to be . . . less complicated. I hope you don't mind?'

Darren couldn't stop the smile from spreading across his face. 'No, Char,' he said. 'I don't mind at all.'

Jill

She was taken aback to see a stranger sitting by Andrea's bed when she walked into the hospital room. He was tall, well-built, and he had hold of one of Andrea's hands.

'Hello?' Jill said, making the man jump and drop Andrea's hand. But when he turned she saw that he had kind eyes and a warm smile.

'Oh, hi there.' He stood and offered his hand. 'My name's Shaun. I'm sorry, I was hoping to be able to speak to Andrea, but I see she's still . . .'

'Yes. No change, is what I've been told. I'm Jill, her mother-in-law. How do you know Andrea? They're only meant to allow family in here.'

He cringed. 'I know, I know, I shouldn't be in here but I talked my way in. I really wanted to see her for myself. We met at her building. We had . . . shared concerns about Violet.'

'Oh. I see. Well . . . I'm sorry. I know Andrea did the wrong thing when she took Violet on Christmas Eve, but you have to understand, her heart would have been in the right place.' Jill was becoming flustered, her hands dancing by her side, but Shaun gave her a small smile.

'It's okay,' he said. 'I'm not here to cause trouble. I know Andrea only ever wanted to protect Violet. She never wanted any harm to come to her. And I was hoping to let her know that I've convinced Heather to drop the kidnapping charges against her. She's told the police that she was mistaken about Andrea taking Violet without her permission, that she'd forgotten she agreed to the trip up the coast.'

'Really? How did you do that?'

'It's a long story, but Heather knew she wasn't blameless in all of this. Listen, when . . . if Andrea wakes, could you please tell her that Violet is very safe with her grandparents and I know they're going to help Heather through her rehab. So now I think it's time for both of us to step back and leave it to family. Do you know what I mean?'

Jill nodded. 'I do,' she said. 'I know exactly what you mean.'

Shaun moved towards Andrea again, gazed intently at her for several seconds and then turned away with a look on his face that told Jill it was hard for him to do so.

'When she wakes,' he said, and this time he put a strong

emphasis on the word *when*, 'please tell her I'd love to talk . . . if she wants.'

'Of course,' said Jill. 'I'll make sure she knows you were here.'

Shaun left the room and Jill moved in closer to Andrea. 'Well, that was certainly interesting,' she said, taking hold of Andrea's hand. 'I wonder if you're going to want to tell me about Shaun or not?' She paused. 'You know you do have to wake though, right? You absolutely have to. It's been almost two weeks and that is *quite* enough, do you hear me? The doctors are saying you should have woken by now. They're getting worried. But not me. I'm not worried. I refuse to give up and I'm going to sit right here next to you, talking and talking until you –'

That was when Andrea squeezed Jill's hand.

Andrea

It felt as though everything was taking place around her in scenes from a stop motion film. She would open her eyes and see a doctor moving towards her. Open her eyes again and the doctor would be right up close, examining her face. Open her eyes again and the doctor would have moved back away.

There were voices, beeps, and things prodding her. Her throat felt painfully dry and she wanted to ask for water but couldn't find her voice.

There was Jill, beaming but crying, all at once. Her face was different though, it was blemished by a long, thick scar down the side.

Eventually, she fell back to sleep and when she woke again, the world seemed clearer.

Jill leaned over her and stroked her hair. 'You're back with us,' she said.

Andrea cleared her throat. 'Yes,' she said, her voice raspy. 'I guess so . . .' She faltered, there was something important she needed to ask, but she couldn't think. She closed her eyes and three images appeared in rapid succession.

Tablets on a palm.

Her own hand knocking them into the air.

Violet's confused face.

Her eyes flew open and she tried to grab at Jill's arm. 'Violet?' she said urgently. 'She was with me, she –'

Jill spoke over her. 'She's fine. Absolutely fine.'

Andrea's eyes filled with tears. 'It was my fault,' she said. 'All of it. I lost control . . . there was nothing I could do. Oh God, I could have killed somebody.'

It was impossible to miss the look that crossed her mother-in-law's face.

'Jill?'

'Maybe you should get some more rest, darling. Everyone is so desperate to come and see you now that you're awake. They've all been so worried.'

'*Jill?*'

'Mimi and Pete and the kids are coming tomorrow morning, Darren said if you're up for it he'll come by tonight . . .'

The tears were sliding down Andrea's face. She knew the worst possible news was coming. And she was realising how odd it was that her husband wasn't by her side right now. Jill was listing all of these names, trying to distract her. But instead it was like she was holding up a neon sign. Because she wasn't saying his name.

'Please,' she said. 'You have to tell me. Where's Tony?'

Jill's face crumpled.

25

Saturday 9 January

Andrea

Her eyes were fixed on the top of the gum tree she could see through the window. She still couldn't quite comprehend what Jill had told her about her husband earlier today. For the past couple of days, Andrea had been grieving the death of the man she had loved.

But now, her feelings had been upended. Her grief had to shift sideways and make room for shock, anger, fear, guilt.

At first, Andrea fought against it.

'There has to be a mistake,' she said. 'A misunderstanding. I know he lied about his stupid book, I was beginning to suspect he wasn't the person I thought he was, but not this. This is impossible.'

So Jill had talked her through it. Gently explained that there was no denying it.

They'd continued to talk for several hours. Andrea asked question after question as she tried to make sense of the idea that her husband was a monster. Eventually, she asked to be alone.

She lay still and stared at the tree and considered her relationship with Tony. Was all of it a lie? Did he ever truly love her? Was the love she felt for him real? She thought about the way he had perfectly positioned himself as the polar opposite of the men she'd dated before him. Was it genuine? Or was it a careful manipulation?

She lifted one hand and touched it to the side of her head, rubbed her fingers across the patch of shaved skin.

The day he'd proposed, she'd thought his speech showed her how much he cared:

I'm going to take care of you. I'm going to treat you the way you've always deserved to be treated. No one else could ever love you as much as I love you.

But now she reconsidered those words in a new light.

No one else could ever love you.

Was it romantic? Or was it cruel?

She'd believed he was showing her she deserved better. Maybe he was actually warning her that she'd never find anyone else. And she'd bought into it.

It wasn't that she wanted to lie there and dismantle her marriage, piece by piece, it was that she wanted to understand. And she wanted to know if she'd somehow missed the signs. She was his wife. Should she have somehow realised what he was capable of? She thought about the cracks that had already begun to form in their relationship. The way he'd started out so adventurous in the bedroom, but then their sex-life had petered out. Was it because the only way he could be attracted to her was to pretend? To play games? And when she didn't want to play along anymore, had he completely lost interest in her?

Or was the explanation even more sickening? Because if she thought about it . . . it was possible the timing of his assault on Callie lined up with the beginning of things changing in their marriage. As though something monstrous inside him had been awakened and there was no turning back. So the terrifying question was this: if there had never been an accident, if Tony was still alive today and the truth had remained hidden, would this have only been the very beginning?

She fixed her eyes on the tree again. The gently swaying branches. It was all too much.

When she heard footsteps, she didn't turn to look. She was used to nurses coming in and out of her room all through the day and night. Tapping on buttons, scribbling notes, taking her blood pressure or changing the bag on her drip, disappearing. But then she heard the sound of a chair being pulled up to the bed. She tore her eyes away from the tree and saw the doctor she'd got to know over the past few days sitting down to face her. His expression was grim. She wasn't sure if she could handle anymore bad news.

Yesterday, two police officers had been in to talk with her. After questioning her about the accident, they'd eventually explained that she was being charged with negligent driving occasioning death. It would likely be several months before she would have to attend court, but when she did, there was the possibility she would be up for jail time.

Yet another thing she was struggling to understand: her husband had apparently committed a horrific crime, yet she was the one who was facing potential incarceration. It seemed like such a cruel twist of fate.

'How are you feeling today, Andrea?' said the doctor,

his eyes sweeping across her face before looking back down at the chart in his hands.

She shrugged. 'Okay, I guess. I still feel slow, groggy.'

'That's to be expected. You'll probably feel that way for some time. You told one of the nurses you think your menstrual cycle has been disrupted?'

Andrea nodded. 'Yeah, my period was due . . . I think . . . a week or so ago? But maybe while I was in the coma –'

The doctor cut her off. 'We ran a blood test after you mentioned it. Andrea, I have some news for you, but you need to understand your body has been through an enormous amount of stress, not to mention all the drugs you've received over the past few weeks. On the one hand, it's still early days and it may therefore be fine.' He hesitated. 'But on the other hand, it's important that you prepare yourself for the possibility that it may not progress.'

Andrea stared back at him in confusion. 'What might not progress? What do you mean?'

'Andrea, you're pregnant.'

Epilogue

Christmas in July

Mimi

Andrea grabbed her hand as they walked towards the restaurant and gave it a gentle squeeze. 'This is about new beginnings,' she said. 'New traditions.'

'I know,' said Mimi, 'but I've still got this resentment towards her. I know it isn't fair, I know that Jill didn't know everything, that she couldn't have foreseen what Tony would do. I've forgiven her . . . I think. But then I still sometimes get this rage when I see her.'

'Jesus,' said Andrea. They stopped at the front door. 'You've forgiven her but you get ragey when you see her? I think you still need more therapy.'

'Ha,' said Mimi. 'Trust me, I'm still having fortnightly appointments since the accident. And Callie goes weekly.'

'God. Poor girl. I'm so sorry.'

'It's okay, her psychologist is amazing. Callie's made so much progress. She's finally stopped scratching her skin to pieces. Sometimes I look back at all the signs and I can't believe I missed them.'

Mimi reached out for the door, but Andrea touched her shoulder. 'Before we go in, can I ask . . . Do you sometimes feel that way when you look at me?'

'No,' said Mimi. 'You didn't know. You couldn't.'

Andrea twisted her mouth. For a moment, it looked like she was about to say something but then she stopped. Mimi pulled Andrea to the side, away from the door of the restaurant. 'I promise,' she said. 'I don't blame you.'

'But why? The day that he did . . . what he did . . . your daughters were under my care. I was responsible for them. Why don't you blame me?'

Mimi wasn't sure why Andrea was pushing for this. Maybe it was to divert some of her attention away from Jill? But the truth was, Mimi really didn't hold Andrea responsible – at least, not anymore. In the early days, when everything first happened, there were times when Mimi could have turned her anger towards just about anyone. Against Pete or Darren for not seeing what their brother was capable of. Against herself for letting Callie and Tara go to their place that day. And of course, against Andrea for being his wife. For not seeing the signs or watching more closely that day.

But as time had gone on, she'd slowly come to realise that there was only one person to blame. Tony. And while she might still harbour a level of resentment towards Jill, she had come a long way.

'I don't blame you because I believe you were basically a victim, too. He hid his true self from everyone. Besides, you were there for Callie that day, remember? It was you and Tara coming back upstairs that stopped him from taking it any further.'

'Can I tell you something? I hate that I fell for him. I hate that I ever loved him.'

'He was your husband,' said Mimi. 'Of course you loved him.' She licked her lips, reluctant to say the next thing.

'It's okay,' said Andrea.

'I just found myself wondering, do you ever miss him . . . now?'

Andrea shook her head. 'I don't miss him. I miss the man that I thought he was when we first met. Back when I believed he genuinely cared for me and wanted the best for me. But now I think the only reason he married me was so he could tick that box. Show the world he was normal. Or maybe it was because he was trying to fight against those desires because he knew they were wrong . . . and he thought that if he was married . . .'

Mimi interrupted her. 'I don't think we'll ever know what was going on in his head and I don't think we want to.'

Andrea gave her a sad smile. 'Yes, you're right. Listen, I know it's hard with Jill. And I know that you may never feel the same way about her. But she's family. We're all family. And when this new baby arrives, I want him to have his grandmother in his life at the same time as his aunt.'

'I should have known you'd pull the baby card on me.'

'Yep, gotta use it when I can. Come on. Let's get inside. It's freezing out here.' She swung open the door and let Mimi walk in first.

Andrea

As she followed Mimi, Andrea touched a hand to her stomach and considered the secret she was keeping. It was true that she wanted Jill to be a part of her baby's life, but it was a lie that Jill was the baby's grandmother. She'd triple-checked the dates and there was no denying it. Tony was not the father of this baby.

When Andrea met up with Shaun at that bar, she never meant for things to get so out of control. But everything was whirling through her mind that night. The knowledge that Tony had stolen his father's book after his death and was using it to make himself rich, successful, popular; the realisation she didn't know who he was anymore.

She'd seen Shaun sitting in the corner and felt that sting of attraction flash through her body. When he'd kissed her on the cheek, she'd thought she was in trouble. She'd been right.

'What can I get you to drink?' he'd asked.

'You don't have to buy,' she'd said.

He'd waved it off. 'You can get the next round.'

When they were sitting with their drinks in front of them, he'd explained his part in Violet's life. 'Heather is my ex. I met her when Violet was four and we dated for two years. Pretty much throughout the whole relationship, it was clear that she was struggling. I kept granting her second chances. I didn't want to give up on her, but drugs . . . they're not my thing and I could see they were affecting her ability to look after Violet.

'Eventually, she broke up with me. I think she worked out if there wasn't someone holding her accountable, she could do whatever she wanted without consequences. The thing was, I'd been like a father to Violet for those two years and I didn't want to just leave. I told Heather I still wanted to be a part of Violet's life, so she made a deal – I could see Violet if I wanted to drive her to and from school every day. I'm sure she figured I'd turn her down, but I said I'd do it.'

Andrea had been amazed at his determination to stay in Violet's life, at the way he cared for her and stuck by her.

And to be honest, seeing those fatherly instincts in him was a turn on. In the end, they'd had more drinks and started chatting about other things.

The more Andrea had to drink, the more she opened up to Shaun. He was so laid back and easy to talk to. He was nothing like the men she'd dated before Tony, but he was also nothing like Tony.

And he was flirting with her. Every now and then, he would reach across and touch her arm or her hand. With each touch, it was as though an electric current zipped right through her body. When she spoke, he held her gaze. Sometimes it was so intense that she would dip her head or turn away, her cheeks warming. But then she would look back and he would catch her eye again and a dimple would appear in his left cheek.

So she flirted back. And drank some more.

Eventually, the words tumbled out: 'I found out today that my husband lied to me about something really big.'

'That's awful,' he said, his face full of genuine concern.

'And now I don't know if I can trust him about anything anymore. I mean . . . if he lied about that, what else is he keeping from me? And what if I don't know him like I thought I did? What if my marriage is in trouble? Real trouble.' And next thing, Shaun had leaned across the table, taken her face in his hands and kissed her.

It was one of the best damned kisses she'd ever had.

Long and slow and soft. It woke her up and filled her with desire.

When they pulled apart, he'd tried to apologise, assuring her it wasn't his style to hit on a married woman and that he'd kissed her without thinking. But she'd silenced him by leaning in and kissing him back. Another long, slow kiss that had him pulling her up out of her seat and around to his side of the table to sit next to him.

When he asked her if she wanted to come back to his place for another drink, she'd said yes without stopping to think.

After the accident Jill had let her know that Shaun had been to visit her in the hospital, that he was hoping to see her again when she woke. But Andrea had been putting it off. She was nervous about his reaction when he found out she was pregnant – let alone that he was the father.

Plus it would complicate things with her family. They might not be her family by blood or even by marriage anymore, but they were still the best family she'd ever known and she didn't want to lose them. Would they forgive her if they knew that she had cheated?

But yesterday, Shaun had called her. He'd been thinking about her a lot, he said, and he was hopeful they could meet up.

So perhaps the truth would come out after all.

Darren

Darren thought Christmas in July was one of the smartest ideas his mum had ever come up with. And he was impressed that she was finally ready to break tradition. None of them were going to want to celebrate next Christmas. Too many bad memories; it would likely take a long time for those feelings to fade. So, shifting celebrations to the winter was the perfect way for their family to still have Christmas together. Besides, this December Pete and Mimi were taking their family to England so the twins could finally meet their other grandparents.

Darren and Sage hadn't talked about what they might do at Christmas time yet. They were taking things one day at a time. She wasn't the type to plan ahead, but that was fine with Darren. It made for a nice change of pace after his relationship with Charlotte, which had always been about planning for the future. He hadn't seen Charlotte in several months now, but he'd heard that Steph was pregnant and he was happy for them.

Pete and the kids were already in the restaurant when he and Sage arrived.

'Where's Mimi?' he asked as they pulled out their chairs and sat down.

'She's picking up Andrea, she's still not allowed to . . .'

Darren nodded. Andrea's licence had been suspended for twelve months when she'd finally been well enough to go to court and face her charges. She'd also been hit with a large fine, but had been granted leniency due to the fact there were no drugs or alcohol involved, no prior record, and that the reason she'd been distracted was because she was attempting to stop a minor from mistakenly taking drugs. Due to all of this, she'd been served a suspended sentence, which meant no jail time.

They were all relieved; none of them had wanted to see her behind bars for Tony's death.

'So,' said Pete, 'have you got it for me?'

Darren pulled a USB stick out of his pocket and passed it across. 'Remember, it's only the first draft,' he said.

'First draft is still a hell of a lot better than no draft. Well done.'

'Yeah, well, we'll see. I still don't know if the publisher's going to give me another chance. They might not even want to read it.'

'They'll read it. Trust me, Elizabeth is a gun when it comes to dealing with publishers. She'll talk 'em round. Besides, they'll want the opportunity to make back all the money they lost on you.'

'Jeez, thanks, mate.'

'No worries. Still can't believe you decided to make your main character a bloody dog.'

'Don't knock it till you read it,' Sage interrupted. 'Your boy here's got some serious game. This book made me cry in a way I never have while reading before. I'm talking snot bubbles. He's onto something. Trust me.'

'Can I read it too?' Callie asked.

'Love you to,' said Darren. 'Wouldn't mind knowing if this book might cross over into the YA market too. Just make sure you're honest with me.' He reached across the table and held out his pinkie.

Callie looked mildly embarrassed but she twisted her own pinkie around his and shook. 'Promise.'

Sage winked at Callie. 'Don't worry, I bet you'll love it.' She paused then added, 'How's the singing going, babe? Are you a famous YouTuber yet or what?'

Callie laughed. 'Oh my God, not even close.' She got up from her chair and walked around the table to sit next to Sage. 'But I do have a few more questions for you, if you don't mind?'

'Of course. Hit me with them.'

Callie had found out that Sage had attended one of the biggest performing arts schools in Sydney when she was younger, before she'd had to give up dancing. It was clear Callie had real talent, yet she was modest about it – and she tried to be realistic too; she was aware of how hard it would be to turn it into a career.

But Mimi was determined to give her daughter all the support in the world and she'd suggested that Callie consider applying to study music at that same performing arts school after she finished Year Twelve. So, Callie regularly sought Sage's advice.

Darren pulled his phone out and waved it at Tara. 'I have new Leo videos,' he said.

Tara reached across the table and grabbed it. 'And I have new videos of Scorpio, on Dad's phone.'

Scorpio was Tara's pet rabbit, which she'd decided to name after a star sign as well.

'Excellent,' said Darren, grabbing the phone off Pete. 'Scorpio is the best. Ah look, here comes your mum and Aunty Andrea.'

Tara looked up and Darren couldn't help clocking the way she visibly relaxed as she saw her mum walking towards them. He hadn't even realised she'd been slightly tensed up as she waited for Mimi. Darren felt a sting in his eyes. While Tara might have seemed like a perfectly happy kid, she'd obviously been left with some anxiety after the accident. He supposed the repercussions of what had happened would stay with their family for some time to come.

Mimi

'Wine?' Sage offered the bottle to Mimi.

'Not for me, thanks,' Mimi said with a smile. For Mimi, Dry January had turned into Feb Fast. By March she finally felt comfortable enough to enjoy the odd glass of wine with dinner, but she was being careful not to fall back on old habits and use alcohol as a way to escape from life. And when she was driving, she stuck to a zero limit.

She glanced over at the video of Scorpio that Tara was showing Darren and felt pleased that her face was glowing with pride. Mimi had come up with the idea of a pet rabbit as a way to help take some of Tara's focus away from the twins. She wanted her to enjoy Elliot and James as their big sister and nothing more.

She'd also picked up on some nerves from Tara when it came to car trips. Especially if she was separated from Pete or Mimi. Mimi had been working hard to ease her back into the idea of riding in a car without her parents so that she wouldn't be afraid if the parent of a school friend needed to give her a lift to a band event or a playdate. It was a slow process, but they were getting there.

Mimi's attention was pulled away as she saw Jill walking through the tables towards them. Jill caught her eye and Mimi tipped her head slightly to the side and then managed to smile at her. *New beginnings*, she thought. It was time to put the past behind them.

Jill

Dear Frank,

I know I haven't written to you for a while. I guess after the funeral, I wasn't sure what I should say. I wasn't sure if writing these letters was doing me more harm than good. But tonight I felt compelled to talk to you.

You see, tonight, something happened. I think our family finally started to piece itself back together. And I could have cried with happiness.

We all went out to dinner together – Christmas in July, we called it. And we talked, about everything. You, for instance. About how much we all still miss you and about how incredible your book is. It hit the shelves last month. There was a slight delay from the original publishing date; a bit of chaos when the publishers found out Tony wasn't the author. In the end though, they still wanted to publish it.

And we found more of your writing, you cheeky thing. Why did you keep it all hidden? Why didn't you tell any of us that it was your true passion? Why didn't you tell me? I still can't believe you were writing in secret. Don't you see that we could have shared in it together? Your talent, your achievement. We could have celebrated it.

But I still love you anyway, you old fool.

Anyway, Pete and Darren are working together to turn the rest of your notes and half-written stories into more books, and they'll be published under your name as well. The publishers were relieved they weren't investing in an author who couldn't keep providing them with more work.

It's a bestseller by the way, Don't Breathe. *The royalties are going to Andrea. I know it's going to be tough for her being a single mother and I don't want her to have financial worries on top of that. So I insisted. The money for the next book will be split between Darren and Pete, of course, seeing as they're working so hard to pull it all together. Pete and Mimi will have a new book out soon, too. You should see the gorgeous illustrations in this one. Mimi's absolutely outdone herself. There's this adorable little monkey, cheekiest thing I've ever seen. I love it.*

And we talked about Andrea's pregnancy. It's a boy, by the way. I wonder if she'll ever feel ready to tell me the truth. That Tony's not the father. She thinks I don't know, but she has no idea that Tony told me he'd already had a vasectomy. That he was pretending there was still a chance for them to have children when he knew full well it was never going to happen. I was going to tell her, but then I thought, does she really need to know that there was yet one more lie in her marriage?

So who was the father? Well, I saw the way that man looked at her in the hospital that day. Shaun was his name and it was clear that he cared strongly for Andrea. So, I've put two and two together. Of course, I could be wrong, but I don't think I am. I'm learning to trust my instincts from now on. I don't blame Andrea for being unfaithful. Knowing everything that Tony has done, I can hardly judge her for straying.

I really do hope Andrea calls Shaun one day.

I suspect he might be the one to make her happy.

I just want to say to her, it's okay, no one is going to be upset with you. Because we all just want her to be happy now. But she'll have to come to it in her own time, when she's ready.

Do you want to know what else we talked about tonight? We talked about Robin. And it was wonderful. It was the kind of conversation I've always wanted to have. They asked me questions about her, what she was like, the colour of her eyes, her hair. We imagined who she might have been had she had the chance to grow up. We guessed that maybe she would have dated one of her brothers' friends in high school, or that she might have gone through a rebellious teenage phase. We wondered if she would have been a writer too, perhaps the best one of the lot, or if she would have chosen a different path altogether.

I know you thought the ony way to deal with our loss was to shut it out. But I realise now I did the wrong thing by letting you do that. I should have encouraged you to remember her and to celebrate who she was. I thought I was sparing you the pain and helping you to cope, but instead I made it worse for both of us. It's never good to bottle up feelings and it's never good to keep secrets. I know that now. I wish you could have been there for tonight's conversation, because it really was glorious. It made my heart sing to know that she was finally being remembered, the way she should have been.

And you know what else? I've stopped doing all those Hail Marys. And I'm finding I'm sleeping a lot better these days.

Love,
Jill

Mimi

'Mimi! You can't leave me here. Mimi!'

She woke up and lay still, breathing hard. She often dreamed about that moment in Tony's car. Not every night, but maybe once every two or three weeks. Just enough to make sure she would never forget it.

It was ironic. Now that the twins often slept through the night, here she was waking from nightmares and unable to fall back to sleep. She didn't know if she'd call it guilt exactly. Because she didn't feel guilty. He deserved to die.

No, what she felt wasn't guilt. It was fear. Fear that one day, the truth would come out. Because she didn't simply leave Tony in the car. She did much, much worse than that.

It was as she was crouching down, ready to climb out, that she saw it. Callie's mobile phone in the centre console. For some reason, she automatically reached for it. It was silly, possessions were the last thing on her mind, but that phone was Callie's whole world. As she tried to grab it, she realised it was stuck, jammed in place by part of the console that had been bent out of shape. She pulled it free and heard a tiny click. It was the car's cigarette lighter. It had obviously been held in place by the phone jammed up against it. It had been heating up this whole time and once she'd moved the phone, it had popped out.

Then she heard the words Callie had said. *I could smell something in there . . . petrol.*

A strange sensation came over her. It was as though a thin layer of ice had coated her body from her head to her toes. Her limbs switched to autopilot. She watched her hand reach for the cigarette lighter and take it out. Check to see it was still glowing red. Hot. She looked around for the source of the smell. There, down low . . . liquid dripping into the car from under the bonnet. She didn't stop to think. She crouched down and placed the lighter near the growing puddle. Perhaps the heat would be gone by the time it touched the petrol. Maybe without a spark, it wouldn't even ignite. She couldn't be sure. But she left it there anyway.

She crawled back through the windscreen.

Then she walked away from the car and didn't look back.

Acknowledgements

My heartfelt gratitude to every single person who helped me along the way with this novel, and, as always, I apologise profusely if I miss someone in the following acknowledgements. First, a gigantic thank you to my wonderful friend Sabeeha Toynton. Sabeeha was kind enough to give me hours of her time, answering my questions about her expertise as a paramedic and even reading a full draft of the book to check my work. Any mistakes are entirely my own fault and would have been introduced *after* she read it. I'm also lucky enough to have an amazing group of friends that happens to include a firefighter, several nurses, a high school teacher and a police officer. This comes in quite handy with most of my writing. Thank you to Mark Zullo, Kristen Zullo, Kerry Lockwood, Brooke Macdonald, Alex Wilson and Andy Lyttle for all being so patient with me when I ask inane questions about seemingly random things such as 'Can I set this on fire?' or 'What injury would put me in a coma, but I want to survive, please.' Thank you to my family GP, Doctor Vilkins, who looked slightly bemused at the end of an appointment when I suddenly asked, 'If I was a man who wanted to donate sperm, what questions would you ask me?'

As always, I am extremely grateful to the huge team of people behind the scenes, including, but not limited to, my extraordinary publisher and gorgeous friend Anna Valdinger, along with everyone else at HarperCollins Australia, including Dianne Blacklock, Jordan Weaver-Keeney and Belinda Yuille; as well as my equally extraordinary UK publisher, Maxine Hitchcock, and everyone else at Penguin Michael Joseph, including Rebecca Hilsdon and Clare Bowron. Further gratitude to my agents, the excellent Sheila Crowley at Curtis Brown UK, the lovely Stacy Testa at Writers House US and of course my fabulous friend who has been with me since day one, Pippa Masson at Curtis Brown Australia. My books would not exist without any of you.

I'm also very appreciative of Pamela Allen's kindness in allowing me to quote her beautiful book, *Who Sank the Boat*. When I first came up with the original concept for this book, I would lie awake at night, wondering which character would end up being the one to have caused the car accident. As I lay there trying to work it out, I would mutter to myself, 'Who sank the boat?'

As always, thank you to Pete and Leesa at Mini Espresso Bar, who are kind enough to provide me with delicious food, amazing coffee, great conversation, a place to sit and write for hours on end and also several character names, including their own.

Love and gratitude to my remarkable mum and all of my sisters (Diane Moriarty, Liane Moriarty, Jaclyn Moriarty, Katrina Harrington and Fiona Ostric) for simply being my mum and all of my sisters. But particularly to Liane, Jaci and Kati, who all read early drafts and answered questions and provided invaluable feedback. Thank you also to my marvellous parents-in-law,

Madeleine and Arthur Menasse, for the ongoing love, support and babysitting.

All of my love to my family: Steve Menasse, Maddie Menasse and Piper Menasse – I am extremely lucky to have you, and thank you, Steve for (eventually) reading one of my earlier drafts even though it wasn't quite fast enough for me to ask you any questions before it was time to hand in the next draft. Never mind, next time faster?

Finally, this book was dedicated to my late father, Bernie Moriarty. Dad, you always gave the best reaction when I gave you good news. When I told you that I'd finished a book or had a new book deal or sold film rights . . . telling you and seeing your eyes light up and hearing you laugh and say, 'Get'em, Nic' was always the absolute best part. I wish you didn't have to go, but I'm glad you're no longer hurting. I love you and I miss you, from your Nic-a-lic.

He just wanted a decent book to read ...

Not too much to ask, is it? It was in 1935 when Allen Lane, Managing Director of Bodley Head Publishers, stood on a platform at Exeter railway station looking for something good to read on his journey back to London. His choice was limited to popular magazines and poor-quality paperbacks – the same choice faced every day by the vast majority of readers, few of whom could afford hardbacks. Lane's disappointment and subsequent anger at the range of books generally available led him to found a company – and change the world.

'We believed in the existence in this country of a vast reading public for intelligent books at a low price, and staked everything on it'
Sir Allen Lane, 1902–1970, founder of Penguin Books

The quality paperback had arrived – and not just in bookshops. Lane was adamant that his Penguins should appear in chain stores and tobacconists, and should cost no more than a packet of cigarettes.

Reading habits (and cigarette prices) have changed since 1935, but Penguin still believes in publishing the best books for everybody to enjoy. We still believe that good design costs no more than bad design, and we still believe that quality books published passionately and responsibly make the world a better place.

So wherever you see the little bird – whether it's on a piece of prize-winning literary fiction or a celebrity autobiography, political tour de force or historical masterpiece, a serial-killer thriller, reference book, world classic or a piece of pure escapism – you can bet that it represents the very best that the genre has to offer.

Whatever you like to read – trust Penguin.